## BATTLETECH:
# FOREVER FAITHFUL

## BY BLAINE LEE PARDOE

BATTLETECH: FOREVER FAITHFUL
Edited by John Helfers
Cover art by Anthony Scroggins
Design by Matt Heerdt & David Kerber

Published by Catalyst Game Labs,
an imprint of InMediaRes Productions, LLC
113 Cherry Street #93897 • Seattle, Washington 98104-2205

I dedicate this to my grandson, Trenton Davis Hester—future MechWarrior. And to the Catalyst Demo Team, who always invites me to play at Gen Con and makes sure my ego is properly boosted. *Seyla!*

# ACKNOWLEDGMENTS

## BLAINE LEE PARDOE

This book ties together a number of novels, starting with the *Twilight of the Clans* series (especially *Exodus Road*), *Impetus of War*, and *Surrender Your Dreams*. They are not required reading, but will add to your enjoyment of this novel.

I also realized that a lot of fans want to be a part of *BattleTech* too, part of the canon. My solution was to randomly pull names off my Facebook friends list to include as characters and places in the book. This was all done at random. Sure, they are just cameo roles, but what the hell—why should I be the only one to have fun?

They deserve acknowledgment here for my heist (and in some cases tweaking) of their names or character descriptions.

Jose Alvarez
Ray Arrastia
Dustin Ballard
James Bixby
Brian Blaney
Shawn Bruno
Brian Chiasson
Alex Clarke
Alexander JW DeSantis
Colin Duffy
Josh Ellis
Eric Eny
Peter Farland
Todd Farnholtz
Patrick Finnegan
Brandon Fisher
Andrew Gardenhire
Aaron Gregory
Craig Gulledge
Shane Jaskowiak

Camille Klein
Oliver Kraft
Thomas Lagemann
Mike Lubowitzki
Dean Manning
James McHenry
Adam Mckern
Clifford McKinney
James Eyres Mclean Miller
Av Paredes
Nathan Pelchat
Trixter Phillips
Bradley Proffitt
Devin Ramsey
Craig Reed
Keegan Reid
Jamie Rife
David Shell
Sam Snell
Benjamin Starkey

# PROLOGUE

SANTA FE, NEW MEXICO
TERRA
REPUBLIC OF THE SPHERE
10 DECEMBER 3130

Paladin Victor Steiner-Davion looked at the screen and drew a long, deep breath. His study was loneliest at night. There was a hint of smoke in the air from the fireplace, the kind of aroma that invited an afternoon nap. There were always people who wanted his time or opinion, but the number of friends was dwindling as the years passed.

*That is part of the price I must pay for outliving so many of my contemporaries.* While comrades had crumbled in time, it seemed that enemies were always easily replaced. *We always felt the Clansmen were bred for war, but in reality, it turns out it is a trait we all share.* Memories of the Clan Invasion, the Word of Blake Jihad, and the subsequent wars tugged at him like ghosts, beckoning him to remember them. Victor suppressed those thoughts. *It would be unworthy of me to remember fondly the battles I've fought.*

His knee ached as he adjusted his position in the thick leather chair. *Old injuries, like memories, have a way of coming back when you least expect them.*

The former Archon-Prince of the Federated Commonwealth had been working on his memoirs for three years, and there was a gap in his material that he sought to fill. Tackling the task alone in the dark of night seemed most appropriate to Victor. It was not easy to face. He had skipped over it during his first pass of the text, secretly hoping the memory of the events would have faded, or that no one would notice the omission. *Maybe no one will care about that now. It really was worthy of a footnote–little more.*

His editor felt differently, and had insisted that more be said about the planning for the strike on Huntress that destroyed the

Smoke Jaguars and bought the Inner Sphere some much-needed peace. In particular, the editor wanted to know the story of Trent, the former Smoke Jaguar who had betrayed his Clan.

Old guilt washed over Victor every time he thought of that man. *I was young still, I didn't realize what I was setting in motion. How could I have known?* Memories of his behavior then, of the anguish he had caused, gnawed at him along with regret. *I should have been more understanding at the time. Not as rash...*

Now the time had come. *People will judge me by my actions and the repercussions.* Some of the information he knew he could not put in print. *Stone and I struck a devil's bargain, one that still binds me to some degree of secrecy.* Still, the story of the Exodus Road needed to be clarified for the readers—at least, that was the prodding of his editor. *I am one of the few alive who knows the details, knows the full truth.*

Victor cleared his throat and hit the transcribe button.

"The opportunity to strike at the Clan Smoke Jaguar homeworld came to us fortuitously, at just the right time. One of their warriors, Trent, believed the ways of his people to be corrupt. According to reports provided by a ComStar agent who had infiltrated the Clan with the purpose of turning some of their troops, the Jaguars were pompous, political pariahs. They had twisted the words of Nicholas Kerensky into a cudgel and used it to pummel their best warriors.

"Trent had fought in the Battle of Tukayyid, and was horribly injured during the Jaguars' loss there. The scalp on the right side of his head was so scarred that no hair grew there. His cheek- and jawbones were disfigured, and he had a bionic eye and an arm replacement.

"From what Precentor Focht told me, Trent was tormented by his commanding officer, an Elemental named Paul Moon. He deemed Trent too old to be of use to the Jaguars, and sent him back to the homeworld of Huntress. Trent, with the help of his ComStar handler, created a rudimentary chart of the Exodus Road. He managed to get himself rotated back to Inner Sphere duty—while carrying a map of General Kerensky's route.

"When Trent defected to ComStar, Focht struck a deal with him. He would be given a command of his own and a chance to fight in battle, in exchange for the map to Huntress. Focht understood the man better than I, understood the MechWarrior he was, the man whose honor was beyond reproach. I was so focused on defeating the Clans, challenging their invasion of the Inner Sphere, I couldn't see past the fact that Trent was a traitor to his own people.

"When we reached Strana Mechty for our inevitable confrontation with the Clans, I did something that I regret to this day. I denied Trent his chance to fight with us. I believed we couldn't have a traitor on the field of battle. Doing so would introduce an unknown and possibly unstable element to the fighting. I mistook his desire to lead troops into a battle for revenge against his former Clan. At the time,

I didn't understand that all he wanted was the opportunity to prove himself a worthy MechWarrior. I assumed what drove him was vengeance.

"I was naïve, now that I look back at the entire affair. I was so fixated on finishing our quest, bringing an end to the Smoke Jaguars and stopping the Clan invasion, that I failed to comprehend the desires or heart of a single warrior—one who had made the entire operation and invasion possible. Instead, I treated him as a pariah. One man, one warrior, who gave up his people for all the right reasons, was denied what he desired—merely a chance to prove himself worthy. I labeled him 'traitor' without fully understanding him. I won't justify my thinking with hindsight. Anyone might have made the same call I did and revoked the promise Focht made to him.

"What I didn't factor in was that entirely destroying one Clan had consequences. Our actions to protect the Inner Sphere were like casting a stone in a pond. There were ripples. Destroying the Smoke Jaguars in such a brutal manner caused events years later. Destroying them created a void that had to be filled in some way.

"Nature abhors imbalances like that. The universe always finds ways to set things back into balance...I know that now. My denial of Trent set things in motion that I never could have foreseen. It's odd how one moment of letting your emotions get ahead of your logic can have ramifications for decades. I tipped over the first domino with Trent, and once the rest started to topple, the reaction was impossible to stop. This string of reactions I set in motion impacted the Jihad years later."

After a moment, Victor deleted the last sentence. Some secrets still needed to be kept.

"Little did I realize the role he had to play in affairs, and how one day I, and the entire Republic of the Sphere, might be indebted to him. But on that day in 3060, on the sacred soil of Strana Mechty, all I saw was a vile traitor.

"Rarely have I been so wrong."

# CHAPTER 1

Trent, formerly of Clan Smoke Jaguar, stood awash in anger as he glared at the short Inner Sphere prince. Trent had long seen the corruption of his people, how they had twisted the teachings of Nicholas Kerensky, turning it into a justification for naked brutality. Gone was the path where honor had prevailed. Now petty politics and backstabbing were the norm. *We have wandered so far from the tenets of honor that we are now just brutality.*

This depravity had driven him to do the unthinkable. He had provided ComStar with the route to the Clan homeworlds, the Exodus Road. It was to be an exchange. He provided the Inner Sphere with the first chance to strike at the heart of the Clans and purge his former people, and they were to provide him a chance to fight in battle once more. He had assumed the role of traitor to regain honor. The irony was not lost on him.

And now Victor Steiner-Davion was denying him that. The shorter man looked at him as a lesser man. The Inner Sphere warlord didn't understand him at all. He wanted to join battle again; not out of vengeance, but to purge the anger and guilt that boiled within him. Trent's returning to battle had nothing to do with revenge. But the glare he got from the prince was that of a man who saw him as an untrustworthy traitor—nothing more.

Worse, while Victor denied Trent his chance to join the fight against the remaining Smoke Jaguars, he was accepting the help of Clan Nova Cat. *Are they not traitors as well,* quiaff? It was too much to bear. Trent's heart pounded in his ears, and he felt his face flush.

"Do you have *no* honor, Victor Davion?" He stepped forward, reaching for the prince's throat. Davion's Elemental bondsman shifted, but Trent's warrior mind had already calculated that he would be on top of the prince before she could react. *She will try to protect him, and I will need to incapacitate her quickly.*

Suddenly a blow struck him in the face, just under his bionic ocular implant, sending him reeling before he reached his target. Khan Severen Leroux of the Nova Cats had slapped his face so hard he lost his balance in mid-lunge and tumbled to the floor. He felt something land on top of him. A knee to his solar plexus drove the air out of his lungs, and in a moment of panic he struggled to get air.

Trent felt Leroux grab his right wrist, felt something wrap around it. His bionic arm, cocooned in myomer muscle, picked up only a faint sensation of something there. Looking at his hand, he saw a bondcord wrapped around his skinny wrist, its ends in the hands of the Nova Cat Khan. If it had been his real arm, he would have felt the cord digging into his skin. As it was, the image of the cord there and what it symbolized was clear. They had taken him as one of their own. Neg! *This is not supposed to happen!* He struggled for the words as he gasped for air.

"Trent, you are my bondsman. You belong to the Nova Cats." The bald Khan rose from his chest and let the bondcord fall off...the symbolic gesture when a bondsman becomes a full-fledged warrior. "I now accept you as a warrior in our Clan. If you wish, you may join us in fighting the Ice Hellions."

Trent coughed once to get air back into his lungs and rubbed his still-stinging cheek. Victor Steiner-Davion had misinterpreted his motivation; worse, he had refused to listen. *This was never about revenge; all I desired was the chance to fight in battle. The Nova Cats are offering me that.* "Ice Hellions? I will fight them for you."

"Good. Go to Alpha Galaxy headquarters. They are waiting for you."

Hands reached out to help Trent up: Precentor Martial Anastasius Focht. Trent staggered to his feet, allowing one more icy glance back at Victor Steiner-Davion.

His new Khan, Leroux, turned to the precentor martial as well. "You have no objections?"

Focht shook his head. "He will fight well for you. Go, Trent, you have what you wanted. Finish what you have started."

Trent saw another Nova Cat warrior near the entrance to the tent. She opened the flap and gestured for Trent to walk with her.

*"Finish what you have started..."* Focht's words dug deeply into his mind as he pushed through the tent flap. *What I started was to set the Smoke Jaguars on the right path. What I have done is become the instrument of their destruction.*

The Nova Cat warrior walked alongside him. She was younger than he, much younger, and shorter. Yet she looked up at him with wide eyes, as if he were some sort of celebrity. Her short black hair caught the wind and fluttered in the breeze. She was small but muscular, her chest solid, making her breasts look small. For a moment, Trent remembered Judith, the ComStar operative who had helped him find his way to ComStar with the Exodus Road. He wondered for a moment where she was...if he would ever see her again.

"I am Star Captain Inanna," she said as she led him toward a waiting Anhur VTOL transport. Once away from the tent where Victor Steiner-Davion had so grossly disrespected him, Trent suddenly felt a sense of familiarity and comfort with a military tarmac, a *Clan* military base. As they walked at a brisk pace along the ferrocrete, he allowed himself to drink in, if only for a few moments, the feeling of belonging. The air stank of coolant, lubricant, and the slight tang of sweat as he passed other warriors. Those who spoke as they passed spoke like brethren, using Clan language and proper wording. Trent suddenly realized, in that moment, how much he had missed such places. Two years huddled in seclusion with ComStar made him long for the life he once had. It made Khan Leroux's gesture feel like a welcome gift.

Trent unconsciously rubbed his wrist where the bondcord should have dug into his skin, but instead had only tugged at myomer replacement muscle. "Why did he do that? Why take me into your Clan?"

The younger warrior's grin only broadened. "We are Nova Cats. Our journey is different than the Jaguars', which brought you into the world. Your role in affairs was, dare I say, foreseen."

Trent had heard since his inception that the Nova Cats gave credence to mysticism, but he had never experienced it firsthand. "How could he have known what would happen?" *It was all so fast, I am not sure I fully understand just yet.*

"He was told of your arrival by one of us who pierced the mists of the future."

Trent looked at her and saw her wide-eyed gaze on him. "It was you, *quiaff?*"

"*Aff*," she replied. "My vision is why I am here. It is also why preparations were made in advance."

His brow furrowed at the thought of someone predicting that he was coming with the Star League Defense Force; yet there he walked, into his new Clan. *Perhaps I need to challenge my own beliefs.* "Where are you taking me?"

"Your new home, of course," Inanna responded. "You will serve in Khan Leroux's Star."

"Such a place should be reserved for those who have earned honor in the Nova Cats—not for a new warrior." To fight alongside a

Khan in battle was a right for which many warriors vied. Now it was being given to him. While Trent was grateful, it did not feel right.

"The honor is yours, Warrior Trent," Inanna replied, her tone light, almost casual. "Who other than you is worthy? If our Watch is to be believed, you alone are responsible for the events that are unfolding. The destiny of our Clan, indeed, the future of the Clans is changed because of your actions. None of our warriors have held such sway over the power structure of known space."

Trent had never framed his actions in such a way. *I never set out to change the universe. I simply wanted to restore the honor of my Clan, and for the Jaguars who strayed from the true path of Kerensky to pay the price for their insolence. That is all. Not...not what she is saying.*

Despite his resistance, there was no point in debating his life choices with Inanna. She saw him through her own goggles, attuned to the views of the Nova Cats. *Now that I am one of this Clan, I need to adopt their perspective.*

"You give me too much credit," he said in a low tone that betrayed his dark feelings. "What I am responsible for is the death of many warriors."

"*Neg*," Inanna replied. "You are responsible for the destruction of Clan Smoke Jaguar. You and you alone." Her voice held no judgment. Instead it was calm, factual, as if reading a passage from a book.

Trent stopped in mid-stride, as did his guide. "I prefer to believe that I have set matters right. The Jaguars had wandered far from the teachings of Nicholas Kerensky. They had lost every shred of honor. My leaders—*neg*—*their* leaders were brutal, and had sold their honor for power and prestige. I was left with no choice."

Inanna nodded once. "We all have a choice. I understand, as do your brothers and sisters in your new Clan. We saw what the Jaguars had become. As I saw matters unfold in my darkest dreams, others made your choice for you. You were the instrument that set many things in motion."

They passed two Nova Cat Star Commanders who saw him and nodded as if they knew him. His gaze lingered on them; their complete lack of surprise at seeing someone in the base wearing a ComStar jumpsuit confused him.

Inanna stopped in front of the Anhur. Above the personnel hatch was stenciled the logo of Alpha Galaxy. The motto, *Victory Over Delusion*, caught his eye more than the insignia's image of a Nova Cat twisted into a dragon's tail. *It will take time to get used to their customs and beliefs.* As a Smoke Jaguar warrior, he had learned to dismiss the mystical ways of the Nova Cats as proof of their weakness. He was beginning to see that their belief system intertwined with their path as warriors.

"They will shuttle you to our encampment," Inanna said.

Trent paused and looked inside, feeling almost wary of how he was being treated. *I have been called traitor for so long that I have allowed myself to believe it.*

"The Khan will expect you to be properly equipped with a 'Mech. What is your preferred configuration?"

Trent nearly chuckled. It had been more than two years since he had piloted a BattleMech. ComStar had granted him access to simulators, but it wasn't the same as sitting in the cockpit. He was excited by the thought of piloting a 'Mech again. "My last one was an *Ebon Jaguar*. I also have experience in a *Timber Wolf*—at Tukayyid."

Inanna's forehead wrinkled. "The *Ebon Jaguar* is of Smoke Jaguar design, and is not one that we have available."

"I understand." He allowed himself a wry grin.

"Why the smile?"

"You seem to have such a grasp on things, so I assumed you already knew what kind of BattleMech I prefer."

Inanna's face stiffened. "My gift is a view through the veil of the future, Trent. I have remarkably little control over what I see. The past is for others to view, usually our Loremasters."

"I meant no offense, Inanna. I have only been a Nova Cat for a few minutes."

She nodded. "I sometimes forget that you have undergone a number of changes. 'The man who fights under four flags.'"

"Four flags?"

"I knew you were the one because I saw four flags in my vision, and a lone warrior beneath them. It is you. Smoke Jaguar, ComStar, Star League Defense Force, and now Nova Cat."

He had not thought of his journey in that context. "I sometimes forget the road I have chosen to walk. I hope your insight saw that this was the last flag I would fight under."

Inanna said nothing for a few seconds, enough to disturb him. *She is not telling me everything.* She checked her noteputer, then locked her green eyes onto his own eye. "If you are to be of use to our Khan, you will need a BattleMech to pilot. I ask again, what is your preference, Star Captain?"

"I will be pleased with whatever 'Mech is available." Just talking about it made his excitement rise again. The time spent in simulators had honed his skill, but that was nothing compared to the feeling of raw power a real BattleMech provided. *It is finally happening. I am fulfilling my dream of returning to battle.*

Inanna studied her pad. "We have a *Timber Wolf*, captured *isorla* from a trial with Clan Wolf. It is operational, but an older model. I also have a *Supernova* available for your use. Perhaps that will fulfill your needs better, *quiaff*?"

"*Neg*," Trent replied. He had never piloted a 'Mech that large, but knew it was a killing machine at ninety tons, and jump-capable. "As much as I would be honored to pilot a *Supernova*, I will take the smaller *Timber Wolf*. I am accustomed to it, and I am sure there are others more worthy of an assault-class 'Mech."

"You must do as you wish. If you are concerned that others would feel slighted by your taking the larger 'Mech, dismiss that thought. I doubt any would challenge you to a trial for it." Her voice rang with confidence.

"Is that not the Clan way, *quiaff*?"

Inanna offered another flash of a smile. "*Aff*. It is the Nova Cat way, however, to respect another's vision. Word of your arrival preceded you."

*I must learn the ways of this Clan, and soon. Their reliance on visions and mysticism seems archaic. If this is indeed my new home, I must learn to trust their ways.* "I would be wrong to refuse such an opportunity then. I accept the *Supernova*, if it is agreeable to those of my new Clan."

"Smartly bargained and done. I will arrange for us to train together, and I will brief you on our fighting formations and style differences. I will arrange for your codex to be updated, and that will grant you access to our entire complex."

Trent nodded. "Thank you."

"Thanks are unnecessary. You are a Nova Cat now, we share a bond that others cannot see or comprehend. I will be joining you shortly, after I take care of a few matters here on which the Khan has asked for my perspective. Should you need anything, contact me over our Galaxy's net." She bowed her head, as if he were somehow revered in her eyes.

*If I need anything?* Trent pondered. *I have been a foreigner, a traitor in the eyes of the Inner Sphere for the last two years. Now I am welcomed back into the Clans, albeit a Clan fighting against the other Crusader Clans.*

It was almost too good to be true. The only thing that tempered his excitement was Khan Leroux's commitment that he would be fighting Clan Ice Hellion.

# CHAPTER 2

Trent juked hard right and felt the *Supernova* skid on the soil, digging a furrow with the side torque of his turn. The low center of gravity threw off his sense of balance, but he immediately realized his mistake and compensated, nearly to the point of overcompensating. The 'Mech listed uneasily in the high-speed turn, and for a millisecond he wondered if he was going to fall.

A lifetime of training took over his body. He maneuvered his left leg further out mid-stride, pushing the hip actuator to its maximum but giving him the support he needed on the turn. The ninety-ton 'Mech swayed but stayed upright as he turned his attention to the next leg of the course. Sweat formed on the left side of his face under his neurohelmet as he focused on sprinting ahead 200 meters, making a mental note on how to compensate for the next high-speed turn, based on his new understanding of the *Supernova*'s handling.

He made it through the next set of turns with no problem, gaining a little more confidence in handling tight turns at higher speeds. The assault 'Mech was no sprinter to begin with, but he had to learn its feel, its characteristics, and its limits if he was going to take on the Ice Hellions.

He came to a stop twenty minutes later in front of Inanna's *Mad Dog*. Her 'Mech was painted the same as his, a base of canvas tan with camouflaged streaks of browns and greens. The Jaguars in his former Cluster favored gray patterns, so seeing the *Mad Dog* standing in front of him reinforced that he was no longer in his former Clan.

The earpiece in his neurohelmet snapped as Inanna's voice came on. "Your pace was better than your last run, but still off from where it needs to be, Star Captain."

"*Aff*, I am aware," he replied with disappointment. Inanna had partnered with him to assist him in mastering his new 'Mech; in many respects, she was as demanding as a sibko trainer—minus the abuse. "The gait on this *Supernova* is taking me some time to master. It rides much lower than a *Timber Wolf* and its mass changes the energy it builds up in a sprint. I am having to unlearn as much as adapt to it."

"I suggest a break. You have done eleven laps...progressively faster and better on each one."

Trent wanted to press on, but as he flexed his legs, he felt an ache in his muscles. *I forget at times that I am older than many warriors. I do not want her or anyone else to think of me as anything other than prime.* Clearly, two years out of the cockpit had softened him, dulling some of his skills. "I agree. Let us run back to the bivouac and take in liquids there." He didn't wait for a response, immediately thrusting the massive *Supernova* forward into a run, its birdlike feet thundering on the ground under him.

Twenty minutes later, the pair arrived at the Nova Cat bivouac on the fringe of the rolling Duergar Plains. Trent felt the wash from the heat sinks as he climbed down. When he reached the ground, he patted the leg of the *Supernova* reassuringly, as if it were a pet rather than a machine of war. After hours of training in the simulator and the cockpit, he was developing a fondness for the capabilities of the 'Mech. With six extended-range large lasers, it could inflict considerable damage at long distances. After two full salvos on the move, however, the *Supernova* became an oven, overwhelming its heat sinks. He had already learned the key was to manage his heat carefully. It was easy to do in simulated combat: in a real firefight, the tendency to shoot whenever he had a shot could lead to the 'Mech shutting down if he was not careful.

They put their neurohelmets and coolant vests next to other warriors' gear on a table outside of a hard-shell temporary structure. Stripped down to their shorts, Trent saw tight muscles on the compact Inanna. She caught him looking and flashed a narrow smile back. *It has been years since I have coupled with another.* That thought hit him like a well-aimed shot. *I have been so consumed with my circumstances in life, I have forgotten how to live.*

Looking down to avoid her gaze, he saw his right arm, a replacement for the one he had lost on Tukayyid. It was skinnier, wrapped in synthskin, looking more robotic than human. He reached up and touched his sunken right cheek, then lowered his hand. He did not need a mirror to remember the horrific damage he had suffered in the name of the Jaguars. *I am deformed. A twisted survivor of a failed crusade. While the scars mark my duty as a warrior, I am repulsive.* Thoughts of coupling with Inanna evaporated with the mental acknowledgment. His disfigurement was further physical proof of the failure of the Smoke Jaguars.

Inanna handed him a green bottle of what warriors called "Flush," a sweet-tasting drink packed with electrolytes and vitamins. He sat across from her, taking a long drink. Some of the fluid missed his reconstructed lower lip and dripped down onto his sweat-soaked chest.

Two more warriors sat on the bench seats, one next to him, one next to Inanna. They both had short black hair, apparently of the same genetic stock, though one of the men was old, even older than Trent. He recalled that Khan Leroux was older than him as well, and it struck him as odd. *The Smoke Jaguars spurn age; they treat it as a disease, a weakness. It was one of the reasons they discarded me. Here, things are different.*

"You are Trent, the former Smoke Jaguar, *quiaff?*" the younger of the pair asked.

Trent eyed him for a moment, then nodded. "*Aff.*" He wondered if an insult would be forthcoming; he expected one. So far, none of the Nova Cats except Inanna had engaged him in conversation other than simple greetings.

"I am Star Captain Clifford Keating," he said, extending his hand. Trent shook it with his bionic appendage. "This is Antony Oberg. We serve in the Keshik." Oberg nodded. "We saw you working with the *Supernova*. They can be tricky to handle at speed. Even trickier on landings when you fire up the jump jets," Keating said.

"*Aff,*" Trent replied, relaxing slightly. "I practiced for an hour with the jets yesterday. Some of my landings were less than spectacular." While he had not fallen upon landing, he found the *Supernova* to be an ungainly 'Mech in the air.

"You will be fighting in my Binary," Star Captain Keating said. "We will need to incorporate you into our exercises. Our tactics are no doubt different than what you were used to in the Jaguars."

Inanna piped up. "He needs more practice, but he is ready for you, Star Captain." Trent looked across the table at her, and she allowed her deep green eyes to drift to him as she spoke.

"We should begin this afternoon, then," Keating replied. "Trent, have you ever fought Ice Hellions before?"

"*Neg.* I am familiar with their preferences in combat, but I have no experience against them."

"That is too bad," Oberg said. "Only two of our warriors have experience battling them."

"Khan Leroux has devised a plan for our trial," the Star Captain said. "One that will require us to turn their style of combat against them. I have been given a specific role in that battle, one I believe you can assist in."

"What is the plan?" Trent pressed.

The Star Captain leaned toward him. "The Ice Hellions favor co-ordinated attacks and rely on striking with speed...a blitzkrieg. We know, from their comments during the bidding for this trial, that they despise our Clan and our leaders for our choice to support the Star League. Our Khans will be their primary objective—it is the nature of the Hellions. They will do what they can to kill them in battle."

Trent nodded as Star Captain Keating continued. "Our Khan has only bid his *Keshik*, a Binary, for this battle. Knowing this, they will direct the brunt of their assault at our Khans. Khan Leroux plans to draw the Ice Hellions to the far north end of the Duergar Plains along the edge of the Lyod Glacier.

"The glacier is a solid vertical wall of ice rising nearly one hundred meters. Along it are many canyons, narrow cracks that cut deep into the glacier itself. The wall will limit their maneuverability, something their tactics rely heavily on for a quick victory. We can use the walls of the glacier for cover. We shall gnaw at them one bite at time, hit them with distractions that will confuse them, and cause them to lose the cohesion that is one of their strengths."

"What if they do not drive toward the glacier?" Trent posed. "They are Ice Hellions, not ignorant bilge bores. They will realize the glacier is a trap. It is hardly something that they can ignore."

"*Aff*," Keating replied. "Khan Leroux will pilot his *Scytha* OmniFighter and will remain far enough back as to compel them to drive deep into our starting position. If need be, he will challenge Khan Asa Taney. The Hellions' hatred of Khan Leroux runs deep, and for Khan Taney, Leroux's leadership of our people is a direct personal affront. Such a challenge cannot be ignored. No matter what the risks, they will come at the Khan."

Trent understood far too well the rage a warrior could feel, and how it could nearly blind them. "Their battle will be in the skies, ours is on the ground. How do we ensure their defeat there?"

"Distraction combined with skill. While the Ice Hellions are under orders to destroy our Khans, the strength of their Clan is coordinated tactics. If any component breaks off or fails to follow the plan, their attacks become fragmented and easier to shatter. We need a distraction that would compel some of the Ice Hellions to abandon their designated plan. Something that is as great, if not greater, an affront to their honor as our Khans."

Trent felt the left side of his face blush as all eyes turned to him. *It is me. I am to be the distraction.* "You refer to me, *quiaff*?"

"*Aff*, Star Captain. You, the person who brought the Smoke Jaguars to heel. You, who are seen as a traitor to the Clan cause. You, who brought the Star League to our homeworlds. You are the perfect distraction."

"I prefer to see my role in the battle as contributing with my skill as a warrior, not merely as bait for the enemy," he replied flatly. *Is this the only way they see me as being useful,* quiaff?

This time it was Star Captain Keating who appeared embarrassed. "You misunderstand, Star Captain. Your being here can accomplish more than what Khan Leroux might be thinking. Your presence is exactly what we need to give us the edge. You will use your consummate skills in combat, as is our way. Your presence, however, will be too tempting for the Ice Hellions to ignore. Once they know you are here, their ire will boil to rage. Timed properly, spurring them into that rage could spell the difference between defeat and victory." His voice rang with respect, something Trent was still unused to.

"I am to announce myself to them, draw some of them to fight me rather than our Khans, *quiaff?*" he asked slowly, carefully, listening for subtext in their response.

"Affirmative, Star Captain. You will get the battle you seek. Some, if not all, of the Ice Hellions will be unable to resist going after you."

Trent considered the implications of what he was saying. Of course the Ice Hellions would come at him, the betrayer of not only the Smoke Jaguars, but of all the Clans. They were now forced to fight a unified Star League for the right to conquer the Inner Sphere. That would have been impossible if he had not given the Exodus Road to ComStar. *I served up not only my own Clan to the Star League, but the whole of the Clan invasion effort.* He lowered his head slightly at the new insight that his role as traitor had such far-reaching effects.

"I mean no disrespect, Trent," the Star Captain continued. "Even you must admit that this plan of battle offers a good opportunity to confuse our foes at a critical moment."

"*Aff.* Assuming they know the role I played in matters. Other than a few Smoke Jaguars, none know who I am or what I have done." Trent's betrayal was not widely known. What was known was that the Smoke Jaguars had brought the wrath of the Star League to Clan space. How that had unfolded was something few seemed to question.

"We could let them know, in advance, that we have taken you in. We will tell them what you did. Their Watch will confirm it. Their Loremaster, Jonas Cage, has displayed little cunning in the past, but we will make it easy for him to confirm your placement and your presence in our Clan. This will further fuel their outrage. All that remains is for us to let them know you are actually on the field of battle. That is something we will surprise them with, at just the right moment—if you are agreeable."

From what he knew of the Ice Hellions' blitzkrieg approach to warfare, Trent thought the plan had merit. The thought of a Binary of warriors rushing at him gave him a pang of dread. It was never his intention to die in battle, only to fight once more. Trent's desire to be in combat again tempered that trepidation. If anything, the last few days' familiar strain on his muscles reminded him how much he loved combat.

"They will come at me for vengeance," he said coolly.

Both Nova Cat warriors nodded. "Some will," Antony Oberg said, "some will stick to their drive against our Khans. It will divide them and allow us to crush them."

"I have no desire to die, only to fight," Trent replied.

Inanna reached out and covered his left hand with her right. "Death stalks us all. It is the shadow of every true Clan warrior. You can no more shake it than you can your own shadow."

Trent turned to her, his bionically enhanced eyepiece showing her thermal readings, which made her seem to glow slightly in his gaze. "You have foreseen my death in this fight, *quiaff?*"

She said nothing for a moment, then met his eye. "The future is always unclear. I see you, the true man that you are, emerging from this fight." It was clear that she was choosing her words carefully.

"What say you, Trent?" Star Captain Keating asked. "I need to know, if I am to take this plan to our Khans."

Trent looked at Inanna then to the pair of Nova Cats. "I live to serve the true vision of Nicholas Kerensky. I am a Nova Cat, and my fate is intertwined with yours. I will fulfill the role you would have me play. Together, we shall crush the Ice Hellions."

"Well bargained and done," Keating replied, flashing a smile.

Trent rose to his feet and took a long gulp of his Flush. "I must go. I must use every hour possible to train for this task you have asked me to take as my own."

Inanna rose as well. "Go ahead, Trent, I will join you shortly."

Trent nodded once and walked off. His *Supernova* came into view, and seemed smaller to him now, more in his control. Having a role to play in the upcoming trial, and an important one, despite the risks, made him feel good. He understood that feeling: it was purpose.

As Trent walked away, Star Captain Keating turned to Inanna and his forehead immediately wrinkled. "Inanna, you did not tell him the truth."

Inanna looked back at Keating, then at Oberg, and nodded. "How did you know?"

"Khan Leroux told me about these visions you had regarding Trent. You told the Khan that Trent was going to die at the hands of the Ice Hellions. I was there when you said it. You said that his death would be his final release, did you not, *quiaff?*"

Inanna nodded. "I did say that to the Khan, and more. He did not share with you all of what I saw in my visions."

"What are you withholding from us, from Trent?" Antony Oberg demanded. "He is one of us now, a brother warrior."

Inanna turned to the older warrior. "No one should know the details of their future. We as a Clan are just beginning to understand the ways of visions. I did not want to risk corrupting the future."

"He should know the truth," the Star Captain interjected. "If you knew my fate, *I* would want to know. It is only right—only fair."

Inanna put her fists on her hips in defiance. "These visions are mine to do with as I please. If you tell Trent what may happen to him, it will alter his path. He still has a greater role to play, even beyond death. If either of you choose to interfere, you may set things in motion that cannot be understood or controlled."

Keating shook his head. "It does not feel right to me."

"Nor to me," Inanna replied. "I feel no joy in these matters. You must trust my judgment. If you do not, we will face each other in a Circle of Equals, and I *will* win."

Star Captain Keating rose to his feet. "The path you are walking is dangerous, Inanna."

She glared back at him. "I know. The future, by its very nature, is perilous." She pivoted and walked off after Trent.

# CHAPTER 3

DUERGAR PLAINS, NEAR THE LYOD GLACIER
STRANA MECHTY
THE KERENSKY CLUSTER, CLAN SPACE
23 APRIL 3060

A quarter of a kilometer behind Trent rose the Lyod Glacier—a dominating wall of ice that was cloudy at the top as the warmer season
melted off the surface snow. Before him was an undulating sea of rolling hills covered in two-meter-tall green spring grasses that rippled in
waves as the wind swept across them.

This was the day chosen for the Inner Sphere's Star League forces
to face off against the Clans. At stake was the end of hostilities if the
Clans lost. The Nova Cats had thrown in their lot with the Star League,
which was nearly an act of war on its own. Trent had been surprised
that in the last three days he had heard only minor griping about the
decision, and those who did complain found themselves in Circles
of Equals to battle for their spoken words. *As a people, they seem to
have accepted the decision to face off against their former brethren for a
sustained peace. They trust their leaders, which is something I can comprehend. If they fail, the Clans will come at them and devour them—purge them
like the Unspoken Clan.* It added gravity to the battle that was to come
for him. *Every shot counts in this fight.*

The Nova Cats had bid a Binary for the trial, the Keshik that
was led by both Khans. They had been slightly underbid by the Ice
Hellions. Trent had heard the rantings of Ice Hellion Khan Asa Taney.
It had been filled with flowery bravado, none of which had impressed
or frightened the Nova Cats.

"We, the Ice Hellions, following the true sight and path of
Nicholas Kerensky, are proud to defend the honor of our people and
our ultimate destiny: to rule the Inner Sphere. This false Star League is

a deceptive ruse, a lie perpetrated for the sole purpose of a genocidal war against our brothers and sisters of the Smoke Jaguars.

"And whom do we face? A betrayer as sinister as Stefan Ukris Amaris, the Usurper: Clan Nova Cat. These traitors conspired with our enemies to bring about this trial. They stabbed the Smoke Jaguars in the back. Now they have in the ranks of their warriors the very snake, the Judas that sold out our people—the traitor Trent.

"We face them with honor, and will defeat them. When we are done crushing the rule of Khan Leroux and his ilk, we shall call for their annihilation. Against these forces, I bid one Star and three Points of the Seventh Attack Cluster. This shall be settled with blood and honor, in the name of the great Kerenskys. Our pack shall tear the meat from your very bones for your decision to side with this false Star League."

Trent was happy that Star Captain Keating's plan had worked thus far; the Ice Hellions knew he was in the Nova Cat force. Soon, at the right time, they would learn that he was on the field of battle, too.

Over an open frequency, Khan Leroux declined to shower his foes with prose. "Ice Hellions, we await you, if you have the intestinal fortitude to face us. We anxiously await the inevitable." There was something in the last sentence that struck Trent. *Does he know already if we are going to win or lose,* quineg?

The Nova Cat Khan switched to tactical channel two. "As we planned, Nova Cats. I shall see you in the mists of time..."

Before Trent could process what Leroux had said, Star Captain Keating's voice rang over the same channel. "Pouncer Star, per our plan, follow me."

He saw Keating's *Executioner* painted in the same colors as the waving sea of grass. Adorning the side of its cockpit was a Nova Cat emblazoned on the star of the Star League. The Khan had had each of the 'Mechs painted with the symbol, homage to the new League the Cats were fighting for. The lumbering *Executioner* led the charge to the west, and Trent followed.

There was a low roar overhead as a sleek OmniFighter raced toward where Khan Leroux circled in his *Scytha*. *If nothing else, the Ice Hellions are predictable.* The Hellion *Visigoth* left a twisting contrail in the sky over their position. He ignored the raging dogfight in the distance and focused on his own movements. *Leroux can take care of himself.*

Trent's *Supernova* tore up the sod as he followed Star Captain Keating. The rolling, grass-covered hills were deceptive. At first glance they appeared to be shallow hills and ridges, but the depressions were, in some cases, deep enough to conceal a BattleMech. They broke up the line of sight, forcing combat to be up close and personal.

Keating and the rest of his Star stopped. "Trent, proceed to Waypoint Bravo and wait there."

"*Aff*, Star Captain," Trent replied, and checked his tactical display, which mapped out the second waypoint, some three kilometers south into the rolling plains.

When he reached the designated waypoint, he stood in a depression between two massive hills that concealed him. Checking his display, he saw the red, pulsing lights marking the Ice Hellions hitting the Star commanded by the Nova Cat Khans. The aerospace fighter dogfight was only visible as contrails in the air, but the chatter on the tactical channel spoke of a vicious battle being waged.

The remainder of the Hellion assault bore down on the Khans while Star Captain Keating's Star, sans Trent, pivoted slightly, preparing to hit them in the flank. The Ice Hellions were moving fast, adhering to the straight line boring in on the glacier face where the *Keshik* defenses were anchored. *Their lust for vengeance makes them predictable.* That was something Trent understood. He had faced the same with his own Smoke Jaguars. Rage could cloud logic, thinking, and tactics.

"In position," Trent signaled. Watching the tactical display, he saw Khan Taney's red dot of light on the tactical display flicker off. A few seconds later, the same happened to Khan Leroux's signal.

SaKhan Lucian Carns's deep, rolling voice came on the channel. "Khan Leroux has fallen. Now we shred these Hellions for supporting a false vision!"

A chorus of "*aff*s" rang out on the channel, including Trent's.

Keating's voice came over the tactical channel. "Star Captain Trent, it is time. They are bleeding us here, one plate of armor at a time. Get their attention."

Trent found himself smiling as he switched to the broadband channel to transmit into the clear. "This is Star Captain Trent, formerly of Clan Smoke Jaguar. It is I who brought the Star League to your doorstep, Ice Hellions and the rest of the Clans. It is I who was the fuel on the funeral pyre of the Jaguars. It is I who gave the Exodus Road to your enemies. Come to me, if you have the courage!" He had gone over the statement several times in his head prior to the battle. As he said it, he did so with vigor and energy that he had not felt in a long time. *That should do it.*

On the tactical display, two red dots closed on his position within a half-minute. Their reactor signatures and scans from the other Nova Cats told him what he was up against. *A Naga...they must have won it from Clan Wolf. That is their artillery support.*

The other approaching signal was a 100-ton *Dire Wolf*. Bristling with weapons, the OmniMech was a formidable foe. As a Smoke Jaguar, Trent had experienced the 'Mech up close many times. Even his *Supernova* seemed dwarfed near it.

One-on-one, each of these would be equal to his 'Mech. Two of them meant he would have to be decisive in his victory. *I trained my entire life for this moment: a chance at redemption in a new Clan, one not marred by arrogance and brutality.* He hit the warmers on his six extended-range large lasers and flexed his muscles against his safety harness.

The first Ice Hellion to crest the ridge of hills was the *Naga*. It looked like a hooded cobra, with fanlike arms ending in boxy Arrow IV missile racks where its hands should be. It unleashed a pair of salvos the moment it locked onto him. The Arrow IV missiles roared through the air between them as Trent broke into a sideways run, heading perpendicular to the incoming warheads. It was to no avail; the explosions tore into his upper torso and right arm. Shards of armor fragments from the hit peppered his cockpit like hailstones.

"I am Benjamin Rood of Clan Ice Hellion. Prepare to die, defiler!" a voice broadcast on the direct channel in his neurohelmet's earpiece.

"Not yet," Trent replied, more to himself than his Bloodnamed foe. "You disappoint me, Rood. I expected better than you in response to the litany of my crimes against the Clans. Perhaps intelligence was something they forgot to mix into your iron womb."

The *Naga* paused in mid-step at his response. "You are unworthy of taunts, defiler. You are barely worth the ammunition needed to kill you."

"Words do not cut, but I will," Trent said through gritted teeth. His training brought to mind the *Naga*'s specifications. *If I'm going to take this out, I need to negate its firepower and maybe cook off its ammo.* The key was to concentrate his fire on the target 'Mech, not easy while being shot at.

He raised his right arm, bringing his targeting reticle onto the right arm of his enemy, and unleashed three of his large lasers. The searing crimson beams stabbed outward like lances, one hitting the center torso of the 'Mech, the others cutting deep, black scars in the hood and arm actuator, sending armor plates spinning off behind it.

The *Naga* sidestepped along the ridge of the line of hills, keeping its waist pivoted and locked on Trent. Trent ignored the slight rise in his 'Mech's temperature and reversed his stride as another salvo of Arrow IV missiles launched. He had timed it just right. Only one of the large missiles hit him, this time in his left leg. The explosion rocked his 'Mech while the other missiles hit the hillside behind him, sending a thundering concussion that pushed him forward as he coped with the hit to his leg. It altered his balance, and he had the presence of mind to hold his shot until he was sure he could make it count.

Raising both arms, he zoomed his targeting reticle in on the right side of the *Naga*. This time he unleashed four of his large extended-range lasers, once more favoring the right side of his target. One shot went high, just above the large hood of the *Naga*. One lanced again into the Hellion's center torso just under the cockpit. It made a crater-like hole there, shimmering red as it punched into the myomer muscles. Smoke curled out of the gouge he had burned.

The other two lasers hit the already-damaged torso and arm of the *Naga*. The impacts seemed to make the 'Mech stagger back, if only a half-step.

Trent juked his stride again, backstepping out of the shallow low ground and moving up the hillside opposite his Ice Hellion foe. The heat was now nearly impossible to ignore. *I have to manage this, give myself some time to cool.* He slowed his gait, then pivoted sideways.

The air between the two 'Mechs filled with the thin, snakelike smoke trails of Arrow IV missiles. One explosion tore up the sod behind him, raining grass and clumps of dirt on his *Supernova*, while a huge explosion tore into his right leg. The damage display chirped, and amber warnings appeared on the outline of his 'Mech's right thigh. Trent still held his fire as his 'Mech continued to vent heat.

He angled his climb along the hillside, gaining altitude as he moved. It was tempting to run, but he wanted to cool down as much as possible. He stopped suddenly, as another salvo rained down on him, one explosion rocking the left torso of his 'Mech and a blast hitting his right foot. The hit staggered him slightly, and he fought to maintain his balance. The Arrow IV missiles brutalized him with each impact.

He checked his temperature, and a smile rose on his twisted lips. *It is time.*

He switched the massive lasers in both arms to a single target-interlock circuit, allowing him to fire them all in one salvo. He knew the heat would hit a critical spike, but he ran the calculations in his mind unconsciously. Trent moved the targeting reticle onto the center of the Ice Hellion 'Mech and fired.

There was a whining hum as the lasers fired and the air filled with scarlet beams stabbing out at his foe. One missed, going high into the air. The other five found their marks on the *Naga*.

The Ice Hellion's right torso erupted from within as the remaining missile ammunition cooked off from the damage. The destruction made the entire arm of the 'Mech go limp. Even with cellular ammunition storage, the explosion still did some damage to its torso.

The rest of the shots stitched into the body of the 'Mech just under the cockpit. The *Naga* seemed to shake violently—*damage to its gyro.* Trent's tactical display showed a severe heat spike in his foe's 'Mech. Either the lasers or the exploding ammunition had savaged the heart of the 'Mech, its fusion reactor. As his own cockpit became a furnace around him from the heat of the weapons fire, he stopped moving—mostly an attempt to bleed off some heat, but also some out of awe.

The vibrating *Naga* tried to step toward him, but it was as if the 'Mech itself was fighting Benjamin Rood. Its massive footpad wobbled, then locked up as the *Naga* fell. He thought it might topple over backward from the laser impacts, but instead it slumped forward, down the long slope of the hill. As it slid, it furrowed the turf with its shoulders as if they were bulldozers.

*He might still stand up—still fight.* Trent moved his *Supernova* forward slowly, his body wet with sweat except for where his coolant vest struggled to keep him conscious. His muscles, despite the last few days of working out, strained as he moved the 'Mech to point-blank range.

Trent's tactical display chirped a warning—the *Dire Wolf* was closing on his position. Trent switched one laser in his 'Mech's left arm to a single target-interlock trigger. He aimed it at the *Naga* as Benjamin Rood struggled to rock his crippled war machine to its side.

He fired at the rear left torso as the *Naga* finally rolled enough to get to its knees. He had to admire Rood—he was still fighting not only Trent, but the laws of physics to try to kill him.

The brilliant red beam stabbed into the armor, searing a blackened hole. He aimed right at the loading hatch for the Arrow IV missiles—searing inward and setting off the remaining warheads and fuel housed there. There was a loud, semi-muffled *whump!* as the majority of the explosion blew out of the torso. The rest channeled into the already mauled internal structure of the *Naga*. Trent saw a momentary spike in his crippled foe's reactor heat, then a complete shutdown of the fusion reactor, leaving the powerless *Naga* crouched on one knee and one foot.

"Benjamin Rood, you are defeated," he said. Trying to ignore the wavering heat of his cockpit, he twisted to face the new threat. As he glanced at his tactical display, he came to the grim realization that he would not have enough time to cool down before the *Dire Wolf* was on him.

"I would rather be dead than face this indignity," Rood spat back.

Trent maneuvered his *Supernova* so the *Naga* was between him and the approaching *Dire Wolf*. He bent the knees of his 'Mech to lower its profile, using the *Naga* as cover.

"Be quiet," he replied, "or I will make you my bondsman." It was one thing to have been beaten by Trent, quite another to be made his chattel.

The *Dire Wolf* lumbered over the crest of the hill. Looking like a forward-hunched man bristling with weapons, the 'Mech was painted in off-white and light-blue streaks, not entirely unlike lightning bolts, but somehow not quite the same. Dark-blue jagged striping, narrow and erratic, ran vertically like lightning-like camouflage, breaking up the lines of the 'Mech. Trent's tactical readout told him it was loaded out with lasers—medium pulse and extended-range large lasers like his own. The autocannons the *Dire Wolf* also carried made it even more menacing.

"Behold the defiler, cowering behind a Bloodnamed warrior. You truly have no honor in you, false Jaguar," a voice said over his broadband channel. "I am Star Captain Adam Bragg, and I am here to kill you, traitor."

Trent eyed his heat levels. *Time...I need more time.* "You call me a traitor, yet you know nothing of me. What I have faced—what I have endured. I am not a traitor to the vision of Nicholas Kerensky, I am its keeper," he said, goading Bragg into conversation rather than combat. He knew that as he spoke, Star Captain Bragg was adjusting his targeting reticle on the *Supernova*, preparing to unleash a barrage. The only thing holding him back was that he might hit his fellow Ice Hellion.

"If that were the case, you would not be hiding behind a true warrior. Benjamin Rood will not protect you. You are and will always be a coward. Step out, Trent. If you are indeed what you say, prove it in battle."

*He is right; he could still hit me despite the cover. It is enough to give him pause, and that purchases time for me to cool.*

His tactical channel crackled to life for a moment. "Trent, we are on our way to your position. The plan worked. Your contact is the only Ice Hellion left standing." Star Captain Keating's voice was oddly reassuring. Trent saw on his tactical display that the Star Captain was still precious minutes away. *I have fulfilled my role, and have proven to the Nova Cats that I am still worthy of being a warrior.*

"You could fire now," he taunted Bragg.

"*Aff*, I could. My aim is exceptional. I have no desire for Benjamin Rood to suffer further insult and injury in this contest. It is enough that he was defeated by a character as low as you. Step out, and we shall end the façade that is your life. Stand tall, and I will kill you quickly."

His taunts made Trent grin. *We are a people given to bravado and poetry when it comes to battle.* He waited for a few seconds, then rose slowly to the full height of his *Supernova*. His lower torso was still protected by Rood's kneeling *Naga*, but he was standing upright, ready for battle. "You question my honor, *quiaff*?"

"*Neg*. I say you have none, now or ever. You have sold out our people to a false Star League. You have cast your own blood into the ashbin of history by stabbing them in the back. For that, you will die."

Trent watched his heat drop into the green. "So be it, Star Captain Bragg," he said, assigning three lasers to two of his target-interlock triggers. He stepped to the side of Rood's *Naga*.

Bragg opened fire as he charged down the hill with a speed that pushed the Clan OmniMech to its limits. The emerald-green pulse lasers peppered Trent's *Supernova* in several spots, while one of the large lasers came so close to its mark that it seared the camouflage paint on Trent's right arm. The pulse lasers tore into his 'Mech's hulking body, pockmarking numerous armor plates.

Trent extended his right arm and brought his targeting sight onto the looming *Dire Wolf*, unleashing three of the large lasers. The red beams lanced into the assault OmniMech, hitting it on the left side, in the leg, and carving a scar up its torso. As the heat rose, Trent stepped again, moving sideways to the charging *Dire Wolf*, trying to maintain some distance.

Bragg did not relent. He fired his four large lasers and his pair of autocannons, catching Trent as his eyes darted to his heat readout. The autocannon rounds rocked his 'Mech hard, almost toppling him to the side, and the two of the large lasers tore into his left arm while the others hit his legs. Looking out of his cockpit, he saw smoke rising from his left arm, and the yellow damage indicator on his display flashed to crimson.

Trent swung both of his arms toward the Ice Hellion and adjusted his trigger settings, firing four of his lasers. One missed, hitting near the left foot of the *Dire Wolf* and flaming the grass. Two of the beams hit the rounded left leg of the 'Mech, gnarling the armor and twisting it under the heat. The other hit the *Dire Wolf* in the cockpit just above the canopy, causing the 'Mech to jerk momentarily to one side. *That seems to have gotten Bragg's attention.*

The Ice Hellion warrior moved in beside Rood's *Naga* and fired another barrage of pulse lasers. Two hit his 'Mech's bulky body, the emerald bursts searing off small chunks of armor and sending them flying. One hit his left torso, the other hit his left arm. A warning light flared on his damage display. Two of his lasers were out of commission from the impact. Trent killed the power feed to those weapons. *At least that will help my heat buildup.*

Trent brought two of his right-arm lasers onto a trigger and fired, aiming for the *Dire Wolf*'s legs. Both hit the already-damaged left leg, one high and one low. The upper one left a nasty blackened gouge in the armor up into the crotch of the OmniMech, while the other simply burned in deep. A thin green ooze boiled out of the hole—coolant.

Star Captain Bragg fired his autocannons, both into Trent's left side. One hit his damaged arm, while the other hit his leg. His last laser on the left side was lost in the assault, as was most of the arm from the elbow actuator down. The forearm flew off in bits and pieces, leaving a bundle of myomer and bits of internal structure dangling in the air.

Another pair of large lasers followed the autocannon shell impacts, slicing across his *Supernova*'s center torso just under the cockpit. Trent's body ached against his restraining straps. Damage indicators flickered from yellow to red as he staggered under the barrage. The *Supernova* fought him, and he tried to compensate for the shift in his center of gravity from losing the arm, but overdid his efforts.

His 'Mech toppled, falling backward, mangling his rear armor in the process.

Trent was tossed hard against his safety harness, and despite the padding, it dug deep into his left shoulder. His coolant vest tore open and began leaking, the stench of the gel penetrating his neurohelmet. Immediately, instinctively, he extended the right arm of the 'Mech and tried to get to his feet.

Bragg did not relent as Trent struggled to stand the *Supernova*. Damage warnings flashed in Trent's heat-soaked cockpit as pulse lasers peppered his legs and torso, melting armor plating as he rocked the 'Mech to its side, then slowly got to its feet. His muscles protested every move.

As he rose to his full height, another barrage of autocannon fire blasted his right arm and center torso. Each round exploding on his Omega Heavy Stellarguard armor made the big Nova Cat 'Mech quake and rattle. There were other explosions, too, hitting every-where—long-range missiles. Even at this range they speckled damage all over his *Supernova*. His damage display readout showed almost every part of his 'Mech was damaged, badly in some areas.

He unleashed his remaining trio of large lasers at the looming *Dire Wolf*, which seemed to walk toward him almost casually, closing the distance to a brutal point-blank range. It would be nearly impossible for Bragg to miss. Trent's scarlet lasers seared into the left torso of the Ice Hellion, punching deep. There was a low, thunderous rumble as he hit the long-range missiles stored there. While the force of the blast channeled out the rear of the 'Mech, it still tore a nasty hole and created some internal damage. Black smoke billowed out of the laser holes.

If the damage shook the Ice Hellion warrior, he did not show it. Instead, Bragg let go with another pair of large lasers, ravaging Trent's already riddled legs. His right knee actuator protested as he tried to backstep to keep some distance from the advancing *Dire Wolf*, an indication that the damage was worse than his readout was telling him.

His training and combat experience told him he was losing the fight. Between the damage from the *Naga* and what the *Dire Wolf* had poured into him, he was on the edge of complete destruction. He checked his tactical display and saw two Nova Cat 'Mechs closing on his position—but a mental calculation told him they were still too far to be there in time. His options were diminishing with each beat of his heart.

"This has come to an end, traitor," Adam Bragg's voice boomed. "I shall be written in *The Remembrance* for slaying the great Betrayer of the Clans." He closed to thirty meters and seemed to hold his fire for a few seconds, no doubt cooling down before unleashing a killing salvo of hellfire.

Trent licked his lips and tasted the salt in the corners of his mouth. Glancing down at his damage display, he saw there was still one system he had not used.

"Perhaps," he replied on the open channel, half hoping the other Nova Cats were listening in. His jaw locked and his teeth gritted as he managed the next words. "Perhaps not."

Trent fired his 'Mech's jump jets.

The thrust to lift the 'Mech into the air was considerable and the jets' range was short—but Bragg had gotten so close Trent felt he couldn't miss. Heat rippled through the scorching cockpit as his *Supernova* took off straight at the *Dire Wolf*. Trent ignored the blast of heat and concentrated on his enemy.

Star Captain Bragg seemed stunned for a moment, but regained his composure and unleashed his weapons one after the other, trying to pluck Trent from the air as he loomed up and over him. The *Dire Wolf*'s pulse lasers tore off the last bits of the *Supernova*'s leg armor and the autocannon hit Trent's right arm, taking out a laser.

Trent felt the 'Mech rock in the air and saw two of the large lasers streak into the sky near him, while the other punched a cut deep into his *Supernova*'s torso, searing a heat sink in the process. He didn't waver, though, fighting the control sticks and foot pedals with the skill that came from a lifetime of Clan training.

As he came over the *Dire Wolf*, he killed the jets, dropping down like a 90-ton pile driver on his Ice Hellion prey. He felt the jarring impact under his right footpad, and the *Supernova* toppled off to the right side. There was a tremendous grinding sound, metal and armor twisting and protesting as the two 'Mechs collided. He felt weightless, if only for a millisecond, as his entire body weight slammed into his safety harness.

The *Supernova* toppled to the ground, the grass filling his cockpit view as he went facedown. Darkness and the crimson damage display dominated his view through the hot air all around Trent.

He checked his tactical display and saw that the *Dire Wolf* was down as well, only a few meters away. He had done a great deal of damage to the Ice Hellion 'Mech, but had failed to come down on its cockpit and crush it.

Trent pushed with the stump of his 'Mech's mangled left arm to twist to the side. His right leg was slow to respond, then he saw why. The knee actuator was gone. Like his left arm, his leg had been blown away. It would make standing difficult, if not impossible. Regardless, he tried. *My entire life has been about doing the impossible.* He knew Star Captain Bragg would be attempting to stand, too.

Trent got to his knees, and daylight streamed through his fractured cockpit canopy. Twisting his torso and pushing off, this time with his right arm, he managed to shift his weight out enough to rise. He stood on one leg, with one arm, his 'Mech mangled, burned, and blown apart. What little armor he still had was random plates that looked like islands in a sea of carnage, all twisted metal and seared myomer bundles.

As the heat slowly dissipated, Trent twisted slightly to turn enough to see the *Dire Wolf*. He had come down on its right side, shearing down the torso and into the arm. It hung limp at the side of the Hellion's 'Mech, twisted and dangling off a lone myomer muscle that was sparking from electrical damage. The autocannon barrel was twisted and dragging on the ground as Bragg moved like a drunken freebirth.

Trent had two large lasers left, though he wondered how reliable they might be, given the condition of the arm. He raised his arm and fired them both, embracing the wave of heat that hit him. The shots both found their mark, hitting the already-mauled leg of the *Dire Wolf* and sending a gray cloud of smoke rising from what was left of its hip actuator. Bragg's attempt to move was in vain—the hip seized and melted into place.

"You fought well, traitor, but no one will ever know. Now, before you die, know that I will tell them that you pleaded with me in the end. That you begged for *bondsref*. I will tell your brethren that in the end you turned on them, sold them out, told me they were followers on a misguided path of ruin. You will be remembered as a criminal, and your name will be spoken only in the same breath as the Usurper's." Bragg raised his remaining arm slightly and fired.

The autocannon rounds shattered Trent's fusion reactor. He saw it go offline and felt his *Supernova* start to topple. The cockpit exploded all around him, torn by lasers and autocannon rounds. Cool air rushed in as the 'Mech fell hard to the ground. Smoke and pain greeted him. For a moment he blacked out, almost happy to embrace the darkness. *I died a true warrior, but no one will know.* He coughed and tasted the coppery hint of blood on his gnarled lips.

In the darkness, he experienced a flashback to Tukayyid, where he had been so badly burned and injured. The feelings were nearly the same, though the pains were in different parts of his body.

He opened his human eye; his bionic one didn't respond. Blood filled half of it, oozing in his neurohelmet. He tried to wipe it away, but his arm sent a hot ripple of pain to his brain. Coughing, more blood came up. *Broken ribs—punctured lung.* From the way his head was twisted, he saw his bionic arm, now burned off just below the shoulder—probably from a pulse laser hit.

The canopy of his cockpit was gone, torn open to the sky. He saw the *Dire Wolf* still standing in the distance. Trent tried to shift his body, but the agony was too great. His vision tunneled, and a tinny sound filled his ears. *Is this death?*

There was an explosion in the distance, and a plume of fire and smoke rose from behind the Ice Hellion 'Mech. His Nova Cat brothers and sisters—they had arrived!

Trent grinned as the *Dire Wolf* fell forward, crashing some dozen meters from his broken cockpit. His last moment of consciousness before the tunnel of light collapsed on him was the sight of a Nova Cat *Timber Wolf* standing on the hill in the distance.

*I am now ready to face death...*

Then the darkness took him and pulled him down.

# CHAPTER 4

Paul Moon, formerly a Star Colonel of Clan Smoke Jaguar, sat up in his hospital bed and inspected his replacement arm. It was unlike the bionic replacements the Smoke Jaguars used. This arm looked just like the one he had lost, right down to the tone of its synthskin covering. *These Inner Spherers place emphasis on appearance. That was not the way of our warrior caste.* He flexed his new hand and was pleased to feel the sensors in his new fingertips sensing each other.

The replacement of his arm and shoulder made him look whole again—scarred, but whole. While his body was complete, his heart was not. Sleep had proven nearly impossible in the hospital. Not because of the wounded, but because of the memories of what he, Paul Moon, had done. *I lost Huntress to this new Star League.* Defeat was never easy to accept, but this was the battle that had mattered the most. His defeat spelled the end of his Clan. *Khan Osis still lives and should be on Strana Mechty...perhaps a counterstrike may yet come, with the help of the other Clans.* While he hoped such a strike might come, he did not take such thoughts seriously. *We were left here to fend for ourselves. Only a brain-addled* surat *would think the other Clans would come to our defense at this point.*

The conquerors treated him well enough. They medicated him with painkillers, despite his requests that they not. The ComStar and Eridani Light Horse doctors had insisted, and he no longer had the fight in him to resist. *I wanted to feel the pain. If nothing else, it would remind me of my failures.*

There was more that kept him awake in the darkness of night, more than the guilt of losing the Smoke Jaguar homeworld. Words echoed in his mind: *"You, Paul Moon, caused your own destruction, and that of your Clan."* Nothing he did could shake those words, nor the memory of the man who had spoken them.

*Trent.*

The traitor had come to him on his second day in the hospital, not to gloat, but simply to show that he was indeed still alive. Trent had been an older warrior; one Moon had despised from the moment he had met him. Trent's generation of warriors had failed in their invasion of the Inner Sphere, and he had been badly maimed at the Battle of Tukayyid, which had forestalled the invasion.

Paul Moon had sent him back to Huntress. The journey was supposed to be one way. Trent was over thirty and unblooded. Returning to the Inner Sphere should have been impossible for him: it was the way of the Smoke Jaguars, opening up opportunities for younger, better-bred warriors.

But Trent had come back, this time with his ComStar bondsman Judith in tow. Trent's fondness for her was always misplaced in Moon's eyes. He had ignored their relationship. In his mind, she was little more than a trained pet. *I did not realize that she had corrupted him, turned him against his own people. That mistake is mine and mine alone.*

Despite his age and the deformities he carried from Tukayyid, Trent had returned. Moon had been infuriated that he had come back, like a shadow that stalked him. During a battle on Maldonado, Moon had sent Trent into a battle that was sure to kill him. Then came word that Trent had been working with another disgraced warrior on Huntress, and that he might have been turned. Moon had led the troops to capture or kill Trent, only to have ComStar's illustrious Com Guards arrive. *The victors of Tukayyid came to rub salt in our open wounds.* Trent was supposed to have died in that battle. *I never checked for his body; there was no need.* Then later, when he reviewed the battleROM footage, it never occurred to him that Trent could have escaped the explosion that devoured his 'Mech. Again, the blame rested solely with him.

Moon had dismissed Trent after that day. He had lost his leg in the battle, and he liked to tell himself that that loss had distracted him. The doctors had grown him a new leg, but it had taken him months to get back into fighting form. In Moon's mind, Trent had proven himself unworthy and had been killed by his own people in the battle; it was as if he had pulled the trigger himself. Paul Moon had purged all thoughts of the traitor. In hindsight, that also was an error.

The Inner Sphere had formed a new Star League, and their target was his Clan. The Smoke Jaguars had been further betrayed in their invasion corridor when the Nova Cats had refused to fight the Star League to aid them. The injuries he had sustained in fighting Trent had cost him a chance to repel the Inner Sphere barbarians.

*I was supposed to be the hero of Huntress. They would have written passages about me in* The Remembrance. He had mustered the surviving Smoke Jaguars and had set out for Huntress to be its savior... to drive the invaders from the sacred soil of his people. It had never dawned on him that he might lose. Losing would mean the end of his Clan. *I did not understand at the time that we had already lost. Even if I had defeated the invaders, our people were so crippled that the other Clans would have quickly consumed us. It is in our nature, and perhaps it is our greatest weakness.*

The Star League had beaten him. They had taken the jungle world of Huntress for their own, and he had failed to annihilate them. Star Colonel Moon did what he had been raised to do; he fought to destroy those who dared to take his homeworld from him. He had challenged the Eridani Light Horse to a trial on the plains outside Lootera, the capital city, filled with confidence that they would be crushed under his heel. Moon had gone into the fight knowing that it was do-or-die...an all-stakes test of his Clan's doctrine against that of the Inner Sphere.

Now, sitting on his hospital bed, he saw himself in a new light. *Arrogance...that was what filled me. I was so convinced of our superiority I failed my people, again.* Artillery had chewed through his forces and nearly killed him. When the ComStar medtechs had found him, he was nearly dead. His right arm was gone, taken in the battle, and he suffered four broken bones. The Light Horse had won the day, and with that victory came the final fall of Huntress.

The fact that his arm would be replaced by a bionic implant rather than using Clan technology to rebud and grow a new arm was significant. In the Smoke Jaguars, Elemental warriors with artificial limb replacements were barred from frontline combat units. Tradition held that the bionics made them less than a perfect warrior. *Even if our Clan were to survive, I would be relegated to some* solahma *garrison unit, or Zeta Galaxy. If Zeta Galaxy even still exists.* The damage to the *touman* of the Smoke Jaguars by this new Star League had been considerable. *There may not be a home for me, even if somehow we become victorious.*

In the pit of his stomach, he knew sudden victory was an illusion. He had battled the Inner Spherers, and they had proven themselves cunning, devious, and adept. *Our arrogance–my arrogance...was our weakness, and they exploited it perfectly.*

Worse, Trent had come to him in the hospital, wearing a jumpsuit uniform of the new Star League. The traitor had told Moon that the fall of the Jaguars was *his* fault—not Trent's. *Worse yet, he was correct. None of this would have happened if I had not treated him so poorly. I made him the traitor he became.*

Guilt knotted Moon's stomach as he sat in the bed and looked at his bionic replacement arm. *Fate has even seen fit to remake me in the very image of the man who took down our Clan.*

Moon had asked Trent for *bondsref*, ceremonial suicide. Trent had denied him. His old adversary's words still stung his ragged memory. *"Kill you? Oh no, Star Colonel Paul Moon. Why should I grant you the release you seek when I will have to live with my own shame? No, I believe you should live a long and useless and miserable life, wallowing in the bitter poison of the knowledge that you failed as a warrior."* With those words, Trent had truly defeated him.

The former Star Colonel had contemplated killing himself. There had been rumors of some warriors doing that after Huntress fell. Suicide outside of the rite of *bondsref* was rare for trueborn warriors. It was seen as a waste, and waste was abhorrent to the Clans. *With the fall of Huntress, are we even Clan warriors any longer?* Taking his own life or compelling the guards at the hospital to kill him felt wrong to him, against his nature. Death outside of combat would be far too easy a path to walk down. *Trent was right. I need to live a long life to purge the horrible things I have done that led to this time.* Nonetheless, he was miserable.

Major Kris Blau appeared in the ward and walked to the foot of Moon's bed. Blau had been a liaison trooper between the Eridani Light Horse and Com Guard forces on Huntress, and wore both insignia on his uniform. Moon knew the older man far too well; in the last few weeks, he had claimed Moon as his bondsman. Their talks had always been short, not by the major's choice, but because of Moon's brooding. He resented the older man, despite his claim to being Moon's bondholder. Moreover, Blau's white sideburns and salt-and-pepper hair served to remind him that the man was old by Moon's standards, making Blau's domination over him even more insulting. *Were I to have myself killed, I would take him, too, so that I do not have to suffer under the memories that he bested me in battle.*

"Good day," Blau said, rocking on his heels slightly, at parade rest at the end of Moon's bed.

"As you say," Moon replied flatly.

"They tell me you are ready to be discharged. I thought I would come check with you myself."

"The doctors have told me the same."

"How do you feel?"

Paul shook his head slightly. "Does it matter, *quineg*?"

Blau blinked in immediate response. "I think it does. You led the counterattack against us quite effectively. You are the most senior of the Smoke Jaguars to have survived."

"Do not mock me. If I had been effective, you and the rest of this 'Star League' would have been destroyed." His words were not threatening, but flat, almost lifeless, just as he felt at that moment.

"You were the one who initiated a Trial of Annihilation. You set the terms and conditions of the battle. Our victory was fairly won."

Paul Moon said nothing for a few moments. "As you say," he finally repeated.

"Paul, there was a reason I made you my bondsman." Blau pressed the conversation forward despite Moon's clear desire to end it. The fact that he called him "Paul" made it feel like a derogatory phrase. No longer Star Colonel—not Paul Moon, a Bloodnamed and honored warrior of a proud Clan. *I am now merely a 'Paul' in his and other's eyes.*

"To demonstrate the degree of my failure as a commander, *quiaff?*"

Major Blau frowned slightly. "I did it to save you."

Moon cocked his right eyebrow involuntarily as the major continued. "Many of the Jaguar warriors are 'unattached'. They are leaderless and forced to live out their lives here with no Clan to rule them, no battles to fight, no wars to win. I couldn't stand to see someone like you end up like that. It didn't seem right to me...like a waste of materiel."

Moon allowed Blau's words to penetrate, and felt his face get red. He had been treating the visits by the major with disdain. *How would I fare as a Dark Caste bandit?* The thought of being adrift on Huntress under occupation was horrible.

"Besides," continued the major, "you are a leader of your people. Some of them are chafing under our occupation. They need someone to show them that life can and will continue. Otherwise, they may take actions that result in senseless slaughter on both sides. A group of us officers discussed it, and we felt that making you a bondsman to the Light Horse was a way to preserve you so that you can be a living example to your people that this is not the end—but a new beginning."

*A beginning without the Clan that was their family and home.* "My people do not look up to me. I am a failure. I have been made the possession of an enemy I failed to kill. The only example I set is one of defeat at the hands of an inferior foe."

The major seemed stung by his words and crossed his arms. "Paul, you think of us as inferior. We defeated your Clan at its own game—on its own turf. We drove you out of the Inner Sphere, then we came all the way here and crushed you. I know you've had a lifetime of training and brainwashing that says we are beneath you, but in reality, we *have* bested the Jags. That may not be to your liking, but you should consider that in your thought process."

The major was right, and Paul hated it. Clan doctrine often referred to Inner Sphere warriors as barbarians. It was a mindset that had prevailed even when ComStar had won the trial at Tukayyid. Changing that perception was hard; it had been pounded into him from his earliest days in a sibko.

"I hear your words, Major," Paul said. "The fact that you stand on our sacred soil of Huntress is proof of your determination in battle.

What you are asking me to do is forsake a lifetime of thinking, training, and experience. Perhaps you only bested my people because of the failings of a few—such as me, *quiaff*?"

"I saw you in the counterattack, Paul Moon," Major Blau said coolly. "You were no failure. If you were, we wouldn't be having this conversation. We beat you, but you came damn close to whipping us. We defeated you fair and square, but that defeat is not on your head."

Moon nodded once, acknowledging his bondholder's words. *Perhaps he is correct. We did put up a glorious battle.* There had been moments when the Star Colonel thought victory was in sight, especially when they first dropped on Huntress. Now it was a fading memory.

"In the whole of my life I never saw myself as being a bondsman. I am not sure I am suited for this," he said.

The major nodded. "I understand. You led these people here, Paul. Many will be torn between settling into a new existence or trying to take up arms against us in some ill-conceived guerrilla war. We have won this battle and the trial, and the price of that is peace. I need to know if you can help me lead your people again. This time the battle is against change—changing their lives and futures."

Paul Moon sat quietly and contemplated what the major was offering. *I have lain here long enough. My mood was not driven just by guilt, but by lack of purpose.* While the major was not offering resolution for his guilt, he was giving the Elemental warrior a new purpose. "I will accept you as my bondholder, Major Blau. I will play the role you require me to. This is not easy for me. I cannot imagine how it is for my people."

"Good," Blau replied with a hint of enthusiasm. "There is something that you should know, something we have kept quiet so far. The representatives of the Star League have gone to Strana Mechty, and are fighting a Trial of Refusal to stop the invasion of the Inner Sphere. That trial is happening as we speak, with representatives of the Clans fighting the Star League and Nova Cat forces."

The news brought feelings of excitement and dread. "What of Lincoln Osis? He is fighting in this trial with the Smoke Jaguars, *quiaff*?"

"Yes, he is. The results will not change what happened here on Huntress, but they will possibly lead to a standing peace between our peoples." The Light Horse officer spoke with hope in his voice.

The mention of the Nova Cats irritated Moon. When the Star League struck, the Nova Cats had all but changed sides to join them. That they were fighting for the Star League's cause meant they were no longer of the Clans. *They betrayed us when we needed them the most. Blinded by their drunken visions and their souvenirs of battles, they sold our people out. We should have seen that coming from them much sooner.*

"Peace is the antithesis of the Clans," Moon replied. "Our entire culture is centered on the warrior caste and battle. Our liberation of the Inner Sphere is the cornerstone of our people's beliefs. Take that away, or stop it, and what is left of us? We risk becoming obsolete or turning against ourselves simply to maintain our existence as warriors."

Blau nodded again. "You see what's at stake, then. Peace always requires those who are willing to defend it. There will always be a need for men like you and I, who stand ready to defend our way of life."

It was still unnerving that Blau saw himself as Moon's equal, if not superior, but he was slowly coming to terms with it. "This Trial of Refusal, when will we know the results?"

"Soon, I hope. Can you tell me how your people will react if the Clans lose?"

Moon paused for a moment to contemplate. "It will harden some of them, anger others. If the ilKhan and the last of the Smoke Jaguars in the field fall, those here on Huntress will be nervous about the future. Most will assume that the other Clans will ravage our carcass and collect the spoils. They all will wonder what this Star League will do when that happens."

"We will fight," Major Blau said firmly. "Our blood spilled on this soil, the same as yours. I find it hard to believe that once this is over, we will just pack up and leave Huntress to be sacked like Rome."

Paul nodded. "That is what they need to hear. If your people do not provide them with hope, they will seek to make their own. My former Clansmen do not deal well with a void in leadership. You do not want hundreds of former warriors seeking ways to rebuild what you have fought to take down."

"I—no, *we* will need your help, Paul."

"Well bargained and done," Moon replied almost unconsciously. "There is something I need from you, though."

"And that is?"

"A bondcord. If I am to be your bondsman, my people should see the symbol of my role. That cord will tell them that I fought honorably against an enemy and am respected enough to be made part of the enemy Clan."

Major Blau smiled. "I will get you one before you are discharged. When you are released from the hospital later today, report to the Light Horse encampment. You'll find me with the intel team."

Paul Moon watched Blau walk out of the hospital wing, and found himself oddly invigorated, with more energy than he had felt since the fall of Huntress. *Perhaps this is what it is to have purpose...even though that purpose is not my own.*

# CHAPTER 5

FIELD HOSPITAL, NOVA CAT ENCAMPMENT
DUERGAR PLAINS
STRANA MECHTY
THE KERENSKY CLUSTER, CLAN SPACE
24 APRIL 3060

"We lost him," Doctor De Santis said to Inanna.

Hearing Trent was dead drained the blood from her face and she suddenly felt numb. Inanna gazed at the burly doctor, blood smears and splatters dotting his operating gown and even his mask. He had been operating on Trent for several hours, leading a team of medtechs who struggled with him.

De Santis looked at the floor, then back to her. "Three times, in fact. There's something in him that refuses to let go."

Star Captain Keating stood at her side, his thick arms crossed. He had been with her since the battle and had personally carried Trent into the field hospital. The air around him was an invisible mist mixing a hint of coolant, sweat, grease—the cologne of a MechWarrior.

"He is a fighter, this one," he commented to both the doctor and Inanna. "He dispatched one Ice Hellion and did considerable damage to another."

Inanna knew Keating had finished off the last of the Ice Hellions, destroying the Hellion's OmniMech but leaving the warrior alive. As he had put it, "So that he could carry back with him the disgrace of having failed in so important a trial." It was a sentiment she agreed with.

Now she collected her thoughts and suppressed her emotions. "Will he live, Doctor?"

"Unknown. How he has lived this long is something of a mystery to us."

"His fate on that field of battle was foreseen," she replied in a soft tone. *As is his role going forward.*

"I will do what I can. For now, we need to keep him in a coma. His body will need time to recover." With that the doctor stepped away, heading back to his patient.

Inanna moved closer to the clear plastic window that led into the field hospital. Lying on a table near Trent's body was his bionic arm, burned nearly through at the elbow joint. Blood-splattered myomer hung down, dripping crimson gore on the floor. Trent himself was almost like a mummy, wrapped in gauze and medpacks.

Star Captain Clifford Keating put his beefy hand on her shoulder. She glanced up at him. "The Star League won the day. You have brought us great honor," she said to him.

"I have? Both of our Khans perished. My plan worked, but look at the cost. If this is the price of victory, I am not sure I wish to celebrate it." He nodded at the window where the medtechs were adjusting Trent's IVs. "This is not the victory I envisioned."

"*Neg.* It is the victory the Khans foresaw," she replied. *Right down to Trent's participation in the trial.*

"Khan Leroux told me as much, though I did not think of it until after the battle. He said, 'For history to continue, chapters must be closed so that new ones can begin.' At the time, I thought he was merely waxing philosophical. Now I understand differently." There was longing in Keating's voice, which Inanna understood. The Nova Cat Khans had both alluded that they were prepared for their passing, that their deaths were inevitable. She had prepared for the pain of their passing; not so much for warriors like Keating.

"They have laid the foundation of a new future for us, both of them."

"*Aff,*" Keating replied as he watched the medtechs shift Trent to another bed, one for transportation. "Where does this warrior fit in that future, Inanna?"

"Trent does not belong there," she replied. "He is with the past."

"You say that with such resolve, such confidence. We accept him. He accounted for himself with honor in fighting the Ice Hellions. There are others outside of our Clan who will not. In his own mind, he is a traitor. The Ice Hellions called him the Defiler, and in the eyes of the surviving Smoke Jaguars and the rest of the Clans, that is what he will always be—the man who turned against the Clans and gave the homeworlds to the Star League."

She paused for a moment, letting his words sink in. *This too was part of what I saw. I just never thought it would be like this.* Sharing too much of her vision was wrong. Biccon Winters, Oathmaster of the Nova Cats, once told her that speaking a vision could contaminate it, set things in motion that could not be controlled. Rather than risk the future, she kept it to herself. *That is part of the burden I must bear in these events.* "You are correct. The answer, I believe, is before us both."

"What do you mean?"

"The doctor told us that Trent had died. For him to have any sort of existence, even among our people, this must be what the rest of the universe believes."

"A lie."

"*Neg.* It is a truth. As you have heard, he died at this hospital. His codex will be taken and reflect that death. Word must be sent, per our rede, to the Ice Hellions as well. They will help spread the word that Trent the Defiler has perished."

"It still feels like a lie to me, Inanna."

"Deception is not an uncommon tactic with warriors. You used it yourself to a certain extent during the trial. To save Trent, he must perish here. We will recreate him as a new warrior, with a new past. Then he will be able to survive and be one of our people." *...and fulfill the visions I have seen.*

"What you propose...it is something we have never done before."

"We are Nova Cats. We are treading a new path into the future. We have been on this road since the invasion."

Several hours later, she found herself before Galaxy Commander Santin West in the Nova Cat command center, a temporary domed shelter in the middle of their bivouac. She saw several laborers packing up gear and recognized the signs of the Clan preparing to move out. West was large, even for an Elemental, his hair cropped and spiked with precision. His piercing gaze met hers as she moved in front of the holotable that was being carefully packed in its transport crate.

"Inanna, reporting as ordered, Galaxy Commander," she said, standing at attention.

"Leave us," he said in a deep voice to the laborers. "This warrior and I have things to discuss in private."

The technicians did not need to verbally respond; they simply followed orders. The three warriors who were in the command center also left silently. In four heartbeats, the two of them stood alone.

The summons was not unexpected. Santin West was a Nova Cat *ristar.* He had proved himself many times in combat, and had a reputation for being a solid commander. *Which is why I am here.*

"At ease," he said. "What we need to discuss does not require formality."

"How may I serve you, Galaxy Commander?" she said.

"We have two matters to discuss. Just prior to the trial with the Ice Hellions, Khan Carns sent me a private message. He told me to seek you out should he fall in battle. He claimed that you possessed a glimpse of the future, and could tell me my role in it. I am hoping you can shed some light on this for me."

"I can," Inanna said. "I understand that you too share the Gift of Sight."

His large jaw extended forward, locking for only a moment. She saw him blush slightly, a sight she was not used to. *An embarrassed Elemental is a rarity indeed.* "I have had dreams in the past which may or may not have come true. How do you know this?"

"Biccon Winters shared it with me," Inanna replied.

"She should not have," West said. "You, better than most, know that it is a private matter when one gets a glimpse into the future."

"Except when it is not. In this case, Galaxy Commander West, my insights were seen as useful. The Khans both acknowledged that. In the event of their passing, I was to tell you what I saw for you."

West said nothing for a second, letting the silence become static between them—she could feel it in his stare. "Do not speak in riddles. Tell me, Inanna, what is it that you saw?"

"You will be the new Khan of the Nova Cats," she said flatly.

After a momentary pause, West chuckled, the kind of deep, thundering chuckle that only an Elemental could produce. It took him a moment to regain his composure. "I am a Galaxy Commander, and I know the warrior caste is often seen as being driven and opportunistic. I would be a candidate, that much is assured. Perhaps, just perhaps, I am not inclined to take the trials to become our Khan. It may be that I am one of those rare commanders who is content with the unit he leads and his place in the Clan."

"That is why you must be the new Khan. You do not seek it out. Khans Carns and Leroux knew a great truth with our people, that the rank of Khan was not something to be coveted. It is a role warriors are bred for. You are such a man. I have seen it—as did Khan Carns." She handed him a small orange-colored data disk.

"What is this?" the Elemental asked.

"Our Khans prepared for such an eventuality. They left word with me that if they perished in the trial, I was to pass this on to you."

"What does it contain?"

"Plans—contingencies that they anticipated their successors would need."

West looked at the disk and some of the stony resolve washed from his face. "I would have done almost anything to not have this fate befall me. I have never been a power-hungry man. This is the worst time for anyone to lead our Clan. We have severed our ties with those who share our past. There will be those out there who want our blood—who will demand it. We will face threats from every direction. Our only ally is a new Star League, and even that is precarious. What you ask is incredible."

"*Aff*. It is not my role to weigh this decision, but instead to pass that information on to you."

"We have only met once before," Santin West said, "but I am already beginning to dislike you, Inanna." Sarcasm rang in his voice.

"I was told to pass on my vision, and have done so. The rest—that is up to you to come to terms with."

He wet his lips slightly and eyed her from the top of her head to her feet. As he stared at her, she became hyperaware of the difference in their masses. West was a mountain of muscle, and she was small for a warrior. He finally spoke, shattering the momentary silence. "Very well. You have done what was required of you. Now then, we should talk about the other matter...this warrior, Trent."

"How did this come to you, Galaxy Commander?"

"The doctors came to me, as did Star Captain Keating. He and I are old comrades. He served in my Galaxy before testing for the Keshik. With our Khans both dead, they were unsure whom to take the matter to. I was available. This Trent still lives, *quiaff*?"

"To the best of my knowledge, *aff*. He is gravely injured."

"Indeed," West said, picking up a sheet of paper. "According to the physicians, his spine is fractured in two places, requiring a reinforced carbon-nanotube replacement. His bionic arm has been ripped off. His face has been badly burned, on top of the scarring already there. His other arm is broken in two places and will need additional reinforcement to be usable. His bionic eye is damaged. He has a skull fracture, a concussion, two broken ribs, a punctured lung, and several other injuries that seem to be pulling him toward death."

"Yet he fights on."

"*Aff*, that he does. Khan Leroux thought enough of him to take him into our fold and make him one of us. He fought with honor and gallantry against the Ice Hellions. Now I am told that you want to see him repaired and remade—to the point where he will take on a new identity. Tell me, Inanna, if I am to be Khan, how am I to respond to such a request, to deceive not only our own people, but the rest of the Clans? I am most curious."

Inanna felt her face redden at his query, but maintained her composure. "The man who was Trent died on the Duergar Plains. We have the surgical skill to rebuild him—generations of repairing combat injuries make that possible. Our surgeons who work on the other castes have the ability to reshape his face and body, give him a new identity. We are clearly more skilled in cosmetic surgery than the Inner Sphere or most of the other Clans. I believe this is something we are not just capable of doing—it is something that we must do."

"He is barely alive, and you ask that we remold him as a new man—without his input in the matter, *quiaff*?"

"*Aff*, that *is* what I am asking. If we leave him as he is, the other Clans will come at him and at us for harboring him as one of our own.

Trent, in their eyes, is the greatest criminal since the Usurper or the khan of the Unspoken-Clan. His actions not only doomed the Smoke Jaguars, they set matters in motion that led to the defeat of the Clans today.

"You have said we are facing difficult times. Why add to that by making Trent suffer more? Why invite the other Clans to come at us like a pack of rabid dogs seeking vengeance? My proposed course of action preserves us all and saves Trent's life."

Santin West listened carefully to her words. "I hear what you are saying, but that does not mean that I agree with you. Is this part of a vision you have had, Inanna? What are you not telling me?"

She adjusted her stance as she tried to form an answer. *What can I say that won't imperil the future?* "You of all people know the risks of saying too much about what we have seen, Galaxy Commander. What I can tell you is that this is the right thing to do, morally. No matter what the other Clans feel about us, we are a people given to doing what is right. That is our way, and always has been."

"You speak the truth. What you ask for...it is not the norm."

"These are not normal times, Galaxy Commander. The universe is changing, and the Clans with it. The Nova Cats are embarking on a long journey, and we make this trip alone. All that I am asking is that we save the life of one warrior, the man who made this voyage possible for our people."

Santin West cocked his right eyebrow in thought as he looked at her. He wadded up the paper in his hand and tossed it into the recycler, landing it perfectly without even looking in that direction. "I am still just a Galaxy Commander. But for now, I authorize your plan. Keep it secret. Do what you must. Who am I to deny a warrior redemption?"

"Thank you, sir," she said. *There will come a time when I ask for more, but for today, this suffices.*

Inanna stood over Trent's unconscious body as the doctor checked his readings. The air stank of disinfectant, cleanser, and burn salve, like every other field hospital she had visited in her life. *How people can choose to work in such places is beyond my comprehension.* Such was the fate of the lower castes, relegated to certain specialties and careers. "Is he any better, Dr. De Santis?"

"Negative. He is no worse, though, and that alone is something."

"I trust that Galaxy Commander West informed you of his decision, *quiaff*?"

"Affirmative. I meant no disrespect going over your head to him, but what you asked was out of the ordinary. It is beyond my skills, and requires several specialized surgeons. My role is to save the lives of injured warriors. What you have asked for is extreme cosmetic surgery."

"It can be done though," she stated flatly.

"Affirmative," the doctor replied. "We do this work less with our warriors and more with the other castes. In many respects, it is easier to make him look different than it would be to make him look as he did before these injuries. We will reconstruct his jawline, grow new ears, reshape his facial bone structure as part of our repairs, and graft new skin for his face and scalp. From what I can tell, the Smoke Jaguars did little to repair his appearance from his battle on Tukayyid."

"And the rest of him...you can make it so he can fight again, *quiaff*?" *It is his fate.*

The doctor's eyes widened at her request. "Affirmative. We can—I believe. The only outstanding issue is his fractured spine. Reinforcing it and regenerating the nerve connections is delicate work, but is possible. I have seen worse damage be repaired and warriors return to the fray."

"Excellent. When can we begin?"

"We? Inanna, with all due respect, this is not something where your skills are needed. Our surgeons will need to perform their work here before some of his injuries begin to heal and cause more problems than we can solve. We will keep him in a coma to assist the recovery time. It will take some time, but he will wake up looking very different from before, unidentifiable as his former self except by genetic testing."

"This needs to be kept secret, Doctor. Select only those in your caste who can be trusted."

"Galaxy Commander West told me as much. It will be done with utmost discretion."

"Then I will leave you to your work. Contact me when you are ready to move him, Dr. De Santis." She turned and walked out before the doctor could reply. She paused at the doorway and took one last look at Trent. *We have a long journey ahead of us—together.*

# CHAPTER 6

ERIDANI LIGHT HORSE HQ
LOOTERA, HUNTRESS
THE KERENSKY CLUSTER, CLAN SPACE
24 APRIL 3060

Paul Moon found his walk through Lootera surreal that morning. Banners of the new Star League were draped over the symbols of his former Clan. Signs of the fighting appeared everywhere, but repairs and reconstruction had begun.

The people looked as they always did when going about their lives, yet there was a sullen expression on their faces, especially when a member of the Star League passed. It was a look of shame. Even the lower castes seemed to understand the fate that had befallen them. With the defeat of the Jaguars on Huntress, any prospect of them returning to the Clans were no more than idle fantasy. *They fear they are adrift in the chaos of change, their lives at the mercy of conquering strangers who we have told them are inferior to us. This is something we caused as much as the invaders.*

The walk galvanized Paul's thinking about his role with the invaders. *Being a bondsman for the Star League is perfectly demeaning for me... an excellent punishment for the man who lost Huntress.*

He entered the Eridani Light Horse intelligence center in search of Major Blau. The chamber was a stark reminder of his former status. A massive holotank filled the center of the room, fed by a dozen different workstations. It was not unlike the command posts of the Smoke Jaguars, yet, oddly, it seemed more primitive to him. There were more cables than he was used to seeing, the holotank seemed larger, bulkier, and cruder.

Uniformed soldiers went about their work, each noticing him when he entered the room. He could smell them, the aroma of the soaps they used, even the scent of their boots. Paul Moon could feel their eyes penetrating him, trying to determine if he was a threat of some sort. There were no looks of comradeship. He was the enemy in their eyes, despite the end of formal hostilities.

Paul Moon knew his return gaze was likely not helping. He made a point of concealing his emotion. Moon glared back at them silently, making sure he made tight eye contact with each of them as they looked at him. *I may be a bondsman, but I am still a warrior. One day I hope to prove that again.*

On the far wall was a concrete relief that had been chiseled off. The outline was one Moon knew too well, the symbol of the Smoke Jaguars. The Light Horse troops had taken the time to remove it from the wall. The image struck him deeply and personally. *We are to be erased, unless Lincoln Osis and the other invader Clans secure a victory on Strana Mechty.*

He stood at parade rest until one officer, an ebony-skinned captain, stepped up in front of him, clearly not intimidated by his dominating size. It surprised him to see her as an officer—she was much smaller than Clan warriors. *Their standards are so much lower than ours, yet they defeated us. How?* "May I help you?"

"I am Paul Moon, bondsman of Major Blau, reporting for assignment," he said. He held out his right arm, and on his wrist was the bondcord the major had provided. It still seemed strange to wear it on his bionic arm. The arm itself was thick with myomer muscles, but not nearly as thick as his old arm. Even with the synthskin, it seemed scrawny to him, misshapen. The bondcord hung limp on his wrist.

Every time he noticed the arm, he thought back to Trent, who had shared a similar injury. That seemed only just to him, a twist of fate, yet still depressing. *It is as if the universe wants to constantly remind me of my failures.*

The captain pivoted and left the room. A few moments later the major stepped in. "Ah, Paul, good to see you today."

"I am here to serve," Moon said with as little emotion as possible.

"Yes. I am going to have you report to 'Mech Bay Five. They are replacing the arm on my 'Mech, and I want you to work with the technicians to help them."

*Work with the technicians—lower caste members? This cannot be what he has in mind for me.* "How am I able to assist them, Major?"

"You can assist with the replacement of the arm, as I said."

"I am not trained in technical work. My skills are more suited for combat."

Blau gave him a quick nod. "I understand. At the same time, you are my bondsman. We are not fighting a war, not here anyway. Now, south of here, that's a different story—guerrilla activity from some of your former colleagues. What I need you to do is work with my lead technician and provide him whatever assistance he requires."

Moon felt his face redden slightly, and he realized that the composure he had maintained was now beginning to fade. "While I understand the workings of a BattleMech and can make field repairs, I am ill-suited for work as a common technician. This is not an appropriate task for an Elemental bondsman."

Major Blau's face tensed; his jaw slid slowly forward. "It is work suitable for you as *my* bondsman. We are short on technicians, given the number of vehicles and 'Mechs we have to repair."

Paul understood, and more importantly, he wanted Blau to understand. "Each Clan views bondsmen differently. Some see them as below the laborer caste. Others, like the Smoke Jaguars, only take in Bloodnamed warriors as bondsmen and use them for military purposes—coordinating training exercises, analyzing intelligence data, and so on. What you ask is for me to do something foreign to me."

The major seemed to comprehend, but was unwavering. "I appreciate your customs, but they no longer apply. My lead technician, Sergeant Gardenhire, needs help, and we do not have the resources to assist him, so that is what you will do. You *do* understand that, don't you?"

Paul waited for the "*quiaff*" at the end of Blau's question, but it never came. "I meant no disrespect, Major. This is work that traditionally has been beneath a Smoke Jaguar bondsman. I will serve as you deem appropriate."

Blau stood down, at least in terms of his facial expressions. "One of the hardest things you are going to have to deal with is that the caste system you were raised under has no place under the Star League. We're not going to force changes for individuals, but you will need to accept the orders I give you, regardless of your feelings on the matter. That is the only way you will earn the respect and trust needed for you to one day be a warrior again."

Moon did not like what he heard, but understood it. *They are the victors, and he is within his rights. Smashing the castes will cause them problems they cannot fully comprehend. It is clear they are picking and choosing which traditions to maintain.* "My apologies, Major Blau. I am your bondsman and part of that is my pledge to serve you. If you feel that my considerable skills are best suited to manual technical work, I will do that out of honor for our traditions."

Blau shook his head slightly. "Very well. I will be by later to check on your progress."

Moon snapped to attention, then did an about-face to leave. *They have won the war, and as the victors, they will dismantle our very culture piece by piece. This Star League will need to be careful. Unraveling years of traditions and breeding may mean that they win the war, but will eventually lose the peace.*

Sergeant Trixster Gardenhire seemed genuinely happy to see Moon when he arrived. "You're a big lad, aren't ya?" he said as he looked him over.

"I was bred as an Elemental."

"I figured as much," Gardenhire replied with a big grin that split his thick, twisted black beard and mustache. The older sergeant's working coveralls were stained with a variety of colors, some years old, no doubt.

The repair bay had been used by the Jaguars, but Paul only saw a few OmniMechs in various stages of reconstruction...no doubt the *isorla* of the battle. The distant sounds of hammers falling on metal and of grinders being used bounced off the walls. Every bay was filled with a 'Mech and covered with anywhere from two to five workers. A fluorescent light above the nearest 'Mech flickered on and off, almost like a strobe. *There is a reason I never spent a lot of time in such places.*

The major's 'Mech was a *Black Knight*, and it loomed over him. The model dated back to the original Star League—the *real* Star League. This one had been rebuilt, possibly a dozen times from what Paul could see. Some of the armored plates didn't quite match, and there were signs of things having been attached or removed. The logo for the Seventeenth Recon Battalion, Seventh Light Horse Regiment had been pitted and seared in the fighting but was still visible. As it stood, this BattleMech lacked its left arm, which hung from an overhead gantry crane, just a few meters from the shoulder.

Sergeant Gardenhire moved in beside him as Moon looked over the humanoid war machine. "She's a beaut, ain't she? This one is an antique-plus. You cats tore her all to hell. It's taken me days to get her this far along."

"Jaguars," Paul corrected. "'Cats' implies the Nova Cats."

The beefy sergeant grinned. "Same to me."

Moon held his tongue. *I must remember my new station.* "My bondholder ordered me to help you. How may I assist?"

"I'll need some brute strength to get the replacement arm into place. Then we'll have to rebundle the myomer. You ever work with a bundle-stretcher before?

"*Neg.*"

"A welder unit?"

"*Neg.*"

"Ever done any electrical wiring?"

"*Neg.*"

Sergeant Gardenhire paused for a moment. "So it's the basics, eh? Well, I'll train you as we go."

Paul almost felt as if he were looking down at him, mocking his lack of skills. *How I will ever adapt to this?* Then he girded himself. *I will do it as a Smoke Jaguar warrior would...with dignity and pride.*

The two men worked for the better part of three hours to simply get the arm properly positioned and attached to the shoulder actuator. It was hot, sweaty work in spaces Moon found cramped. The sergeant had insisted that Paul call him Trixster, which was easy for the Clansman. *I will never get used to people having a surname they have not won in battle.*

What surprised him was that after five hours of hard work, learning new tools and skills along the way, he found himself almost enjoying the repair. The hulking Elemental was almost embarrassed by the feeling of accomplishment he got when he and Trixster finished attaching the arm. It was the first time since the fighting that he had felt even close to normal. *I will never admit it to these freebirths, though.* While it felt great to do physical labor, he longed for the sting and thrills of battle.

They broke for food, and Trixster led him to join the other techs for lunch. Their cafeteria had been used by the laborer caste before the war. A tattered and battle-burned flag of the Star League hung on the far wall, where it covered a carved quote from the Smoke Jaguar's *Remembrance*. Paul felt the stares of many in the dining area—including his own people, who were also repairing 'Mechs and vehicles. He ignored their gawks as he ate. *I am a bondsman to Inner Spherers; this is my role now, until I prove myself.*

Trixster was friendly and cordial to him, though some of his colleagues kept their distance. Paul did not take part in idle chatter, despite their efforts to include him. He could smell their fear—could read it in their faces. It was understandable. *A month ago, I led the war to defeat their armies and retake this world.*

A vidscreen on the wall spat out news about food distribution and rebuilding efforts in the city. Paul ignored it for the most part. A red banner and an announcement of breaking news did manage to catch his attention and that of everyone else in the room.

The reporter was a frail-looking woman whose voice wavered slightly as she spoke. "We have just received word from the Star League Defense Force regarding the Trial of Refusal on Strana Mechty. The forces of the Clans honorably faced the members of the Star League and Clan Nova Cat in battle." She paused, reading the paper in her hands, which started to tremble. "The Clans have lost this trial. IlKhan Lincoln Osis was slain after the battle in an altercation with Prince Victor Steiner-Davion in one-on-one combat."

Her words drew the air out of the cafeteria. There were murmurs of rejoicing from the Star League technicians there. Almost to a person, the Smoke Jaguars in the room went pale. Several mouths hung open.

Paul Moon understood what the Inner Spherers could not. It was one thing for a lone Clan to face the Star League and be utterly defeated. The Trial of Refusal was against all of the invading Clans. It invalidated the Crusade to liberate the Inner Sphere. It smothered Nicholas Kerensky's vision with a wet blanket of peace. *Peace! We are a warrior people. Peace will turn us against each other.*

The newscaster regained her composure, but still looked shaky. "Lincoln Osis led the last unit of our Clan into the trial. His death—" she stared at the paper nervously. "—marks a new beginning for the former Smoke Jaguars. We will have a statement from the Star League commanders within the hour. To repeat our breaking story..." Her words trailed off into nothingness for Moon as he tried to process what he was hearing.

Some of the technicians became awkwardly conscious of the mixed company and went silent as a measure of respect. Moon sat back in his chair and crossed his arms in thought. There would be no relief for Huntress. Gone was any thought that somehow the Smoke Jaguars might return and liberate the world he had failed to free. *I am no longer alone in my failure. Every Clan warrior living or dead now shares the humiliation I have felt. Even the ilKhan could not turn the tide and return to save us.*

Paul Moon was almost numb from the news, unsure how to react or what to say. Trixster seemed to comprehend that. "Look, I can finish up the major's 'Mech. With all this, I'm sure there'll be some celebrating. I'll let the major know you're done. You should go over and report to him for your next assignment."

*Celebrating? Neg! Could they be that heartless?* After he processed what Sergeant Gardenhire said, he understood. For the Star League the war was over, a complete victory. For the battered and scattered remnants of the Smoke Jaguars, it was a deep and burning humiliation. "Thank you, Sergeant. I will report to his command center." Moon slid his chair out and left the cafeteria, feeling the eyes of everyone follow each footstep.

As he walked out into the streets of Lootera, it struck him that it was oddly silent. He saw members of his former Clan, most with drawn and sullen faces, others with tears and expressions of anger. As an Elemental, he caught their attention, and they looked at him with a mix of scorn and confusion.

One man, a merchant from the clothing he wore, stepped in front of Moon and angrily planted his fists on his hips as he looked up at him. "You are a warrior. How did this come to pass?" Almost immediately the people on the sidewalk stopped and gathered around him.

"We did all that we could to save our Clan," he replied.

The man was clearly unsatisfied with his answer, and from the murmur of the crowd, he was not alone. "We have been told since birth we were the forebears of Kerensky's legacy. Our Khan was the *ilKhan*. We were told that this Star League was nothing but fiction, a ruse. When they landed here, we were assured that they would be quickly defeated—that we had nothing to worry about. Now look at us! My store was destroyed in the fighting. My neighbor's daughter was killed. War was never supposed to reach us—that is the Clan way, yet members of my caste died in the battles. What is going to happen to us, now that our Clan has been broken?"

Moon had no immediate response. He blurted out a confused "I do not know," but those words were not well received by the crowd.

"You are a warrior—your role was to protect us. Now we will be devoured by the other Clans. They will come and scoop us up like chattel," a woman bitterly joined the now very public debate.

*They believe my caste failed them.* "The Star League warriors proved themselves our betters," Paul tried to reason.

"Where were you when they hit us?" another man, a laborer joined in. Others muttered "yes" in support of the man's question.

Paul stood taller and more defiant at that question. "I led the counterattack against the Star League. I traveled from the Inner Sphere with the survivors of the assaults there in an attempt to save all of you."

His response only angered the crowd more. They circled him, closing to within two meters. His warrior training kicked in, and he mentally plotted out a physical fight with them—while at the same time appalled at the concept of fighting the lower castes. Months ago, an angry mob would have been unheard of on the streets of Lootera.

"You were supposed to protect us," another woman said. "Now foreign soldiers patrol our city. Why did you not fight harder?"

"You are a *coward*," another cursed.

That comment pressed Paul too far. He snap-pivoted in the direction of the voice and pulled back the sleeve of his right arm on his jumpsuit, revealing his bionic replacement arm. All eyes fell to it.

"Do not accuse me of cowardice. I had my arm blown off while fighting to drive this Star League off Huntress. I nearly died, more than once. I shed my blood and poured out my soul to try to save our homeworld...to save you. I nearly died, and most of my command was slaughtered giving their all. Call me coward again, and regardless of your caste, I will take you on in a Circle of Equals."

"You are now working for our enemies," an older man called out.

"You have sold out your people," another added.

Moon held up his arm so they could see his wrist. "I was made a bondsman to one of their officers. I am not disloyal to you or my Clan. I honor them by upholding our traditions—traditions that these Star Leaguers seem to also respect." While it was tempting to say something bad about the SLDF, even Moon had to admit they had acquitted themselves righteously. The sight of his bondcord quelled some of the tension in the crowd.

His booming and immediate response drew some of the anger from the gathering crowd. "What is our future?" another woman asked from within the throng. "What will become of us?"

*What indeed?* "I do not know. Other Clans will eventually come and battle to take this world and what is left of our Clan. It is the way of our former people. They will sense prizes and *isorla* and believe themselves better able to defeat the Star League...if only to prove they were superior to us."

"What will happen then?" a younger woman in the gathering asked.

"They will learn the same lessons that our warrior caste did. This Star League is not to be trifled with."

# CHAPTER 7

Alpha Galaxy Commander Rik Myers of Clan Goliath Scorpion stood opposite Khan Ariel Suvorov's desk, his arms crossed in angry defiance. His Khan's Asian features were common to her Bloodline, and she bore the tattoo of her sibko on her neck, an ancient radiation symbol with a hammer in the middle of it. She was angry too; he could see that in her face. Myers and the other two commanders from Alpha Galaxy shared her feelings. *How has it come to this?*

"So the invasion is halted—a peace is forced upon us all?" he finally asked.

"Affirmative," the Khan replied. "The Star League triumphed fairly. The Crusaders have doomed us all by underestimating these Inner Spherers."

"I am satisfied that at least the traitorous Nova Cats suffered. Two Khans downed in the battle—both dead," replied Star Colonel Ahrissta Lunde of the Eighth Scorpion Dragoons, the Whip-Tail Brigade. "They are leaderless for the time being, ripe for the wrath of those of us who did not fail our cause."

Khan Suvorov frowned. "If you think the Nova Cats are crippled, you are misguided. They are still a potent threat. Any Clan going after them seeking vengeance will likely find itself as humiliated as the Ice Hellions were. We did not become the Clan we are by making rash mistakes." While her words were for Lunde, her eyes drifted to Myers.

*She knows me well.* "I concur," Myers said. "The Nova Cats follow visions as we do—regardless of how false theirs may be. They would not have taken the actions they did if they did not see it in their destiny to make those choices. To attempt to disrupt such visions is dangerous."

Khan Suvorov's left eyebrow cocked in surprise at his words.

"Where does this leave us?" Star Colonel Adam Yeh asked from the far end of the trio of Alpha Galaxy officers. His sibko tattoo on the right side of his neck was smaller than most, a sword crossed over a skeleton key.

"Where indeed?" Khan Suvorov replied, leaning back in her chair. The old chair had been carried from the Inner Sphere during the Exodus, and was one of the many sacred relics so deeply prized by the Goliath Scorpions. Its oak and leather creaked in protest as she tilted back in it. "Each Clan is attempting to do what we are discussing—find a path in a universe now forced into peace."

"Will the Inner Spherers remain on Huntress?" Star Colonel Moreau asked.

"Affirmative," Suvorov replied. "They are going to garrison the world. They view it as some sort of liaison office or embassy. It is not. It is a reminder that they came here and defeated our people."

Myers shook his head. "Negative. Not all of us failed. We did not take part in this trial. We may be bound by its results, but our actions did not force this peace. And that enclave on Huntress, it is a threat."

"A threat, *quineg*? I doubt that," the Goliath Scorpion Khan replied. "They took Huntress, but at a high cost. It will take some time for the Star League units rebuilding there to present a threat to the rest of us."

Myers was not convinced. "We would be prudent to go after them before they have the chance," he fired back.

"I believe Prince Victor's commitment to peace. For now, the Star League is not a threat to us or the path we walk," the Khan replied.

"While I trust you, I do not trust these invaders," Myers said. "The Inner Sphere has been embroiled in war since the Exodus. While they desire peace now, I believe that is at best a temporary state. They purged the Smoke Jaguars from the roll of the Clans. How long before they target another?"

Khan Suvorov pounded her fist on the desk with such force that the sound boomed in the confines of the Spartan office. "Negative, Galaxy Commander. Striking at the Star League to preempt a perceived threat that may never come is not our way. They are primitive, but have proven themselves effective. Striking at them in an effort to destroy them would be akin to kicking a beehive."

"So we do nothing, *quineg*?" Myers pressed.

"Of course not," she said, glaring up at him. "We have time and patience on our side. The Clans have never faced this before—a forced peace. It defies everything we have been taught for generations. The Crusade is stalled. The Smoke Jaguars have been crushed. The Nova Cats have turned against our people. As a result, my alleged peers are in confusion and disarray. I must formulate a course of action that will not precipitate a war with this new Star League. I will not preside over the same fate that befell the Jaguars because of arrogance and conceit."

"My Khan," Myers said, treading carefully. "Not taking action is an action in and of itself. The longer we vacillate, the more time we provide for the other Clans to take action. We need to move now, strike quickly, before the spoils are lost to us."

Suvorov's face stiffened at his words. "Do not assume that I am not taking action, Galaxy Commander. Do so, and you and I will square off in a Circle of Equals, and that is something you do not want." That much was true. Ariel Suvorov was not a physically imposing figure, but she moved like the namesake insect of the Clan—with lightning speed and ferocity. When she fought, she was a blur of blows and counterblows.

"I meant no slight, my Khan. I am only fulfilling my obligation as one of your senior commanders." He felt his subordinates' eyes on him as well, wondering where the conversation was going.

Suvorov's voice took on a frigidly crisp tone. "I have no desire to sit back and do nothing. Our people struggled with indecision in the past and paid a price for it. We will not do so again."

Myers understood all too well what his Khan said. The Goliath Scorpion *Remembrance* spoke of his people's struggles to capture the OmniMech technology that the other Clans possessed. It had cost many warriors' lives over the years, and was a blemish every member of the Clan was painfully aware of. *We will not go down that path again.*

Star Colonel Lunde shifted his stance slightly. "What is your desire, my Khan?"

"Galaxy Commander Myers, you must contemplate several courses of action. I need plans that will demonstrate our strength to our sibling Clans, without provoking a critical response from the Star League that we would regret."

Myers and the others stood to attention, and he nodded. "I will find us the right course of action."

Myers usually enjoyed his trips to Strana Mechty. The Warrior Quarter had history. There was a museum dedicated to the Pentagon Wars: some of the artifacts there, including the bloodstained coolant vest Nicholas Kerensky wore in battle, were near to religious relics for a Goliath Scorpion.

This trip, however, allowed him no opportunity to take in the sights. *I am here at a moment in history. Our invasion has been hamstrung by the very people we sought to liberate.* History and context was something the members of his Clan understood and embraced.

He sat alone in his small temporary quarters and tried to relax in the quiet. *We must take some action. If we do not, the other Clans will, and we will be left looking weak.*

He understood the Khan's caution, though. The Star League might look exhausted on the surface, after battling both the Smoke Jaguars and the Crusader Clans, but they had been victorious. *I know Ariel Suvorov. She will not be impulsive. She will want something to believe in before she will take action.* It was a dilemma. Take too much action and risk vicious retribution. Take no action and be seen as weak. *I must find a middle ground.*

For Rik Myers, there was only one place to turn for such a solution. He pulled a small flask out of his kit bag. It contained his custom-mixed cocktail of necrosia, a derivative of Goliath Scorpion venom. He held the flask like it was an old friend. Every member of his Clan's warrior caste had access to the narcotic. Some, like Suvorov and Yeh, took it from a needle, using their tattoos to conceal their use. Myers preferred to ingest the drug in a drink.

Goliath Scorpion warriors believed strongly in the vision quests that the narcotic brought on. In the early days of the Clan, warriors would allow themselves to be stung by their namesake arachnid, but that method often caused overdose and death. The Clan adapted, not abandoning the risky ritual, but instead regulating it, to preserve the lives of the warriors who indulged.

He had won the flask in a Trial of Possession with a Nova Cat warrior. The antique had been brought back as *isorla* from the Inner Sphere. Ornately etched, it bore the symbol of a dragon, no doubt taken from a Draconis Combine world. To a Goliath Scorpion like Myers, artifacts from the Inner Sphere were cherished items—direct links to the past. He held it for a few moments in his hands, turning it, admiring the intricate craftsmanship.

Drinking necrosia was fraught with risk, even diluted as much as it was in his flask. Too little, and the drug would merely numb your extremities. Too much, and you risked damage to your internal organs—mostly the liver and kidneys—or death. The mistake novices made was that they thought they drank too little at first, then gulped more, only to suffer an overdose.

The drug was also highly addictive—though that information was kept from the other Clans. The Galaxy Commander had seen the sullen faces and deep brown bags under the eyes of necrosia addicts. They were often assigned to special units, treated in a similar way to *solahma* units. They entered battle in a drug-induced haze, which sometimes had spectacular effects in combat. *I will never end up that way. Though I doubt many of them thought they would find themselves in such a state, either.*

He knew the exact amount that induced the mental haze that made visions possible. Myers poured out the drink in the flask's shot-glass cap as he had many times before. He drank it, and it stung his lips and gums. The necrosia was bitter, leaving a dry feeling on the back of his tongue. *Onions, and perhaps garlic*—that was what it tasted like to him. The Galaxy Commander lay back on his bed and closed his eyes.

The room pitched slightly—a dizzy feeling tainted with nausea, similar to getting a pulse of neurofeedback from damage in his 'Mech. There was a millisecond of panic as the ripple of imbalance swept him, a panic he suppressed. A cold sweat racked his body a minute later as the dizziness became more manageable.

The darkness behind his closed eyes erupted with bursts of different colored lights. The blackness became a swirl, a fog, a white-gray mist. It wasn't in his room, it was in his mind. Opening his eyes—at least, he thought they were open—didn't change things. The colors grew brighter, the mist much thicker.

In the mental haze he saw an outline of Huntress. The silhouette of a sleeping cat, gray and black, hovered in the distance. Then his mental gaze fell on a jagged, rocky continent on the map: Abysmal. As he recognized it, the map became clear. The mountains—the Lunar Range on the east, the swirling yellow and streaked black sands of the Hatya Desert to the west. In the middle were Jaguar settlements, production and parts storage.

*This means something.* Myers tried to process it. His heart pounded in his ears like an engine, the throbbing making the image distort. *What does this mean? Why am I seeing this?* The more he focused on the map in his mind, the more it faded into the fog. A part of him reached out for it, and it was gone.

An hour later he stirred, his joints aching from his muscles locking up, a common effect of necrosia. He tasted something coppery in his mouth and realized he had bitten his tongue. A dried trickle of blood ran down his jawline, flaking off in his beard as he scratched at it.

Sitting up was painful, as his joints protested his every movement. *Abysmal. That continent is the secret—but what is it?*

He rose, and almost toppled from a last wave of dizziness that hit him. His head ached as if he were in the depths of a hangover. Each time the aftereffects of the drug worsened. Myers fought them back, swallowing hard, mustering his return of control of both his mind and body.

Heading to the small bathroom, he looked in the mirror. Remnants of the dried blood from the corner of his mouth to his chin were visible. His short blond hair was a tangled mess, wet from sweat. He ran his fingers through it in an attempt to make it presentable, but he gave up the effort in a matter of seconds.

Turning on the water, he splashed his face several times. The water was cold and seemed to stir him, give him more control over the downside of the necrosia's effects. His beard was longer than he had expected, and through the open door to where he slept, he saw that nighttime had come to Strana Mechty. *I was under the influence for a long time, longer than usual.*

As he dried his face on a towel, he walked back into the compact bed chamber. At the desk he activated the comms unit. "Find Rife Nagy," he said with a dry, crackling voice.

Star Commander Rife Nagy was head of the Goliath Scorpion's Watch, their intelligence bureau. He had been a Seeker early in life, venturing out in search of artifacts for the Clan. His return had earned him the honor of being appointed to the Watch.

The vid-unit displayed Star Commander Nagy on the screen, his black hair perfectly trimmed and combed. *We are in contrast, Nagy and I, at least physically.*

"Galaxy Commander Myers," Nagy said, leaning back in his chair slightly. "I am surprised to hear from you at this hour."

"I was...*consumed* with some research for Khan Suvorov."

"How can the Watch serve you?"

"I need information on Huntress, specifically what the Smoke Jaguars have on the Abysmal continent—their facilities there, any damage they may have suffered in their fight with the Star League, et cetera."

"What you ask is difficult. Travel to and from Huntress has been all but stopped since the arrival of this Star League. Our intelligence is, as such, dated."

"I know you, Star Captain. I saw your Trial of Bloodright. As a Seeker, you have gone far and wide. I am confident you have eyes and ears on Huntress. I need to know what is there on Abysmal."

Nagy nodded and flashed a faint smile of appreciation at the compliment. "I will have a comprehensive report prepared for you by the end of the day tomorrow."

"Well bargained and done," Rik Myers said. He shut off the comms unit and leaned forward on his palms, grinding them into his eyes. The pain in his head had peaked, but still clung to his every movement.

"There is a reason I saw that image of that continent," he muttered. "And when I learn it, it will unleash the fury of the Goliath Scorpions once more."

# CHAPTER 8

Inanna finished reading the chapter of the old book and carefully slid the bookmark in and closed it. *Norse Mythology: Tales of Ragnarök.* It had been an antique when the Exodus fleet left the Inner Sphere. Every day since the battle she had read Trent passages from it. His coma didn't matter to her; she knew he could hear her voice—or at least she hoped that was the case. *Tales of heroes and gods seem appropriate to one who has done so much and impacted so many lives. One day, someone might yet write Trent's tale.*

She watched him carefully. The surgery had gone well, and the growth accelerators attached to his skin grafts and his reconstructed face all had green indicators. The doctors had assured her that his new face would be noticeably different from his old, but a part of her was reluctant to take them at their word. One had even said Trent would be slightly taller thanks to the carbon-nanotube rods reinforcing his spine. *I will be the judge if they have done their work well, not them.*

Word had reached her the day before—Clan Star Adder had called for the Grand Council to "purge the cancer that is the Nova Cats from our body." A Trial of Annihilation. Inanna and most Nova Cats had expected it. *It is the price we must pay for the path we chose to tread.* The brothers and sisters of their fellow Warden Clans had intervened. The Nova Cats would not be destroyed as the Smoke Jaguars had been. Instead, they had three months to leave the Clan homeworlds. *We have become outcasts, as Khan Leroux had foreseen.*

The Nova Cats accepted the will of the Grand Council without resistance or complaint. Inanna understood this better than most. As one of the seers of the Clan, the visions had been relatively clear, starting with the destruction of the Smoke Jaguars. *We will travel to our new home in the Inner Sphere. And from there, we shall become something more.* It was with an almost eerie resolve that the Clan packed and prepared to leave.

She reached for Trent's natural hand and squeezed it slightly for the hundredth time. It was a warm hand, muscular, a hand that had spent a lifetime in calisthenics and holding controls in battle. *He too has a path to walk.* Despite the damage done to him, his recovery had impressed the doctors. "This warrior has a will to live." Inanna understood that better than the physician. *Fate has plans for him. The circle he began must be completed.*

She felt the hand shift in her own, and looked up. Trent gave a low moan, almost inaudible. He stirred—not a lot, but he moved. Then he coughed once and moaned louder. Inanna activated the call button for the physician and moved to stand in front of his still-bandaged face. "Can you hear me?"

It was as if he tried to form words but couldn't. The special healing mask he wore impaired his lips—but she heard him groan and saw him nod slightly. "You are in a hospital."

The physician entered and asked her to move aside. He and a nurse hovered over Trent, drilling him with questions. Inanna was asked to leave the room as more medtechs came in. She stepped out, and as the door closed behind her, realized she was smiling.

It was like waking from a long sleep—a long, *painful* sleep. Every joint and muscle protested his efforts to move them. The doctors had barraged him with questions, finally getting him some water for his parched throat. He could see from both eyes, though sight in the right one, where his bionic eye had been, was different—the outer edges seemed larger than before, and his field of vision was expanded.

The air stung of cold oxygen mixed with a faint aroma of disinfectant. *A hospital.* It was the only place he had ever smelled that mix of cleansers. Trent struggled to focus.

*What was my last memory?* There was the salvo from the Ice Hellion *Dire Wolf.* He remembered the smell of bacon...then the realization that the smell had been his own flesh. There was an echo in his memories, a scream that penetrated every fiber of his being. It had been him. The pain had been excruciating, and had surpassed even what he had experienced after the fighting on Tukayyid that left his body and face deformed. Trent was sure he had been dying in the cockpit of his *Supernova.* The lighting above him and the sensations that penetrated his long sleep told him otherwise.

The doctors and nurses swarmed over him like a hive of disturbed bees. They told him he had been gravely injured. It wasn't the first time he had come close to death, but they also said he had died several times on the operating table—which was a first. He remembered nothing of that experience, which seemed odd to him. He had always heard there was a sensation, a bright light. None of that had awaited him. *It must not have been my time to go.*

They adjusted the bed so that he was half sitting, and that was when he spotted Inanna. Her smile glowed at seeing him. The fog of his coma was hard to shake, but bit by bit, sentences spoken to him started to make sense. When the physicians eventually left, Inanna remained.

"We won, *quiaff?*" his voice cracked slightly. He reached out with his right arm to get a drink and noticed that his bionic arm had been replaced. No longer a crude prosthetic of myomer and artificial bone, this one looked like a human arm, almost indistinguishable from the real thing. Trent paused in mid-reach and turned it, examining it as if he were unsure that it was really his. *It looks human.* He held the glass as if in his natural hand and took a long gulp of cool water.

Inanna nodded, though the joy on her face faded quickly. "The Ice Hellions were defeated. You performed brilliantly. We lost both of our Khans in the assault, though."

Trent barely knew the men, yet Severn Leroux had taken him in when the Star League and Victor Steiner-Davion had betrayed him. The Nova Cat leaders had honor, and had shared it with him to allow him to fight the Hellions. "I am sorry."

"They understood what was going to happen," she said. "The Star League triumphed over the Clans. There is a price we are forced to pay. In the next three months, we must leave Clan space entirely."

The Star League had won. "And the last of the Smoke Jaguars—and the ilKhan?"

"They are gone. Your former people have been vanquished along with the invasion. The Crusade has been blunted. There is word from Huntress that some warriors are unaccounted for and still fighting... but their efforts stand no chance of success. They cling to a lost cause."

"They do it because it is all they have left," Trent said, adjusting his position slightly in the bed.

"Regardless of their determination, the Smoke Jaguars as you knew them are gone—nothing more than lines in *The Remembrance*, a fading memory in Clan history. Lincoln Osis himself was slain by Prince Victor when Osis attempted to strike at him after the trial. What was the great gray stalking cat is gone."

*And it is my fault.* Inanna did not say it, but Trent felt it. *I lived while my former Clan died. Ironically—I have become the last Jaguar.* "What is to become of me now?"

She moved in closer to him, beside his bed. "You were badly injured, Trent. The physicians only told you about the injuries, not all of the damage. Your head, face, and body were burned horribly in the battle. The battle left you more scarred than before."

Tukayyid had scarred him badly enough. Half of his face had been little more than gnarled scar tissue *before* the trial with the Ice Hellions. *I must look like a monster now. Somehow, that is fitting, given what I have brought down upon the Clans.* "I understand" was all he could say.

"*Neg*, you do not—not fully. Our physicians are more skilled in cosmetic surgery than your former Clan. I had them work on you, rebuild your face and body. It took many hours of work, but they have given you a new face."

Trent reached up and felt the bandages still wrapping his face. "I will look...normal, *quineg*?"

"*Aff*. From what they tell me, you will have some scarring, but it will be minimal. They have given you a new chin, new cheeks, a new brow. Even now, you have hair growing where you once only had burn scars."

Trent reached up and felt several spots on top of his head. Before the trial, he had hair on only half his head. Now he was growing hair again, it seemed. Once his looks had been lost, they had ceased to matter to him. The Smoke Jaguars never used resources to rebuild damaged skin. *I have been told that scars mark a warrior's experience.* "Thank you. This was unnecessary."

"*Neg*, Trent, it was necessary," she replied firmly. "You are known throughout the Clans for what you did. When you died during surgery, we allowed that word to leak out. To the Clans, you *are* dead. Allowing that belief to stand prevents warriors coming after you to glean honor from killing you. Giving you a new face was necessary to provide you with a new identity."

"But I am not dead."

"They must believe you are. Even the Star League has been told that the Ice Hellions slew you during the trial."

*I am a dead man, either in fact or reality. These decisions were made without my input. I cannot change them. I must accept this as my new life. I must imagine there are many, Prince Steiner-Davion among them, who rejoiced that I was no longer around to question their honor.* "So I am dead to the universe."

"So it would seem."

"And your Khans support this?"

"Yesterday Santin West was elected Khan of the Nova Cats, despite his lack of desire to assume that mantle," Inanna replied. "I have apprised him of your situation, and he agrees that it is necessary for you to take this course of action in order to fit in with our people—and survive."

"Then what becomes of me?" He asked the question out loud, but it was spoken as much to himself as it was to Inanna.

"You will be given a new identity, first and foremost. A codex will be created for your new name. You will become a Nova Cat warrior, and none will be aware of your past."

"An identity?" Trent pondered that thought. A new name. "How does one go about choosing a new name?"

His question surprised Inanna, and for a moment, she seemed as perplexed as he was on the matter. She glanced at the chair next to his bed. Trent saw a book there, an old one with a leather cover and well-worn pages.

She turned back to him. "Are you familiar with the Norse legend of Baldur?"

"*Neg*," Trent muttered. His stomach growled, and a wave of fatigue washed over him. *I am weaker than I imagined.*

"He was the son of Odin," she explained. "He was invulnerable to every substance except mistletoe. Loki, the trickster god, learned of this weakness, and tricked Baldur's blind brother Hodr into shooting Baldur with an arrow of mistletoe. Baldur served next to the death-goddess Hel, despite the gods' attempts to bring him back to the land of the living. He eventually returned during Ragnarök."

"Ragnarök?"

"An epic battle where the universe was destroyed and remade. Baldur was seen to represent strength, energy, and the beauty of life."

Trent heard her words and even managed a chuckle. "Beauty and I have never been compared."

"Many believe Clan warriors have no appreciation of beauty. We are always cast in the role of combatants. The lower castes think we do not understand what has appeal and what does not. They are mistaken, of course. Beauty is not the skin you wear, it is within you. In that respect, you are one of the most pure and beautiful people I have ever met."

Trent smiled slightly under his medical wraps and attachments. "You propose I become 'Baldur,' *quiaff*?"

"It is a name that befits you. You have died as he did. The Nova Cats have faced their Ragnarök, and the universe is being remade with us and this new Star League."

The name did not resonate with him, but it meant something to Inanna, and that was enough for him. "We Nova Cats are given to symbolism and mysticism. I am part of this Clan and to fit in, I will become the warrior Baldur."

"Excellent," she said. "I will have your new codex prepared for you to learn. Clan Nova Cat embraces you, Baldur," she said as she slipped away.

As she left the room, the realization hit him. *I am no longer Trent. Trent died on the Duergar Plains at the hands of the Ice Hellions. The universe must believe I am dead, not just for my sake but for that of my Clan.* It bothered him that Star Captain Adam Bragg would be able to boast that he had slain him, *neg*, Trent. It was equally disturbing that Trent, the Traitor, the Defiler, would be remembered only as a demon in the annals of Clan history. *They will never understand the burden that I...that Trent...bore. None will care that he did what he did for the sake of honor.*

"Oddly, my fate, for now, is tied to the Clan that turned against the other Clans. I am Baldur of the Nova Cats," he said out loud to himself. "And today I am born anew."

Khan Santin West looked down at Inanna with his arms crossed and a gaze of defiance he wanted her to see—she was sure of that. She stood to attention when she saw him in the hospital hallway. "Inanna," was all he said in the way of a greeting.

"Khan West. Congratulations on your ascension to your new rank."

His brow furrowed at the mention of his new position. "Thank you. I heard that this Trent has recovered consciousness."

"Trent is dead," she said flatly. "I *have* met with Baldur, the newest warrior in our *touman*."

West said nothing for two heartbeats. "I take it he is comfortable with this deception, *quiaff*?"

"*Aff*. He understands the necessity of this course of action," she replied.

"Inanna, I am not entirely comfortable with this. My predecessor trusted your visions. I have embarked on vision quests myself over the years, some with better results than others. If the other Clans learn of Baldur's true origins, they will come, and with a ferocity that may imperil brother and sister warriors. I am giving you a wide latitude out of respect for those who came before me."

"I understand. I appreciate your trust."

"We should hide Baldur," West said. "Assign him a posting that will keep him from prying eyes. Even our fellow Warden Clans view us suspiciously after we sided with the Star League in these recent matters."

"I concur, my Khan. Yet I am also guided by a need to not do anything that would draw undue attention. You agree, *quiaff*? There is an old saying: sometimes the best place to hide is in plain sight. You have heard this before, *quiaff*?"

West's eyes narrowed as he glared down at her. "What are you saying, Inanna?"

"I have a plan. One that requires your approval..."

# CHAPTER 9

Paul Moon entered the intelligence command center for the Eridani Light Horse and stood out of the way. He had been working for several days under the tutelage of Sergeant Gardenhire, repairing the Light Horse's BattleMechs. While he had disliked the thought of doing the work of a laborer at first, he was quickly coming to enjoy it. The tools were easy, and there was a sense of satisfaction with completed work. That was something he had not anticipated.

Major Blau had been to the repair bay several times to check with Trixster on Moon's progress. He overheard one of the conversations, and it appeared the technician was generally pleased with the services Paul performed. When he heard the words, it made him feel a little proud, and at the same time, disgraced. *I can perform this work, but ultimately, I am a warrior. My lot in life is on the battlefield, not working with myomer stretchers.* But bondsmen were often asked to perform menial tasks—some more menial than others, depending on the Clan.

Most of the Light Horse troops he met were cordial to him. A few looked at him scornfully, something he understood. A few months ago, they had been locked in battle against each other. Both sides had lost good friends and comrades. Paul ignored their icy stares. *It is not my role as a bondsman to persuade them I am now part of their Clan.*

Trixster understood this. Two days ago, he gave Paul a project closer to his liking—repairing two Stars' worth of Elemental armor. The suits were Smoke Jaguar, and some still carried the blood of their warriors, dried and caked where the men had bled out in battle. Sergeant Gardenhire had a pile of suits and a larger mound of parts, all salvaged from the fighting. They were charred, twisted, smashed, and had the burned aroma of battle damage. Their splotched gray, white, and black Smoke Jaguar camouflage was barely visible on some of the parts.

Touching the suits, even in their mangled condition, was oddly pleasing to him, familiar, and it stirred his longing to get away from repairs. The sensation reminded him of who he was, a warrior. Honor was all that prevented him from refusing the tasks given him. Paul understood that a bondsman was honor bound to their bondholder. *Major Blau could have left me to die on the battlefield. He saw enough in me to allow me the opportunity to serve.*

Working on the Elemental suits became a bit of an obsession with him. He was most familiar with their systems and workings, and was the right size to test them. Restoring them was difficult and challenging, testing his skills. Laser damage had fried electrical components, and locating the faulty part was often tricky. Some had been nearly crushed in whatever battle they had fought. Moon organized all of the parts and components and meticulously worked on fixing them one limb at a time—often toiling into the night, long after the other technicians had left. Bit by bit, part by part, he managed to finish six of the suits and took the extra measure of testing them himself. The experience made him smile—not just from the accomplishment, but from once more piloting the suits for which he had been genetically engineered.

As he lingered near the door of the intelligence center, he saw the major conversing with a trio of officers. Blau spotted Paul from across the room and motioned for him to join them. When Moon arrived at the group, he realized his size dominated the small gathering.

"Lieutenants Fisher and Farnholtz, this is Paul Moon, the bondsman I told you about," he said, making a quick introduction.

Lieutenant Farnholtz, a crimson-haired, battle-scarred MechWarrior, extended his hand, and Moon took it, dwarfing it with his own giant fist. Lieutenant Fisher, a tall, wild-eyed man, shook his hand hard, but his clasp was nowhere near as strong as Moon's grip.

"Paul," Blau said, making eye contact with him. "How are things going in the repair bay?"

"They go well, Major. The sergeant seems pleased with my progress." Paul did not want to say that he enjoyed the assignments he had been given.

"That was what I heard," Blau said. "The sergeant said he would like to have you there on full-time assignment."

Moon surveyed the major's face, trying to interpret his bondholder's intention. He chose a proper response. "I am here to serve as you deem best."

Blau paused for a moment. "I was just telling these two that I think there may be a better use of your skills here in the intel center."

"As your bondsman, I am sworn by honor to accept the duties you assign me."

The major shook his head. "I'm asking you how you would *feel* about reassignment."

*Feel? He places value on my opinion regarding my fate.* "My feelings are irrelevant, but since you place value upon them, I was raised to be a warrior. For me, anything that applies that lifetime of training is a better use of resources. Working here, with other officers, would be pleasing."

"Good," Kris Blau replied. "We are having some challenges with which you may be able to assist us."

"What kind of challenges?"

Lieutenant Farnholtz cleared his throat. "We have been raided, three times, by what appear to be Smoke Jaguar forces. They hit us, steal some supplies, damage our defense force, then fade away into the mountains."

"Smoke Jaguars? It cannot be. We were defeated in the trial," Paul replied.

"Seems to us that they are guerrillas, not content with the results of the trial. We've lost a few good men and women so far to them. Their last raid hit the Knights of the Inner Sphere and took out two of their BattleMechs."

"How heavily armed are they?" Paul pressed.

Lieutenant Fisher took a step closer to him. "Our intelligence shows at least two Stars worth of OmniMechs, and some Elemental troops. Their unit insignias have been painted over, but what we have been able to enhance from battleROM footage shows they are from widely different units."

Blau joined in. "Our analysis shows that a significant number of Jaguar warriors are unaccounted for. That is not uncommon in a battle on the scale of what was fought here, but it is disturbing. We had not contemplated that the Jaguars would fight some sort of guerrilla war against our occupation forces. These raids have grown in their audacity, too. Senior command is concerned that it may force a start of hostilities again."

"Guerrilla warfare is not the Clan way," Paul said flatly. He thought for a moment. "Then again, this is a situation no Clan has been forced to face—a foreign invader soundly defeating them on their home-world. It is possible they have abandoned honor in favor of continuing the war against the Star League."

Blau's brow furrowed at Moon's words. "That's what I suspected. There are intricacies of Clan honor that, even after all of this fighting, we are still learning."

"By the Star League targeting the Smoke Jaguars for annihilation, you are forcing the survivors to adapt. For some, this may be difficult, if not impossible. Warriors bred for battle may not adapt well to a life where that is not their purpose. Our society was highly structured, and with the dissolution of that structure, chaos can ensue." His words were factual. "I have been fortunate. I was made a bondsman. I have a purpose. Many warriors do not."

"I feel the same way," the major replied. "I sent a report along those lines up the chain of command a few weeks ago. Now that we have had these raids, the brass might pay attention to it."

"This is the result of unintended consequences," Paul continued. "We have forced some Smoke Jaguars to believe that honor has no place in fighting the Star League. If they accept that, they will continue to strike. And if they do, others will that see their course of action as the best solution. As word of this spreads, dissatisfied and disowned warriors will seek out these guerrillas to join them."

"So what do you suggest?" Lieutenant Farnholtz asked.

"Word of these attacks must be suppressed," Moon said. "News will leak, but you must not allow media coverage of these attacks. That will make it harder for them to garner support from the disenfranchised warriors."

"That makes sense," the major said. "We also need to address keeping all of the warriors occupied with something else—so that support for these attackers can't build."

"As you did with me, they need to be put to work doing something tied to the occupation forces—something that will appeal to their military training. Even forming them into companies of reserve troops may help."

"That still leaves us dealing with these guerrillas. Their actions will make them more open and more brazen as they try to get public attention," Blau said.

"Affirmative. That is what I would do in their situation."

"We'll have to go out after them...in force," Lieutenant Fisher said.

Paul nodded once, solemnly. "It will be necessary to take the fight to them."

Major Blau shifted his stance so that he was directly in front of the Elemental. "That was what I thought you may be able to assist us with. I'd like you to determine exactly which warriors are unaccounted for. I also want a full inventory of 'Mechs, to determine what they may have. You know Huntress better than we ever could. We will need to determine where they may be operating—what kind of supplies they have access to. I will also need you to work with the lieutenants to determine where they may have bases of operations. Right now, we are working in the dark. Many territories on Huntress we haven't even visited yet. You know these warriors, you know their thinking. I need you to help us figure out who they are, where they are based, and how best to deal with them. Are you up to the challenge? I mean—" he hesitated, "—these are your former people."

"My responsibilities as a bondsman require my highest level of honor, Major," Moon replied. "My honor is all I possess. I fought for the Smoke Jaguars with every bit of my energy and determination. I was defeated honorably. I am now part of your Clan, the Eridani Light Horse. I bear no animosity to the Smoke Jaguars. I understand why they feel the way they do. My role for now is to do as ordered. My free will is wrapped in this." He held up his wrist with the bondcord on it. *That will change if I become a warrior again. For now, I play the role they demand of me.*

The major considered him cautiously. *They do not have the same definitions of honor that we had as a Clan.* Finally, he nodded. "Very well then. Paul, you work with the lieutenants here. See what you can come up with that might help us get a handle on this situation."

Lieutenant Farnholtz gestured to a conference room, and the three of them entered, Moon taking a seat opposite the two Star League officers.

"What do you think their endgame is, Paul?" Farnholtz asked as soon as they all were seated.

*What indeed?* "I believe whoever is leading this effort hopes to eventually make it impossible for the Star League to remain on Huntress, thus allowing them to reestablish Clan Smoke Jaguar."

"I was hoping they would have some other goal," Lieutenant Fisher replied. "They have to realize that's impossible. There's no way that we would allow the Jaguars to return to power. That was the point of us targeting them—to destroy them, to make a point with the Clans."

*A point? Aff. That has been accomplished–but what point? An entire people deprived of meaning and purpose? A once-proud Clan now to be consumed by the remaining Clans?* "I am not saying it is a strategy that will succeed. I am merely answering your question. Should I be leading such an effort, it is what I would attempt to accomplish."

"Guerrilla movements generally require the support of the populace to have any chance of succeeding," said Farnholtz. "Will the former Smoke Jaguars support this kind of effort?"

Moon took note of the word *former;* it rang like a bell tolling the demise of his Clan.

He pondered the question for a moment. "I cannot say. This is unlike the destruction of the Unspoken Clan. There is a substantial population that is suddenly cut off from its culture and past. When you press any person too far and too hard, they will cling to any hope, regardless of how false. As such, some will support these raiders."

"I thought the Jags would be bound by honor once we won the trial," Lieutenant Fisher said.

*Jags.* It stung to hear that slang. "Warriors should be bound by the trial's outcome. The civilian population places less emphasis on honor than our caste does. Some are not going to feel bound by the results of the trial because it was against an entity that they still do not recognize—this new Star League. The lower castes will see this as a chance to restore their former status quo, and for them that is far more comfortable than an unknown foreign invader."

Paul wondered longingly what he would be doing had he not been taken as a bondsman. *Would I have taken up arms as they have?* It was a seductive thought, but reality blunted such thinking. The odds of toppling a victorious Star League would be further hindered by the fact that the Clans did not rush in to save the Smoke Jaguars in the time of their greatest need. *With no allies, we are alone in the jungle at night.* With the demise of the Jaguars, plenty of warriors no longer had a profession, a Clan, a purpose, or a home. They would be the easiest to recruit.

The orange-haired Farnholtz shattered his moment of silence. "I think we need to concentrate our efforts. Our first priority should be to determine where these Jaguars might be operating from. They have to have bases to repair their 'Mechs and to hide. Then we need to do a census of the warrior population, try to determine who among the unaccounted for might be part of these raiders."

Paul nodded, as did Fisher. "Do you have any idea where we should start looking, Paul?" the lieutenant asked.

"*Aff,*" Moon said. "If you will pull up a map of Huntress." Fisher quickly complied, and the holographic topographical map of the world came to life on the table before them. "Can you overlay where these raids have taken place?" Small crimson dots appeared as Fisher stabbed at the holotable's controls.

"They are spread out over pretty far distances," Farnholtz observed. "Maybe we are looking at more than one cell."

"That's logical," Fisher weighed in. "It would reduce the chances of us taking them out in one strike. But if that's the case, that means they have multiple possible bases of operations."

"Where would those bases be?" Lieutenant Farnholtz asked. "There's no cities or towns in those areas, just jungle. It's possible they are camping out there, but to keep 'Mechs and men operationally ready, they would need some sort of facility to operate from."

Paul looked at the map for a few moments, remembering that the last time he had looked at one like this was while planning the counterstrike against the Star League. "Something is missing," he said. "Your map does not show the sibko centers."

"Where you train your warriors?" Farnholtz asked.

"*Aff,*" Paul said. "You show the civilian population centers, but we had eighteen or so sibko centers scattered across both continents. Each has the kind of facilities you speak of. All would have 'Mechs and the means of supporting guerrilla operations. If the Star League did not recover the sibkos at the start of the occupation, they would provide the insurgents with potentially willing and enthusiastic warriors as well."

Lieutenant Fisher scrolled down the list of papers for the holotable, then looked up. "We don't seem to have that data. I thought we did at one point, right after the start of the occupation. I remember seeing something on the sibkos."

"It's been erased," Farnholtz replied with a cold realization. "It makes sense. Once this insurgency got underway, someone must have deleted the map so we wouldn't have the means to easily track them down."

It made sense, though Moon felt the two officers look at him suspiciously. "Lieutenant Farnholtz's assumption is logical. You may check with security on my access. I have not violated the honor of my bondcord."

"We're not saying you have," Farnholtz replied. "It's now just hitting us though—someone with access to the Star League's data may be working for these raiders."

Moon waved his hand over the map. "I can give you general coordinates for the locations that I remember. I suggest restricting access to your data, not just from warriors but from the lower castes as well. It is impossible to know who might be posing as what to sabotage our efforts."

There were nods. Fisher spoke with a striking command tone that Paul respected. "Mark up the map, and I will order the satellite tasking. It won't be easy—with that number of bases, they could be on the move, shuffling from one sibko center to another, but we can at least get a start and narrow our patrols. Good work, Paul."

Moon nodded. "To Lieutenant Farnholtz's point, we will need to canvas which warriors are unaccounted for. I can undertake that effort, if it will help, *quiaff*?"

The work continued for several hours. When they finished, Paul had updated their map. The Light Horse officers were genuinely thankful; he could hear it in their voices. He was as well. For the first time since his failed counterattack on Huntress, he had a purpose befitting a warrior. While he still yearned for battle, the intelligence work—even against his former warriors—made him feel whole again.

# CHAPTER 10

DROPSHIP *WANDERER*
INBOUND FROM THE NADIR JUMP POINT
HUNTRESS
THE KERENSKY CLUSTER, CLAN SPACE
28 MAY 3060

Baldur hovered just above the dining area bench across from Inanna, eating an apple. Other warriors greeted him warmly as they entered. He nodded back, acknowledging them, but was still caught off guard by the Nova Cats' friendliness. Inanna was elusive about their motivations, which made him slightly suspicious. No matter how hard he tried to ignore his nagging feelings, he could not. *I have had a lifetime as a Smoke Jaguar to build my mistrust.*

As he glanced out the small porthole into the darkness, he saw the stars and the blackness of space and remembered his long journey on the Exodus Road. He thought of Judith, the ComStar bondsman who had convinced him of the corruption of the Smoke Jaguars. She had done much to teach him a true path of honor. ComStar had reassigned her after he defected. *It is as if the cosmos is working against me.* He looked at Inanna and wondered how long it would be before she too was ripped from his life.

Staring into space, he allowed his mind to wander. Khan West had ordered the Nova Cats to send a diplomatic delegation to the Star League on Huntress—and Inanna had convinced West to include the two of them. Baldur's protests that he knew nothing of diplomacy were dismissed when the Khan told him, "Diplomacy is politics, Baldur. You, above all others, understand the pitfalls and dangers of politics. And you have had more exposure to the Star League than any of us." Baldur had no choice but to acquiesce to the order; the Khan was right, and he obeyed out of respect for the people who had taken him in. West himself was scheduled to visit Huntress before the Nova Cats' departure.

Baldur knew the stars were familiar. *I was raised under these dots of light.* It was a reminder to him of where he was going. Huntress. The former homeworld of the Smoke Jaguars. *This is not a place for a Nova Cat, nor for me.*

"You are thinking of where we are going, *quiaff*?" Inanna asked.

"*Aff.* I am not sure I subscribe to your thinking that this is a good idea."

"As I said before, the best place to hide you is in plain sight. No one suspects you are alive. And if you were, they would never expect you to set foot on Huntress."

Baldur understood her logic, but could not shake the thoughts of what the Jaguars might do if they learned that he was Trent, the Traitor. *They would rend the meat from my bones. There is no fate darker than that of a turncoat.*

"It is hard for me to come here," he finally replied. "These people turned against me once. I am not justifying what I did in response, but the Smoke Jaguars wandered off the Honor Road. They became political beasts stalking the jungles and battlefields. Seeing them again will only stir up memories I had hoped to forget."

"One cannot hide from their past, nor their memories. You are Baldur now, a warrior remade. Our personal history defines who we are. It does not necessarily set our course for the future." She spoke with a serene confidence that sometimes frustrated him.

"I look in the mirror and see a new face," Baldur replied. "It is hard to accept some days."

Inanna reached into her jumpsuit and pulled out a small leather pouch. "I have been meaning to give these to you. Now seems as good a time as any."

She extended her hand, and he took the pouch and opened it. The contents he saw were fragments of cloth. One was a tag that bore his former name, Trent. It had been stitched into the combat shorts he had worn during the fighting on Strana Mechty. The small white cloth was stained a dark brown—his blood. The other was a Star League patch, crumpled and wrinkled. There was also a uniform button bearing the symbol of the Smoke Jaguars.

Trent held the objects and then turned to Inanna. "What are these for?"

Her smile offered him comfort. "They are your *vineers*, Baldur. Nova Cats keep physical tokens of their lives. These tokens play a ceremonial role on vision quests. They are the bits and pieces of our existence, fragments of what has been, physical bits of memory. Every Nova Cat has them. They are deeply personal items that only have meaning to that warrior. I salvaged these from the hospital. While the button was not yours personally, I thought that it adequately represented where you came from."

Baldur looked at the objects and felt them with both his organic and bionic hands, rubbing the Star League patch, taking in its texture and noting the difference between his natural sense of touch and his artificial tactile sensors. *My past fits into a small leather pouch.*

The button floated in the zero-g environment, and he reached out and took hold of it. The pouncing smoke jaguar on the brass button seemed so majestic, yet so small in his palm. A part of him thought the objects were pointless junk, yet he held them with a bit of reverence. As a warrior, he had no personal effects except for his shaving kit, and even that was new. He had never possessed much, and the things he once had were long gone as he shed alliances and lives. Now he had something else that was his, and the feeling was odd, stirring emotions in an unfamiliar way. *My new Clan understands much of how people think and feel.*

He returned the objects to the leather pouch and cinched it tight. He put it in his breast pocket and secured that. "Thank you, Inanna."

"We still have three days' journey. I suggest we get in some exercise and zero-g sparring," she said.

Baldur smiled at the suggestion. The damage to his body had been extensive, and rebuilding those muscles, mastering a new range of motion and a new bionic arm had proven challenging. He finished his apple, and they headed to the exercise room and changed into T-shirts and shorts.

Inanna's sparring style was demanding. Though short in stature, she was lightning fast. Just attempting to block her blows forced him to react almost as quickly—and she still managed to land jabs. His swings were, in her words, "Jaguar-like": direct, stabbing shots where he recoiled his arm before the strike. She compensated with the skill possessed only by a trained warrior.

After a half hour she paused, sweat beading on her brow. "You still fight like a Jaguar. Your fighting style betrays you. When you pull your arm back, I am able to anticipate where the blow is going to come and can block or avoid it most of the time." She drifted to the back wall and pushed off slightly, floating slowly toward him.

"Like you, I was reared from birth to fight this way," Baldur replied, running his forearm over his own brow to wipe off the sweat. He felt the stubble of the new hair growing on his head. "And when my blows hit, they are stronger than yours."

"*Aff*, they are," she said. "I need you to move like a Nova Cat warrior. Our blows are not vicious stabs, but quick, precise strikes. Move your hands and legs from where they are. Your blows will lack some striking power, but you will not broadcast your intentions." She demonstrated the attacks she was referring to. "It creates the illusion of speed, and gives your foe less time to react."

Turning around, she motioned for an Elemental warrior to join them. "Woodall, will you assist us?"

"*Aff*," the hulking Elemental said, floating over.

Baldur introduced himself, extending his hand.

The massive Elemental hand took his and squeezed hard. "I know who you are, Baldur. I welcome the chance to spar with you. I am Woodall Winters of the Forty-fourth Nova Cat Cavaliers, Delta Galaxy."

*They all seem to know my past and identity and are content with that,* Baldur mused. *I wish I could be.*

"Baldur needs practice fighting someone other than me," Inanna said.

"I was watching you—*aff*, he does," Woodall said. "I mean no disrespect, Baldur. Your style can lead to victory, but your movements betray your origins."

Memories of his sibko training came back to him. *I must learn to be a warrior anew.* "Very well. Teach me then."

Woodall and Inanna worked with him, not sparring, but training him how to react—how a Nova Cat reacted in battle. It was hard changing a lifetime's worth of training. They spent hours practicing attacks and blocking the Nova Cat way. The more they worked with him, the more he understood what they saw as different in his approach to battle. Where the Smoke Jaguar style was to strike hard and direct, the Nova Cats were more reactive. They thought through the fight more than his previous Clan, anticipating reactions. Rather than boldly rushing in, they maneuvered more, striking from the sides and rear if possible. In doing so, if they could achieve initiative, they could more easily hold it than in the Smoke Jaguar fighting style. *It is odd that we studied them as a Clan, but never fully appreciated their style of combat.*

Baldur learned that the weight of his new arm was different than the old one, and that threw off his style. Woodall Winters made him practice with it until he became comfortable with the change in weight distribution. It was also more powerful than his previous prosthetic, and that difference he also learned to embrace.

Inanna watched and sometimes joined in the coaching. "You still resist. Do not. Find the middle ground between the way the Jaguars fight and our way. Make that your style."

Woodall agreed. "Change is not easy, but rather than fight it, let it find you." Training continued, and despite moments of frustration, Baldur found himself adjusting to the Nova Cat way.

After several long sessions over two weeks, Woodall Winters crossed his arms. "Let us see if you have become the Nova Cat we all believe you are. You and I will spar."

Fighting an Elemental conjured up memories of the last time he did it—against Paul Moon. MechWarriors were at a distinct disadvantage against the genetically engineered giants. For Elementals, hand-to-hand combat was much more of a way of life than for a MechWarrior. "I am not sure I will be much of a challenge for you," Baldur said, nudging himself off a wall to drift slowly in front of Woodall.

"No honor is at stake," the hulking fighter replied. "We fight to learn."

Baldur became aware that several other warriors were paying attention to their sparring match, floating around the edges of the workout space. He could feel their eyes on him—not Woodall.

Baldur closed his eyes for a moment and cleared his mind. *I am a Nova Cat now...I must make my own place with them...starting now.*

Opening his eyes, he saw Woodall open his arms and spread his stance as he floated in the open space, drifting toward the floor. "Let us begin," he said in a deep voice, a smile crossing the chiseled muscles of his face.

Baldur drifted to the side wall of the gym. Woodall reached the floor first and sprang at him. He came in fast, but not nearly as fast as he could have had he used all the strength in his thick, treelike legs.

Baldur understood. His eyes darted to Winters's hands and saw the first blow come as Winters closed on him, dominating his space. He blocked, not so much to deflect the impact, but to get a push toward the wall. His left leg made contact as he spun from Baldur's hit to his left forearm. The blow was not from a fist but the edge of his massive hand. It felt like a club hitting him, but Baldur ignored the pain and struggled with his balance in zero-g.

He kicked off the wall, moving past Woodall, catching him with a light kick to the side of his neck as he passed—one that gave him a spin and caught the Elemental off guard. He tried to grab at his foot, but Baldur had already passed.

As he neared the floor, Baldur twisted slightly, just in time to see Winters heading at him, his arm drawn back for a strike. *He's broadcasting his attack.*

Baldur hit the floor and pushed off with both legs parallel to the surface. The long reach of the Elemental's fist caught him in his rib cage. There was pain, but his ribs had been replaced as part of his surgeries, and the impact, while bouncing him off the floor, was not as painful as it could have been. He managed to kick off at the last moment, adding to his speed.

Winters sprang to the bulkhead as Baldur reached the middle of the room. He tracked his trajectory and mentally calculated the angles from where the Elemental might spring. Woodall's experience surpassed him, however. Using the edge of his foot, he moved along the wall, then shot off to Baldur's side.

Baldur lost sight of him as he spun, and remembered his new training. His bionic arm stabbed where he thought the Elemental might be, catching him just below the rib cage. Baldur twisted from a stunning blow to his neck, a knee from Winters that made him spin. As he spun in the open space, he kicked off of Woodall's chest, hitting the thinly padded wall hard. Drifting away, he kicked again.

*Time to mislead him.* As he bore in on the Elemental, he balled up his left fist and pulled it back for a powerful punch...but it was deception. *That was the Jaguar way—not the Nova Cat.*

Winters saw it and quickly moved to block the blow before it was thrown. Baldur did not throw the punch but held it; then, at the last possible moment, he struck with his right arm, hitting the Elemental hard in the solar plexus. He heard the *woof* of air rush out from the blow, and Winters momentarily curled up.

Then a massive hand grabbed his ankle. The jerk toward his foe, from behind, momentarily panicked him. He tried to twist, but the beefy forearm of the Nova Cat Elemental wrapped around his neck and squeezed to cut off his air.

Baldur jabbed his bionic arm back hard into Winters' chest, jamming it like a pile driver over and over as the two spun through the room. He struggled, fighting for air, but he was no match for his huge opponent. His vision tunneled, and a low rumble filled his ears. The slick sweat of the Elemental's arm was not enough to give him a chance at escape.

*I need another line of attack, and fast.* Mentally he pictured where his opponent was behind him. Reaching back with both arms, he slapped the sides of Winters' head hard. He caught the other man's cheek with his left hand, but his right hand was on target—his ear. The hit was hard, but his cupped hand sent a rush of air into the big Elemental's eardrum.

Instinctively Woodall recoiled, releasing Baldur. As air rushed into his lungs, he felt dizzy, nearly passing out. He drifted away from his fellow Nova Cat and struggled to breathe. His eyes tried to focus. As they did, he saw that Winters too was recovering. Baldur gasped to suck in more air, then held out his hand.

"I concede," he spat out, drawing in another ragged breath. "Well fought."

Winters shook his head, still struggling with the blow he had taken to the ear. "Well fought indeed."

The other Nova Cats around them were all smiling; some nodded at Baldur as he rubbed his throat. The skin was raw where Winters had held him, and stung to the touch. *He held nothing back at the end.* That made him feel good. To fight unaugmented against an Elemental was good—especially in zero-g.

Woodall Winters drifted up in front of him, dominating his field of view, and Inanna joined them. He offered a slight smile and put his big hand on Baldur's shoulder. "You deliberately deceived me with that blow."

"*Aff*," he said, his vision finally clearing. "I knew you would think I was falling back on my Jaguar training. It was a calculated strategy."

"You have adapted quickly," his foe commented.

"I have much to learn still. I found myself wanting to fall back into my old style. Can we work out again soon?"

"Affirmative," Winters said. "I look forward to it, Baldur. You are rough still, but much further along than I would have expected. You began this fight as an unknown. You did well, though you still have a way to go. You anticipate well, but do not have a full vision of the fight. That will come with time and practice. You ended this fight as a Nova Cat. Know that when you sleep tonight." With those words, he pushed off from Baldur as Inanna drifted with him.

"You never cease to find ways to impress me," she said to him as another warrior along the wall patted him on the shoulder. "Woodall Winters is a highly skilled opponent."

"Why is he here?" Baldur pressed. "A warrior with his skills should be in the Inner Sphere."

"He came here as a result of his Rite of the Vision. It is a ritual that some of our warriors choose to undergo. His vision told him he needed to be here—that he had a role to play more important than battles elsewhere."

"What could be so important here?" Baldur asked, wiping the sweat from his brow again. His heart still pounded though his breathing was much more regular.

"*You* are here," Inanna replied.

Baldur said nothing in response. *Me? He came here to train me? Why would that be important?* While he grasped the basics of the Nova Cat fighting style, there was still a long journey ahead to understand his new people as a whole.

# CHAPTER 11

Galaxy Commander Rik Myers quietly entered the inner chamber of the Temple of Eternal Memories. The temple was one of a dozen or so shrines that Clan Goliath Scorpion had established for meditation and contemplation. Khan Ariel Suvorov knelt at a bench three rows ahead of him, her head bowed in personal reflection. As he knelt, he studied her from behind. *She has come here for mental guidance. I hope these walls give her the true vision she needs.*

It had been hard for Myers to admit that he had made a mistake, but he had. In pressing his Khan to seize the remains of the Smoke Jaguars, he had reached too far. Suvorov was a strong leader, but calculating. *I should have positioned it with her differently, so she would be unable to resist my plan. It was a mistake I will not make again.* While he wanted to absorb as many Smoke Jaguars as possible before the other Clans did, simply stating that goal was the wrong approach.

His knee ached on the kneeling bench, but Myers ignored the twinge of pain, a remnant of a battle five years ago with then–Star Captain Pelchat of Clan Fire Mandrill over a Star League field manual. While the trial had cost Myers a knee joint, it had cost Pelchat his life. His death was necessary in the contest, at least in Myers's mind. *Had he survived, his fellow Clansmen never would have learned an important lesson about dealing with the Goliath Scorpions.*

As he stared at the back of his Khan's head, Myers wondered what lessons Suvorov might need teaching. *Certainly she needs to understand the importance of speed.*

The Khan rose, her formal robe draped over her as she stepped into the aisle and spotted Myers. He rose, partly out of respect, but mostly for the confrontation.

She paused near him. "Odd that you would come all this way at the same time I am here." Ariel stared ate him with an icy expression. Her face betrayed no anger he could see.

"I came with purpose."

"This is a sacred place," she replied.

"I came to speak with you about sacred things."

Turning slowly, she faced him square on. The silk robe she wore, adorned with the emblem of their Clan, shimmered in the candlelight. "I compliment you on your research. My comings and goings here are kept private. Have you corrupted some of the Watch to start following their own Khan, *quineg*?"

*I will not reveal how I know your whereabouts.* "Neg. But as commander of Alpha Galaxy, it is imperative that I know your whereabouts at all times—should the need arise."

"Has the need arisen?"

"I believe that time has come and is nearly gone."

Her eyes narrowed. "The Smoke Jaguars...again."

"Still," he replied proudly. "May I show you something, my Khan?"

She nodded. He took out an envelope and produced a series of satellite images. "I took the precaution of doing some research. This set of images was taken over the Abysmal continent of Huntress in 3048." The image showed dense jungle growth near a secondary spaceport. He handed her the images to review.

"I see nothing here but jungle," she said flatly.

"Affirmative," Myers replied. He handed her another pair of images. "This was taken just a month ago by one of our merchant DropShips over the same region." The new images showed a long line of structures and an enlarged spaceport with roads leading to the new buildings."

"Warehouses, *quiaff*?"

"Affirmative," Myers replied.

"What does this prove, Galaxy Commander?"

"Before the Crusade in the Inner Sphere, there was nothing. But after the Smoke Jaguars went on their rampage in the Inner Sphere, behold, these warehouses appear. One can draw many conclusions, but what I surmise is that the Smoke Jaguars have built these structures to hold *isorla* taken from the Inner Sphere." His words were chosen carefully, as he had rehearsed the discussion in front of his mirror.

"Speculation," Khan Suvorov replied.

"Is it? This is the only major expansion the Smoke Jaguars undertook once the invasion started. Think of the worlds they conquered, the history they had access to. Some of the very jewels of the old Star

League were in their grasp. Who knows what treasures they took and brought back here?"

Suvorov stared at the images for a long time before replying. "If this is why you came, you did not bring enough to sway me, Galaxy Commander. So far none of the Clans have opted to strike at Huntress. For us to be first, I need more."

*More? Negative! She wastes our time with such folly!* "Consider this, my Khan. Remember the Not-Named Clan? They were cast into the darkness of history. Nearly everything about them has been purged from our rolls. Gone is our understanding of their betrayal, their motivations, and even their artifacts. We did nothing then, yet now Seekers of our Clan look for artifacts from that era for study and preservation."

"Go on," she said, handing him back the photographs.

Myers could tell she was hanging on his words. *She is a student of history, as we all are. I must play off that to convince her.* "Clan Smoke Jaguar is no more. This farce of a Star League will never be able to hold Huntress against the rest of the Clans as they come to pick at the rotting carcass of the Jaguars' arrogance. Everything that was Smoke Jaguar will be lost. They are the antiques of the future. Unless someone acts. Unless *we* act."

"Yes," she replied, in deep thought. Myers suppressed his grin; she had been drawn into his logic. He had been planning her manipulation for days, ever since he had received the new images.

"Generations from now, Goliath Scorpion Seekers will travel far and wide to recover the artifacts of this dead Clan. You have a chance to make history. I can go there with Alpha Galaxy and take the Abysmal continent along with those warehouses. In the process, I will secure countless Jaguar artifacts to bring back here. The Smoke Jaguar officers are living artifacts of a dead Clan. Only we understand and appreciate the value of such relics."

"Our focus has always been the pursuit of *Star League* artifacts," she countered.

"Affirmative. The Star League defenders include the Eridani Light Horse, a storied unit that traces its heritage back to the Star League of old. No doubt some of their forces will be thrown into the battle. We will not only have the relics of a dead Clan to hold, but we can also possess some of those held by the Light Horse—or better yet, take some of their warriors as bondsmen. They would be *living history* among our people."

"I sense there is more," the Khan said, narrowing her eyes.

"*Aff*, there is," Myers replied. "The warrior caste of the Jaguars. I aim to claim as many as I can. Their Bloodlines are the most precious future-antiquity that the Smoke Jaguars possess. With them in our possession, we can ensure that their Clan is never fully erased from history." *And with it, I can breed a new generation of warriors that will make me even more powerful.*

She remained unconvinced. "There are those on the Grand Council who would say that the Jaguar Bloodlines were flawed—that their genetic material is forfeit, given their utter defeat by the Star League."

Myers shook his head. "You know better than that, my Khan. We are stewards of history. Their Bloodlines are not the fault. They are victims of fate and of poor leadership. You of all people know that."

Khan Suvorov's eyes flared wider, ever so slightly, but enough for him to notice. "If I were to authorize such a strike, it would need to be limited in nature. I have no desire to stir the ire of this new League to prompt them to strike at us as they did the Jaguars."

"Abysmal supports a *Warhawk* factory, the pride of the Jaguars. The Star League has made it operational again. I will emphasize it in my bid so they will believe that is our true interest." His grin was becoming harder to hide.

"You presume much, Galaxy Commander Myers," Suvorov cautioned. "Yours is not the only Galaxy in the Clan. You will be bidding against your peers. There is no guarantee you will win."

"I assure you, my Khan, I *will* win the right to take the Abysmal continent. And I will be victorious. The Smoke Jaguars' heritage will be ours to possess."

"You see yourself as a *ristar*. I am not so sure that your comrades feel the same way. I have known you since you tested for your rank. You are smart, but not nearly as smart as you like to think you are," she replied curtly.

*Ristars are not made by the gaze of others. They are created out of ambition and vision.* "I believe you will see me in a different light when all of this is over." *And perhaps you will no longer be the Khan...*

His words did not change Khan Suvorov's ice-cold expression. "Your pride may yet lead to your destruction," she countered. "I will not put our Clan in jeopardy in the process—that I assure you. Do not think me a malleable fool, Myers. I did not become Khan by ignorance or blind trust. I know your motivations have not changed when it comes to the Smoke Jaguars. You have merely found a way to make your argument more pleasing to my ears. You may think you have swayed me by playing to things you know I am sensitive to. You would be wrong. That was your first mistake in this contest—let it be your last."

Her words hit him hard. While earlier he had been able to hide his smile, it was much harder to hide his blush. "A good warrior pursues all avenues of attack to achieve victory. I will muster my Galaxy and depart immediately."

"*Neg.* You will not. The Star League Defense Force is here now, in number. They are a long way from their homes. Eventually they will depart, at least some of them will. You will not strike until that time, when they have left for the long road back through the stars. It reduces the risk to our Clan."

"Striking now, in a limited way, would make an immediate move practical *before* the other Clans act."

"Negative. My orders stand. You reach far, Galaxy Commander. I both admire that and am wary of it. You will get your chance to bid on the rotting carcass of the Jaguars. If you succeed, you will be the hero you believe yourself to be. If you fail, you will find your subordinates ready and willing to test you in a Trial of Position. I advise you to tread carefully."

# CHAPTER 12

TIPSY MCSTAGGERS
WARRIOR QUARTER
LOOTERA, HUNTRESS
THE KERENSKY CLUSTER, CLAN SPACE
5 JUNE 3060

Paul Moon sat in the back of the bar and cooled his palm on the ice-cold beer bottle. McStaggers had been a popular bar with warriors before the arrival of the Star League. Lower castes had been allowed in, but their numbers were small. Now things were different. As he glanced around the quasi-darkness of the old bar, he saw a mix of all of the castes. Gone from the walls were the images of the Smoke Jaguar. *The Purge has reached here as well.*

For the last week or so, he had been conducting a census of the warrior caste for Major Blau's team, and the results had surprised him. Far too many warriors were missing or dead. The Star League publicly contended that "some" warriors were unaccounted for. The actual number was over a hundred. Moon had begun to frequent places like McStaggers to find some of the missing.

Another Elemental entered the door at the far end of the room—she was easy to spot, given her girth. He knew her, Star Captain Shane; big, brawny, dark-skinned, and a wall of pure muscle. She had been in his relief force from the Inner Sphere. On the census, she was unaccounted for.

Shane went to the bar and ordered a beer, then surveyed the room. Paul locked eyes with her, raising his bottle and tipping it toward her. She saw him and crossed the room to his table.

"Star Colonel Moon," she said.

"No longer," he said, lifting his bionic arm to show her his bond-cord. "Please join me."

She pulled out a chair and sat, though the creaking told him that the wooden chair protested her weight. Shane was not like many female Elementals, who were muscled to the point where you could no longer tell they were female. She still looked feminine—yet powerful. Her red hair was longer than when he had last seen her. *The Star Captain no longer wears her armor, so short hair is not a necessity.* The long hair was not a fashion, it was a statement: *I am no longer a warrior.*

"So, you are bonded to an Inner Spherer?" she said, taking a long drink of her beer. "The once-savior of Huntress, now part of the occupation force. Times, it seems, have changed."

Her words stung, but Paul did not take the bait. *She is the same old Shane.* "I did not ask to be a bondsman. The Star League can take many things from me, but not my honor."

"So you say," she replied. "At least you have purpose."

Moon took a sip of his own beer. He looked deeply into her green eyes. "So tell me, Shane, what do you do with your time now?"

She shrugged her broad shoulders. "There is nothing for me as a warrior. I live with Camille. She used to be in Delta's Crimson Jaguars. We have taken a home in the Dire Quarter. Our days are filled with wondering what will happen to us, now that the Smoke Jaguars are a thing of history. We are fed by a senior laborer who has given us work on his loading docks. It is manual labor, but it keeps us fit and provides us something to do."

Her words hung in the air between them. Paul understood her feelings; they were not so different from what he had experienced as a bondsman. "We live in difficult times."

"It is only a matter of time before these Star Leaguers find themselves beset by the other Clans," Shane said, taking another long drink of her beer. "You know the Clans. They will see us as tempting *isorla*. They will rain down on us and reap us like crops in a field. Every essence of what was Smoke Jaguar will be lost."

"Our unattached are what I worry about," Moon said, matching her sip for sip. "Warriors who lack purpose are dangerous."

"Those of us without a caste do not speak of going Dark," she said with reference to the bandit caste. In Clan society, the so-called Dark Caste were the lowest of the castes...the discarded human refuse from the other castes.

"I have heard," Moon said slowly, "that some warriors have organized and have been raiding the Star League forces."

Shane's eyes studied his face carefully. "Do you bring this up as one of their bondsmen, or as a former Smoke Jaguar?"

"Both."

She leaned back in her wooden chair, and it creaked again. "Do you seek them out to destroy them?"

"I want to understand what they want, and what our former warriors see them as." It was a direct and honest answer.

"They are led by a former Star Colonel you may know—Russou Howell," she said.

Moon tipped back his chair. He knew Russou Howell. In his census, Howell was said to have died in the defense of Huntress. Howell had been a compatriot of Trent the Traitor, and when he thought he had killed Trent, had turned to a bottle to ease his guilt. The defense of Huntress had apparently rekindled the warrior spirit in Russou Howell. "I thought him dead."

"He lives," she said.

*How did Russou survive? How many others live and may be with him—dozens?* Paul had more questions than answers.

"Is he rallying those warriors who are displaced, *quiaff*?"

Shane took another long gulp from her bottle. "*Neg*. He does not recruit in the traditional sense—it is not necessary. Some seek him out in the jungle. They are the disenfranchised who harbor the illusion that he can win. He has gathered all the numbers he can support. As you know, the jungles of Huntress are unforgiving on men and materiel."

"What of you? Do you find his cause appealing?"

She eyed him carefully again. "You know our people, Moon. The Star League has stripped them of what it is to be a warrior. You also know of the threat coming from the other Clans. Former Smoke Jaguars see his cause as a means to an end. We were created to fight, and Howell offers that chance. The Star League does not. It is seductive, I will grant you that. At the same time, he fights like a bandit, running and sniping at an enemy he cannot defeat. *Neg*. I find his cause a dead end. Ultimately, he will be cornered and killed. Those with him seek death in battle rather than living under peace. I am not that kind of warrior. I do not enjoy manual labor, but I am counting on an invading Clan taking us in and giving us a chance to fight again—even as a *solahma* unit. In my eyes, there is no honor in fighting a lost cause."

She voiced a sentiment Moon understood. Many of the warrior caste had died in battle, but enough survived to cause a problem. *If left without a venue to apply their skills, the surviving warriors will attempt to make their own solutions. That is how raiders like Russou Howell come to be.* "I have been conducting a census of the surviving warriors. While the Star League likes to perpetuate the myth that most of our warrior caste is dead, a significant number are still alive."

"If we had been annihilated by a Clan, the defeat would have been complete—to the last warrior. The Star League was not as efficient. They spared us, thinking they did us a favor. In reality they cursed us to a slow death, a miserable existence. Warriors working as laborers, technicians, and other lower-caste roles. An attacking Clan would have incorporated us as spoils of war. There is no place for us in this Star League."

Paul thought back with a bit of fondness to when he worked as a technician. While the work was traditionally below him, he had found it oddly rewarding and satisfying. "I agree with some of what you say, Shane. I too have worked as a lower casteman, a technician fixing BattleMechs and repairing battle armor. I thought I would hate it, yet it was satisfying. I know that sounds strange. You have worked as a laborer. What is that like for you?"

Shane stared at her bottle, turning the beer in slow thought. "I would not insult you by lying. I find the work somewhat enjoyable—much more than doing nothing. It fills my time, and I can see what I have accomplished when done. The work *does* fill a gap. It does not in the least diminish my desire to be a warrior. "

*I am not alone in my thinking.* "Why *wouldn't* you join the 'Jaguar,' if that is indeed what they call Russou Howell?"

"I have been tempted. Any warrior living in the city would lie if they said they found nothing alluring in what he is doing. As I said before, I am no fan of lost causes. What makes us Clan is victories. The Smoke Jaguars are gone. Attempting to rekindle that flame into a fire while occupied by an invading army is merely wishful thinking." Shane did all she could to avoid eye contact with him. She ended her last sentence by finishing her beer and signaling for the bartender to bring another. Paul did the same.

"What is the future of the remnants of our people, then?" Moon pressed.

"I do not know. There is no precedent for our plight." The bartender arrived quickly with their drinks. Both Elementals took a deep gulp of the amber fluid. It did not yet have the numbing effect that Moon so desperately sought. "You, Paul Moon, you came to liberate Huntress. What do *you* see as our future?"

Her question was complex. *What* do *I think?* He had not put it into words before, mostly because he was trying to figure it out for himself. "I am not entirely sure. I do not think our future is with this Star League, though. They view us still as if we were alien creatures. Even when they give us trust, it is with caution and a bit of fear."

He took another long sip of the cold beer, then continued. "Waiting for the Star League to figure out where we fit in their universe is not the answer. Nor is Russou Howell's choice. Even if he were to somehow drive the Leaguers off-planet, we would be ripe for the other Clans to devour us. I have no doubt of that—their betrayal of their own kind is something we are not likely to forget."

"*Aff,*" Shane replied, clinking her bottle neck against his own. "I have had conversations with many others who voiced the same. No one came to stand with us in our hour of darkest need. The other Clans left us to die. Some may have relished it."

"So we no longer belong in the Clans, and cannot tolerate life under the boot of the Star League," Moon said thoughtfully. "That means we must carve out our own solution."

"How is that possible?"

Paul paused. *How indeed?* "I do not know—yet. It will require some thought, and likely some daring on our part." *This is no minor matter that can be solved around a conference table and through* stravag *negotiations. Any solution with merit and purpose will need to be decisive in its nature.* That realization hit him squarely and made his brow furrow in thought.

"You had better think quickly. The Clans will come to Huntress, you can be assured of that. When they do, they will absorb what is left—without the honor of a battle. *Aff*, the Star League will fight, but in their mind we are still the enemy. That perspective is not helped by the Jaguar's raids. A bit of irony, *quiaff?* There is time now for action to preserve what is the essence of our people. That time is fading."

*Essence? What is the essence of the Smoke Jaguars?* "*Aff.* Howell's actions will never result in a restoration of the Jaguars. There *is* no restoration possible—we cannot be what we were."

"I wish there was," Shane replied in a deep tone. "The age of the Smoke Jaguar has passed."

Paul Moon allowed her a moment of silent contemplation before speaking again. "What our people need is direction and a vision of the future. With that, there can be hope. With hope, they can galvanize around a cause and make the future happen."

"I cannot picture a universe without our Clan. I have tried, but it eludes me. Then again, that problem does not fall to me."

"What exempts you, Shane?" Paul asked bitterly. "These are your people too."

"*You* came from the Inner Sphere to save Huntress," she said, taking a long drink from her beer, the condensation dripping onto her tight T-shirt. She brought the bottle down hard enough to make a sound that was deliberately penetrating. "This job falls to you, Paul Moon. It was your mission to save us. With the death of our Khans, there is no one to countermand your orders. *You* will need to set that vision for the future and plot our course of action."

The weight of her words smothered him. He had thought his mission had ended in the battle that made him a bondsman. Shane was telling him something he struggled with. *I am likely the ranking survivor of my Clan. Does this mission fall to me?*

"Shane, you are not fun to drink with," he said, taking three big chugs and finishing off his beer.

His comrade did the same. "These are not fun times. My words hurt, but are true. You see that, I know it. It is written in the lines on your face, Paul Moon. If there is to be a future for us, you will need to make it from the scrap heap that is all that remains of the Jaguars."

She even dared to flash him a grin, releasing the burden she placed on him with her words.

"If I were to do such a thing, I would have to say that we would never quite be Clan again."

"Every other Clan has already turned their backs on us. If even one had bid to join in the defense of Huntress, we would have survived as a people. Instead they hid in the shadows, like Abysmal swamp monkeys. They put up a sham fight on Strana Mechty and allowed the Inner Sphere to win, mocking us all. They may have doomed Nicholas Kerensky's vision, but that does not mean they have doomed our people. You say we cannot be Clan. I will tell you that our people, in every caste, do not want to be like the surviving Clans."

"We were far from perfect," Paul replied coolly. Memories of Trent telling him how he had set matters in motion that led to the Jaguars' defeat still stung in his ears and mind. "I have come to realize that our arrogance is what brought defeat to our doorstep."

Shane nodded. "I would like to argue with you over that point, but I agree. We were leading the fight against the Inner Sphere in the race for Terra. We were frustrated with our progress then—remember? Who would have thought that those years were the good years—our peak? Now the Inner Sphere sits on a Clan homeworld, and we spin as dust in a whirlwind. The Nova Cats are leaving, and the Clans are more fragmented than ever. Times have changed. To your point, we must change as well, if we are to survive."

Moon remembered the invasion and the euphoria that went with it. *It all died on Tukayyid at our loss to ComStar. That brought about the end of our drive for Terra.* "Change is hard. I sense some tough choices ahead of us, Shane."

"The warriors need a voice, a leader," she said. "You may be a bondsman, but to the warriors, your voice is still loud and crisp if you would only use it, Paul Moon."

"I cannot do this alone," he admitted.

"You have never been alone." Shane reached out and touched the hand still holding his beer. "You have been silent, though. We need your voice, Paul. Without a choice, Russou Howell becomes the only hope, and his cause is forlorn and ultimately doomed. Some prefer death to being adrift. If you offer nothing to the surviving warriors, they will find their own paths, and in a matter of months we will be no more, as a caste or as a people. Then everything we were will truly be lost.

"This impacts more than just the warrior caste. *All* of our people need something to cling to, something beyond these foreign invaders. If people do not have a vision of the future, they will go off and make their own—and that can lead to little more than chaos and destruction for our people."

Paul rested his hand on hers for a long moment. "I came here to see if I could find any wayward warriors. I did not realize that *I* was the one who was lost. I would thank you, Shane, but what you have told me places the burden on my shoulders."

"You are an Elemental. Your shoulders are more than up to the job."

"I alone am not enough. I will need your help, if you are willing."

"*Aff.* If you are the man I think you are, I will do what I can to assist."

# CHAPTER 13

Baldur grimly looked down the debarkation stairs at Huntress. He surveyed the tarmac and noticed where blast craters had been recently patched. The city itself loomed in the distance, and he saw the cratered and burned Smoke Jaguar Command Center. Parts of the former operational command building had crumbled onto the parade grounds where he had once proudly marched his OmniMech in review. The command center was little more than a gaping hole in the city, a shell crater ringed in debris. He had noticed it during his last trip there, with Anastasius Focht.

What struck him the most was that nothing had been done to clear the ruins. The same was true of the old spaceport control tower, now just a charred stub of a structure surrounded by shattered ferrocrete blocks and armored sheets. The new Star League temporary tower was right next to it, casting a shadow over the ruins. *They are leaving evidence of the destruction as a reminder of what was, a monument to the war I brought here.*

He rubbed his shoulder, where the bruise was still fresh. He, Woodall Winters, and Inanna had been training twelve hours a day during the burn in-system from the jump point. They had taught him how to think and fight as a Nova Cat. The lessons were sometimes painful, especially when taking on an Elemental. Winters had been patient, though—as had Inanna. Bit by bit, he was unlearning the techniques of a Smoke Jaguar to become a true Nova Cat.

At the landing stood an older man in his late forties, though there was more age furrowed around the crow's-feet surrounding his eyes. He wore a Star League dress uniform, with the symbol of the Knights of the Inner Sphere on his shoulder, the up-thrust sword in the hand of the Lady of the Lake. At his side were other officers wearing SLDF uniforms marked with the symbols of their respective units.

Behind them were lower ranking officers. Lurking behind that row was one man who stood taller than all the others. Baldur recognized him instantly. Paul Moon. The Elemental Star Colonel who had tormented him, had driven him to the point where he had turned against his own people. Seeing Moon gave him a momentary start: *Will he recognize me?* Baldur curbed that thought. He didn't recognize his own self in the mirror. *There is no way he will know who I am.*

His nostrils caught a whiff of garbage in the air, which surprised him. Lootera had impeccable municipal services. Looking around, Baldur saw several mounds of garbage piled at intersections, with clouds of flies swarming over them. The trees were just starting to turn as autumn loomed—a faint hint of red appeared on some of the palm leaves in the distance.

*This was my home. Now it is a world under occupation.* As he reached the landing, he and Inanna both stood at attention in front of the Knight of the Inner Sphere.

He returned the courtesy. "I am Paul Masters, commander of the Star League forces on Huntress and commanding officer of the First Knights of the Inner Sphere."

"Inanna and Baldur," Inanna replied. "And this is Star Captain Woodall Winters." The hulking Elemental bowed his head respectfully. "We come at the behest of our Khan, Santin West of Clan Nova Cat. He offers his greetings to the Star League and sends us to be the Nova Cat liaisons with your occupation forces."

Masters studied them both for a moment. "May I present Colonel Charles Antonescu of the Eridani Light Horse." An even older officer gave the two Nova Cats a courteous nod and a stern frown. There was some venom there; Baldur knew it when he saw it. *This one still sees us as Clan, and as Clan we are the enemy.* It was the one flaw in the Inner Sphere tradition of combat: honor served to purge such feelings.

Colonel Antonescu made several introductions, the last of which was Major Blau, his intelligence officer. The major pivoted and pointed to the hulking form of Paul Moon. "This is my bondsman, Paul Moon."

"A Smoke Jaguar as a bondsman, *quiaff*?" Inanna asked.

*She knows who he is; I shared that with her.* Baldur's eyes drifted to the bondcord on Moon's right wrist.

Moon came forward one step, a somber expression on his face. "*Neg.* There are no Smoke Jaguars. I am merely a bondsman of the Eridani Light Horse. I but serve." His voice offered no inflection, but at the same time seemed dark, almost grim.

Baldur studied the face of the man he had grown to loathe. His arrogance seemed muted, if not gone. What he saw was someone masking pain...something Baldur understood. The Elemental seemed neither happy nor remorseful, simply beaten. *I thought I would enjoy seeing him like this. Instead, my own guilt in these affairs is personified in him.* Moon's expression was bleak, as if his will had been shattered. *Being a bondsman to Inner Sphere troops, especially a mercenary unit, must sting his honor on some level I cannot fathom.* Baldur averted his eyes from Moon. He hated having any empathy for Moon, yet could not completely smother that feeling.

"We have arranged billets for you," Masters said, then paused. "I am not sure I understand your presence here. With the Nova Cats being forced to leave Clan space, I am surprised that your Khan sent a delegation at this time. I would have thought your people would be busy migrating to your new homes."

"Thank you," Inanna replied. "Santin West recognizes the importance of the Star League presence here, and seeks to maintain positive relations with your people. We have come bearing supplies and equipment we thought you might need, which we do not have space to transport on our journey to the Inner Sphere."

Baldur jumped in. "We were also curious as to the condition of the former Smoke Jaguars, as a people." He felt Inanna turn her head, and knew she was shooting him a warning look. *Yes, I spoke out of turn. I want to know.*

Masters motioned for them to follow him as he continued to speak. "We have had some challenges as of late. The laborer caste has had issues with how we handle rations. As a result, they have opted to go on strike—specifically, over garbage removal. We are trying to work with them on the matter, but for the moment, they have chosen to push the responsibility for removal back on us."

"A strike, *quineg*?" Winters asked, as if the word were foreign to him. "That is almost unheard of in the Clans."

Major Blau spoke up as the entourage crossed the tarmac. "They are not Clan now, but a free people. That is proving a bit of a challenge for some."

"The strike is a nuisance, as are some of the crime issues we've had," Masters continued. "It is not entirely unexpected. These people are adjusting to a new way of life and a new way of thinking."

*"These people."* Baldur heard the words, and they sparked an ember of anger in him. *This Knight does not see himself as an equal with these people. And crime?* Crimes happened in the Clans, but they were rare. Rigid order imposed for centuries ensured most criminal activity was suppressed. *Now that the Star League rules Huntress, all of that is unraveling.*

"Change can be hard for a people so entrenched in their patterns of behavior," Baldur replied.

He saw the muscles on Masters's neck clench at his words. "Well, they are no longer part of the Clans, Baldur. They brought the war to us, and we returned it to them. They have been beaten. That means they must adapt to our culture now. It is no different than when the Clans conquered an Inner Sphere world and imposed their society on the occupied people."

Inanna spoke before Baldur could offer a rebuttal. "What my esteemed colleague is trying to say is that taking such a rigidly structured society and imposing greater freedoms often results in discord." She made eye contact with Baldur, and he caught her message clearly: *do not push this warrior.*

Masters gave a slight shrug. "I am sympathetic, to a point. We won Huntress through blood and death. The Jags fought hard, downright viciously, but we won. There are consequences for losing, and one of those is that the victors can impose their way of living—complete with all of the freedoms that come with it."

Baldur understood the logic, but also understood the former Smoke Jaguars. Freedom had appeal—if you desired it. His former Clan had not been chafing for freedom when the Star League had arrived in force to wrestle the planet from them. He was about to argue the point but, remembering Inanna's icy glare, held back. "I am sure this poses some challenges. We stand ready to assist in any way possible." His words were diplomatic enough, and masked his true feelings.

"I appreciate that. Maybe you can provide us some insight. We've had a minor insurgency here," Masters said as they neared the edge of the spaceport. The painted image of a Smoke Jaguar on the tarmac had been mostly stripped off, with only the faint outline of the springing feline remaining.

"Insurgency? That is un-Clanlike," Inanna replied.

"It's led by someone calling himself the Jaguar. We've been hit about six times, minor raids, mostly against supply convoys. His band of merry men seems pretty small, but they are a persistent point of pain for us. Perhaps after you get settled in, you could offer your thoughts on how to deal with him."

"We will be glad to offer our perspective," Inanna said as Baldur processed the information. Huntress was lost in a trial. Resistance should have ended the moment the Jaguars conceded defeat. *Whoever this Jaguar is, his honor is tainted. Why continue to fight? There is no victory possible here.* He looked around the spaceport again and saw the telltale signs of battle that had not been repaired. *The existence of a resistance movement is a sign of other problems.*

He kept his thoughts to himself. As much as he saw himself as a Nova Cat, a part of him felt a bond to this place and these people. The scars of battle he saw dotting the city were as much on his hands as they were Paul Moon's.

When they reached their quarters in the Warrior Quarter of Lootera, Baldur found himself in eerily familiar yet surreal surroundings. *I stayed in this very building for a week during my upbringing.* Gone were any symbols or signage of the Clan that had occupied the structures. Some of those were obliterated, while other were merely spray-painted over.

Their assigned quarters were clean and Spartan, just what he expected, right down to the military sheets on the single flat mattress.

Winters shattered the silence. "This Star League is not what I expected."

Inanna tossed her bag on her bed. "They are struggling. For a decade they have fought us, and yet they still do not fully understand the Clans."

Baldur set his own bag down. "An insurgency? Even the Not-Named Clan did not wage such a conflict. And labor strikes...those would never be allowed. This Paul Masters and the rest of the Star League are setting things in motion that they do not fully understand."

Inanna nodded. "Which is one of the reasons we are here—to help them. Khan West understands what they are facing. We can offer them guidance."

"What if they do not want it?" Winters asked, crossing his massive arms.

Baldur felt frustration brewing in him. He didn't want to hear Inanna attempt to explain their mission; he knew it as well as she did. Seeing Huntress under occupation was not like when he had arrived with Task Force Bulldog. It had been a battlefield then. This was different. Now the Star League was an army of occupation. "I need to get out of here—get some fresh air...I need to clear my head."

He left the room before either of his comrades could offer to join him. Once out on the streets, he wandered the Warrior Quarter. It took a moment to realize one of the differences. When he had been a Smoke Jaguar, the Warrior Quarter had been full, always bustling with personnel. Now it was oddly quiet and empty. It felt abandoned. The humid air cooled as the evening began, another sign of autumn.

Walking through the quarter, he came across a lone warrior. She wore half uniform, half rags, with signs of wear and tear that would have never been acceptable when the Clan still existed. The Smoke Jaguar shoulder patch had been ripped off, leaving a slightly lighter patch of cloth on her sleeve. She was physically dirty, not from combat drills, but from manual labor. He paused, trying to see if hers was a face he remembered. *Too young...a sibko far newer than my own.*

"What are you looking at, Nova Cat?" she said, leaning against the wall.

"I was just out for a walk," Baldur replied.

"Come to gloat, *quiaff*? Come to see what is left of your former ally?" Bitterness colored her words.

"*Neg*," he replied, taking a step closer. "I get no joy out of seeing what happened to Huntress."

"Of course you do. All of the Clans do. When we needed you the most, all of you turned your backs on us. You left us here to fight and die. Especially the Nova Cats. We shared your invasion corridor—we were fellow warriors, yet when the time came, you left us here to face these barbarians alone. You Nova Cats even turned against the rest of the Clans."

Baldur took no offense at her insult. "Our motives are our own, and not for you to question." He took another step closer. "I did not come here to insult our former brethren. We came to see if we could somehow help."

She laughed. "A little late, *quiaff*? Look around you. This is what has become of one of the greatest of the Clans." The warrior waved her torn sleeve in a sweeping gesture. "Behold the glory that is the Star League."

"Who are you?" Baldur asked, narrowing his gaze on her.

"I am no one," she said flatly. "I was a warrior, an excellent one. I was named Bix, of the DesCastris Bloodline. Formerly of the Fourth Jaguar Dragoons." There was a hint of pride in her words, something that had not yet been smothered from her soul.

"I am Baldur," he replied flatly. "What have you been doing since the fighting stopped?"

"You mean after I disgraced centuries of my Bloodheritage? I have been surviving. I was assigned to a work detail clearing rubble on the south side of the city. It is not work worthy of a warrior, but I am no longer a warrior, am I?"

"What are you then?" Baldur asked.

Bix paused in thought, her green eyes staring at him. "I am not sure any more, Baldur. This Star League came to fight a war, but they know nothing of how to wage peace. They told us we are free now—that we are no longer bound to our castes. They act as if the castes were chains of some sort. You are Clan, you know that is not the case. This so-called freedom they have imposed on us has caused chaos. Just the other night, a former warrior was killed three blocks from here, murdered for the food rations he carried."

"Members of the Dark Caste?" he asked.

She drew a sarcastic frown across her face. "*Neg*. You are still thinking like a Clansman, and Huntress is no longer Clan. It was members of the laborer caste. They were drunk and hungry, and the warrior crossed them, and he paid for it with his life."

"They were caught?"

"Oh yes, the Star League was swift in catching them, but less swift in justice. In the past, no laborer would ever even consider killing a warrior, let alone robbing him. The Star League arrested them, and is going to place them on trial. This should have never happened in the first place. Who holds the Star League accountable? No one, that is the answer."

"I was unaware how things are here," he said.

"At least the Nova Cats have come to bear witness to the price of defeat," Bix said with a deep sigh. "The other Clans apparently do not want to come. Perhaps they cannot bear the guilt of what they allowed to happen...that, or they do not care."

*I care.* Baldur absorbed her words, and each one hurt him more. "What has become of the warriors who survived?"

"Most are like me," Bix said. "We are given work assignments by the Star League. Only a handful were made bondsmen, and they are the only ones doing work worthy of their caste. The rest of us do what is necessary to survive. I have heard stories that some members of my unit have even turned to prostitution as a means to get by—though I have not confirmed that myself. Rumors and stories are cheap and plentiful here in Lootera."

*Prostitution? Neg! This cannot be the fate of these people.* The guilt of his treason settled over him like a wet blanket draped over his shoulders—a pressing weight that wrapped around him, constricted his body and mind. "What of this Jaguar who is staging raids?"

Bix frowned. "What of him?"

"Does he have the support of the former warrior caste?"

She paused for a moment, then shook her head. "*Neg.* Those who follow him have shed their last remnant of honor to fight a war they cannot win. I know of one warrior, Bruno Dimitrov. He said he was leaving to find this bandit because he could not stomach living as a mere laborer under the Star League's heel. In reality, Bruno was looking for death. He told me that before he disappeared into the jungles. He looked forward to death fighting a hopeless cause rather than change."

"Why did you not follow him?"

Bix's emerald eyes narrowed slightly as she looked at him. "You ask a lot of personal questions, Baldur of the Nova Cats."

"I came to learn and to help where I can." The downward tug of his guilt grew as she countered him. *These are all things I have set in motion...I and Paul Moon.*

She seemed content with his response, at least for the time being. "He asked me to come with him, but I declined. I would not impugn my honor by continuing to fight a trial that had been fairly won. Whether I like the Star League or not, they battled justly and defeated us. To fight a guerrilla war with no objectives, no hope of victory— that has no appeal for me. No one can take my pride and honor from me. When my *Warhawk* was blasted apart in the Battle of the Jaguar's Fangs, I rode it right into the ground and continued to fire until they destroyed my 'Mech around me. The Star League fought hard and bitterly, as did we. It was a trial though, well bargained and done.

Besides, I have no inclination to continue the fight simply to die for a lost cause."

"What is the future of our—*your* people?"

"I do not know. Change is upon us, whether we like it or not. Some will adapt. Others will not. In between those two states, there will be suffering. I intend to continue on. I do not know what those two states mean for me yet, but I will not succumb. What I dread most is the other Clans coming to feast on our remains. You know our people. They will descend at some point to scoop up what is left of the mighty Smoke Jaguars. The Star League has no idea what is about to rain down on them. They may have won Huntress for now, but the other Clans see us as raw materiel and manpower to capture in Trials of Possession. It is coming—I can feel it."

"I believe you are correct," he said. "Even damaged, Huntress is a prized jewel in Clan space."

"Where does that leave us? Those of us Jaguars who remain will either join the Dark Caste to live out our days as criminals, or be taken captive by other Clans. Unless someone can devise another solution, that is our fate. It is only a matter of time."

Baldur stared at her in silence for a long moment. The vision of the Star League future would never fully stick on Huntress...he understood that clearly. Bix, he felt, represented the other displaced warriors—and even the lower castes. *They seek hope, they crave it. But what kind of vision can save an entire people from the fate Bix described?*

# CHAPTER 14

ERIDANI LIGHT HORSE HQ
LOOTERA, HUNTRESS
THE KERENSKY CLUSTER, CLAN SPACE
10 JUNE 3060

Paul Moon sat facing a trio of Nova Cat warriors across the large conference table, along with other members of the Eridani Light Horse, including Colonel Charles Antonescu. The older colonel sat rigidly in his chair, an icy glare on his face. As always, he regarded Moon as a leper, viewing him with intentional disdain. In the few times he had seen Antonescu, the man had never come close to a smile, and it appeared that was not about to change. It didn't matter to Paul, but was merely an observation. The older officer's expression was a mix of pain and anger. Combined with the humidity that hung in the air of the conference room, it guaranteed Paul's presentation would seem gloomy.

The Nova Cats had spoken little to him since their arrival, and he was comfortable with that. He had almost wished for them to be smug and condescending. That would have given him a reason to despise them. Instead, they had been sympathetic, which was almost as bad. The former Smoke Jaguar did not want their sympathy or support. *We are not weak, merely beaten. That is a misapprehension those in this room must come to grips with, or we will all slide into mayhem.*

Lieutenants Fisher and Farnholtz flanked the Nova Cats and controlled the flow of data to his bondholder. Major Blau was responsible for managing the intelligence briefing, outlining the recent attack in the Shikari Jungle by the elusive Jaguar. The raid had been stunningly fast and left one ComStar 'Mech destroyed, three others damaged, and resulted in the loss of three trucks carrying supplies. Moon's own presentation was to follow the major's.

Colonel Antonescu rested his elbows on the table and tented his fingers in front of his chin as the major spoke. "Have we had any luck in taking out this Jaguar's bases of operation?"

"We have," Major Blau replied, glancing at Paul. "Thanks to the intel provided by my bondsman, we found two sibko training bases these raiders had recently occupied. We recovered some munitions and supplies and razed the structures. The problem is the dense jungle provides the enemy with ample cover. They stay on the move, and we estimate they use these sibko bases for only a night or two at a time."

"Worse yet, we don't have a comprehensive list of training facilities—thanks to some sabotage. If we did, we could push more forces out, knock out the rest of these potential bases," the colonel said, thinking out loud.

"We've given that some thought, sir. Based on the 'Mechs and vehicles we've seen, we might be facing as much as a Trinary's worth of forces. For us to hit all those bases would spread our units thin and leave us susceptible to attack. The most efficient plan is to hit one base at a time with superior force, then fall back. It's a slow process, but one that provides us with the most security and still keeps pressure on this Jaguar."

"I thought your people were honorable," Antonescu said, turning first to Paul Moon, then to the trio of Nova Cats. "We won Huntress fair and square. We've never seen the Clans fight a guerrilla war. I thought this was against your nature." His words were deliberately offensive.

Paul's face flushed with a mix of anger and frustration. Inanna of the Nova Cats spoke up first. "You have never fully defeated a Clan before this, Colonel. In fact, no Clan has ever been defeated on this scale—not by the Inner Sphere, at least. Your estimates and predictions of how these people could and should react to an occupying army has no historical baseline."

"A relatively small number of the surviving warriors have sided with these rebels," Major Blau added. "The rest are slowly adapting to our presence here."

"They will not for long," Paul Moon said. For a moment, there was silence as every eye turned to him.

Major Blau jumped in immediately. "What my bondsman means is that we have been evaluating the risks associated with the unattached former Smoke Jaguar warriors. There may be a way to deprive the rebellious forces of additional troops."

All eyes focused on Paul Moon. "I have spent time with several warriors, interviewing them about the attitudes of the displaced troops. The warriors still have their pride, despite the victory of the SLDF. Dissolving the caste system has generated much chaos, not just with the warriors—you must acknowledge that reality. On top of that, you have essentially stripped a genetically bred military force of its duties and forced its members to perform menial tasks to survive. I have no doubt that the Jaguar has a ready supply of replacement troops. The occupation created that situation."

"What solution do you propose?" Baldur asked.

Moon looked at the dark-haired man for a moment. There was something familiar in his voice, but he couldn't quite place it. He fixed his gaze on the Nova Cat. "I suggest we rearm these troops as militia forces. Form them into units. Give them meaning and purpose each day. It would reinforce the garrison here, and at the same time deprive the Jaguar of any additional troops. Furthermore, it would improve the way the people of Huntress feel about their occupiers."

"You are suggesting that we rearm the Smoke Jaguars?" Colonel Antonescu asked. "We just spent a hell of a lot of men and women's lives to disarm them."

"They are no longer Smoke Jaguars. You have successfully stripped them of their identity and their purpose. And in doing so, *you* have created an insurgency...however small," Paul replied curtly. "If you provide them with something to do, something they were bred to do, it will give them a reason to ignore any cries for assistance from the rebels. The Jaguar and his people will wither and fade away with time."

"Colonel," Major Blau said. "I know it seems contrary to our thinking, but my people have all evaluated the proposal. It makes a lot of sense. It deprives the enemy and helps settle some of the tensions here, especially in Lootera."

The Light Horse colonel bristled at the suggestion. "A lot of our troops out there don't want these people armed, not in any way. They lost comrades in the fighting—a lot of them. They waged a war to defeat the Smoke Jaguars and won it. Arming those defeated survivors would be a slap in the face to them."

Paul Moon shifted in his seat. "I believe I understand, Colonel. I fought against you myself. I have a purpose here, a military purpose. It fits my training and upbringing. The majority of my former caste do not have that. They are being used in work gangs to repair damage and work in construction—tasks they see as beneath them. While it appalls you that we would rearm these troops, by the same token, you do not want to fight an ongoing war in the jungles against an armed insurgent force. More men and women would die. This plan does not defeat the Jaguar on the field of battle, but it wins the war against him, sir."

The Light Horse colonel turned to the Nova Cat warriors. "As our guests and special advisors, what do you think of this proposal?"

Baldur spoke up quickly. "I too have met with some of the warriors in the few days I have been here. Paul Moon is correct. You have a small army of warriors in your midst. You have disbanded them, taken away their weapons, but you have forgotten that they *are*, by their very nature, weapons. If you do nothing to give them meaning and purpose, you will face more difficult times in the future."

Paul studied the Nova Cat carefully. Ignoring his nagging feeling about the man's voice, he gave the warrior a slow nod of approval.

The black-haired Inanna joined in. "If I were you, Colonel, I would also find this a difficult course of action to pursue. The Star League Defense Force fought admirably here on Huntress and on Strana Mechty. The battle for Huntress has been won. Now you must win the peace, or you risk undoing everything your people fought for. It is only a matter of time before the remaining Clans see Huntress as an opportunity to secure equipment, territory, and key personnel."

Antonescu chuckled, a rare display of humor. "After what we have done to the Jags? None of them will risk that, not while we are here in force. They won't want to get a dose of what we gave the Jags here."

The deep voice of Woodall Winters stirred eyes in his direction. "In your Trial of Refusal on Strana Mechty, you denied the Clans the goal of the Inner Sphere. Again, this is a victory. At the same time, these are a warrior people. You have taken away one place for them to fight. They will likely turn on each other—and on you and your people. You may think they are intimidated by what you accomplished on Huntress. In fact, the defeat of the Smoke Jaguars will encourage them to strike with enough force to ensure victory. They will come, Colonel. It is only a matter of time. We have foreseen it."

His last words made Moon cock his head slightly. *They have foreseen it, quineg? The Nova Cats always had a preoccupation with visions and seers. Now I am experiencing it firsthand. I agree that the other Clans are coming, but I would not wager that based on visions.* "Where was this Nova Cat foresight when the Star League came to prowl here?" Moon fired at Winters.

Inanna spoke before Winters could open his mouth. "Everything that transpired here was foreseen, Paul Moon, including your role. It is not for us to use our perceptions to attempt to sway the course of affairs. Some things are ordained in the stars and cannot be averted. Had we come to you, you would have mocked us."

*My role in matters? What role could she be speaking of?* "I place no value on visions. I *do* know the Clans, though. What the Nova Cats say has merit. The Clans will come to Huntress, if only to prove they do not walk in the footsteps of the Smoke Jaguars."

Colonel Antonescu turned to his intelligence officer. "Major Blau, what do you think of this?"

Blau's eyes swept the room, stopping the longest on Paul Moon. "I think Moon's suggestion of rearming the warriors is the best way to deal with the insurgents, sir. I know it isn't going to be easy to sell to Masters, but we have to try."

The aged colonel leaned back in his chair. "I will take your proposal to Masters. I don't know if he'll go for it or not. The man wants peace above all—maybe this will help convince him." He paused for a moment, then turned to Inanna. "Do you really believe the Clans will come to Huntress after the ass-kicking we gave the Jags?"

Moon bristled at the term "ass-kicking," but held his silence. *We very nearly defeated these invaders—but already they are crafting the history of the events here.*

Inanna nodded slowly as she spoke. "We are a warrior people, ruled by warriors, created for war. Affirmative, they will come. They will not try to take the entire planet from you. Even the boldest of the Clans has to know that such an action, with your armies poised here in Clan space, would be a foolish move. *Neg.* They will come here to take this place from you one bite at a time, slowly consuming it until your victory is merely a footnote. As you have proven the vulnerability of a single Clan, none will press you far enough to warrant a full retaliation. Our people are calculating, trained at birth to weigh the odds of battle and the outcomes. We are also creatures of politics."

Paul Moon found himself in agreement. *My own political aspirations caused Trent to turn against our people and led to this outcome. He said as much to me when I lay in the hospital. I will not let my own goals put my people in danger.* "We will need to prepare your senior officers for counterbidding a Clan attack force."

Lieutenant Fisher joined in. "We can begin drawing up a list of high-priority targets that the Clans may attempt to seize—starting with our own target list from when we invaded."

"What else can we do?" the grizzled colonel asked.

"We can prepare defensive positions around the higher-priority targets, something they might be expecting from the Jaguars," Major Blau replied. "It might be enough to throw them off when they do arrive. Furthermore, we can identify battlefields that give us an edge in any Trials of Possession."

"They will not want matters to escalate," Inanna added. "No one yet knows how your SLDF will respond. If I were to come to Huntress, I would limit the objectives of a Trial of Possession. I would not want to force the entire SLDF into a defensive posture, where they would commit all of their resources."

Moon agreed with a nod.

The colonel, then pushed his chair back from the table. "Major, you and I will go see Paul Masters and present this idea of arming the warriors. I also want an assessment of the possibilities of other Clans attacking Huntress." He rose, as did the others in the room, and left.

The Light Horse officers gathered together quickly to chat among themselves, with Major Blau handing out a string of orders. The Nova Cats walked around the table toward Paul Moon.

Baldur stopped before him, arms crossed. Moon looked down at him and saw the man's facial lines were drawn tight, as if his jaw was clenched in deep thought. "Your assessment of how to deal with the warriors here was dead-on, Paul Moon. I have been out in the city several times and have talked to the disenfranchised and unattached. Your suggestion should go a long way in easing their frustrations," he said. His voice still tugged at the Elemental's memory.

"I do not care what you think or what your opinions are," Moon replied, crossing his own burly arms.

"Have I offended you in some way, *quiaff*?" Baldur asked, turning his head slightly to focus with his right eye.

Moon gave a humorless chuckle. "*Aff.* We fought here—alone. You did not come to our aid. Clan Nova Cat not only turned its back on the Smoke Jaguars, but on the Clans as a whole."

Inanna stepped forward one stride and into the conversation. "We did what we were compelled to do. We apologize to no one for our actions. I assure you, our leaders did not take this matter lightly. It cost us our relationship with the Clans and our worlds in Clan space, which we are now abandoning."

Major Blau may not have heard the words, but clearly caught the tone of the conversation. He broke off from his sidebar discussion and moved to join Paul Moon.

*I do not require his help in this. It is a matter of opinion.* "You betrayed the Clans," he said flatly.

"No more than you betrayed your Smoke Jaguars, Paul Moon," Baldur snapped back. His skin reddened, but more deeply on the left side of his face.

*Synthskin—he has been deeply scarred in battle,* Moon realized. "What do you mean by that, Baldur?"

"Trent fought and died for the Nova Cats on Strana Mechty," Baldur said. "He spoke of how you tormented him—how you set things in motion that led to him revealing the Exodus Road to the Star League. You of all people are in no position to speak of the Nova Cats' infidelity." There was anger in the Nova Cat warrior's voice—raw, unnerving.

Moon leaned forward and narrowed his gaze. "I suffer every day I am alive to atone for my actions. That battle is one I fight alone, in my head. We all have guilt we bear. My burden was not purged in the Battle of Huntress." A part of Paul Moon had hoped that his conflict with Trent was gone, a memory. Baldur's words reopened that wound and ground salt into it.

The major stepped between the parties. "Let's watch our tone here. We're all on the same side, no matter our pasts."

Paul cast him a quick glare and uncrossed his arms. "I meant no offense."

"Nor did I," Baldur replied.

Something in his voice told Moon that Baldur was not quite telling the truth. *No matter—he is merely a Nova Cat. In my current state, I could not fight in a Circle of Equals regardless—I am but a bondsman. Even that bit of honor is lost to me.*

Hearing that Trent was dead was news to him. A part of him wanted to be happy about it, but he could not. *He fought in the Great Refusal and died; at least he got the final release from all of this. He managed to achieve something I could not, an honorable death.* It brought him no joy. *I can never set things right between us now. Not that it was ever possible. Our battle was one that could not easily be resolved.* He imagined Trent would have enjoyed seeing him as a bondsman to the Light Horse, a mercenary unit. *He would have relished my current status.*

Paul Moon drew in a long breath, turned, and left the conference room. *I wonder if this is how the Romans felt as the Visigoths closed on their capital.* A growing sense of impending doom found fertile growth in his anger at the Nova Cats. *While I despise them, they are correct—the Clans will come. And when they do, I am not sure we are prepared for what that will bring.*

# CHAPTER 15

Baldur got up early, as he did every morning for a run. The streets were generally empty, as others were just starting to awaken, and the unemployed did not bother to leave their housing. Inanna liked to run with him, and he didn't protest. He welcomed her company.

Lootera felt dangerous now, even in the Warrior Quarter. The SLDF forces had said muggings and beatings were not uncommon. Gangs were forming, too. The tighter the Star League' grip, the more seemed to slip through their fingers. Baldur saw this as the by-product of forced social engineering. *If you impose a new order on people who do not desire it, resistance is natural.*

They had spent days in briefings, and more time traveling to the sites where the SLDF had fought the Smoke Jaguars. Several times he had been in Paul Moon's presence. Each time prompted a roller coaster of emotions. He still was angry at Moon, yet looking at his former antagonist, Baldur found himself pitying him. Despite his character flaws, Moon had tried to do the right thing—the Clan thing, in battling to retake Huntress. The effort had failed, and the cost had been the cream of the warrior caste. The legacy of that failed counterattack physically wore on Moon—Baldur could see that. He had grown sullen, less argumentative. There were bags under his bloodshot eyes. Moon now had a bionic implant—not as cosmetically appealing as Baldur's, but proof of the ferocity of the battle he had waged. To have struggled so hard and lost seemed to have humbled the arrogant Elemental.

One thing Baldur did learn from the myriad of meetings and briefings was the Star League had been prepared to fight and defeat the Smoke Jaguars, but not for what to do with Huntress once they had it. The military leaders struggled to understand the administration of a world. *They usually do not have to do it. They conquer and move on. Now they are staying, and in doing so, they must learn to live with the results of their decisions.* It was an important lesson.

As he and Inanna ran, they passed a monument to the civil war that had brought about the formation of the Clans. It commemorated the lives lost in Operation Klondike, the Clans' retaking of the Pentagon Worlds. Baldur remembered the statue of the springing smoke jaguar carved from black marble that once adorned the top of it. The Star League had seen fit to chisel the magnificent cat off the top. In some places in the city, entire monuments had been removed and presumably destroyed. Such actions felt wrong to him, and the sight of the monument without the commemorative jaguar was gut-wrenching enough for him to pause his run and stare at it. *This is part of the League's problem. They do not understand that defacing or destroying a monument or destroying other ones does not change history. In fact, it often ends up reinforcing that history. Rewriting the history books to impose a new social order rarely works in the long term.*

"What is it?" Inanna asked as she caught her breath.

"This Star League seeks to remove every aspect of the Smoke Jaguars. It is the wrong approach. These people have a rich past. Taking it away from them is merely going to make matters easier for those who seek to resist the occupation."

"Paul Masters and the other commanders are not likely to change their stance on this," she said, sucking in another long gulp of air and wiping the sweat from her brow. "They believe purging everything related to the Jaguars is the key to their future."

Baldur looked into her eyes, making sure she was looking right back at him. "It is a mistake that will cost them. These people will never have the pride in the Star League that they felt with the Smoke Jaguars. Taking that away from them is wrong—in fact, it is criminal."

"Baldur," she said, putting her balled fists on her hips. "Much like the jaguar, the Star League cannot change its spots. What would you do if you were in charge?"

The question hit him hard, and he had no immediate answer. "I would not walk the same path as the occupation forces. They are losing control of Huntress, and do not fully comprehend it yet. And with the other Clans destined to come at some point, I am not sure there is an easy answer."

"Perhaps," Inanna offered, "the solution may not involve Huntress at all."

"Explain."

"You cannot hide Huntress. It will always be a symbol for both the Clans and the new Star League. The world itself is a physical representation of what was once here, and how the Clans' ultimate defeat was forged. This puts the people in the crosshairs of both sides for decades to come."

He nodded and wiped sweat from his forehead. His head felt hotter on the right side than the left, a result of the metal plate covering the missing portions of his skull and the fact that he now had hair on both sides of his head again. "You are correct. Huntress itself is a monument. So the answer lies with the people..."

His mind raced, trying to figure out the problem. He bent at the waist for a moment, then righted himself. "Let us continue," Baldur said, and the pair set off to continue their run. Each footfall jarred his body, but failed to shatter his concentration as he struggled with Inanna's query. *There must be an answer for my former people.*

They ran for six kilometers before Inanna motioned for them to stop. The early autumn air was already wet, common at that time of year. At the end of the Warrior Quarter of the city, both pulled out their collapsible water flasks and took long, cool drinks.

Baldur's muscles ached, especially his back. The surgeons had told him that was likely to be an ongoing issue—arthritis near his spinal implants. *A disease of the old...which I am becoming.* The Nova Cats were far more accepting of age than the Smoke Jaguars, where he had been marked as obsolete in his thirties. *Not so in the Nova Cats. But that does not mean I do not feel the aches that come with age.* For a long moment, he wondered just how long he had before he would truly be of no value as a warrior.

As his lungs strained to get air between mouthfuls of water, Baldur looked across the wide boulevard. Its grass, no longer maintained, was tall and browning from the cool air that nipped at the city.

He saw a young girl, probably ten or twelve years old. Her hair was short, shaggy, and a bit of a mess. He recognized the T-shirt she wore, despite the grime on it: one belonging to a Smoke Jaguar sibling company. He could not make out the logo on her left breast, but he was sure of it. Recognizing her origins, he instantly felt a bond with her.

Baldur's gaze focused on her intently, tuning out the sounds of the city and even his own breathing. The young girl was unkempt. Her fatigue pants were torn in both knees and stained a myriad of dark colors that splotched and streaked their normal gray. She wore standard-issue boots, and strangely, they were polished.

The girl seemed startled at the arrival of the two Nova Cats. As soon as Baldur locked gazes with her dark-brown eyes, she bolted, rounding the corner of some now-abandoned administrative building.

He broke into a sprint, a surprised Inanna following, dropping her water flask in the process. Baldur didn't care. He ran now with a purpose more than just attempting to clear his mind. *Who is this girl?*

He bounded around the corner and caught sight of her dodging into the next building down the block. When he reached the door, he found it ajar and forced it open fast—almost too fast. It hit the stop and came back at him as he darted inside.

It was some sort of an apartment building; from the markings, it had been used by members of the technicians that once supported Smoke Jaguar warriors. Now it showed signs of being abandoned. Garbage littered the floor, including dumped-open folders of paperwork covered with a thin layer of dust. Pausing, he listened for sounds ahead as Inanna reached the door behind him. Baldur held up his hand for silence, and she obeyed instinctively.

Noise, scraping and the sound of footfalls, came from a room down the hall. He saw a worn path in the dust on the floor, and moved down the hallway more slowly than before. Inanna followed him, getting control of her breath from the running. "Why are you following her?" she whispered.

Baldur paused and turned to face her. "Because she ran," he replied in a voice just louder than his own breathing. *There had to be a reason she ran.* That was what he really wanted to know. He resumed his cautious advance down the hall, careful where he placed his feet so as to suppress any sounds.

He came to a set of doors that were closed and locked. Looking down at the floor, he saw papers leaning up against the doors. The girl had not run in there. He crouched down and crept to the second door.

Baldur tried the doorknob slowly, only to find it locked. From the footprints in the dust, it was clear this was where his target had gone. Looking back at Inanna, he nodded at the door. She gave him a nod in response.

Leaning away from the door, he eyed where he would plant his shoulder and braced for the impact. He hit it low, just above the knob, with the full force of his body. It flew open, and he almost stumbled into the room, with Inanna right behind him; he had anticipated more effort would be required. He righted himself within three staggering steps and then caught movement to his right.

Looking around the large space, he realized it had been a classroom at one time. There were nearly a dozen youngsters there, including the girl he had chased. They moved along the wall with terror in their eyes. Three did not cower: they stepped forward, fists balled in the same low fighting stances he had been trained for in his sibko.

One figure, taller, a woman, stepped forward. In her hand was a holdout pistol. From the way she held the weapon, and how it was shaking, he could tell she was unfamiliar with its use. *If she shoots, it will recoil right back at her chin.*

The air was musty, with a hint of urine. That was overlaid by the smell of youngsters, that sweaty aroma children had—multiplied by twenty. It smelled sweet, sticky, and filthy all at once. Through the doorway dust filtered down in the light. *This place has fallen apart in a short period of time. Without the order of the Clan, no one has cared for these facilities.*

"Stay right where you are," the woman commanded.

Baldur raised his arms to show he was no threat, as did Inanna. "We mean no harm," he said in as calming a tone as he could muster.

"Who are you? What are you doing here?" the woman demanded. She was relatively well-kempt, in her early fifties, hair more gray than its original black. Her tunic top bore the shoulder patch of a technician.

"I am Baldur, this is Inanna. We are from Clan Nova Cat. We saw the girl running and came to see why."

"Nova Cats, *quiaff*?" one of the boys standing ready to fight demanded in an arrogant tone. "Have the Nova Cats invaded?"

"Invaded? *Neg*," Inanna replied. "There has been no trial since the Star League's. We came here on a diplomatic mission." The youth that held his fists ready for battle relaxed them ever so slightly.

"You should lower that weapon," Baldur said to the woman. "I am patient. I am also a warrior, and you are threatening me, which I am sure is not your intent. I can see that your goal is to protect these young Jaguars. No harm needs to come to anyone here."

Her hand shook even more, and she quickly surveyed the children. Baldur mentally calculated their distance, his speed, her aim and possible reaction times. He could have rushed the woman and disarmed her three different ways. The risk of her firing was high; the risk of her hitting him was moderate to low. Despite that, he held his position. *If I do not disarm her, an innocent might be injured.* He controlled his breathing to calm her.

The woman jiggled the pistol in his direction. "What do you want?"

"We mean no harm," Inanna replied. "My compatriot saw the girl and was concerned for her."

Baldur piped in. "I wanted to make sure she was not an orphan on the street with no protection."

The woman forced an angry smile. "Sure, *now* you Cats are concerned. Where were you and the rest of our people when the invaders landed? The Star League smashed our homes and businesses. These children are all I could care for from the Lurking Jaguar sibko. Their facilities were burned to the ground in the fighting."

"There were more than this, *quiaff*?" Baldur asked. Now that the woman was talking, she seemed less threatening.

The girl Baldur and Inanna had been chasing spoke up, her fists in front of her and still ready for a fight. "*Aff*. There were another ten of us."

"What happened to the others?" Inanna asked.

Her query was met with uncomfortable and tense silence for a few moments. The woman with the gun lowered it slightly as she spoke. "Their sibko officers left the children to join the counterattack. When the city fell, so did law and order. Gangs formed. Some of them were looking for food...others for..." Her voice trailed off.

"Rape," Baldur said. Two of the girls backed further into the shadows at his use of the word, and he regretted it the moment he said it. *It may have been worse than rape...*

She nodded, lowering the pistol the rest of the way.

Another young boy spoke up. "We were attacked several times. We killed three of the men that came for us. We fought with honor." Despite his slovenly appearance, the boy spoke as he had been reared to do—like a warrior.

"I am sure you did," Baldur replied. *These children were left to fend for themselves in a city with no order after centuries of firm rule.* A wave of guilt washed over him. *This is because of my actions.*

"When I found them, they had not eaten in days. Their sibko was destroyed, they had no homes," the woman said nervously. "I could not take them all in, so I took the ones I could. My neighbors and I made sure they were fed."

"Why not take them to the Star League?" Inanna asked.

She shook her head. "*Neg.* We are not beggars. This Star League may have conquered us, but they cannot take our pride from us. Going to them would mean admitting they had defeated us. We spoke with the children, and they agreed."

"What happened to the ones you did not take in—the ones not assaulted," Baldur asked, avoiding the word "rape" again after the reaction when he'd first said it.

The woman's eyes filled with tears. "We could not take them all, it simply wasn't possible. They were left to fend for themselves." The images that came to Baldur's mind were not pleasant.

"How did you choose who would go?" Inanna asked.

"We wanted to do it the Clan way," the young girl he had pursued replied. "Circles of Equals. Olivia and her mate did not allow it. They simply picked who would go with them and who would remain," she spoke in a flat tone.

"Do you know what became of the others?" Inanna asked.

The young girl released her fists slowly as she shrugged. "We do not know. We have not seen any of them. If they were strong, they still live."

The woman interrupted. "The streets were not safe during the first weeks of the occupation—nor are they now. With much of the Warrior Quarter deserted, and some of it used by the Star League, it is difficult to say what parts of the city are safe—especially at night. We protect the children as best we can, taking shifts to make sure they are under our watch. The Star League provides rations, but I have not been able to convince them that we are sheltering all of these children. Mindless bureaucrats, they refuse to acknowledge what they caused. We are forced to feed them from our own stores—and it is not enough. There simply are not enough of us to take in all of them." Inanna's response was a deep nod. "You have done well—" "Olivia," she said, offering her name. "I am Olivia."

"Olivia. You have all done well under difficult circumstances." One of the young boys, dressed in the dirty gray jumpsuit common to sibkos, stepped forward. "We honored the Smoke Jaguars as we were trained to do. Those who came for us after Olivia took us in were dealt with as warriors deal with them," he boasted, brandishing a field knife. The other children nodded in agreement, most stepping out of the shadows.

*It would be wrong to underestimate them. They are warriors in training.* Baldur remembered his own youth. *At that age, I could have killed as well.* Whoever had dared to go after the children had no doubt met their deserved fate.

"Whatever happened to those who preyed on you, I am sure you gave them more honor than they deserved," Baldur said. The boy nodded firmly.

"We cannot leave them here, not like this," Inanna said to him.

She was right, and her words hurt. *They are here because of my actions. If I had not given the Star League the map to Huntress, they would not be in this situation.* "I agree."

"You cannot simply take them," Olivia replied nervously. "I have cared for them—they are like my own children."

Inanna tried to soothe her. "We have a DropShip at the spaceport, with facilities and full provisions. You do not have to be separated from them, Olivia. You and your mate can come with them, to ensure they are safe."

The young girl spoke up. "We will not be taken as *isorla* of the Nova Cats—not without a fair contest." Her bravado was such that it actually brought a smile to Baldur's face. *This is the true spirit of the Smoke Jaguars—it still exists.* He had no doubt she would fight if forced.

"You are not *isorla*," Baldur replied. "You remain what you are. We are offering food and safety."

"And what do you want for this?" Olivia asked suspiciously.

"Nothing. We merely do not wish to see these children struggling for food and shelter. Our DropShip has both." *They do not trust us—and I do not blame them.*

Olivia's eyes darted between the children and the Nova Cats, carefully weighing her options. She moved to the girl they had followed and spoke quietly to her. There were nods from some children, headshakes from others.

"How can I know we can trust you?" Olivia asked.

Baldur had no quick answer. Inanna broke the moment of silence. "Nothing we can say will earn your trust. There are no words we can speak that will calm you. We came here because we saw this girl running away from us, and we were curious. Neither of us carry a weapon—we were not out hunting you. All we desire is to help. We are able to provide food and shelter and wish to...nothing more or less."

Olivia's body sagged. "I have come to think of them as my own children. I only want them to be safe."

"They will be with us," Baldur said. "And if you wish to come, you can." *The choice is not easy for her. She struggles with it—I can see it in her face.*

"It is the right thing to do," the woman admitted. "I have already made difficult choices in who we took under our wing to begin with. Memories of that keep me up at night. I do not want to think of how I would feel if I turned down your offer."

She motioned to the children. "Go with them. They can take care of you better than I can." Tears trickled down Olivia's face as each of the children gave her a hug.

Baldur watched the children line up with military precision in front of him and Inanna. His eyes fell on their filthy uniforms. They were missing the Smoke Jaguar patches on their shoulders. On two of the uniforms, the missing patch left a cleaner circle of cloth where it had been. *They have not lost their pride, only their identity.* He began to mentally question the approach of the Star League in purging the symbol. *I understand they want to impress upon the populace that the old regime is a thing of the past. But in doing so, they have disenfranchised these people.*

It took an hour for them to get to the DropShip *Wanderer*. They marched through the Warrior Quarter to the spaceport as if on parade. The sibko children ignored the stares as they followed Baldur and Inanna. Strangely, no one from the SLDF stopped them or questioned what was going on.

Aboard the ship, Inanna assigned staff to prepare meals and billets for the children, along with a fresh change of clothing. There were some minor incidents: any clothing provided that bore the mark of the Nova Cats generated immediate protests, but removing the patches calmed the children quickly. Most ate as if they had not been fed in weeks. *Olivia and her kin took care of them remarkably well, given the circumstances.*

Baldur and Inanna quickly showered and, after making sure the children were in good hands, left the ship. He led her toward the pyramid, the huge genetic repository in the city. It was one vestige of the Jaguars that had been left alone. In it was the genetic material of his former Clan. The building had Star League patrols stationed near it, which he understood. *Our genetic material is all that remains of the Smoke Jaguars. While some Clans will think of them as failed Bloodlines, others will come and try to seize that material for their own use.*

"We did well, getting those children to safety," Inanna said as they walked along the perimeter of the pyramid.

Baldur said nothing for a moment. "They were living in squalor. Anything we did to help them was better than what they had."

"You are brooding," Inanna said.

"I am angry."

"At the Star League, *quiaff?*"

"*Neg*," Baldur said flatly. "At myself." He stopped his stride and looked around to make sure no one was in earshot. "I caused this, Inanna. I set all of this in motion."

"*Aff*," Inanna replied—surprising him slightly. He had half expected her to refute his admission. "We *all* set things in motion every day, some big, some small. You had a large impact here—there is no denying it. What remains is what we do from this point forward."

He reluctantly nodded. "I want to save these people. What the Star League is doing is well-intended, but it will not succeed long-term. You saw the children. Pride has not been taken from them in this defeat. What made them Smoke Jaguars was not the symbol, but how they felt."

"What do you propose?" Inanna asked.

"That essence of who they are, that pride in themselves, it must be preserved. It cannot be done here, not under the boot of the Star League. The victors do not trust the conquered, and are licking their wounds from the fighting to take Huntress. They do not care about the people they defeated. All they want is the peace they won." Baldur did not blame them: the war with the Smoke Jaguars had been vicious and brutal. From the Star League's perspective, the population simply needed to adapt to a more Inner Sphere way of thinking—but that was not going to happen. Adapting was not a trait that the Clans valued or practiced. *Rigid order, rules, strict governance–those are our hallmarks. The change will come, but it will be slow and must come naturally, not be forced upon them.*

"You cannot remove the Star League from Huntress," Inanna said firmly. "It is a symbol of their victory—a jewel in their crown. Any attempt to do so would trigger massive retaliation."

"Agreed," he said while considering options. "If I cannot save them all, we can save some of them."

"How?"

"Olivia understood what had to be done. She chose those she thought stood the best chance of surviving. We could do the same, select the parts of the former Clan that were its best and brightest. They would go somewhere else and rebuild." *The choices would be difficult, but necessary.*

Inanna moved a half step closer. "You are talking an exodus. To where?"

"We cannot stay in Clan space. The other Clans would attack us anywhere else, just as they eventually will on Huntress. Going to the Inner Sphere would force the Star League to react."

"Where does that leave us?"

"We need a world that is in neither place—somewhere along the Exodus Road."

Inanna paused, listening carefully to his words. "You would rebuild the Smoke Jaguars, *quineg*?"

"Negative," Baldur replied. "Doing so would only invite problems with both the Clans and the Star League. The Smoke Jaguars, for all of their strengths, had flaws as well, which led to their downfall. The Clans, if they found us, would never stand for it—nor could the League. Whatever we become—it must be something different. Not Inner Sphere, not Clan, but perhaps the best of both."

"You say 'we,' Baldur."

*Did I?* He said nothing for a moment as he gathered his thoughts. *This was my fault. I need to be the one to fix it.* "I think this is something I must do, Inanna. These people are suffering because of my decisions. This is a role I have to play."

"This will not be easy. Our Clan can help, but we are in the middle of our own exodus now. If we go down this road, we will need a great deal of help. The logistics alone are staggering." Inanna paused. "Remember our briefing with the Star League two days ago? A number of the Smoke Jaguar JumpShips and even WarShips are unaccounted for. The Star League cannot find them, but perhaps we can."

"We have a great deal of planning to do. First though, we need a destination."

"What do you need?"

Baldur stiffened. "I made the trip to and from the Inner Sphere and documented the Smoke Jaguar route for ComStar. That is not enough. I need a detailed map of the Exodus Road."

# CHAPTER 16

Paul Moon swatted the massive mosquito on his neck, leaving a smear of his own blood in its wake. He glanced at the crushed insect on his bionic hand and disregarded it. The mosquitoes only had another month or so before autumn set in and their numbers dropped. Its sting was a minor victory that had cost the insect its life.

He had chosen the meeting place carefully. The large flat rock that came up to his waist was the Paseena Stone. It was the end of the journey for sibko warriors undergoing jungle-survival training. Those who made it to the boulder continued their warrior training. It was unremarkable other than as a symbolic stepping stone in the life of the Smoke Jaguars. Paul touched it; the stone was still warm from the early autumn sun. It felt coarse and slightly damp under his fingers. There was a moss on it he had never seen before. *That was because when we were still a Clan, we were here often. Now the jungle is reclaiming it, absorbing it. In a few years no one will be able to find it.*

The foliage rustled around him, and Moon turned. Three warriors emerged from the undergrowth. At first he recognized none of them, but then realized he knew the bearded, bald man. That man strode forward and stopped in front of Moon, crossing his arms. "Paul Moon."

"Russou Howell. Or should I call you 'the Jaguar,' *quiaff?*"

He chuckled. "*Neg.* That is not my name, just one given to me by the people. The people both of us swore to protect." The older warrior turned to his two comrades. "This is Oliver Howell." He gestured to the blond warrior dressed in a dirty, sweat-soaked, olive-drab T-shirt. "And this is Jester, of the Stiles Bloodline." The warrior wore his black hair back in a tight bun. Like Russou, he wore a beard. Moon did not recognize Jester as one of the warriors he commanded on Huntress.

Paul could see the gray streaks in Russou's twisted curl of a beard. *He has aged considerably since I last saw him–his hairline is in full rout.* "People look for leaders in times of uncertainty. 'The Jaguar' is an apt name...a proud one."

Howell gave a crooked grin of pride, then said with a hint of suspicion in his voice, "I was surprised to hear from you."

"Contacting you was not easy. You and your people are highly mobile. I congratulate you on evading the SLDF patrols for as long as you have."

Howell stepped forward to stand closer to him, and Moon noticed his limp. "I learned my lesson defending this planet when they arrived, and I will continue my fight until the Star League departs. But from what I see—" he leaned to the side and looked at the SLDF patch on Moon's shoulder "—others have found solace with our invaders."

Paul's eyes narrowed with anger and frustration "Do not impugn my honor, Russou Howell. I was made a bondsman, and am fulfilling my obligations as such."

Howell barked a laugh, loud and without humor. "Bondsman? You are not bound by these barbarians, no matter how much they twist our rede and traditions. They are Inner Spherers—unworthy of taking a Smoke Jaguar as a bondsman."

Paul curbed his anger and replied through gritted teeth. "There is little honor in waging war like a bandit—striking and running away. You of all people are in no position to question my integrity."

Russou Howell pondered his words. "I fight the only war left to me. At least my people and I still fight, Paul Moon. I do not break bread with these invaders—I kill them. You may not approve of my fighting style, but it is all that is left to me. As long as I live, the Smoke Jaguars live."

There was an element of seductive truth in what Howell said, but not strong enough to sway Paul. "I did not come to squabble with you, Russou Howell. Both of us led the fight for Huntress, and in the end, both of us lost. Together, we failed the Khan and our Clan."

"The difference is," Howell pressed, "I continue to fight."

"*Aff.* You do. To what end?"

"I will bleed our enemies, one pinprick at a time. I will drive this Star League off Huntress and restore the Smoke Jaguars." Passion rang in his voice, which Paul fully understood.

It was also misdirected.

"*Neg*, old comrade. You irritate the Star League, but you do not have the presence or forces to be a real threat. They view you as a bandit, and paint you as such with the population. That is why you do not get the popular support you need to succeed. We lost Huntress.

We lost the Smoke Jaguars. The Inner Spherers dealt with us justly and used our own rede against us. We cannot go back."

Howell's mouth hung open as he stared up at Moon. "You have given up. They have crushed your soul and bled your honor out of you."

"Negative," Paul snapped back. "My fighting for Huntress cost me an arm, an eye, and gave me new insights into our enemies. You paint them as oppressors, but they are not. They simply struggle with administering a world that has been set in its ways for centuries. They have not crushed my soul, and my honor is intact."

Howell shook his head and once more crossed his arms. "When I heard you wanted to meet with me, I had hoped you would join our cause. What did you come to do, dissuade me, *quiaff*? Try to convince me my efforts are a waste?"

Paul Moon shook his own head. "Negative, Russou. I am in no position to try convincing you of anything. I came here to try to understand your plan. I, too, seek a future for our people. I am not convinced yours is the right path to travel."

"My plan is simple—wear down my enemy until I am victorious, and Huntress is free."

"It lacks substance," Paul replied. "The Star League traveled more than a year to come here and defeat us. They are not likely to leave so easily. If anything, they may escalate their campaign against you—treat you like a virus and attempt to eradicate you and your followers." His eyes drifted to the two other warriors. While wet with sweat and moisture from traveling in the jungle, they still wore Smoke Jaguar markings. They stood defiant, with their assault rifles at the ready to protect Howell if necessary.

"At least I have a plan and am trying. What of you, Paul? What are you doing? You cuddle up with our enemy as a kept prize. I will grant you, the road I march is a dangerous one, but it exists. You have been beaten, just as I was. The difference is, I kept on fighting, and will do so until my dying breath."

His words stung. Paul was in no position to fight—that was the restriction laid on a bondsman until they were once more made a warrior. *Who would I fight if I was free?* Blindly lashing out at the Star League occupation forces made little sense.

"There is no path to victory for you, no outcome where you succeed," he said. "Your attacks cause minor damage. The populace does not side with you because of the taint of banditry. The only ones who come to your side are warriors who lack any sort of vision for how to survive other than to meet their fate in battle."

His words clearly rankled the other two warriors. Oliver Howell got red in the face at Moon's speech. They both took a step forward, their weapons at the ready. Russou signaled them to hold their position. Paul swatted another mosquito before it could draw blood from his shoulder.

"Tough words from a traitor to his people," Jester replied in a deep tone.

Paul did not let the other warrior goad him. "I cannot challenge you to a Circle of Equals, Jester, given you are of the Bandit Caste. As such, I suggest you remain quiet and let Russou and I speak."

The man opened his mouth to refute Moon's words, but again Russou waved him off. "Why meet with us just to mock us, Paul? I know you to be a tormentor. Look at what you did to Trent. Is that why you came here—to insult us?"

"*Neg*," he said. "I came with the hope that you had a path to victory—one I could subscribe to. You do not. Fighting a hopeless battle against all odds plays well for holovid movies, but not for true warriors like us."

"I can only offer you the chance to fight on and die as a warrior should," Howell said.

"It is not enough," Moon replied. "Our people deserve more than that forlorn hope. I have proposed to the SLDF that our warriors be allowed to fight in their ranks as militia. It is better than having them roam the streets in gangs or fall to the bottle."

"Or join up with my cause, *quiaff*?"

"*Neg*. That was not my intent, Russou. I have been in Lootera. The warriors there have no purpose, and that is dangerous to the lower castes."

The bald warrior shook his head. "Your action would put our people at war with each other—your warriors against mine."

"Negative. Not necessarily. It *does* give them purpose. You will be the least of our concerns once the other Clans come to pillage what is left of us. At least I am offering them an alternative to the raiding you lead."

"We have a cause—an endgame. Once the Star League leaves this world, we can return to our former greatness."

Paul shook his head. "Your cause is a lost one. They will not give up this prize. As viciously as we defended Huntress, they fought harder to take it. Their blood soaks the soil with our own. Even if they leave today, our warrior ranks have been gutted. The other Clans betrayed us on Strana Mechty. They will come to harvest us like summer crops—you know that in your heart, Russou. They will come regardless of the presence of the Star League. Huntress has a target on it."

"So our future is not here," Russou said. "There are many points of light in the night sky. We simply have to pick one and take it for our own."

His words hit Paul hard. Huntress was *not* a viable solution, regardless of who ruled it. Even the SLDF knew that. He glanced skyward, but it was still daytime. Russou Howell was right—there were many places to go instead of remaining on Huntress.

"Why not take your warriors and do just that—go out and colonize a planet?"

"This is our home," Oliver Howell responded proudly. "We swore to protect Huntress with our lives."

Moon cocked a wry frown. *He speaks the words because he believes them. He is too blind to see the reality of matters.* "That was an oath to a Clan that has been annihilated. Time has moved on. You are fighting a cause for a people that are no more."

Howell puffed up his chest. "As long as we live and fight, the Smoke Jaguars exist."

"I did not come to convince you of the folly of your ways. I came with the hope of finding hope for our people." As Paul spoke, he could not help thinking about what Russou had suggested. There must be a place where his people could go and survive. Yet it seemed daunting. *Moving millions of people and the equipment necessary for survival is akin to what the Great Father did in the Exodus. How could I save all the people?*

"I can offer you battle—a fight," Russou said, as if trying to seduce Paul. "A chance for honor. We both lost Huntress. My path is the only way to ever have a chance of getting it back."

"*Neg.* I must decline. You and I agree on one thing, Russou—our people need hope. Maybe the solution is out there on another world—I do not know for sure. What I do know is that running and sniping at a superior foe will not wear them down, it will only strengthen their resolve. That is what you are doing with the Star League. I speak from experience."

"You serve them as a bondsman, Paul. Will you be coming after me?"

"I will do as commanded. If I were going to betray you, Russou, I would have done it when setting up this meeting," he snapped back. "I serve Major Blau of the Eridani Light Horse. If he commands me to fight you, I will. And if we meet in battle, I will defeat you." His eyes narrowed as he watched the older officer.

Russou chuckled once, almost nervously. "You will try. I am not the same man you sent back to Huntress, Paul Moon. That Russou Howell sought solace in a bottle. I am now powered by vengeance."

"I hope we do not have to fight," Paul replied.

"This is my fate. I was charged with leading these warriors, and will do so until dead."

"*Seyla,*" Paul said in a soft tone. He extended his hand and shook with Russou. The trio of warriors left the small clearing around the Paseena Stone. He watched them disappear into the dense jungle, then turned and began his own return trek.

It was a two-hour walk back to the road where his vehicle was parked. By the time he reached it, darkness had set in. Paul paused long enough to kill another large mosquito, then climbed behind the wheel.

Russou had been right about one thing, Moon was sure of it: the answer for the Smoke Jaguar people did not lie on Huntress. *This world which was our home is now a burden. It attracts our enemies like a light draws a moth.* The Star League would never give it up entirely, and the Clans were destined to come and reap its people and holdings. It pained him to think of his homeworld as an encumbrance, a deadly inconvenience, a target of opportunity—but that was what it had become.

Paul looked up through the bug-splattered windshield at the night sky. There were no clouds, only the stars. *Our people belong out there, somewhere safe. But where? Not Clan space. The Clans would never tolerate the Smoke Jaguars rebuilding. Our competitive nature does not invite the Smoke Jaguars returning to their former place of glory—not now, at least.*

The logistics staggered him. *Millions will need to be relocated, even if a home planet can be found. What do I know of colonization?* General Kerensky had migrated more than six million on his Exodus; he knew what he was doing, and they still nearly starved to death on the Exodus Road. *I am no Kerensky—by blood or competency.*

Paul Moon shook his head and tried to clear it as he started the transport, but it was to no avail.

The answer was out there, in the sky. He merely needed to find a way to get to it.

# CHAPTER 17

Baldur loomed over the holodisplay of the Nova Cats' map of the Exodus Road. It was a nightly ritual for him. His days were busy, attending meetings and briefings with SLDF officers, offering suggestions, reviewing countless reports and presentations on everything from reconstruction efforts to crop yields. Being a liaison officer was more of an administrative role than he had envisioned—unworthy of a true warrior.

In the evening hours, he considered the maps of the Exodus Road in relative privacy and contemplated the logistics of moving some of his people off Huntress. There were gaps in the information he possessed: dividing up the knowledge of the Exodus Road had been part of how the Clans kept the homeworlds' location secure. Since the time of the Not-Named Clan, the full route of the Exodus Road had been kept a secret. That had all changed when he provided the Star League with the map he had compiled. As he looked at the star charts, even with the gaps, Baldur remembered when he traveled to and from Huntress. More than once he caught himself wondering, if he had to do it all over again, would he?

*Affirmative.*

The Smoke Jaguars had become corrupt, rotting from within. Egos and politics had trumped honor. Seeing what his actions had done to the people—he felt guilt, but did not regret what he had done, only the results. He and Inanna spent time with the sibko children every day. They had freedom to come and go as they pleased, but they also had a safe home aboard the DropShip. Spending time with them helped his sometimes dark mood—or so Inanna claimed.

As he looked at the holographic display, Inanna hovered on the far side of the table, watching him and the stars at the same time. He could feel her gaze on him. There was something in the way that she looked at him that was unnerving, though he was hard-pressed to say what. *It is as if she knows something I do not–and is watching me try to figure it out.*

"Any potentials yet?" she asked.

"*Neg,*" Baldur replied. "None that I am pleased with. Apparently one of the reasons the Exodus Fleet continued on was that they did not come across an abundance of worlds capable of supporting large populations. The few out there are staging worlds for the Clans in the Inner Sphere—which rules them out."

"Agreed. You do not want the other Clans knowing where you are. You would be too tempting a target."

Baldur straightened and crossed his arms as he concentrated on the map. "Between my notes on the Exodus Road and the Nova Cat maps, I have filled in many details. None of the worlds jump out as a possibility yet."

As he spoke, he overlaid the Nova Cat map on his own. Some parts overlapped, while others did not. Those that did overlap showed up in a brighter blue in the space over the tabletop, and drew his eyes.

One world stood out. Wayside V. That was its designation on the original Star League astrogation charts. Baldur had heard of the world before, but mostly rumor rather than fact. He zoomed in on the system, and Inanna leaned in to see it as well. "You found something, *quiaff?*"

"Perhaps," he muttered. "Wayside V. It was one of our forward staging bases, code-named Wildcat. We staged Zeta Galaxy there until it was attacked by the Draconis Combine, the Northwind Highlanders, and the Nova Cats. After we lost the world, we accepted the Inner Sphere name for it, so embarrassing was our defeat there. I remember being told we were not to mention the world in the presence of ilKhan Lincoln Osis. He was livid about being defeated by mercenaries and your—our Clan."

Inanna leaned in and studied the data. "The planet has ample plant and animal life. We abandoned the world shortly after taking it. The real prize was the Zeta Galaxy forces." She paused for a moment and grinned. "Fascinating. The leader of the attack forces there was Khan Santin West."

"The planet's atmosphere is low and relatively thin. The Smoke Jaguars set up some atmospheric processors, but I have no data indicating if they are manned. In fact, I don't know if anyone even retook the world."

"I will cross-reference our Watch reports," she said as her fingers flew over the controls. It took a few seconds for the data to scroll through the air between them. Inanna's eyes locked onto it. "We only occupied the world for a short time before abandoning it. From our last intel report, a small force of Smoke Jaguars returned to garrison Wayside V. None of the other Clans seem to know about it."

Baldur stared at his own data. "The atmosphere of this world was badly damaged at one point, most likely a near miss by a comet or asteroid. The air is breathable only over what was the oceans. The continents remain lifeless. The seas were severely depleted by whatever happened. The only place where life exists now is the dry seabed floors. Despite that, there is an abundance of plant and animal life. I have to imagine that the Jaguars seeded it with organics to make it possible for any occupation forces to be self-sufficient. That is—*was* their way."

"Your thoughts?" Inanna asked.

"Right now, barring any new information—Wayside V seems viable. It is out of the way, not along a well-traveled route. The only other Clan that knows about it is ours. There should be existing facilities we can use. The world itself is not highly desirable, but possesses ample mineral and metal deposits under the old seas that would allow for industrial mining. A colony could be established there."

"It is a considerable distance from here—much closer to the Inner Sphere than to Clan space," she cautioned.

"*Aff*, but that works well. I would prefer to be far away from the other Clans during this time of rebuilding. The farther away we are, the less likely anyone is to come searching for us."

Inanna's watch beeped. "Ah, we need to go and attend the welcoming ceremony."

Baldur's jaw set. "I would prefer to not attend."

"We represent the Nova Cats. To not attend would cast suspicion."

"That man is insufferable," he responded in the tone of an unhappy child.

"I understand your feelings, but tonight you must leave them here on the ship. We need to put on our dress uniforms and go for cocktails. We do not have to stay long—just long enough for him to know we are a presence the Star League must contend with."

Baldur hated it when she was right and he was wrong—and this was clearly one of those occasions. Throwing her an icy glare, he went to put on his dress uniform. It was the first time he had worn the outfit, and it felt uncomfortable.

There was a small leather pouch on the dress belt which was for his *vineers*. From the leather bag he kept them in, he took out the Smoke Jaguar uniform button and rolled it in his fingers. It seemed like a lifetime ago that he had been Trent. The bloodstained fabric from his old uniform fit into the pouch, as well as the SLDF patch he had worn on the voyage back to Huntress. *My life summed up in trinkets—bits and pieces of memories that are no longer mine.* A part of him wanted to drop the façade and return to his old name and life—but on Huntress or in Clan space, that would be a death sentence. It was a burning secret that he yearned to tell, but he had to use his new identity carefully. *There will be a time and place to reveal myself to someone other than Inanna. Tonight is not that night.*

The hall chosen for the welcoming ceremony had once been the Smoke Jaguar leadership's formal dining area. Baldur had only seen glimpses of the room through an open door when he had been a Jaguar. Now that he stood inside, the room embarrassed him. Unlike the usually Spartan Jaguar décor, the room seemed opulent. The light fixtures were bronze and more decorative than he felt comfortable with, as was the inlaid flooring depicting a map of Huntress in an intricate and colorful mosaic. The statues he remembered of the pouncing jaguars were gone—removed by the Star League. Most of the paintings remained. Executed by highly skilled artists, they depicted BattleMechs and Elementals of his former Clan—though on closer inspection, the symbols of the Smoke Jaguars had been painted over. A few paintings had been removed outright, the blank spots on the gray marble walls standing out more than the paintings that remained. The victors were truly rewriting history.

Punch and hors d'oeuvres were laid out on a table covered with a pristine tablecloth bearing the Cameron Star of the Star League. Baldur got a cup of punch, more for something to do with his hands than because he wanted to drink it. He was uncomfortable with the formality of the gathering, which included all of the Star League officers. Not because of the officers, but because of the guest of honor.

He spotted Victor Steiner-Davion mostly because of his hulking Elemental bodyguard, who hovered along the wall near wherever he stood. The short man was with Paul Masters when Baldur first saw him, engaged in deep discussion, from the stern look on his face. Baldur stared at Victor intently from across the room and remembered their last encounter—when the prince had denied him his promised command in battle. *Like me, he set things in motion that were beyond his understanding and control.* Anger welled up in him.

Officers huddled around the prince, but Baldur kept his distance. Victor Steiner-Davion was the last person he wanted to be close to. *He never understood me at all, nor did he bother to try.* Baldur sipped his punch but barely tasted it; his focus was on the man in the distance.

As he lowered his cup, he noticed Paul Moon's presence. *Odd that I did not see him before.* Moon loomed along a wall next to his bondholder, Major Blau, who was conferring with several other members of the Eridani Light Horse. He looked at Moon and realized he was as uncomfortable at this gathering as Baldur. *He is trying to hide it, but it is in his face.* Wrinkles on Moon's brow highlighted his bioniceye implant, since the skin there did not fold up as Moon brooded. Oddly, seeing Moon made Baldur happy—if only because his former foe disliked the party as much as he did. Baldur grinned slightly at the discomfort of the Elemental. *This may be the only enjoyment I have this evening...*

He walked across the room, and when Inanna saw him moving, she broke off her conversation and followed. Baldur approached and stood beside Moon. "This room seems oddly inappropriate for a Clan, *quiaff?*"

Moon's head snapped around—he had not seen Baldur at his side. "Perhaps to a Nova Cat. For those of us who were in the Smoke Jaguar leadership, this room was called the Victory Chamber. It reminded us of the past glories of our people. Being invited to meet in this room is a distinct honor."

*He thinks I cannot understand that concept, but he is wrong.* "It is lavish by Clan standards, is all I meant." He glanced over at Steiner-Davion. "They all think highly of their beloved prince, *quiaff?*"

Moon eyed Victor Steiner-Davion as well. "He is the architect of the fall of the Smoke Jaguars, and he brought the Clans to heel in the Great Refusal. I do not underestimate such a man."

"Nor do I," Baldur agreed, taking another sip of his punch. "His forces dealt a crushing blow not just to the Smoke Jaguars, but to the Clans as a whole. Such men are to be respected, if not admired."

Paul Moon cocked his left eyebrow and faced Baldur slowly, deliberately. "I respect him as a warrior, but not for his results. I am not surprised the Nova Cats would admire such a man."

Baldur leaned in closer to the tall Elemental. "What do you mean by that, Paul Moon?"

"You turned your back on us, then on the Clans. Surely you view this prince-lord with reverence." His words were intended to sting, but Baldur let them pass. *This is the old Paul Moon I knew, wielding words as if they were swords.*

"The Smoke Jaguars turned against themselves, first and foremost," Baldur said, casually sipping his punch. "That sealed their fate. We had no role in that. I believe you did, though." He wanted to grin, but knew his opponent well enough to not gloat.

Moon opened his mouth to reply, but both men were interrupted by someone approaching on Baldur's left. He turned, saw Victor Steiner-Davion, and immediately a flush of anger rose to his face.

Major Blau stepped forward with a stern look. "Prince Steiner-Davion, may I present my bondsman, Paul Moon, and Baldur of the Clan Nova Cat delegation."

Victor extended his hand, and for an awkward moment neither of them reciprocated. Finally, Baldur took his hand, squeezing hard and surprisingly getting just as firm a grip back. "Prince Victor," was all he said. Victor shifted his hand to Paul Moon, who shook it as well, his own massive hand all but engulfing the prince's. The Elemental said nothing.

Victor sensed the tension; Baldur saw it in his eyes. The prince turned to him. "I was unaware that Khan West was sending a delegation to Huntress."

Baldur wanted to punch him—wanted to tell him who he really was. *Now is not the time or place for him to find out...not with Moon right here.* "Khan West sent us as a gesture of respect, Your Highness."

Victor paused for a heartbeat. "Have we met before?"

"*Neg*," Baldur replied. "I was on Strana Mechty during the Great Refusal. Perhaps you saw me then?"

"Perhaps..." Victor said. His cocked eyebrow indicated he was not entirely sure.

Major Blau stepped a little closer into the circle. "Your Highness, Paul Moon led the counterattack against us here on Huntress. He has since been serving honorably as my bondsman. He has proven himself invaluable to our intelligence staff."

The prince looked up the torso to the face of the Elemental. "From the damage I saw and the reports I read, you conducted yourself with distinction. What have you been working on lately?"

Moon shifted uncomfortably at the prince's genial tone. "I have put together a plan for the creation of several militia units out of the remnants of the warrior caste on Huntress."

The major chimed in. "We have had some issues with the warriors here. Without a purpose, they are prone to criminal activities. On top of that, a minor insurgency has emerged. Paul's plan would allow us to keep the warriors occupied—give them something to do rather than cause trouble."

Victor shook his head at the major's words. "I am against rearming the Smoke Jaguars. I do not want the other Clans to learn that we defeated them and are now using them as troops. Our purpose was to destroy one Clan, the most dangerous and vicious, as an example to the rest. Rearming them undermines what we accomplished."

The major opened his mouth to respond, but Paul Moon spoke first. "Inviting them to once again protect the people they feel responsible for, even a small number of them, will give them hope. A people without hope can be dangerous."

"I am not at all comfortable with it," Victor reiterated in a crisp tone.

*I may not like Paul Moon, but he is right. The prince is still impulsive—this was the same behavior he exhibited with me.* Baldur cleared his throat, then weighed in. "I understand your concern, Your Highness," he said, choosing his words carefully to paint Victor as a bit of a coward. "The Smoke Jaguars were formidable foes. Rearming a large number of them might make some question the Star League's intentions. But arming a small number of them, a single unit of non-Mech-Warriors, would serve Paul Moon's purpose of giving the former warriors hope without causing a political situation for the Star League."

When he finished, even he was surprised by his argument. *I am more Nova Cat than I thought.*

The prince paused and looked at Baldur for a moment, then turned back to Major Blau. "So these displaced warriors are stirring up trouble for our people?"

"Yes, sir," the major replied. "There is a leader out in the jungles, he calls himself 'the Jaguar.' He can recruit idle warriors with some degree of ease. These warriors spent an entire lifetime to become fighters, and our victory has taken that life away from them. That vacuum of purpose has created a large number of problems we did not anticipate."

"I would have thought that Clan honor would keep them in their place." Victor showed he could parry words as well as, if not better than Baldur.

"Your Highness, Clan honor did not anticipate an army of occupation. Simply telling them they are free to choose their direction in life is not enough. This culture is deeply ingrained, and with the warriors, it is at the genetic level. We need to take action."

Victor nodded after a moment of thought. "Arming a single unit of infantry to cut off the flow of manpower to this insurgency? I wouldn't be much of a leader if I didn't consider the implications to the people. I can see moving forward with a single unit, if only to hurt this Jaguar's efforts."

"Well bargained and done," Paul Moon said, dipping his head in a perfunctory bow. The prince nodded and moved on, working the room one group at a time.

A part of Baldur wanted Victor to deny Paul Moon's plan. He wanted another reason to validate his hatred of the prince. His agreeing with the two of them left a bad taste in his mouth. He gulped down the rest of his punch, but it did not help.

Paul Moon stepped in front of him. "Baldur of the Nova Cats, your contribution to the discussion was unnecessary."

*You arrogant freebirth! I helped you!*

Moon continued. "At the same time, it was persuasive. I am compelled to thank you."

"And I am compelled to acknowledge it," Baldur said, walking away. *This is easily the worst party I have ever attended. I have come away respecting someone I hate and having another person I loathe thank me for assisting them.* He ignored the stern look he got from Inanna and left the room.

# CHAPTER 18

Paul Moon sat at what had become his usual booth and surveyed the crowd. Since getting approval for his plan, Major Blau had tasked him with identifying possible candidates for the infantry platoon he was assembling. Normally that would have meant Trials of Position, but there was no way the Star League would countenance that Clan tradition. *Neg*, he had to select a pool of candidates and have them try out for the new unit.

Moon approached the task with mixed feelings. A part of him was pleased that his plan had been approved, though dramatically scaled back. Another part of him believed it would not be enough.

As he sat, he caught the aroma of vein leaf being smoked, its sweet aroma making his eye water. It was popular with the lower castes, but the smoke irritated his human eye and his nose. *A filthy habit to indulge in.*

Star Captain Shane entered and, after grabbing a bottle of beer from the bar, headed to his table. "Good eve to you, Paul," she said, taking a drink as she settled into a seat across from him.

"You received my message," Moon said.

"*Aff.* And I have heard from other warriors what it may be about. You are forming a new unit from what remains of our caste."

Moon nodded to her. "I was thinking someone of your skills might be a good fit for such a platoon, if you are willing to try out for it." He watched her carefully.

Shane took a long gulp of cold beer. "I am unsure. The Light Horse is a mercenary unit. In the eyes of many, working for them demeans what it means to be a warrior."

"In your eyes?"

She nodded and leaned back in her chair. "Somewhat. This is off-set by the chance, however remote, to fight again."

"Then you will try out, *quiaff*?"

She frowned and drew another sip of beer. "*Aff*. While working as a laborer has been satisfying, it is not what I was raised to do. If your Star League will have me, I will fight for you."

He tapped the neck of his beer bottle against hers. "This unit is a start."

Shane looked at him ruefully. "I admire you, Paul, but you can be naïve at times. Your Star League will never let you rearm us, not in any real numbers. This is more about controlling crime here in Lootera or preventing Russou Howell from recruitment. It does not solve the plight of our Clan—our people. Nothing has changed since our last talk."

Neg, *my thinking has*. In the weeks that had passed since he had last seen Shane, he had given the subject a great deal of thought. He had an idea, not entirely fleshed out, but one that might work. "Let me ask you, Shane—do you believe the other Clans will come to Huntress?"

"*Aff*," she said, sipping her beer. "They will come. They did not come when we needed them, but they will come now. Harvesters. They will want every factory, every asset, every person who once was Smoke Jaguar. This Star League is not prepared for the coming storm. I am not alone in thinking this. Those of the lower castes talk about it often. It looms over them like storm clouds, a nagging threat."

"What if we were not on Huntress?" he said, taking a long drink of his own beer, watching her face for her reaction.

"Are you planning a trip, *quineg*?" she quipped.

"What if our Clan left Huntress? Left the world to the Star League and the Clans to fight over. We could go somewhere else, find some unexplored world and settle there—rebuild the Smoke Jaguars." *There, I have voiced it.*

Paul could see she was not moved by his proposal. "You must be a half dozen beers ahead of me tonight, Paul. Wars are won on the battlefield, but you must first get there—which is why logistics are so critical. You cannot escape with the population of Huntress and set off like the Great Father reborn, looking for a home. The Star League would quickly squash your plans. They exist because of the death of our Clan. They would never stand for a resurrection of the Smoke Jaguars. Nor would the other Clans."

"It is just an idea," Paul said in response.

"Well, it is the start of an idea," Shane said. "The Clans do not want the return of the Smoke Jaguars, either. It would be an ugly reminder of how they turned their backs on us. They would come to defeat us and take our warriors. Such a plan on the scale of what you propose would only invite a replay of what happened on Huntress."

Shane was right—and that bothered him. His face flushed at the realization. He cradled the beer bottle with both hands and wished he had consumed more. *She is right, logistics would be the key. Moving millions of people would be a massive undertaking.* Worse yet, it meant that he was wrong, and Paul Moon hated that. "I was in charge of saving Huntress. I only wish to finish that mission."

"I salute that," she said. "We do need salvation. And for what it is worth, none would be better than you to provide it. But the logistics are against you. Huntress has millions of people who would need to be moved without the Star League catching on. And it is not just the people. They would have to be provisioned. We would need our BattleMechs to protect them, and they would need the equipment necessary to build a viable society. There is an old saying among our people—'you cannot fight the math.' Such is the nature of your plan, Paul."

"So we are doomed, *quineg*?" he said flatly.

"*Neg!*" Shane said, grinning broadly. "We simply lack a solution to the problem. We will need it soon, I fear. With Prince Victor Steiner-Davion's departure for the Inner Sphere, the Clans will no longer hold back. They will come, one by one, like carrion birds pecking at a dead animal."

"By then it may be too late."

She shook her head. "Again, *neg*. It is never too late. Perhaps you need to come at this from a different perspective. You should be asking yourself this—what are you trying to save? It is the Smoke Jaguars, *quiaff*? That may be the flaw in your thinking. You think that our former Clan is the sum of all of its parts, all of its people. That is a narrow view."

"What are you saying?"

"Being a Smoke Jaguar is not about the symbol of a pouncing feline. The Star League has erased all of those, yet we are here—still Smoke Jaguars in our hearts. What I am saying is the thing you want to preserve is not millions of people—it is an attitude, a belief."

Her words hit him like an SRM volley. She was right. Even though he was a bondsman, he had never stopped being a Smoke Jaguar. *How does one preserve the soul of an eradicated Clan?*

"You are not making this any easier, Shane."

"It is not my intention to make your life easy, Paul. For what it is worth, you did get one thing right. Huntress is a lure. Our former allies will come here because they are drawn to it. Being here is part of the problem that must be overcome."

"Finding a new home will take time. It would need to be far away from both the Inner Sphere and the Clans to allow our people to thrive."

"Agreed. It is more of a problem than you may realize. Each day would consume food and resources you cannot replenish quickly. Exploration of habitable worlds would be a further drain on your logistics."

"So, do you have a suggestion?"

"*Neg.*" She grinned wryly. "It is an interesting exercise though—contemplating a means of survival. It gives you a deeper respect for what Aleksandr Kerensky accomplished, *quiaff?*"

"*Aff,* it does at that," Paul said, downing the last of his beer. "You have given me a great deal to think about."

"And you have given me a chance to prove myself again. Honor is given and received," Shane replied as she took three gulps and finished her beer, slamming the bottle down next to his empty. "For that, I thank you." She rose and walked toward the doorway.

Paul sat alone at the table. *I want to save my people–that was my mission. Shane is right, though: this is all about logistics, and the logistics are indeed staggering. No one has migrated a planetary population in recent memory, though the Jade Falcons claimed to have done that on Somerset in the Inner Sphere.*

*I must find a way to make this happen. The storm is coming this autumn, and with it will come a rain of fire and hail of death. Our enemies will harvest us, and once that begins, we will be lost. Even the SLDF understood what they were up against.*

*All that remains is a plan and action...*

# CHAPTER 19

As the Goliath Scorpion destroyer *Sagitta* and the other JumpShips emerged from jump space, Galaxy Commander Rik Myers's stomach pitched and rolled. It happened on half the jumps—a wave of nausea accompanied by his face getting red and hot. Clenching his stomach muscles, he rode it out as beads of sweat formed on his brow. He never threw up, but always had the symptoms. Pushing the bile back and fighting the urge to vomit was a demonstration of his will.

"All vessels reporting in-system," the comms officer signaled.

"Very well," he said, regaining his composure. "Any sign of Prince Victor's JumpShip?"

The tactical officer on the *Sagitta*'s bridge worked furiously. "*Neg*, Galaxy Commander. No sign of it or the majority of the Com Guard WarShips, either. There are a large number of JumpShips in system, however—all tagged as former Jaguar merchant caste vessels. We have an encrypted message from Star Commander Rife Nagy being transmitted to us from the local commsat."

"Receive and decrypt," Myers replied.

"It is for your eyes only, Galaxy Commander," the comms officer replied.

Rik floated over to one of the workstations and activated the retinal scan. The message bore the mark of a red scorpion—the Watch.

Rife Nagy appeared on the screen, his black hair in pristine order. "Our operatives on Huntress report the SLDF has departed—there is no way they could be recalled in time to assist the local garrison. I am including the latest intelligence on facilities on the Abysmal continent—chiefly the *Warhawk* factory at Rakt-Jabada and the attached spaceport there. Be forewarned, we have indications the Star League is actively recruiting former Jaguars into their ranks. Unfortunately, we have no details of these efforts, but it allows them to augment their forces with Clan warriors. May you claw and sting your enemies to their graves. Rife out." The image went dark.

Myers broke out a narrow grin. His Khan had been precise: do not risk pushing the Star League to respond with full force. It had been agreed they would not go to Huntress until after the bulk of the SLDF left Clan space for the Inner Sphere. Rik Myers had been chafing for weeks. He wanted Huntress and her surviving warriors. *I must prove to Ariel Suvorov I am worthy of her trust.*

Khan Suvorov had been difficult to convince, and she curtailed some of his original plans. He had proposed bidding for all of the Abysmal continent on Huntress. She cautioned him that seizing such a large percentage of the planet would force the Star League to defend with a substantial portion of their force. "We run the risk of winning the day, but having insufficient force to defend against other Clans that would come." She pointed out that conquest was not just seizing the territory, but administering it. "You have no idea how substantial a task it is to manage a world or a continent of that size." Her words stung. *She falls back on caution too much.* Abysmal is the key—he had seen it while in the throes of a necrosia haze. *What do I care about administration? I am a Goliath Scorpion warrior. I have come here to establish us on Huntress, seize the Smoke Jaguars' prizes, and absorb the remains of their warriors into our ranks.*

Suvorov had forced him to scale back his grand plan. Rather than take the entire continent, he would have to settle for an enclave—one hundred kilometers in every direction of the *Warhawk* factory. The rugged mountain terrain to the east, the Lunar Range, would anchor the new Goliath Scorpion holdings. *All I have to do now is win.*

"Galaxy Commander," the comms officer said. "We are being pinged by the Star League from the jump station. They wish to know our intentions."

He pushed off to drift to her workstation. "Set this transmission in the clear—I want those on the planet to hear it, too."

The officer nodded and stabbed the transmit button. The green bar flickered on at the top of the screen.

"Star League Defense Force in the Huntress system, this is Galaxy Commander Rik Myers of Alpha Galaxy of Clan Goliath Scorpion. I have come to harvest the former Clan Smoke Jaguar holdings on the Abysmal continent and take them in the name of my Clan. The Goliath Scorpions understand the importance of our past, and now that the Jaguars are history—we seek to reap them.

"I come to claim the *Warhawk* factory at Rakt-Jabada and all territory surrounding it for one hundred kilometers in every direction.

This includes the spaceport and all former Jaguar personnel. I do this in the name of the one Clan that remains true to merging our own history with that of the past.

"You fought with honor to take Huntress. I now demand you honor our traditions. Tell me, with what forces will you defend what I intend to take? My Rock Minders stand ready to deliver honor." His *batchall* issued, he nodded and the comms officer killed the transmission.

*Let us see how long it takes for them to respond.* He didn't have to wait long—no more than twenty minutes before a message came back.

"This is Paul Masters, commanding officer of the Knights of the Inner Sphere and the Star League Defense Force on Huntress. We acknowledge your *batchall*. We are prepared to defend with one battalion of combined forces from ComStar and the Eridani Light Horse. We are preparing our list of units at present. In keeping with your traditions, we choose the Hatya Desert as the location for our fight. We shed our blood to take this world, and will honor our dead by fighting to keep it."

Even Rik Myers had to acknowledge that Masters's response was appropriate. *This man understands the importance of history. He seeks to honor his dead warriors, a desire I can respect.* He responded quickly. "I accept your response, Paul Masters. I will contact you with the forces I intend to use in our attack after receiving your *touman*, and apprise you of our arrival schedule."

He drifted back from the communications console. *I did not expect them to choose the Hatya Desert as the venue for our fight. No matter. The Goliath Scorpion is a creature of the hot sands. We shall make them pay for this decision—and take what is left of the Jaguars as our own.*

## STAR LEAGUE DEFENSE FORCE HQ
## LOOTERA, HUNTRESS

The large, circular conference table was ringed with the commanders and intelligence officers of the SLDF units still on Huntress. Paul Moon was pleased that Major Blau had invited him. Word of the Goliath Scorpions' *batchall* had spread like wildfire. While Paul sensed the tension in the room, he also noted that the Star League officers seemed composed. Even the Nova Cat delegation seemed remarkably calm, though he saw the one called Baldur fidgeting at the table. *He has nothing to be anxious about. The Star League, on the other hand, must put up a good fight, or they will pay the price of other Clans rushing in to battle them.*

He had warned them this was coming. While Paul had not guessed the Goliath Scorpions would strike first, he knew the Clans would descend on Huntress sooner rather than later. He had been working out with his platoon of former Jaguar warriors when he got word of the Scorpions' arrival.

The last few weeks had been rewarding. The SLDF would let no more than a Star of his troops don Elemental battle armor. The rest of the force would fight as conventional infantry in standard tactical gear. The anchor of his platoon was the armored Elementals, while the rest was a mix of non-armored Elementals and warriors. It had taken some time to get them back in shape and working together. Months of downtime had left some straining just to do calisthenics. Moon had pushed them hard. They were not a threatening force, but they were worthy of battle. All appreciated the chance to once more ply their trade. *I have done one thing–I have given them purpose.*

Paul Masters looked more exhausted and frustrated than anything else. Moon had been in the room when he had decided to shift the fighting from the area near the *Warhawk* factory to the desert. "I don't want to run the risk of destroying that thing after we got it up and running again," Masters had said. He was a strange commander: he abhorred the thought of fighting, yet was clearly skilled at it. Moon had seen that with his Knights of the Inner Sphere. *Such a man is a paradox, which makes him interesting.*

Masters cleared his throat, and the room quickly went silent. "I promised these Goliath Scorpions a battalion to oppose. We need to decide who should comprise that force. I want a mix of troops, to show him we are a unified League."

A Com Guard precentor, "Jumping" Jimmy McHenry, spoke up in a gravelly voice. "Second Division is still rebuilding, but can provide a Level II of combined arms and a heavy assault Level II. Our combined force is one lance of 'Mechs, one of artillery, one of tanks. I'm afraid that is the best we can do at this point."

Colonel Antonescu spoke up next. "The Seventh Light Horse Regiment's Seventeenth Recon Battalion is only at thirty-five percent strength. I can commit that force." For Paul, that was significant—it was Major Blau's unit. "I have another company of mediums from the One-fifty-first we can add, which should give us a good mix of forces."

Masters nodded. "We have seen the Clans respond poorly to combined-arms attacks, so I like the idea of using artillery, tanks, and infantry in our defense force."

"Sir," the major said. "I would like to include the platoon of former Jaguar infantry in our force." He glanced at Moon, who was surprised.

"Major," Paul Masters said. "Does it make sense for us to do that at this time?"

"It does," Paul Moon answered for his bondholder. "Part of the Goliath Scorpions' goal here will be to gather former Smoke Jaguars. If we are part of the SLDF, we are not subject to that. It also sends a clear message to the rest of Huntress that there is a path for the warrior caste. That the Star League sees value in us."

Masters paused for a moment. "Agreed."

Inanna spoke up. "Clan Nova Cat proposes including a Star of our troops in the fighting as well."

Paul Masters eyed the pair of them. "You are not formally part of the Star League. It might be inappropriate for us to include you."

"True," replied Baldur. "However, we are warriors who support your cause and ideals. Our Clan yielded worlds in the Inner Sphere during Operation Bulldog. We are allies, if not of the same blood."

Master nodded. "Very well then, the two of you may fight as well." He looked back down the table at the Light Horse delegation. "Paul Moon, since you were Clan, are there any other precautions we should be taking?"

"*Aff*," he said. "I heard the *batchall*. Galaxy Commander Myers intends to take the factory and spaceport. We have grounded almost all of the merchant caste DropShips, and that spaceport is packed. I recommend we load them with anything we do not want to fall into the hands of the Goliath Scorpions, including key personnel, and move them here to the Lootera spaceport. The Galaxy Commander would try to claim those ships as *isorla*. Removing them prior to the battle reduces our potential losses."

Masters nodded. "Sounds reasonable. It will pack our spaceport here, but I'd rather not give the Scorpions any more than they deserve, should they win."

Colonel Antonescu spoke up. "We need to get our people in place. These Scorpions are probably burning in-system as we speak. We have a lot of different formations, and will need to get the lay of the land as well as work out command and control."

"Agreed," Masters said. "Gentlemen—ladies—I can't stress enough the need for us to make these Scorpions bleed. We can't afford to have the other Clans think us weak. Victory is important, but I believe hurting them is much more critical. With that in mind, Colonel Antonescu, I'm asking you to take command of our forces in the desert." The seasoned veteran nodded.

With those words, the meeting adjourned. Major Blau walked over to Paul. "That was outstanding, Paul. Good words of advice—and a good idea to get your unit into the fray."

"Thank you, sir."

"We will need a designation for your former Jaguars for responding to the *batchall*. What do you want to be called?"

He was not prepared to answer that question. "We are not the Jaguars—nor should we use that name. It sends the wrong message. We are more like ghosts of that former Clan."

"The First Ghost Platoon? Does that work for you?"

"*Aff*," he replied. Oddly, it did.

"I suppose they will need a commander?" Blau asked.

"*Aff*. I have several suggestions based on their performance and past battle history."

Blau cocked a smile. Reaching down, he took Paul's bionic arm in his hand and lifted it by the wrist. Taking out a small pocket knife, he cut the bondcord. "You have one flaw—you don't recognize sarcasm."

The bondcord dropped to the marble floor, and Paul stared at his wrist.

"You have more than earned it, Paul Moon," Blau said. "You will have an appropriate rank—sergeant. You will lead your Ghosts in battle against these Scorpions. They won't expect us to field Clan troops against them. If anything, you'll catch them off guard."

Moon was unsure how to respond. He raised his gaze to his commanding officer. "Well bargained and done, Kris Blau." He rose slowly to his full height—tall, proud. *I am a warrior once more.*

# CHAPTER 20

HATYA DESERT
ABYSMAL CONTINENT, HUNTRESS
THE KERENSKY CLUSTER, CLAN SPACE
7 AUGUST 3060

Baldur looked out from the cockpit of his recently assigned *Timber Wolf* at the rolling sand seas of the desert with a keen tactical eye. Every dip and rise in the terrain offered potential cover or a spot for an ambush. The desert was deceptive; he had learned that when he trained here as a young Smoke Jaguar. There were wadis, gullies that were almost invisible until you were right on top of them. You could drive armor in them, or move infantry or Elementals through them. There was the Istara Depression, a mostly dried salt marsh that was stony, but a white coating of salt dust made it nearly impossible for vehicles to move through. The depression was a mix of quicksand, mires, and jagged, white-tipped rocks that could devour tank treads. At night, the howls of silver jackals that made the desert their home kept some of the troops awake.

He had offered these suggestions during the planning session for facing the Goliath Scorpions. His descriptions raised Paul Moon's eyebrows. *He must have wondered how a Nova Cat could know the terrain so well.* Baldur's description of the ground was supported when the SLDF visited the site. The autumn winds were dry, whipping the powdery layer of dust at unprotected eyes. *This is not the kind of ground where battles are fought easily.*

He and Inanna being included in the defense force was an honor, and Baldur was excited at the prospect of getting to fight again...this time defending the citizens of Huntress. Woodall Winters had been angry that his Star of Elementals had not been bid in the fight. Inanna had gone off with him for a conversation that resulted in him accepting the decision, though neither shared what she had told him. Baldur had come to respect her powers of persuasion.

Colonel Antonescu had listened intently to the descriptions of the Hatya Desert, then formulated a plan. Rather than go on the offensive, he would let the Goliath Scorpions come to his force. The troops would execute a controlled retreat of the center of the line, luring the Scorpions into the center. There, flanked by their own advance, they would be pummeled.

The plan sounded good on paper, but Baldur was leery. The Goliath Scorpions were known for rapid flanking tactics. Antonescu believed the Istara Depression would prevent the attackers from using flanking maneuvers.

Paul Moon argued against that conclusion. "It is not good ground for vehicles or heavier assault BattleMechs, affirmative, but can be traversed by light 'Mechs. They can move on the salt ground without risk of getting bogged down."

Colonel Antonescu had ignored his suggestion, convinced that his forces would be prepared.

Baldur was not. "This Rik Myers commands the Thirty-fifth Scorpion Cuirassiers," he said. "He did not rise to his position by falling for an elementary ploy."

Antonescu scowled. "We shall see how elementary it is when we crush them." He meant his boast, but Baldur considered it false bravado.

Inanna sought to mediate. "Colonel, we would be honored to provide cover to the artillery in the rear," she offered. Antonescu accepted with a nod.

Baldur understood her move. *That puts us in the best position to blunt a flanking move by the Goliath Scorpions.*

Baldur, wearing a light scarf and sand goggles, ran pre-battle checks on his *Timber Wolf*, as did the other warriors of the defense. The fine, powdery sand created tricky challenges: actuator joints could start grinding if sand particles got in. The dust penetrated every minute gap in the armor plating. His technicians were good, but nothing equaled a warrior checking out his own equipment.

The Eridani Light Horse and ComStar Second Division units were equipped with a larger number of recovered Smoke Jaguar 'Mechs than their older Star League models. Despite the paint jobs, Baldur could see the faint symbols of his old Clan outlined when they caught the light at the right angle. *Try as they might, they cannot quite erase us.*

He caught a glimpse of Paul Moon. His best Elemental troops were outfitted in old Smoke Jaguar armor, repainted in the Light Horse's Seventeenth Recon Battalion camouflage pattern. The unarmored troops, both Elemental and warrior alike, were heavily armed. They wielded twin SRM launchers, man-pack PPCs, assault rifles, and armor cobbled together from scraps.

Moon was in the middle of the mix, checking his troops' gear, giving them encouragement. Baldur watched him and saw a man he should have been able to respect. Their history prevented that. Perhaps Paul Moon had changed. If that was the case, Baldur looked forward to witnessing it.

Moon's Ghosts were positioned on the right-center of the line. He ordered his troops to dig foxholes and trenches in the deep red sands, giving them as much cover as possible. Baldur took his *Timber Wolf* out for a short run to confirm that all systems were functioning, and saw them working on their entrenchments. Tarps were being staked over the holes, then a light layer of sand was thrown on top, hiding the positions almost entirely. *He is making good use of what he has.*

Inanna strode alongside him in her *Mad Dog*, also watching what Moon was doing. "He seems to have adapted to his new lot in life," her voice said in Baldur's neurohelmet.

"Looks can be deceiving," he replied.

"You are only willing to see what you want to see," she replied. "I see a man who is trying to find a future for his people."

"The only future for them is a world on the Exodus Road, I am convinced of that," Baldur replied, thinking again of his plan to save the soul of his former Clan. "Taking the warriors to war serves only to cripple the Jaguar and his raids."

"Perhaps. You need to move past the Paul Moon you knew. This warrior has been through a lot—not as much as you, but a great deal. He has been humbled in defeat and by the loss of his arm and eye—just as you were after Tukayyid."

He heard her words and hated them. He had shared his memories of Tukayyid with her, and now they were coming back to bite him. Making peace with Moon was not easy to contemplate. Still, Inanna had a way with words. *She is planting suggestions with me–and they are not necessarily bad ones. They are just difficult to hear.* "We shall see in the morning when the Goliath Scorpions come."

That night, sleep eluded Baldur. It was nothing new—he had suffered from sleeplessness before battles in the past. What made this different was the location. This was not Tukayyid—this was Huntress. Fighting to protect this planet was the last place he had imagined himself. *In my anger against the Smoke Jaguars, I always thought I would come here to fight them. Now, I find myself fighting to keep a part of Huntress against invaders. The universe has a perverse sense of humor.*

He got up from his hard-shell shelter and went for a stroll. He thought back to when he had trained in this desert before. He had not done well in those tests. The desert was constantly changing; the terrain folded in on itself and reshaped itself in the winds. The cool air of the dry night felt chilly, but he ignored the goose bumps. The Star League encampment was quiet for the most part, lit by a few solar torches on poles around the camp. There were other warriors out in the night—going for their own private walks.

Baldur came around one of the domed tents and saw the hulking figure of Paul Moon standing there, staring into the darkness of the desert. When he saw him, Baldur took a step back. The last person he wanted to see or speak with was the beefy Elemental warrior.

Before he could retreat, Moon turned to him. "Baldur of the Nova Cats—you cannot sleep either, *quiaff?*"

"*Aff,*" he replied, taking two steps forward. Avoiding conversation was now impossible, given that Moon had fired the first salvo. "It is not uncommon for me before a battle."

"I used to sleep like an exhausted sibko student before a fight, but not tonight," Moon said, turning his gaze back to the barren landscape.

"Your troops are ready for the coming fight?"

Moon almost shrugged. "*Aff* and *neg*. While they all look forward to being in the battle, some are looking for honorable release. They feel dying is all they have left. I worry about them the most."

"I understand," Baldur replied. "Their Clan is gone. If they do not die in battle, they run the risk of being *isorla* to the Goliath Scorpions."

"My entire Clan was made *isorla* of the enemy—a prize of war. We have paid that price once. Most do not want to face that again."

"Huntress is untenable. If it is not the Goliath Scorpions, it will be others. You must know that."

"I do," Moon said, turning back to him. "I am seeking a solution, but it is proving as elusive as trying to capture the wind." As if to emphasize his point, a cool breeze whipped between the two warriors.

*He struggles with the same problem Inanna and I are—how to save what was our people.* "I too have been studying the problem of preserving your former Clan. It is...*complicated.*"

"I heard what you did for the children from the sibko," Moon replied, looking intently down at him in the near darkness. "You and Inanna took them into your ships, gave them food and shelter. For that I thank you."

"Thanks are unnecessary," Baldur replied.

"Agreed—but they are offered regardless. But it does make me wonder, Baldur. What is your interest in the former Smoke Jaguars? Is it guilt for your people not coming to our aid and turning against us in the Inner Sphere? Or is it something more?" His tone bordered on accusatory, and Baldur grew defensive as he crossed his arms and looked up at the enormous warrior.

*Does he suspect who I really am? Neg. He is suspicious of our intentions.* "I am fulfilling a debt I feel is owed."

"By you? What debt could you have with my people?"

*They are not your people...they are* our *people.* "Does it matter, Paul Moon? I carry this burden. We took in the children because they had become outcasts, and no one deserves that fate if they have not had the chance to fight for it."

"You and Inanna seem very protective of Smoke Jaguar survivors. It is more than just honor—it is as if you feel a kind of responsibility."

"*Aff.* I knew Trent well enough to know that he felt guilty for what happened. He wished he had not been forced into the course of action he chose."

Moon shook his head. "He had no need for guilt. We met before he left for Strana Mechty. He told me I caused all of this. The fate of the Smoke Jaguars came about because of my arrogance. There was no guilt for him to bear."

"Then you did not truly know Trent," Baldur said solemnly.

"You are right. And he is dead now, and with him any chance to prove to him that I learned my lesson. And come the morning, I will purge more of that guilt with the blood of the Goliath Scorpions."

"The question for you to ponder tonight, Paul Moon—is that enough? Even if we defeat the Scorpions tomorrow, will it be enough for the people of Huntress, *quineg*? Your guilt over Trent is misplaced. Your debt is with what remains of a once great people."

Baldur pivoted and walked into the night before Moon could answer, leaving the Elemental to ponder his future—the same thing he himself was doing with each step into the darkness.

Before dawn, the Star League forces mounted their vehicles to brace for the coming storm. As Baldur approached his *Timber Wolf*, he noticed someone had changed the Nova Cat emblem on the side of his cockpit. Behind the cat was now a silver Cameron Star, the symbol of the old Star League. He stared at it for a long moment as Inanna walked up beside him.

"I had our technicians paint that on last night," she said proudly.

"It seems we have tied our fates to this fledgling League," he replied.

"You are always so dour before a battle," she said. Looking at her, he saw a grin. "This is what you wanted all along, a chance to fight. You fought for our Clan on Strana Mechty, now you fight for the Star League. Even when you get what you want, you are not happy." Her voice was downright jovial.

Baldur found himself grinning back at her. "No one should be happy when people are about to die."

A few minutes later his *Timber Wolf* throbbed to life, and he and Inanna assumed their position with the Long Tom artillery battery near the rear of the SLDF lines. He looked off to the east and saw the brilliant red and yellow plumes of the Goliath Scorpion DropShips beginning their landings. He fidgeted with his natural hand, rubbing his thumb on his fingers. That the Star League officers had been so confident about facing this Clan bothered him still. *They defeated the Smoke Jaguars, and presume the same will happen with the Scorpions. I can only hope they are right.*

He activated his long-range sensors and got a relative reading on the designated battlefield. Baldur took note of where Paul Moon and his Ghosts were, near the right center of the front line.

A voice came over the open comms channel some fifteen minutes later. "This is Galaxy Commander Rik Myers of the Rock Minders. I come with my Scorpions of the Veil, the Thirty-fifth Cuirassiers, to face your Star League in defense of the *Warhawk* factory at Rakt-Jabada. I assure you your people will be dealt with honorably, and I also assure you that your defeat is sealed in the bite and sting of our namesake. *Seyla.*"

Baldur automatically replied "*Seyla*" to himself.

Colonel Antonescu's voice replied a moment later. "This is Colonel Charles Antonescu of the Eridani Light Horse. Our heritage can be tied directly to the Cameron Star League. We stand ready to defend what we won with the blood of our comrades. You want honor, and you shall have it. You can have a dollop of defeat as well. Let's end the chatter—come and face us!"

Watching the sensor, Baldur waited anxiously for the first blow from the enemy, but it was long in coming. *This Myers will not be goaded into a fight.* The first engagements took place at the center of the line—as Antonescu had expected. Because of the terrain, he could not see the battle, but the roar of the pair of Long Tom artillery pieces told him it was underway.

"Look to the flank—out over the Istara," he said on the tactical channel to Inanna. Watching the fighting on the long-range sensors display, it looked as if the Star League forces were slowly starting their retrograde movement. *Falling back while in battle is much harder than pressing forward.*

Inanna's voice cut in. "I picked up something—at zero-eight-two. Reactor signature. It is gone now."

"*Neg*, it is not," Baldur replied. His own sensors picked up a faint reactor signal in the same general area—moving fast. "I have a target ping at zero-niner-three, moving fast to our right."

"You were correct in your assessment of the Scorpions," Inanna said.

"I wish I had not been."

"Do we pursue, *quineg?*"

"*Neg*," he replied. "They want us to chase them into those old salt marshes. We need to shift behind the Long Toms. Signal the colonel that we have enemy forces flanking us on the right."

While Inanna shared the threat with command, Baldur moved his *Timber Wolf* around to the rear of the artillery pieces, which were still firing a steady barrage into the distance. Each blast of the big guns kicked up dust all around them, like a plume marking their position.

His short-range sensors barked to life—five dots of light. "I show one Star, five 'Mechs coming from one-five-five. One *Mist Lynx*, four—neg, make that five *Fire Moth*s. I am going weapons free."

"*Aff*," Inanna replied. "Black Horse Actual, we have a reinforced Star of enemy 'Mechs in our rear."

When he had seen their types, he had cringed. These were fast 'Mechs—some of the fastest produced by the Clans. They were small and weak, but could literally run circles around him and Inanna. He targeted the *Mist Lynx* first and linked his extended-range large and medium lasers on the same target interlock circuit, putting his long-range missiles on the thumb trigger.

The *Mist Lynx* fired its salvo of long-range missiles at him at the same time he unleashed his lasers at it. The missiles and red beams passed each other in the air.

The missiles peppered his legs and the sand around him, tossing it all over his *Timber Wolf*. With the *Mist Lynx* running, only one of his medium lasers caught it, searing its right torso with a smoking black scar through the green Goliath Scorpion painted on a brilliant yellow-orange star.

Two of the *Fire Moth*s unleashed short-range missiles and lasers at the Long Toms, hitting them in the rear. The Light Horse vehicles ceased their barrage and shifted position, moving toward the center of the lines. *They have already negated the artillery by making it move rather than fire.*

The other pair of *Fire Moth*s went after Inanna's *Mad Dog*. She backstepped the bird-like 'Mech as they ran in opposite directions in circles around her. Baldur's own 'Mech shook as another barrage from the *Mist Lynx* tore into his left arm and torso. *I should not have allowed myself to be distracted–Inanna is capable of dealing with this threat.*

He dropped his targeting reticle onto the running *Mist Lynx* and tried to lead it, anticipating its moves. Gritting his teeth, he hit the thumb trigger, unleashing a salvo of forty long-range missiles. His *Timber Wolf* listed back slightly as the missiles surged out and away, while the *Mist Lynx* juked hard and started to double back. The majority of his missiles arced toward the sprinting Scorpion OmniMech but missed, throwing rocks and a mist of salt dust into the wind. Only six found the mark, detonating on the dark-painted 'Mech's arms and legs.

Baldur checked as the two *Fire Moth*s blasted away at the Long Toms. They were turning slowly, trying to bring their machine guns into play. It was a mistake—he could see it. The *Fire Moth*s would run around them while the lumbering artillery would rarely get a shot.

Each passing moment, the artillery pieces were taking enemy fire, slowly being whittled away.

The *Mist Lynx* moved in closer, unleashing its Streak short-range missiles as Baldur brought his medium pulse lasers into play on the upper trigger. He moved the targeting reticle while sidestepping his *Timber Wolf*, making a slow circle counter to the movement of the *Mist Lynx*. A microsecond after he heard weapons-lock tone, he fired.

The air filled with an emerald burst of charged laser energy—catching the *Mist Lynx* in the right arm. Pulses of light shredded the limb, sending myomer and bits of armor flying into the salty dust. There was a flash—some sort of ammunition went off, and the enemy 'Mech rocked hard as smoke trailed from its now-severed arm stump.

To his surprise, it turned and charged straight at him, firing another wave of long-range missiles. He initially recoiled, stopping his sidestep as if to brace for impact. Decades of training kicked in. *It is only twenty-five tons to my seventy-five. On a full run, it will splatter against my cockpit screen like a bug.*

Instead of breaking off, Baldur rushed right at his opponent as the missiles hit, blasting his center and left torso. He shook off the impacts and continued heading toward the onrushing Goliath Scorpion.

And bringing his machine guns onto the same trigger.

No longer dodging, the *Mist Lynx*, its smoking shoulder dangling myomer muscle, came at him fast. The moment it came within range of his machine guns, Baldur opened fire. The tracer rounds marked the bullets' path as they stitched down the left torso and into the 'Mech's dashing, scissor-like legs. Armor fragments sprayed into the sand and dust as it closed the distance.

By the time he collided with the *Lynx*, it had lost all of the armor on its left leg and half on the right. The crash shook his *Timber Wolf*, but he barely felt the impact on his own 'Mech's balance.

He pivoted after the charge and saw the *Mist Lynx* sprawled on its back—it had hit so hard that the rush knocked it backward. The entire front armor of the 'Mech was crumpled and rent. The cockpit glass had a spiderwebbed crack in it.

*That one is down,* he thought—right as a damage warning went off. Two brilliant red bursts of light stabbed at him from the side, barely reflecting in his cockpit, hitting him from the rear. He whipped his massive 'Mech around to see where the shots had come from. Off on the edge of the Istara Depression was one of the *Fire Moths*.

"I took out one of them," Inanna said. "They are nimble machines."

"The *Mist Lynx* is down," Baldur said, bringing his large and medium lasers back onto the same target interlock circuit as he broke into a run, moving to intercept the fast-moving *Fire Moth*. "What is the status on the artillery?"

There was a pause as he strained to get his targeting reticle onto the *Fire Moth* for more than a millisecond. Its warrior was masterful, he had to admit that. It fired a wave of short-range missiles, half of which found their mark on his *Timber Wolf*.

"The artillery is signaling for help," Inanna said, her voice strained. "They are getting torn apart two klicks from here."

Surat's *blood—this ends here and now!* He stopped his *Timber Wolf* and brought all of his weapons onto the same trigger. The *Fire Moth* skirted him, and all he did was pivot his torso, waiting for the right shot.

The *Fire Moth* slowed and fired its medium lasers. As a standing target, Baldur knew they would hit...and they did. The brilliant red beams flashed, burning and melting parts of his armored plate on his center torso. Melted armor splattered the sand at his feet.

The momentary pause while the *Fire Moth* fired was all Baldur needed. The targeting reticle drifted onto his enemy as he had intended. He fired everything he had except his machine guns in a single, concentrated alpha strike against the twenty-ton enemy. The lasers stabbed out first, crimson beams of varying thickness and depth, and the brilliant green bursts from his pulse laser all struck the heart of the *Fire Moth*.

It staggered and spun, almost like a dancer, as its warrior compensated for the incoming fire. Whoever it was, they were skilled and even graceful, as the Goliath Scorpion somehow managed to stay upright under the assault, though it dropped to one knee, facing him squarely, almost defiantly. Sparks flew from the damage on its left side, and armor fragments spun into the air all around it. Its left arm dangled by a few myomer strands.

That was when Baldur's missiles hit.

The long-range missiles' flight time brought them in on the target a second or two after the lasers had all but disemboweled the *Fire Moth*. Many missed their mark, but just the proximity of their explosions rocked the remains of the enemy 'Mech, dusting it with salt and sand. The explosions obscured his view except on infrared, which painted a burning-hot humanoid figure tumbling backward as the world around it erupted.

The *Timber Wolf*'s heat spiked dangerously high, and Baldur worried he had gone too far, as he felt like he was baking in the cockpit. As the heat subsided, so did the dust from where the *Fire Moth* had been. He saw it was down, its reactor off-line—probably destroyed in the assault that had consumed it.

*I should have led with that attack on the Mist Lynx.*

Turning to Inanna, Baldur saw her *Mad Dog* showed signs of battle. Its right missile rack was a gnarled and twisted piece of broken machinery. Smoke rose from hits to her right leg that had burned scars on the camouflage pattern of her OmniMech. "My last foe is down as well," she said with a huffing breath over the tactical channel.

"We need to catch up with the Long Toms," Baldur said. "Inform the colonel we are moving toward the center of the line. Tell him the enemy has penetrated our rear area, and we are moving to pursue."

# CHAPTER 21

In his concealed foxhole, Paul Moon looked through a field periscope at the approaching line of Goliath Scorpion 'Mechs. The sand-covered tarp concealing his Ghosts, made them all but invisible to the attackers. Each footfall from the approaching enemy made their foxholes cave in a little more and kicked up more dirt and dust.

Moon stood in his new Elemental armor, his visor flipped open so he could use the periscope. The Scorpions were closing quickly. On the left flank, Eridani Light Horse tanks had already been routed, hammered into falling back behind the big crimson dunes with a steady barrage of fire. In the desert, 'Mechs had the advantage, and they were more than willing to press it.

The approaching 'Mechs were unfamiliar to him. *Fire Scorpions* were quad-legged war machines armed with deadly autocannons. The *Night Gyr* moving along the far right of the formation blazed away with its particle projector cannons. The *Bowman* he made out through the rising dust unleashed volley after volley of deadly Arrow IV missiles. The lead 'Mech, a *Kodiak*, blasted away with its huge overhead autocannon. The Star was pushing right into the center of the Star League's lines. As much as he hoped Colonel Antonescu was executing his plan to collapse the center, Paul Moon wondered if the SLDF had much of a choice.

It had taken a lot of time and effort to dig a hole deep enough for his Elemental suit, but it would be worth it. *We may be infantry, but we will hit them at point-blank range. They will never see us coming.*

"Sergeant Moon," came the voice of Shane, who was part of his Elemental Star, from her own foxhole to his right. "We stand ready to engage." He could hear the anticipation and excitement in her voice.

"Hold," he said on the tactical channel for his entire force to hear. "Hold until they are on top of us. Wait for my signal."

He rose again to look through the periscope. A wave of long-range missiles roared past overheard and slammed into the *Bowman*, sending it staggering back a step and showering the dune with chunks of armor. The Scorpion warrior had taken a lot of damage, but still maintained his forward movement. *I wish I had a better understanding of how the battle is going.*

Off to the far left, the *Fire Scorpion* moved forward, right on top of Able Team's foxholes. The squat left leg of the 'Mech punched down into the foxhole, and Paul heard anguished screams as his non-Elemental infantry there were squashed. The 'Mech lost balance for a moment, but continued on. *Even in those deaths there was some honor—they died in battle.*

"Sergeant," came the distressed voice of one of his fire-team leaders, Camille. "We must engage or end up like Able Team."

"Agreed," added Blaney, who was rocking back and forth in place, ready to lunge into the fighting.

"*Aff*," he replied. *It is time.*

On the tactical channel for the Light Horse came the grizzled voice of Colonel Antonescu. "Where the hell are you, Ghosts? Hit them!" There was a distinct tone of stress in his voice.

Moon leaned back into his Elemental suit and closed it up. As the seal hissed, he slid his arms into its arms. It felt familiar, like a second skin. "Ghosts, this is Ghost Actual. We move on my mark. Ghost Star, you are with me on the *Night Gyr*. The rest of you go after the *Fire Scorpion*. Remember our plan—target the legs."

A flurry of "*Affs*" came over the channel.

"Engage!" he bellowed.

He fired his leg jets and hit the overhead tarp hard, punching through it. Paul rose into the air on a plume of fire and dust some seventy meters from the *Night Gyr*. He angled his flight path toward the 'Mech as it moved past the line where his people were dug in, firing at a target in the distance. He landed near it, plowing deep into the crimson sand.

Off to his side, Shane landed in her armor. "The legs."

"*Aff*—fire at will."

Paul activated the pair of short-range missiles in the shoulder mounts of his suit and aimed at the right knee and thigh of the Goliath Scorpion OmniMech. The missiles snaked through the air, along with others launched from his Star, and slammed into the *Night Gyr*. Two went high, hitting it in the hip and torso, and one went wide, but the others found their mark. The black-painted 'Mech with brilliant orange designs concealed how bad the damage was, other than the seared-off armor plates. One plate near the knee was peeled back like a banana skin.

The *Night Gyr* paused its advance, pivoting at the waist toward Paul's position. To him, it was as if they had angered the warrior by daring to strike at his 'Mech. The enemy unleashed its Ultra-class autocannon on the Elementals to his right, killing Amon with a direct hit that engulfed his armor in a furious black-and-orange explosion. A piece of bloody flesh splattered against Paul's suit.

"Missiles," he barked on the tactical channel. "Use the last ones now."

The smoke trails caught the desert wind and dissipated as the missiles bore in on the 'Mech's damaged leg. Explosions tore into the armor as Moon detached his now-useless missile rack. This time the *Night Gyr* vibrated under the hits. There was no time to pause and savor the moment—death was close at hand every second on the battlefield.

"Fire again at the leg, then grapple," he commanded.

The remains of his Star joined him in blasting at the already damaged leg of the black-and-orange 'Mech. His own small laser hit the knee actuator dead-on, sending up a gray whiff of smoke as the Goliath Scorpion turned to face him. A PPC barrage from a Light Horse BattleMech in the distance plowed into the *Night Gyr*'s right arm, sending brilliant blue arcs of charged particles dancing across the surface as armor tore free.

Paul fired his jump jets again and angled toward the damaged leg. The right-arm barrel swept nearby, just missing him on his descent. Not so for Shane, who was hit by the swinging arm and sent spiraling through the air.

Moon landed on the footpad of the hulking 'Mech and jumped up, grabbing a torn piece of armor with his claw hand. He jabbed his small laser into the hole and fired into the leg's unprotected internal structure. Smoke—some gray, some white—told him he had blasted the myomer muscle that allowed the 'Mech to move.

The big-barrel right arm of the *Night Gyr* swung downward at the leg above him, where Calypso was hanging on. At the last moment, he swung around the front of the leg to a new position just as the arm hit the leg, mangling the armor where the Elemental had been a second before. The 'Mech swayed under the impact.

Moon pulled himself up farther under the knee, wedging his suit's footpads on a twisted panel of ferro-fibrous armor. He found another burned hole in the armor and stabbed his laser into it, firing upward and inward. The weapon's whine filled his ears as the heat rose from the hit.

The *Night Gyr*'s warrior realized the threat. Turning the massive OnmiMech, they broke into a run. A standard tactic, one Paul had anticipated. His mechanical-claw hand strained as he lost his footing and clung to the leg of the Goliath Scorpion. Calypso held firm, but Brax Chrisholm dropped into the dunes below, leaving a trench in the sand as he skidded on his back.

The 'Mech stopped hard, and Moon swung out wide, but managed to maintain his grip. As he swung back like a pendulum, he wedged his laser into a blast hole for stability and another chance to fire. He unleashed the energy weapon again. This time there was a popping sound, and the armor his laser was wedged under erupted, blowing off completely. His mechanical claw held tight, but he heard the metal groan in protest under the weight of his suit. *That is never a good sound to hear.*

Paul and Calypso held on like ticks, each jabbing their small lasers in and firing. The big autocannon barrel arm swept down again, this time catching Calypso and ripping him free from the thigh where he had been working. Paul didn't see where he landed.

Moon was alone, and for a millisecond memories of the counterattack for Huntress came back, washing his body in a ripple of anger, fear, and terror. His bionic arm tugged tightly at his skin and muscles where it attached to his body, bringing back the horror of losing his arm. The flashback to his defeat was almost overwhelming...almost. He closed his eyes for a moment and gathered his composure, smothering that feeling of failure. *I cannot and will not lead my people to another defeat.*

Flexing his arm, he pulled himself up over the knee actuator just as the *Night Gyr* trotted back toward the battle lines in the distance. At the knee joint itself, he planted the small laser flat and fired—twice. Molten metal splattered out of the hole and onto his armor, sizzling through his camouflage paint. He felt something warm on his thigh, but ignored it and the light warning that his suit had been breached.

The OmniMech suddenly lurched as the knee actuator froze. Each footfall of the right leg was a decisive *thump*, a limp as the warrior tried to flex it but the joint failed.

Paul allowed himself a moment of satisfaction, but continued to climb. At the top of the front thigh, he held onto a hole blown by a short-range missile with his claw while firing his laser into it. A brilliant red flare lit below him as Calypso fired at the damaged leg from a distance.

The *Night Gyr* ignored him, unleashing a barrage of autocannon fire overhead. He glanced over and saw a Light Horse BattleMech topple in the distance. He returned to his task, blasting at the internal structure of the Scorpion 'Mech.

Suddenly there was an explosion above him, and his grip failed. He hit a sand dune on his back, head first. His breath rushed out of his lungs, and he fought to get it back.

Towering above him, the *Night Gyr*'s right shoulder was smoking where an autocannon barrage had ripped a nasty hole. The Scorpion 'Mech returned the favor, unleashing its Ultra autocannon and short-range missiles into the battle raging a half kilometer away. Empty shell casings rained down around him as he finally caught his breath and sat up.

The *Night Gyr* limped forward as Calypso moved in beside him. Paul glanced over and saw his platoon's non-Elemental infantry were pressing their attack on the *Fire Scorpion*. As the unarmored infantry surged forward around the right front leg, one of the 'Mech's antipersonnel pods erupted, raining deadly shrapnel onto the assault troops. A red mist sprayed the air where three men had stood as the explosion and deadly fragments tore them to pieces.

"Orders, Sergeant?" Calypso asked.

"Fire Teams Charlie and Delta need our assistance—we go there," he said.

The squat, spiderlike 'Mech fired a blast of autocannon fire at a Com Guard Burke tank that had crested a dune. The autocannon fire chewed into the front glacis armor plate, forcing it to back down as quickly as it had driven over the dune, leaving a thin wisp of smoke in its wake.

Moon fired his jump jets and angled toward the *Fire Scorpion*. As he rose, he got a glimpse of the battle. His infantry was already in the rear of the Goliath Scorpion advance. Plumes of black smoke rose from destroyed vehicles and 'Mechs—far too many to be a good thing. The Com Guard's Second Division forces were falling back. The Light Horse line was still holding, but was moving backward in a controlled retrograde movement.

Arcing through the air, he landed next to the leg where the antipersonnel pod had decimated his troops. Up close, he got a better understanding of the damage the *Fire Scorpion* had sustained. The man-pack PPCs fired at the front legs had done considerable damage. The armor was burned from the PPC hits and flamer attacks, and holes had been blasted in the 'Mech's knee joints.

Paul fired his jets again and landed on the leg just above the expended antipersonnel pod, using it to brace his footing as he latched onto the enemy 'Mech. From this spot he was able to hit the cockpit of the *Fire Scorpion*, and it was a chance he could not pass up. His laser whined as it discharged, sending a brilliant crimson burst into the cockpit glass, burning a black streak on it. The 'Mech jerked as the warrior reacted to the direct and personal attack.

Paul fired his jets again, going right in front of the Goliath Scorpion war machine and grappling with the side of the cockpit. The MechWarrior knew he was there, either from the sound or from watching him. He pivoted the 'Mech around hard, spinning in place so fast that Moon struggled to hold on. The quad 'Mech's four legs kicked up dust, and Paul saw his infantry fall back, firing with their man-pack PPCs as the 'Mech reeled about. Centrifugal force made it nearly impossible to hold on, but he did.

The *Fire Scorpion* stopped, and Moon fired his small laser at the side hatch to the cockpit, at the upper hinge. The hinge melted away in a burst of brilliant, cherry-bright energy. The pilot started to turn again, this time in the other direction. Dizziness swept over Paul as he clung tight to one of the ladder-holds on the side of the cockpit. Wedging his thick footpad on one of the lower rungs, he jammed the laser through one of the rungs, bending it outward under the stress.

The *Fire Scorpion* lurched forward and suddenly stopped to try to toss him off, but Paul clung to the side with all his might. His back ached as he fought the momentum and the sheer weight of his Elemental suit. The pilot stopped for a moment, and Paul fired another laser discharge at the hatch, searing it to the point where it nearly melted through.

The warrior broke into a run, right at the Star League's lines. A wave of long-range missiles came in from the Light Horse's position, riddling the 'Mech all around him. Some of the shrapnel, including a missile tailfin, peppered his armor, with the fin impaling his suit's arm. *Another centimeter or two and I would have lost my hand.* The *Fire Scorpion* warrior was smart. He was using the tried-and-true tactic of rushing into the heart of the battle, hoping Moon's own troops might accidentally shoot him off the 'Mech.

Moon's options were to stay put and try to finish blasting through, or let go. There was no letting go at this point, not in his mind. The battle had become personal for the former Jaguar.

He fired two more laser bursts at the hatch, his last shot concentrating on the remaining hinge assembly. It glowed a brilliant red before melting, splattering molten metal as the hatch broke free and dropped. His organic arm ached as he clung to the moving 'Mech.

Paul swung his legs in first, his metallic footpads thumping hard inside the cockpit. There was no room for an Elemental and a MechWarrior in the space, but Paul hunched over the warrior, filling the open hatch with his bulk. The Goliath Scorpion warrior reached for his pistol, and Moon struggled to aim his laser in the tight space, somehow managing it.

"You have fought honorably," he said through gritted teeth. "Do not stain that honor with your own blood—I assure you, I will not miss at this range,"

The warrior raised his hands. "I stand defeated."

"Power down," Paul commanded, and the warrior complied. Switching to the tactical channel, he tried to locate the rest of his unit. "This is Ghost Actual, the *Fire Scorpion* is down. Sitrep."

A ragged breath filled the speakers of his Elemental suit. "Ghost Actual, this is Ghost Delta One," came Klein's voice. "The enemy has moved past us and is driving through to the center of the line. They are inflicting heavy casualties."

His own sensors told a similar story. At present, he was closer than the rest of his unit to the brunt of the fighting. "All units, gather your equipment and fall back to my position."

Paul turned back to the broken hatch and looked out at the battle raging all around him. The undulating dunes made taking in the battle difficult—but to his trained eye, it was clear how things were unfolding.

The Goliath Scorpions were not pushing back the left flank of the Star League force, which looked to be holding. In the center and the right flank, however, the Star League was retrograding under heavy fire. Rising, twisted streams of black smoke marked the demise of far too many vehicles and BattleMechs. The smoke mingled with clouds of red dust kicked up from the dunes, making the stalking 'Mechs look like ghostly shadows. Lasers and PPCs firing lit the clouds like fireworks or lightning. Nearby explosions—concussions from missiles and autocannon rounds—made the *Fire Scorpion* he stood in vibrate slightly.

His keen eyes drank in the battlefield as if he were a connoisseur savoring a fine wine. *This was not the plan Colonel Antonescu had envisioned. We are not luring them in, we are collapsing.* There were times he cursed his experience; this was one of them. He saw the defeat from the enemy's rear, and it was almost complete. *Antonescu will fight long and hard, but this is checkmate. All that remains is to see when this is finished.*

Moon fired his jets at 75 percent and dropped down next to the footpad of the defeated Goliath Scorpion 'Mech, landing hard enough to make his legs throb as he bent at the knees in the powdery, ginger-red sand, kicking up a small puff as he rose.

It took some ten minutes for the remains of his unit to arrive. He surveyed the group. Shane was gone. Calypso from his Elemental Point was alive, but his Light Horse-painted armor was torn and rent from his legs to his head. The rest of his infantry was coated in a sweaty paste of sand and perspiration. Most carried their SRM launchers, though little ammunition remained, judging from the empty bandoliers. He did a mental count and calculated that almost a third of his troops were gone, either dead or casualties.

Corporal Kevin of Fire Team Charlie saluted. "Star—er, Sergeant Moon. We stand ready to serve."

Paul returned the salute, despite it not being necessary, given his new rank. "We will mourn the dead when this battle is over...and it is not over until we finish the fight." His weary troops flashed white smiles from under the crust of filth on their faces.

Before he could issue a single order, the ground shook and they turned. Cresting a dune was a squat, egg-shaped BattleMech—an

*UrbanMech IIC.* It had a black undercoating, with jagged yellow, orange, and red striping across its body like uneven lightning bolts. The 'Mech showed some signs of damage, but the Goliath Scorpion's camouflage scheme was excellent at covering the scars of battle.

"Scatter!" Paul barked, and his people instinctively did as ordered. A series of explosions from the Ultra autocannon rained death and carnage all around him. One of his men was consumed by a blast, leaving only an arm spinning in the air over the crimson dunes.

Moon aimed his small laser up at the *UrbanMech IIC* and fired. Neg, surat-*spawn! I still have fight in my blood...*

# CHAPTER 22

Baldur moved his limping *Timber Wolf* as fast as he dared, given the steep angles of the sand dunes. They had lost one of the Long Tom launchers to the Goliath Scorpions. The other, while battered, had been saved.

It had been a difficult fight. The last *Fire Moth* had literally run circles around both Nova Cats, peppering them from every angle. The arrival of a fresh *Black Lanner* had forced Inanna's 'Mech to shut down and had cost his own *Timber Wolf* much of its armor and a badly damaged right-hip actuator, which gave the OmniMech's movement more of a limp than its usual birdlike gait.

Still, he had forced the *Lanner* to fall back, horribly damaged but still operational. A barrage of Arrow IV artillery missiles from an unknown source had twisted one of Baldur's long-range missile launchers into useless metal. *I never even saw the spotter 'Mech that directed that salvo.* He had a grudging but growing respect for the Goliath Scorpions.

The Star League's well-conceived plan had disintegrated upon contact with the enemy. The Goliath Scorpions had been cunning, sending fast, lighter 'Mechs to the rear and along the right flank. They had made a good showing along the left flank, but concentrated on the center. When Antonescu had ordered his center to fall back, they found themselves engaged at nearly point-blank range. In some places, namely the Com Guard Second Division, it had been a near rout.

Antonescu was wily, and adapted to the enemy's plan—something Baldur admired, though it happened too late. He reformed the lines into a new position near the rear. Baldur found himself suddenly out of alignment with the rest of the Star League forces. Rather than fall back, he pressed along the right flank. *Until my 'Mech falls, I am still in this fight.*

His long-range sensors kept picking up a faint reactor signal, masked behind the metallic sand of the Hatya Desert dunes. That was what he was after—an isolated Scorpion 'Mech. He stalked the phantom blip on his screen, moving farther into the Goliath Scorpion's deployment zone. The smoke of destroyed vehicles and 'Mechs rose like jagged streaks on the desert winds. *Where are you hiding?* Baldur bit his lower lip as he limped in a wide arc to come up behind the signal he had seen.

The signal came back—a light-to-medium mass signature. He trudged up to the top of the dune and saw it—a black- and yellow-orange streaked *UrbanMech IIC*. It was unleashing fire on a small cluster of infantry, kicking up clouds of dust from autocannon shells. Streaks of shoulder-fired missiles filled the space between the 'Mech and the ground, hitting the enemy BattleMech but doing insignificant damage. The Scorpion warrior was so intent on killing infantry that they ignored Baldur's presence.

He locked his still-functional right shoulder–mounted LRM rack and his large and medium lasers on the *UrbanMech*'s rear. His targeting-and-tracking system had taken damage, and he had to use hard movements on the control stick to bring the targeting reticle onto the stout, round 'Mech that reminded him more of a garbage can with legs than a war machine. The moment he heard the ping tone of the target lock, he hit the thumb trigger.

The *UrbanMech IIC* was not moving, and Baldur's range was dangerously close, thanks to the sand dunes. The lasers tore into the thin rear armor, all of them hitting. The fact that the 'Mech wasn't moving allowed the lasers to bore in deep, hitting its fusion reactor and gyro.

The wave of twenty long-range missiles hit a few seconds later, only some hitting the head and torso of the rotund little 'Mech. Most of the missiles went wide. Smoke billowed out of the pockmarked impacts of those that did hit, and the *UrbanMech* shook hard as its pilot turned to face the new threat. Twisting at the waist, it fired its Ultra autocannon. Most of the rounds shot over Baldur's shoulders, but several found their mark on what was left of his left torso, punching deep and mangling his internal structure.

Baldur's pulse laser spiked his heat even more, due to his damaged heat sinks. The brilliant emerald bursts stitched the side of the 'Mech, rattling its autocannon arm hard, searing smoking holes with each hit.

The Scorpion 'Mech staggered a half step, and Baldur let go again with his machine guns, this time aiming at the cockpit. He didn't even use his targeting reticle, instead relying on tracers to guide his barrage.

The badly injured BattleMech lurched hard to the side, and the warrior finally lost his war with gravity. The *UrbanMech* toppled over slowly, reminding Baldur of the old rhyme about Humpty Dumpty. It hit the sand on its side, shedding more armor in the fall.

The infantry did not relent in their attack. Two Elementals jetted near the collapsed 'Mech, firing their arm-mounted lasers. Baldur joined them, opening up with his machine guns, sending a steady stream of shells and tracers into the exposed rear of the BattleMech. Sparks and smoke rose, and his sensors showed another spike of heat from the fallen Scorpion—more engine-shielding damage, making the ripped insulation shimmer even more than the heat ripples of the desert.

Over the local broadband channel, the fallen *UrbanMech* pilot broadcast in the clear. "I yield to the Star League," he managed to say with a breathy, exhausted gasp.

Baldur held his fire in check—honor had been offered and accepted. Through the reddish haze of blowing sand he made out the Light Horse Elemental armor of Paul Moon's Ghosts. A sinking feeling hit him. *I have saved the life of Paul Moon!* Months ago, that thought would have driven him insane. Now he realized just how different he felt. *He and I are different sides of the same coin.*

As he tried to cope with his new reality, another voice came over the broadband channel—in the clear. It was tired, and sounded down-trodden. "Galaxy Commander Myers, this is Colonel Antonescu. I wish for this trial to end. My forces have suffered sufficient losses to make a further infusion of blood pointless. The Star League Defense Force concedes. Let's stop this test of wills and death. You and your Scorpions have won."

"This is Rik Myers of the Rock Minders. I accept your defeat. It is 'Goliath Scorpions,' Colonel—not merely 'Scorpions,' as we have demonstrated to you and your gallant troops. We are one of the chosen peoples of Nicholas Kerensky's great vision. You fought with honor, and we accept your concession. We will immediately assume possession of the facilities and personnel within the declared target of our *batchall*. We will claim as *isorla* all BattleMechs and vehicles that date to the era of the original Star League, which we understand are among your Com Guards and Light Horse units. Your people are free to go–they are of no interest to us. In the name of the Great Kerensky, we salute the Star League for fighting with such valor."

Antonescu's voice came back quickly. "My forces shall stand down immediately. I regretfully say that you have won your toehold on Huntress. I only hope that we will be good neighbors, and perhaps friends."

"We do not seek friendship, only honor and our past. But your intentions are not lost on us," Myers said. "I look forward to meeting you off the battlefield one day, Colonel. *Seyla*." The channel crackled once and then went silent.

*Defeat.* Baldur had faced defeat and even death several times in his life, but nothing could fully prepare any warrior to accept it. His stomach knotted at the thought of losing. This was worse. It was not just about honorable defeat in battle, it was about Clan Goliath Scorpion getting a foothold on Huntress. *They have come to harvest the Smoke Jaguars...and will do so.* It meant his efforts to try to save his former people had to be accelerated.

Looking down from his cockpit, he saw Paul Moon, now a sergeant in the SLDF, checking over his people, making sure they were safe. Baldur identified with his gesture. *That is where I need to be.*

He undid his coolant-vest hose, some of the liquid drizzling onto the deck of the cockpit. The Nova Cat warrior pulled off his neurohelmet and felt the slightly cooler air wash his sweaty face and soaked hair.

He popped the hatch to his *Timber Wolf* and climbed down, dropping past the last three rungs into the sand. Even the hot desert breeze was cooler than his cockpit. Baldur walked to the remnants of Moon's platoon. They were all covered with a fine reddish dust, their goggles the only clear surface. Towering over them were two Elemental warriors, both with their suits open.

Baldur could see their pride, even in defeat. That was the part of the Smoke Jaguar he still admired and respected. They were checking and clearing their weapons, a few of them field-dressing minor wounds. He walked up to them, and the group parted, eyeing him with suspicion.

Baldur turned to Paul Moon. "Your troops fought well."

Moon put his fists on his hips and glared at Baldur. It was an expression he knew all too well from his former commanding officer. "There was no doubt they would. These are former Smoke Jaguars you stand before. Their Clan is gone, but not their lifeblood. It flows in their veins today. Half of my personnel are casualties, but they did not falter, Nova Cat. You would do well to look upon them and remember where they came from."

The arrogance of the Elemental warrior was familiar. *This is the Paul Moon I know best.* It was a stark contrast to the introspective man he had spoken to the night before. This was the Paul Moon who haunted Baldur's memories.

"I have not—nor will ever—speak ill of the Smoke Jaguars, *Sergeant* Paul Moon. I merely came to acknowledge the performance of you and your troops and to see if I could render any assistance—warrior to warrior." He stressed "sergeant" to highlight the former Star Colonel's new position.

"We do not need your acknowledgement or assistance," Moon replied in a low tone. "These are my people, and I will take care of them. Unlike the Nova Cats, we do not turn our backs on each other as you did with our people, then the Clans. Our Clan may not exist as far as those on Strana Mechty and Terra are concerned, but the heart of the Jaguar still beats. Even these Goliath Scorpions can only take the soil beneath us, not us as a people."

Arrogance had become unmitigated pride. Baldur could identify with that. "I understand your feelings—more than you could ever know. You cannot comprehend why we Nova Cats did what we did. You live in the here and now. We look to the future, and you are in no position to question what we did or why. That is now the past. We are here now, Paul Moon, and your anger at me is misdirected. We are not your enemies. In fact, we are closer to you than you can comprehend. You would be well advised to not let your prejudice and preconceived notions guide your actions. It did not help you with Trent of the Smoke Jaguars, and it does not serve you now."

The mention of his old name stung Moon. With the face plate of his Elemental suit open, Baldur saw his former foe's face redden and his jaw lock. Moon was furious, but held his anger in check. After a tense silence, he finally nodded. "I have made mistakes, and I continue to atone for them. Your use of the Betrayer as a weapon to pummel me is no more damaging than when I use him as a weapon against myself. I bear that burden, Baldur, and I bear it alone. Your words burrow into me like a missile salvo. As crude as they were, you are right. I am prejudiced. We have fought on the same field, but that does not change my perception of you, not yet."

"Understood. If I were you, I would feel the same." Baldur turned toward his 'Mech and saw the damage, especially the twisted and mauled remains of his long-range missile rack, with one missile still dangling half-in, half-out of a tube it had never cleared. The damage was everywhere on his 'Mech except his left torso, which looked oddly pristine. *Such are the contortions of the gods of war.*

*There are so few of us former Jaguars left, Paul Moon. We cannot continue hating each other—not forever.* He did not continue the debate, but instead walked back to his OmniMech, each step sinking deep into the sand.

When he reached the 'Mech, he turned back to look at Moon, who was conferring with an infantry warrior, but apparently sensed Baldur's stare, and looked over at him. The two men locked gazes for a silent moment. *We have a long way to go, Moon, and time is running out for both of us.*

# CHAPTER 23

Galaxy Commander Rik Myers looked with some satisfaction at the massive *Warhawk* factory he and his Scorpions of the Veil had won from the Star League. The OmniMech factory was a prize, but not the one Myers wanted. *I came for the legacy of the Smoke Jaguars–their warriors, their prizes, their people.*

As a Goliath Scorpion, he knew the future was wrapped in the past. Those who controlled the past could set their destiny in the future. His Khan would be happy about the factory—to her that target had the most appeal. *Khan Ariel Suvorov foolishly thinks that possession of a factory will guide our future. She is shortsighted. Once I control the legacy of the Jaguars, I will challenge her to a Trial of Position.*

His thoughts of leading his Clan one day were heady. *But that is the necrosia thinking–not me.* He reined in his ambitions for a moment as he stared at the recently repaired factory. *I should not have indulged so early in the morning, but this is a day to celebrate victory.*

Myers was in control of all he surveyed. The Star League had done him a favor by repairing much of Rakt-Jabada. The *Warhawk* factory had been made operational a month and a half earlier. Now it was his. Not since the Jade Falcons had another Clan held a place of their own on Huntress. *The other Clans will be envious of us, but will fall upon the rest of the Star League before they tangle with us.*

Star Captain Gulledge Brinker stepped into his field of vision, his noteputer in hand. "Galaxy Commander, I trust you are well, *quiaff*?"

"*Aff.* The laborer-caste manager for this factory insists on taking me on a tour. He wants to discuss changes to his work shifts. I get the impression they are nervous about being *isorla* of the Goliath Scorpions. Matters hardly worthy of a conqueror."

Brinker shifted from one foot to the other, his tell that he was about to deliver bad news. "It could be something else, Galaxy Commander."

Myers eyed his subordinate suspiciously. "What have you learned?" He had tasked Star Captain Brinker with an initial survey of what Alpha Galaxy had secured on Huntress.

"It appears that the Star League migrated almost all of their warriors out of our declared territory prior to the battle, along with the most-skilled personnel from the scientist and laborer castes. They were moved by DropShip to Lootera."

A ripple of necrosia-fueled anger swept Myers. Balling his fists, he felt every muscle in his body tense, and his face reddened. After a momentary pause to regain composure, he spoke through clenched teeth. "How many warriors did we gain in our victory?"

"Less than a dozen," Gulledge replied. "The majority of those were in the local hospital still recovering from injuries they received during the Star League's attack on Huntress." The Star Captain hesitated for a moment. "There is more..."

"Proceed," Myers said in a low hiss.

"One of the units we battled, the Ghosts, was made up of former Smoke Jaguar warriors. When you did not claim them as *isorla*, they were evacuated back to Lootera with the rest of the Star League survivors."

*I was in possession of Smoke Jaguar warriors and let them slip through my fingers?* Neg! Myers balled a fist and slammed it into his other palm. *Our Watch failed me...and will not do so again.*

"What of the other lower castes of the Jaguars?" he asked.

"Substantially more, but it appears the more skilled members of the lower castes departed with the warriors."

*I have been cheated of my victory! I never thought the Star League would stoop to such guile.* Neg. *The surviving Smoke Jaguars had to be behind all of this. It is the kind of move one might expect from our kin.* "Have you investigated the warehouses, Star Captain?"

"Affirmative," Gulledge said, his own face getting redder. "We found mostly manufacturing materials and parts for use with the factories that are now in our possession. In one, we did find a number of crates bearing Smoke Jaguar artifacts. It appears the Star League is in the process of purging anything related to the former Clan. Rather than destroy those artifacts, they put many of them in storage. There are paintings, tapestries, flags...crates filled with Jaguar artwork and military symbols."

That took some of the edge off Myers's anger, but not nearly enough. The artifacts of the former Jaguars were one of the pieces of bait he had used to lure Khan Suvorov into permitting him to invade Huntress to begin with. "These artifacts will provide our Clan with honor. We have moved to preserve this history rather than lose it. Khan Suvorov will be pleased with our recovery of these items. I would like to inspect these myself when I am done with this factory tour."

"I shall arrange it, Galaxy Commander," Gulledge replied.

Myers paused for a long moment. "We have been cheated of our victory by the warriors being transported elsewhere. I have no intention of being made a fool of again."

"I understand, sir."

"Good. I want you to arrange for members of our Watch to travel to Jaguar Prime. I want them to infiltrate this Star League and learn all they can about the former Jaguars. When I make my next move, I want to be prepared for any eventuality."

"Your next move, sir? I was unaware this was part of a larger campaign."

*Of course you were not.* "Khan Suvorov knew my objectives when I came to Huntress. Your need to know is whatever I deem appropriate. For now, follow my orders."

"It will be done immediately, Galaxy Commander," Gulledge said, standing to attention for a moment before dismissing himself.

Rik Myers looked out along the freshly repainted exterior wall of the *Warhawk* factory. The sound of equipment operating inside was muffled but still audible. The factory was continuing work. Looking down the long gray wall, he saw where something had been chiseled off the exterior—the pouncing cat symbol of the Smoke Jaguars.

*The Star League seeks to erase a once proud Clan from memory. They want to purge our collective consciousness of the Smoke Jaguars. If they have their way, the Jaguars will be nothing more than what the Not-Named Clan is, just a story to frighten freebirth children at night before they go to sleep.*

Myers shook his head. Neg, *I will not allow that to happen. This is what it means to be a Goliath Scorpion. The other Clans see us as fools for seeking and preserving bits and pieces of antiquity. They see us as archivists, as collectors, as curators of trinkets of our past. They are all wrong. We seek to connect with our past because we know it is the key to the future. The Jaguars may be destined for the dustbins of history, but I will save their warriors—the essence of what made them a Clan. I will absorb them into our ranks.*

The Star Colonel turned toward the long, winding walkway that led to the entrance of the factory. *When I am done, I will be Khan, and I will have a new generation of warriors fighting for me—ones with the ferocity of the Smoke Jaguars and the kinship and patience of the Goliath Scorpions.*

*The other Clans will* become *history under my rule!*

# CHAPTER 24

Baldur stood over the holodisplay, staring at the long lists he and Inanna had prepared. The amount of data they had compiled was formidable. "We were fortunate that historians documented so thoroughly what General Kerensky brought with him on the Exodus," he said with his eyes still fixed on the numerous open virtual windows floating in the space before him.

Inanna leaned in as well, using her fingers to scroll through the list of agricultural requirements. "The general was moving six million people—we are looking at moving far fewer than that. But, *aff*, you are correct, he gave us considerable data to lean upon."

As he straightened up, he felt a dull throb in his lower back...a remnant from the fighting in the desert. Baldur stretched, arching his spine, but it didn't help. *I used to recover from a battle much faster.* He was sure all of the metal implants and bone fusings he had undergone after Strana Mechty contributed to his pains as well. *I am not old by Nova Cat standards, but I feel the icy grip of time much more than I used to.*

"About that," he said. "I was able to adjust some of the space. If we do not bring a full set of iron wombs, but only bring the agricultural reproduction units, I can fit another seventy people aboard." He watched her eyes for a reaction.

Inanna did not disappoint. Her eyes widened. "Not taking the iron wombs is significant," she said in a low tone, as if the words were sacrilegious. "Without those, how will the warriors reproduce?"

Baldur crossed his arms. "Like every other human." He flashed a sarcastic grin. "We will still possess the technical skills to build iron wombs, should we decide to."

The Clan warrior breeding program was a cornerstone of their society. Nicholas Kerensky had built a culture in which the top caste was artificially created: each generation bred from the best genetic material available, genetically engineered to be superior. Baldur understood the implications of what he suggested. "We can only save 3,800 Jaguars. With such a small number, every body counts."

"That would bring an end to the Clan's breeding program," she replied coldly.

"*Aff*, it would. As we say, you cannot fight the math, Inanna. There is only so much room on the DropShips and JumpShips, and we can only carry so many provisions. The journey to Wayside V is a long one. If we are to build a viable colony, we will need every person aboard when we arrive."

"It will not be a true Clan society, not without selective breeding."

He nodded. "*Aff*. It is not my goal to remake the Smoke Jaguars. Doing so would bring down the wrath of the Clans and the Star League upon us. *Neg*, the goal is to become something different... perhaps the best of both societies."

"This will be a difficult reality for the warriors to accept."

"Our breeding program for warriors did not save the Smoke Jaguars when the Star League descended upon them. After centuries of selective breeding, we were defeated on Tukayyid, on Huntress, on Strana Mechty. Our technological edge brought us great victories, but our enemies copied and adopted our tech and turned it against us in a relatively short period of time. Our warriors were bested on the field of combat. Yes, we hold a portion of the Inner Sphere, but for how long?"

He could see she wanted to reject his words, but she kept her composure. "You are talking about building a new society, Baldur. What form will it take?"

The Nova Cat shook his head. "I do not know. The people who create the society will need to be the ones who craft it. The warriors will play a role, I am sure. Again, however, if you look at the numbers, of the 3,800, we can take only 250 warriors. They are a distinct minority. I presume the people themselves will create their own culture and society, as colonists have done for centuries."

"Such an approach could lead to chaos," she countered.

"*Aff*," he conceded. "Or it could lead to something wondrous."

"I am surprised at your concessions," Inanna replied. "Your plan is audacious—and counter to everything in your upbringing."

For a long moment, he said nothing. *She is correct, this is not my nature. I have always let honor mark the boundaries of my life. It has governed everything I have done, every decision I have made. This is beyond what honor can control or define.* "Inanna, I made decisions based on my honor that impacted millions of lives. When I made those decisions, I did not think about the people who would be caught in the backlash of my choices. I acted out of honor. Look at what that accomplished. The Clan culture was not raised to the standard I had in my head, but left to rot and be torn apart by carrion eaters like the Goliath Scorpions. I never wanted to see the Smoke Jaguars end up like this, but that is the price of my vision."

"You cannot blame yourself alone for this."

"*Aff*, and I do not. There were many who put me on the path that led to this moment. I was betrayed by my culture, and responded with betrayal. My actions did not make things better, only different. I know in my heart this is not the fate I or anyone else intended for the Smoke Jaguars. Going to Wayside V, allowing the best of these people to survive and build something new and different...perhaps that is the only course of action that makes any sense. We will find a way to create something better—perhaps actually realize the tenets of honor Nicholas Kerensky believed in. That future is not with the Clans, it is something else." A tear formed in the corner of his eye. He turned from her to wipe it away.

"It is all moot if you cannot get these people to Wayside V unharmed."

*That is the crux of the matter.* Baldur and Inanna had struggled with this problem for long days and nights. The Clans would want the people he took with him, especially the warriors. They also would not want his people to form a new Clan Smoke Jaguar, perhaps one motivated by revenge. *The first few years, when we are at our weakest, will be the most dangerous.*

"We face a number of logistical problems, all of which must be resolved," Baldur replied. "First, we must contact the leaders of the castes and solicit their assistance in identifying those who should make this journey, and the staging of the equipment and supplies we will need. This also means enlisting the aid of the merchant caste JumpShip pilots—they are critical to our plan. Second, we have to devise a means of loading our DropShips and taking off without the Star League intervening."

"Third," Inanna said, "the SLDF still has ships in orbit. I would imagine they will respond to a fleet of DropShips departing."

"Fourth, we need to get to Wayside without the Clans pursuing us. And all of this must be done without raising the suspicions of the Star League or the Goliath Scorpions. We have managed to pre-position the DropShips here in Lootera as a result of the Goliath Scorpions' attack, but I doubt they will be silent neighbors."

"You will not like what I am about to say," Inanna said, watching for his response, "but you need Paul Moon's assistance."

*She's right,* Baldur thought. *I do* not *like it. But what choice do we have?*

"I concur," he said, "Regardless of my personal feelings about him, Moon is the nominal leader of the warrior caste. This Jaguar who is out raiding in the jungles is a good leader, but he does not carry the influence Moon does. Moon was a Star Colonel, likely the ranking officer to survive the fighting for Huntress. I must set aside my personal feelings. We need his cooperation and assistance to pull this off."

"Agreed," Inanna said. "In a few days Santin West will arrive here. Perhaps he can offer some insights that can assist us."

*She did not share this information with me earlier. Why?* "I was unaware the Khan would be visiting. I would have thought he was well on his way to the Inner Sphere." With all he had focused on, he had forgotten his own new Clan, the Nova Cats, had been expelled from Clan space. They too were on an exodus, one taking them much farther than what he was planning. This could be a complicating factor. What if Khan West disapproved of the plan? He could order them to abandon it altogether. *I am a member of this Clan now; I must keep that fact firmly in mind.*

"I received word right before the battle with the Scorpions. I did not think you needed any other thoughts on your mind than fighting them."

Baldur paused for a moment. "You said he was escorting the last of our Clan, *quiaff?*"

"*Aff.* He is stopping at Huntress to pay his respects to the Star League and complete his final provisioning."

"How large is his fleet?"

"I do not know. It will be significant enough to warrant his protection. Why?"

"Santin West has been to Wayside V. The Nova Cats already know its location. If we can join his fleet, the other Clans would be none the wiser. They know the Nova Cats are on their way to the Inner Sphere. Our JumpShips could simply join them. There would be no risk of them revealing our destination because the other Clans have shunned them. It is almost perfect—and solves one of our key problems."

"Assuming Khan West agrees with what we propose," she cautioned. "If he does not, you could expose the plan to someone who can put an immediate end to it."

"I have considered that. If we can convince Paul Moon to join us, even if Khan West orders us to abandon our plans, Paul Moon can carry on without us." There was no way around it; Baldur knew he needed the support of his former rival. "Do you believe the Khan will order us to stop?"

Inanna shrugged. "It is hard to say. He has been on several vision quests in his career. He understands the importance of destiny in matters such as this. While there is no love lost between him and the Smoke Jaguars, I do not think he would be in favor of them dying out as they are now. It is difficult to predict how he will respond."

"If he refuses us, we can still try. As long as he does not tip off the SLDF."

"Khan West knows, as do many of our Clan, that our fate is now intertwined with the Star League. That does not imply loyalty—that is something yet to be earned. The Nova Cats have stood against the Clans with the Star League, so the fate of our Clan is exile. It is impossible to say if he would tell our new allies what we have planned here."

*So, it is a calculated risk—just as is bringing Paul Moon into the fold.* "We have a choice. We could try to take a fleet alone to Wayside V, but the risks would be great, and our people would be vulnerable. It is better to take the risk of sharing our plan and being rebuffed than to cower in fear of the unknown and court death as a result."

Inanna paced around the holotable, staring at the images as she moved. While the data dominated the space between them, he felt her eyes on him. "Baldur, you have not told me just how you intend to sway Paul Moon as to our cause."

"That is because I am not sure yet," he replied with a sigh. "Moon is stubborn. He has, in the past, let his stubbornness blind his actions. It certainly prejudiced him against me. I feel he is no longer the man I knew years ago—there is something different about him. Yes, I see glimpses of the man I grew to hate—" memories of his rebuke by Moon after the fighting in the Hatya Desert reinforced that, "—but I have to believe him losing Huntress to the Star League changed him. I never thought to see him as a bondsman to a mercenary unit, yet he stepped into that role. In his soul, I believe he still holds out hope for the Smoke Jaguars."

"He does not seem to like Nova Cats," Inanna replied.

"*Aff*," Baldur grinned. "He believes we turned on the Jaguars. He does not understand our motives. It will be a hurdle we must cross in order to convince him."

"Your past with the man gives you intimate knowledge of him, but it is also a liability," she pointed out. "When you face him, you will have to shed the memories of the man you once knew. Much like you, Paul Moon has also been remade."

He wondered if her words were true. "Perhaps, but perhaps not, Inanna. My true identity is a secret that could unravel everything if he were to discover it. In that way, my identity is a liability. But it is also an asset. I think the solution to handling Paul Moon may not just be Baldur, it may also be Trent. My true identity could be a weapon—if used correctly."

She walked around the table to stand next to him. "I will support your decision, Baldur, however you choose to implement it. Revealing that you were Trent could have far-reaching implications—not just in your dealings with Paul Moon, but with the other Smoke Jaguar survivors. They would never follow Trent. As it is, many will chafe at following Baldur of the Nova Cats. We have created a potential future for the Jaguar survivors, but it is a fragile thing. All I ask is that you do not let that fall because you want Moon to know you still live."

Baldur grinned. "You misinterpret me, Inanna. Everyone thinks of Trent as focused on revenge. I do not seek it. Like any weapon, my true identity is not to be used indiscriminately. I have no intention of revealing myself to Moon unless it suits our plans. I hope I do not have to tell him. If I do, I will do it in a manner that will work to my advantage."

She put a hand on his shoulder. "I trust you."

"I will not fail that trust," Baldur replied. He looked at the lists hovering in the space above the table and surveyed the data for the thousandth time. *We have gates to cross through that lead us to the future. Inanna is right in warning me to tread carefully. The fate of my former people is at stake, not just my own life.*

# CHAPTER 25

Paul Moon entered Major Blau's hospital room and was stunned at how much of his former bondholder was covered in bandages. Blau had been in a medically induced coma for days while the doctors worked on growing him replacement skin. He had only been awake and able to receive visitors for a day or so.

Paul hated hospitals. He visited Shane several times as she recovered from shattering all of her ribs during the battle, and as much as it pleased him to spend time with her, he still hated where they were. Hospitals had a chemical smell to them. The cleaning solvents used created a disgusting aroma. Once, during his first year as a warrior, he had been hospitalized with a bad wound on his lower arm. Gangrene had set in by the time he made it to the hospital, and the hand had been removed and regrown. Moon still remembered the stink of infection before the hand had been removed. The pain didn't bother him, but the memories of the rotting-flesh smell mixed with disinfectants did.

"Major," he said as he stood beside the warrior in the bed. "How are you?"

Blau stirred, his face bandaged except for his eyes and lips. "Been better..." he managed in a groggy tone. *He is heavily drugged.*

"The physicians told me you will recover to fight again," Paul replied. "Unfortunately, the Goliath Scorpions claimed your BattleMech as *isorla.*"

Major Blau moaned. "It's been in my family for centuries..."

Paul did not understand the sentimentality. Warriors did not have possessions—not many, anyway. The Goliath Scorpions collected antiques and the Nova Cats had their *vineers*, but to him those were exceptions rather than the rule. *As a Smoke Jaguar, I never had an attachment to things–only to people.* "A 'Mech can be replaced," was all he could reply.

"Not that one," Blau countered. "It was special."

"As you say," Paul replied. "What is more important is you live to fight another day."

"Don't remember much," Blau muttered, struggling against the effects of his painkillers. "Damned Scorpions were on top of us before we expected it."

Paul nodded solemnly. "Galaxy Commander Myers swept our right flank and got some light 'Mechs in our rear. The lines collapsed after that." Paul decided not to tell him the details of his own fall, how a Goliath Scorpion *Kodiak* had blasted Blau's *Black Knight* with a barrage of autocannon fire into his cockpit. Major Blau should have died, but had been saved thanks to Clan medical technology. His hand, while bandaged, was already being regrown in the special casing attached to Blau's arm.

"The colonel said we lost," the major mumbled. "Said your Ghosts fought hard as hell, too."

"We lost a significant number in the fight. Those who died found honor on the field of battle. Those who lived found new purpose."

"You did good."

"Not enough to turn the tide of the battle," Moon offered. "From what I have been able to make out, the Goliath Scorpions suffered extensive 'Mech losses—maybe more than the Star League. Galaxy Commander Myers was merely more determined to win than the colonel."

"The old man is getting tired of the fighting here," Blau said in a casual tone. *That is the medication talking...he never would refer to the colonel as an 'old man.'* "Huntress is where the Light Horse came to bleed. His words—not mine." As he finished speaking, Paul thought the major might have drifted off to sleep.

"I wanted to thank you, Major, for making me a warrior again," Paul said.

Blau's eyes half opened. "Had to... You earned it. Didn't want you kept out of the fight. You were right...about the Smoke Jaguars. If we don't give them a purpose...they will go over to the insurgents."

"We have more volunteers than openings. At least there is a chance for my former caste mates. I thank you for supporting me."

"Have to do...what's right for them," the major said, his voice getting weaker as sleep began to overtake him. "Proud people... Can't take that from them. Not if the League...is going to...mean anything."

With those words, he drifted off to sleep, breaking into a soft snore. Paul stared at him for a long moment. *The major is a good man.*

*He actually understands the Smoke Jaguars, unlike some of the other officers.* He turned and left the room.

Baldur and Inanna of the Nova Cats were standing in the hallway. As Paul closed the door to the major's room he said, "He has just gone to sleep."

"We did not come to speak to him," Inanna said.

Moon glanced at her and stared at Baldur. "Then why are you here?"

"We came to speak to you, Paul Moon," Baldur replied.

"Very well then, speak."

"Not here," Inanna said. "We ask that you join us aboard the *Wanderer*."

For a moment, he wondered if the Nova Cats knew of his meeting with Russou Howell. *Why else would they desire to speak with me in private?* "Let us go," he said gesturing down the hall.

During the entire walk to the spaceport nothing was said, and the *Wanderer* itself seemed empty, the exception being a young child who stepped out of a stateroom as he passed. The youngling looked at him and straightened to stiff attention. *It must be one of those sibko children I heard they had taken in.* Paul stopped and stood at attention in response. The child then relaxed and took off down the corridor.

Inanna and Baldur led him into a conference room with a table-top holodisplay. Baldur closed the door behind them.

"I am intrigued," Paul said. "This smacks of cloak-and-dagger. There is no need for such subterfuge."

"Perhaps," Inanna said. "Perhaps not. That always depends on the subject matter, *quiaff?*"

This confirmed his earlier thought. *They must have figured out I met with the Jaguar and believe it to be more than it was.* "*Aff*, I suppose it does. Things sometimes are not what they seem, though. One man's treason might be an act of honor, depending on one's perspective."

"That is something we agree on," Baldur said, moving slowly and deliberately to the opposite side of the table from Moon. The ventilation system pushed cool air onto him. A lesser man might have changed seats for comfort's sake, but Paul simply endured the chill.

"Why am I here?"

Baldur shifted nervously, just enough for Paul to notice. "For some time now, Inanna and I have been contemplating the fate of the former Smoke Jaguars."

*Much like the Goliath Scorpions, I imagine.* He crossed his arms defiantly. "Let me guess. Clan Nova Cat has their eyes on Huntress or its people, *quiaff?*"

"*Neg*," Inanna said from his side. "Not in the way you may be thinking, at least. Like you, we have seen how the other Clans reacted to the crippling of your former people and the taking of Huntress. Clan Nova Cat has no designs on the soul of the Jaguar people."

"Then why I am here?"

Baldur spoke again, this time his voice much firmer. "We have devised a plan to save some of the Smoke Jaguars...to ensure they do not become *isorla* to be fought over. Regardless of your status with the Star League Defense Force, you are a leader, Paul Moon. For this plan to work, we need not only your input, but your assistance as well."

Moon was caught off guard by their words. "What do you have in mind?"

Baldur's fingers drifted to the table displays and pulled up an array of data in a dozen different floating windows. Paul's eyes darted from title to title: food consumption rates and composition; travel routes; DropShip capacities and stowage; construction necessities; seed and farming requirements... *What are these Nova Cats up to?* "What am I looking at?"

"The future," Baldur said proudly. "Huntress is not viable for the long-term survival of the former Smoke Jaguars. We are proposing to take a cross section of the Smoke Jaguar population and relocate them to a colony world outside Clan space. There they can rebuild and grow and become a people who can truly fulfill the vision of Nicholas Kerensky."

Paul Moon was stunned. *They have planned almost what I was thinking...though their planning is far more extensive. Why are they doing this? What is their true intent?* "You are not taking the entire population of Huntress?"

"We cannot," Baldur said flatly. "We have built models that account for the food necessary for the journey, the capacity of the DropShips, the colony's projected ability to support a population, et cetera. We can save just over three thousand former Smoke Jaguars."

"Where would you take them?

Inanna looked at Baldur, then back at Moon. It was as if she were evaluating how much she could trust the Elemental warrior. "Wayside V. It is a staging world in the Periphery once controlled by the Smoke Jaguars. The world sustains life, but is not known by many of the Clans. It is far enough away from both Clan space and the Inner Sphere for your people to thrive and grow."

Wayside V—Paul had heard of the world while posted in the Inner Sphere. For a while the Smoke Jaguars had called it Wildcat, but after the defeat of Zeta Galaxy there, Khan Osis had stripped it of that name. While he did not know its location, he remembered Zeta Galaxy being sent there as a garrison. *Old warriors—washouts unworthy of facing battle alongside younger, better warriors.* He thought about his own plans to head off into unexplored space. *This sounds better. There is a place to go, a destination.*

His eyes fell to Baldur across the holodisplay table. "Why should I trust either of you?" he asked bitterly, and recited the well-known litany of Nova Cat sins. "You are Nova Cats. You have turned your back on the Clans. You came here to cozy up to the Star League. Now you pull me in here and say you have devised a plan to save my former people."

Baldur responded quickly. "Your mistrust is ill-placed. We have done nothing to inspire your distrust since our arrival here. You slander the Nova Cats, but we fought beside you against the Goliath Scorpions. I saved your life, Paul Moon. That *UrbanMech* would have wiped out your Ghosts."

Moon scoffed at his words. "We would not have been wiped out by that 'Mech. It was, after all, only an *UrbanMech*. My troops would have destroyed it without your interference." He shifted his stance, putting his hands on the edge of the table and leaning toward Baldur. "Perhaps it is true that you have behaved honorably here—but you did not come to our aid when the Star League hit us here and in the Inner Sphere. You even fought against the Clans in the Great Refusal. My words stand not as slander, but as reality."

"We are not here to discuss your views of the Nova Cats," Inanna interrupted. "We asked you here to discuss a plan to save the essence of the Smoke Jaguars."

"Yet you are asking me to trust both of you, and assist you in carrying this out," Moon countered. "You are proposing to save only a few thousand of them. What of the others, those not fortunate enough to go on your little exodus?"

"They will remain here on Huntress," the Nova Cat replied. "Their fates will be tied to the Star League forces here."

"They will be consumed, one bite at a time, by the other Clans," Moon spat back. "Any plan to save them must look at the whole population."

"*Neg*," Baldur replied. "It is impossible. It is a larger population than General Kerensky took on his Exodus. He had a whole naval fleet to execute his actions. All we have is the remaining merchant-caste JumpShips and the two WarShips still in orbit."

"You are leaving them to fate."

"We have no choice. Tell me you have not contemplated the logistics involved in moving millions of people, Paul Moon."

"I have," he said in a raised voice. "Of course I have. I played a game similar to the one you have been simulating here. It is impossible to save all of them, but any other plan is folly."

"Why?" Inanna asked.

"Saving some, not all, would doom the masses," Moon replied. "Taking a small number of each caste would mean the Smoke Jaguars would never rebuild, not in my lifetime. It would take several lifetimes before they became a Clan worthy of that name again."

Inanna tilted her head. "Why would they need to be the Smoke Jaguars?"

"What?"

"Reforging the Smoke Jaguars is not our purpose, not for the time being. Our goal is to preserve and save the *essence* of the Jaguars... all of the good parts, the aspects that made them honorable and respected. The people would have to decide whether to become a new version of the Smoke Jaguars."

"You are not reforging the Jaguars, then?"

"*Neg*," Baldur jumped back in. "The Smoke Jaguars had their time. It has passed. This is about giving these people hope and a place to make their future. Perhaps over time, missions could be mounted to recover other survivors from Huntress—but for now, our plan is not to save the Smoke Jaguars in name, but in essence."

"What would they be? Outcasts? Dark Caste? Bandits? That is how they would be seen by the other Clans."

Baldur seemed angered by Moon's words. Part of his face turned crimson. "They will need to forge their own destiny, their own identity. If they are indeed faithful to the vision of Nicholas Kerensky, they will have no problem becoming a people in their own right."

"A few thousand would not be enough if the Clans found them. In Clan eyes, they would be nothing but refugees."

"I do not believe in casting myself by what other Clans perceive. I do not think you do either, Paul Moon," Baldur snapped. "This is not about the other Clans. This is about saving the heart of the Smoke Jaguars."

"By condemning others to the hand of fate," Moon fired back.

"You are a warrior, Paul. We have been raised under the concept of coping with acceptable losses. How many men have died under your command so you could secure a victory? It is the fate of warriors. Yes, I am talking about leaving the bulk of the Smoke Jaguars here under the Star League's wing. This is a chance to take all that was good and pure about the Smoke Jaguars and save it. Can you pass up such an opportunity, *quineg*?"

Moon said nothing for a long moment. *I have struggled long and hard to save all of my people. It was my duty as the last commander to fight here against the Star League. I could not solve this puzzle, but these Nova Cats may have found a path. However, they are asking me to turn our back on the majority to save a select few. Is that wrong?*

Finally, he shook his head. "The Star League would never stand for this. The moment we begin to move our people to DropShips, they would strike."

"*Aff*, they would," Inanna said. "That is one of the reasons we need your help. We need them to be diverted...occupied elsewhere."

"I was their bondsman," he fired back. "I am now one of them. They severed my bondcord."

"They are not Clan," Baldur replied. "The Eridani Light Horse are a mercenary unit *employed* by the Star League. They share a close bond, that is true, but you are not tied to them as you would be to a Clan. At best, any connection to them is subject to your personal interpretation."

Moon's jaw locked, and he clenched his teeth. "This is folly. If we are to plan, we need a plan to save *all* of my people. I cannot agree to a solution that would leave the majority of my people in the hands of Inner Spherers."

"You understand logistics as well as we do," Baldur countered. "You have already crunched the numbers to make your concept work, and it cannot. Adding our brains to that mix will not change facts, Paul Moon. It is impossible to save all of the Jaguars. We can save some, we have the resources to achieve that. That is where we need to concentrate our efforts—on what we can accomplish."

"Wayside V is nearly a year's journey from here. Our people would be exposed to the other Clans and at risk."

"The other Clans will not know what has happened here until long afterward," Inanna said. "Only the Goliath Scorpions would be close enough to try to pursue. They will be confused, unsure of where we are going or what our intentions are. Besides, we have a plan for moving our JumpShip fleet, which might further throw them off."

"You already have a plan in mind," Paul said after a two-second pause. "You do not need me or my approval."

"*Neg.* That is not true," Baldur said. "You are the surviving senior officer, still in a position of respect and honor. The members of the old warrior caste look up to you. Personally, I would prefer to execute this plan without you. But Inanna has pointed out that we stand a much better chance of success with your support. You are a leader, Paul Moon. You always will be. We need you on our side. Neither of us has to like that—but it is the reality of the situation."

"I could tell the Star League about your plan," Paul mused.

"*Aff,*" Baldur said. "And you may. We took you to be a warrior with honor. If that honor comes at our expense, you only confirm what Trent believed about you. *I* think you still want to act in the best interest of your people. You may hate our plan...you may hate working with us. In the end, you know that what we are proposing is the only hope to save even a fragment of the Smoke Jaguars."

"I have a responsibility," Paul snapped.

"To what? A Clan that has been annihilated? A Grand Council that turned its back on you? A Star League that does not represent your values or culture? What exactly do you have a responsibility to, Paul Moon?" Inanna pressed from his flank.

Her words burrowed into him like a Streak-missile salvo. "I am responsible for my people," he said slowly, through gritted teeth.

"So you will not help us?" Inanna asked.

"*Neg.*"

Baldur shook his head, then locked eyes across the table. "Very well, Paul Moon. You leave me no choice but to challenge you to a Circle of Equals and force you to do what is right."

# CHAPTER 26

"You are joking, *quiaff*?" Paul Moon said.

"*Neg*," Baldur replied. "I challenge you to a Circle of Equals. The winner of that contest determines our course of action. The loser must fully support and follow his directions. Both of us have the same goal, Paul Moon—to save the soul of the Jaguars. We come at it from different approaches. This will determine our course of action."

"I am no longer Clan."

"In words and rank you are not, but you fought the Goliath Scorpions under Clan terms and rules. I assume you have not forgotten how we settle our differences. Then again, if you are afraid to face me in a fair contest, I understand." His words were chosen to chide Moon...prod him into the Circle.

"Baldur—" Inanna said, but he held up his hand to signal her to be silent.

The challenge caught Moon off guard, and Baldur enjoyed the moment as the Elemental tried to size up why he would challenge him.

"Your definition of a fair contest shows that you hold me in low regard, Nova Cat," he finally said. "You in a BattleMech and I in my armor would be hardly a fair contest."

"Then we fight unaugmented—warrior to warrior," Baldur said firmly. *He seeks to have the advantage, so the best way to counter that is to give him what he wants and force a concession elsewhere.*

"You would not last five minutes with me man to man," Moon replied with a feral grin. "I am twice your strength and almost twice your size."

"Perhaps," Baldur countered. "But I am more than I seem." *Much more.* "If you wish, we can set the terms of the fight at five minutes. That is more than enough time for me to defeat you—unless you feel you need more."

"I do not need five minutes to crush you."

"Then we shall fight unaugmented for five minutes. I know you have not been a part of a Clan for some time now. I promise you, I will not need five minutes."

His words pummeled Moon, implying he was a lesser a warrior than Baldur. *As intended.*

Moon glared back at him. "I could beat you with one hand tied behind my back," he said, chuckling at his words.

"Accepted."

"What?"

"You bid away one of your arms, and I agreed to your condition."

The grin turned to a frown in an instant. "It was a figure of speech."

"And I accepted," Baldur said. "I have some other terms." *I knew he would overreach. I expected it more during our fight rather than at this stage. Only a fool would not have taken advantage of his misstatement.*

"Very well, but the choice of arms to be restrained is mine," Moon countered.

Baldur grinned. *I know you too well. I can clearly see your bionic arm. I know you intend to use it to your advantage. But my bionic arm looks just like my human one. I am counting on you attempting to tip the balance of our engagement.* "I agree."

Still angered at having been tricked, Moon scowled. "What is it you seek?"

"Anything spoken between us during the trial stays in the Circle," Baldur said, already thinking ahead to the fight and his strategy. "Once this fight is done, our pasts are behind us. We work together to move forward, no matter what."

Moon nodded once. "When I win, your interference in the affairs of the Smoke Jaguars will end, and you will do things as I demand—you understand that, *quiaff?*"

"*Aff,*" Baldur said. "Likewise, should I defeat you, you will give us any and all aid in our plan to save the Jaguars."

"I can agree to that easily, since that will not happen. You cannot win this match. I am younger than you, Baldur—younger, faster, and stronger."

"All that matters is that you agree to the terms of our trial," Baldur said, unshaken by Moon's boasts.

"I do," he said wetting his lips. "All that remains is for us to fight."

"I propose we fight under the DropShip. The Nova Cat warriors aboard will attend as our witnesses. There is no need to involve anyone from the Star League here."

"Agreed," Moon said. Baldur knew he would agree to the terms, since there was a risk that both of their plans might be exposed. "Let us go now," he said confidently.

"In one hour," Baldur said. "As a Nova Cat, there are things I must do to prepare for this contest. As you said, you are stronger and younger than me. I am less prone to rush into things than your generation of warriors." He deliberately played off Moon's words. *Listen to me, Paul Moon. Let your overconfidence grow from a spark to a bonfire.*

"Very well then. Shall we meet at the gangway to this vessel in an hour?"

"Well bargained and done," Baldur said.

Moon left the room, and Baldur grinned as he turned to Inanna.

"Baldur—"

He cut her off. "I know you are going to tell me I was foolish... that I have put our entire plan at risk. That I am letting my feelings about Moon and our past guide my actions. Let me say this, Inanna. I am going to beat him. I am *not* responding with my emotions, but am setting a trap for him. I will win."

"I know you will," she replied.

"You do?"

"Affirmative," she said with her own wicked grin. "Your contest with him was ordained, it was destined to happen. It is the only way we can hope to move forward. I *do* trust you, Baldur. His arrogance and confidence is going to work against him—that much is obvious."

Her response surprised him, but it gave him a sense of confidence. "The one thing I have working for me is I know Paul Moon, and he does not know me. I need to turn that into a weapon."

"Five minutes with an Elemental in a Circle of Equals can be a lifetime."

"That is why I asked for an hour. I need to do some research."

"Research—how may I help?"

Baldur grinned. "I have been waiting for this for a long time. Preparation is the key."

The midday autumn sun cast a shadow where the Circle of Equals was drawn. It was not the blisteringly hot summer sun, but a warming one nevertheless. A cool breeze blew through, and the wind carried the smells of the nearby city. When the wind did not blow, the odors of fuel and lubricants on the tarmac hit Baldur's nostrils. *I have spent far too much of my life in such places. Warriors were meant to be on the battlefield, not here.*

He wore tight-fitting athletic shorts and a T-shirt. No amount of padding would protect him from hits from Paul Moon's bionic fist, so there was no reason to weigh himself down with it. Speed would be key, but Moon was an aggressive brawler—he would keep on top of him. The Elemental's sheer size could dominate the fight. He would be especially determined to make short work of Baldur. *He will not want to chase me around the Circle for five whole minutes.*

Woodall Winters was one of the warriors forming the Circle of Equals. Paul had asked him to assist in tying his human arm behind his back. *Good–as expected.* Winters secured the arm with a length of rope and tugged it to make sure it was secured to Moon's waist. He looked over at his sparring partner and gave Baldur a supportive wink. *He trained me to fight like a Nova Cat, and that is what I am going to do today.*

Baldur and Moon entered the Circle formed by the gathered warriors, and Inanna stepped in to officiate. "As has been done many times in our history," she announced, "a Circle of Equals is where warriors face each other to resolve their differences. These two have sworn their terms for this fight, and enter to end their dispute once and for all time. We face them and mark the boundaries of this fight. Let no warrior question what takes place here or question the integrity with which this trial is fought. In the name of the Great Kerensky, may you fight well and bring honor to the victor. *Seyla.*" She raised her arm for a long few seconds, then lowered it.

Paul Moon dropped into a battler's crouch, his eyes filled with anger. Baldur backed up to the edge of the circle of warriors watching him, dancing sideways with springing hops.

"I look forward to beating your face bloody," Moon spat.

"You have failed before," Baldur fired back. "Talk is cheap—let us fight."

Moon sprang into the air like his namesake jaguar, coming at Baldur with stunning speed. Baldur dodged, but caught a glancing blow to the rib cage from the bionic fist. He was thankful his ribs had been replaced with metal ones, or it would have hurt much more.

He swung around behind Moon, who shifted his footing and swung at him again with the massive bionic arm. It missed by a centimeter, the wind from it lifting Baldur's hair. Baldur spun and threw a punch with his own bionic right arm, hitting Moon hard below the shoulder blade. The Elemental staggered back, shocked at the force of the blow. *He has not yet figured out that I too have a bionic arm.*

Moon closed the gap between them with two steps and sent a powerful kick at Baldur that he could not dodge. It hit him square in the chest and sent him flying into the warriors marking the edge of the circle. His muscles ached at the impact, and for a moment he felt breathless, but his metallic rib cage held. The skin on his thigh was torn from skidding on the pavement, and blood drizzled down his leg as he got back up.

That he rose at all surprised Paul Moon; Baldur could see the stunned expression on his face. "You are stronger than you appear," Moon muttered.

"I am much more than that," Baldur countered, grinning at his larger enemy.

The grin angered the Elemental. Paul Moon swung again, this time connecting hard with Baldur's organic upper arm, sending him flying. He rolled upon impact with the tarmac, coming up on all fours, his arm aching where it had been hit. *Not broken–but I can feel where each finger hit me.*

Paul Moon was instantly on top of him. He raised his arm upward, as if to chop down on Baldur like an axe.

*Now!* He had been waiting for this chance. With all the effort he could muster, Baldur sprang up, catching the underside of Moon's bionic limb and grappling with it.

Moon swung downward in an effort to shake off Baldur. He held tight to the limb, its myomer muscles warm to the touch. Paul Moon pivoted quickly, swinging himself around in another effort to throw off his opponent, but Baldur still clung to him.

Paul Moon's bionic arm was like Baldur's original prosthetic. It was not cosmetically pleasing; it was ugly bundles of myomer with a simple power source and actuator controls in a shielded box. He had used the time before their trial to pull up the statistics and diagrams on Moon's model of arm.

He slid his natural hand into the mass of flexed muscles, feeling the heat singe his skin and hair as he held on tightly. Finding the power supply, he twisted it hard, disconnecting it. The moment it came free, he fell away from the Elemental, rolling on the tarmac to land at the feet of Woodall Winters. Every muscle ached as he got to his feet and sprang to his right to make some room between the two of them.

Moon did not waste time. He came at Baldur as he had before, arm flung back. He swung down in a chopping motion aimed right at Baldur's head. Baldur brought up his own bionic arm in a perfect block.

Without the power cell, Moon's arm only had enough power to lift the arm, not for the chop. It came down hard, but without the force of synthetic muscles to drive it for a killing blow. Moon looked down at his arm and suddenly realized he no longer had complete control over it.

"Missing something?" Baldur said, waggling the power supply in his human hand, then tossing it outside the Circle of Equals.

"*Surat* spawn!" Moon said, standing up. He swung the arm back, and while it remained limp, it was still metal and mass. "I can still crush you!"

He swept it through the air like a massive flail, hitting Baldur hard above his bionic eye. Blood ran down the side of Baldur's face as he took a few steps back, gaining more distance. *He's still dangerous–now is not the time to be cocky.*

Moon tossed his shoulder and arm back for another blow. This time Baldur's Nova Cat training kicked in. Moon was telegraphing his swing—he had no choice, he fought as a Smoke Jaguar. Baldur deflected the blow again with his own bionic arm, though his synthskin ripped as he deflected the strike over his head.

He was breathing hard as he shifted left. Moon loomed over him, and he saw the anger on the Elemental's face. As Moon tossed his arm back for another flailing attack, Baldur jabbed a quick punch at his opponent's face. The blow hit Moon on the forehead, and the Elemental didn't even flinch.

It was not a vicious hit, but a cutting one. Blood flowed down into Paul's organic eye, blinding it. *He still has his bionic eye...but this hinders him somewhat.* It was enough to force him back a step and pause his attack.

"Is that the best you can do?" Moon roared.

"I have a few more tricks," Baldur said, spreading his arms to his sides and moving in a little closer with each beat of his heart in his ears. He remembered to strike from where his arms were, not giving Moon a chance to see where the attack was coming from.

*Now is the time.* Baldur grinned.

"You have no idea who you are fighting," he said as Moon tossed his arm back and swept it forward. It came in low this time, aimed at his knees. Baldur jumped, and the arm went under him. To his credit, Moon continued the sweep, turning completely around. When he stopped, Baldur closed some of the distance again. Moon's bionic arm hung limp at his side while his natural arm was still tightly secured behind his back.

"I fight an old Nova Cat who is meddling in affairs that are none of his business."

"*Neg*, Paul. You fight someone you have known for years. Someone who has bested you at every turn. Someone who will defeat you today."

"We have never fought before, you fool!" Moon said, taking a sidestep himself, twice the length of Baldur's. He flung his arm across his body for a backhanded sweep, which Baldur deflected with his organic arm, albeit with some pain. *Even unpowered, that arm is deadly.*

"Oh, we have. You still do not know, do you?"

"Know what?" Moon said, swinging his arm back again with a twist of his waist and shoulder.

"I am not Baldur, you fool. I am Trent. I never died."

For a moment, time slowed. Moon's face showed a mix of confusion and horror. Bewilderment washed across his face—just as Baldur had anticipated.

Baldur jumped, taking full advantage of his foe's uncertainty. His own bionic limb swept through the air, hitting Paul Moon in his throat, striking his windpipe so hard that it tore flesh.

Without hands to reach for his throat, Moon panicked as he fought for breath that was not coming. He staggered back as Baldur landed on the ground before the giant of a man.

Not waiting to be sure, he launched himself up again, hitting the Elemental's upper body as Moon struggled for breath. He hit him hard, but it was like jumping into a brick wall, a staggering brick wall of muscled flesh. Baldur toppled, as did his foe. Moon fell backward through the boundary of the Circle of Equals and onto his back, his limp bionic arm twisted under him.

As he rose to his feet, Baldur felt the eyes of every Nova Cat in the circle fall to him, then to Moon. "He has broken the Circle. Get him medical attention—now!" he commanded. Within a few seconds the medtechs were on top of Moon.

Inanna stepped forward. "This trial is complete," she said as the Nova Cat medical team worked feverishly to get air into Moon's damaged windpipe. "Baldur of the Nova Cats, you have won. Let no one challenge or question this outcome. *Seyla!*"

The circle of warriors all responded with "*Seyla!*" She approached Baldur, and he sagged as she wrapped an arm around him. Adrenaline still pulsed through his veins, but the pain was starting to creep in.

"How are you?" she asked in a low tone.

He nodded, still breathing hard. "Better than him." Paul Moon coughed from where the medtechs worked on him, and a splatter of blood shot out of his mouth. His massive lungs surged with air.

"He may well wish you had killed him."

"*Aff.* This has been a long time coming. He tried to kill me, more than once. That is the past. He now must cope with the fact that I still live and have beaten him."

"Will he?"

Baldur nodded. "Moon has lost everything but his honor. The old Moon would not cope, but this Paul Moon will. He may twist honor to fit his needs, but he will honor his word."

"You..." Paul said from the sickbay bed aboard the Nova Cat DropShip as soon as he made eye contact with Baldur. His rough voice was filled with venom and anger. *The damage to his throat was considerable.* For a moment, that made Baldur happy.

"*Aff*," he replied. "Me. Baldur and Trent both." There was a hint of pride in his voice that he didn't try to conceal.

"Impossible. You died," Moon said as Baldur's eyes drifted to his emergency tracheotomy. Both warriors bore the scars and bruises of their trial, with Moon being held for a few hours to recover. Inanna entered the room but hovered near the doorway.

"I did—several times, in fact. What was left of me after the Grand Refusal was so badly damaged that cosmetic surgery was necessary. My survival would have spelled my doom, since I was seen as the instrument of the Smoke Jaguars' and the Grand Council's downfall—so Trent died on that table, and Baldur was born."

"I liked it better when I thought you were dead," Moon said, dejected.

"That is behind us. You are bound by our rede. None of what was said in the Circle of Equals is to be repeated. You will not reveal my identity. Furthermore, your defeat means that we move forward with the plan Inanna and I have devised—with your *full cooperation*."

"I am a man of my word."

"You and I have spent half a lifetime hating each other, Paul," Baldur said, moving alongside his bed. "And for what? Look at us. Look at our former Clan. It was not my actions alone that brought about the end of the Smoke Jaguars. You made me the man I am today. Your blood is on them too. You know that."

"*Aff*," Moon said in a bitter, low tone.

"You hated me, and tried to send me into exile on Huntress. Later, you tried to kill me on Maldonado. For me, you became the embodiment of everything wrong with the Smoke Jaguars. I am willing to bet I was the same thing in your eyes."

Moon didn't reply. He didn't have to. Baldur saw it in his face.

"We both contributed to the downfall of the Smoke Jaguars," Baldur said. "Now we are both going to save everything that was good in them. We will do this together."

"What you have planned—it will not be easy," Moon said.

"I need your help. *We* need your help." Baldur shot a quick glance back at Inanna. "I know you want to save them all. I wish we could—but it is impossible."

"You are asking me to turn my back on the Light Horse, who saved me from the Dark Caste."

"I am asking you to act in the interests of your former Clan—to save them. That was your mission when you came from the Inner Sphere back to Huntress. All I want is for you to fulfill that mission."

Moon eyed him carefully. "I want you to know that I do regret how I treated you. Ever since you showed up on Huntress and I knew you betrayed the Smoke Jaguars, I have felt the full weight of responsibility for what I did. If you are expecting an apology—none will be offered. At the time, I felt I was doing what was right and just. It was not until Huntress fell and the Grand Refusal was lost that I came to grips with my role in all of this. It is a burden I have borne since then."

"You no longer bear that burden alone," Baldur said, extending his hand to his former foe.

Paul Moon eyed the hand as if a snake had been put before him. "I cannot shake hands with you, Baldur."

"After all of this, you are still bitter, *quiaff*?" Baldur snapped. "I should have known better than to confide in you—or hope you would truly act honorably. I have been wrong about you. You are still the same Paul Moon, blooded and better than me. Your arrogance is so annoying—"

Moon grinned. "And you are still a rash fool at times," he said, cutting Baldur off. "You tore the power supply out of my arm. They have not yet replaced it."

The two enemies looked at each other for a second in silence.

Then they both broke into laughter.

# CHAPTER 27

"So there you have it," Baldur said. "Our proposed plan to save the soul of the Smoke Jaguars."

The presentation had lasted twenty minutes, hitting the high points of the mini-exodus they were proposing. As he powered down the holotable display, his gaze drifted over each leader of the former Jaguar castes.

The venue had been chosen carefully, honoring the merchant caste. Their JumpShips and DropShips were critical for the planned migration to Wayside V. Inanna had suggested the location, though Paul Moon had chafed at it. But since their trial, he had been much more willing to compromise with the Nova Cats. *He is coming to grips with who he is, his role, and ours in these matters.*

The room had a hint of mustiness in the air, probably from being unused for so long. The merchant caste had been grounded, their fleet of JumpShips held at the nadir jump point, their DropShips parked on the Lootera spaceport. *Like most of the Jaguars, they are struggling with this new order the Star League has imposed.*

Master Technician Udvar, leader of the technician caste, a burly man with as much black curly hair on his body and face as he had muscles, leaned forward on his elbows. "Many of my people will welcome this opportunity. Since the Star League came, we have known only headache and heartache. They have kicked us out of our own repair bays so their people can take over. Without a warrior caste to service, we are idle."

"I concur," came the voice of Senior Laborer Ambrosia, the leader of the laborer caste. "Many of my families are now unemployed, as factories and other businesses were destroyed in the fighting. We just completed the repairs on the 'Mech facility at Rakt-Jabada only to have it fall into the hands of the Goliath Scorpions. None of us want to become chattel of the other Clans, to be fought over and made to toil for them. We were born Smoke Jaguars. These Star League invaders may have smashed our warriors, but our Clan is more than our warrior caste."

Scientist-General Nicasio, the balding head of the scientist caste's governing council, sat with crossed arms and a slight scowl on his face. "My people are being courted by the Star League. They have offered us many things in exchange for our technological secrets... better housing, financial gain, and so on. Speaking for my caste, I must say that these 'invaders,' as you called them, Ambrosia, are offering us a chance at something we never had before—recognition and power."

"What do you mean?" Paul Moon asked from across the table.

Nicasio leaned back in his seat, his arms still defiantly interlaced. "We have always been second to the warrior caste. The warriors of our former Clan are almost gone. The Inner Spherers want our technological advancements, and are willing to advance us to get them. If we remain here, we will be more than a lower caste. We may very well be the ruling caste of Huntress when all of this is done."

Baldur saw Paul Moon bristle at Nicasio's words. "You may be right," Moon said. "Your people may very well have more sway than you have ever had before. But it will be under the yoke of the Star League. Once they have from you every innovation the Smoke Jaguars possess, you will be of no use to them. You will rule over a rotting carcass that was once a proud Clan...one of Nicolas Kerensky's chosen."

The scientist's face reddened at Moon's prophecy. "Again, our warrior caste is all but gone. Would it not be better to rule over the ash heap of Huntress than to serve under warriors who failed us the one time it mattered?" His verbal salvo hit back at Paul Moon just as hard.

"I am a warrior," he said through gritted teeth. "I remind you of that, scientist. I could order you to take part in this plan." Moon's threat was clear.

Nicasio seemed almost amused. "You are *not* a warrior—not any longer, not in the Clan sense of the word. You are a soldier of the Star League now, Paul Moon, if my intelligence is correct. The warrior elite of the Smoke Jaguars wander the streets as unaffiliated, or skulk off in the jungles to fight for the Jaguar and his band of thieves. Your period of rule ended when you lost Huntress to these barbarians."

"*Aff*," Moon said, moving halfway around the holotable. "You are correct, Scientist-General. Perhaps the warriors no longer carry the importance they once did. But I am here, now. There would be little to stop me from killing you if I felt like it—Star League or not." The scientist-general squirmed in his seat at those words.

*We cannot afford petty bickering. Too much is at stake.* "Enough, Paul," Baldur said. "If we turn on each other, then the Star League's victory is truly complete. Nicasio, do all of your former caste feel the same way you do? Do they all believe life will be better for them under the Star League?"

The balding man frowned and uncrossed his arms. "*Neg.* There is a portion of my caste that still yearns for the era of the Smoke Jaguars."

Baldur leaned on the table, propped up by his fists. "We cannot take everyone—you have seen the plan. Would it not be wiser, as the leader of your people, to allow those who do not want to remain to go with us, *quiaff?*"

Nicasio said nothing for a few moments. *He does not want to let his people go–they represent the source of his future power once we depart.* Finally, he nodded, his jowls shaking in the process. "*Aff.* Some of our people still cling to the past. I am sure we can find numbers to meet your projected quotas. I do have some criteria, though."

"Proceed," Paul Moon said.

The scientist glared scornfully up at the towering Elemental. "You spoke of forming a new society. My people will want an equal voice in that. We trusted our warriors to protect us and our way of life. That meant being subservient to them. We did this because it was right and just. There was a balance to our relationship, our roles were defined in our lives. We gave up some control over our destiny for the protection the warrior caste offered. Our warriors failed—" Moon opened his mouth to retort, but Nicasio continued, "—through no fault of their own or their leaders. No one could have foreseen the re-formation of a Star League and a unified strike against one Clan."

Paul Moon slowly nodded.

"If we are going to have people undertake such a journey," Nicasio continued, "it cannot be to reforge the Smoke Jaguars as they were. If we did that, we would condemn ourselves to repeat the failures that brought us to this table. My people will want a voice—an *equal* voice, with the others who make this journey. If they believe they have a future where they control their destiny, I can endorse this proposal."

Baldur spoke before Paul Moon could. "It is not our intent to make a new Clan or to try to make a new Smoke Jaguar. That flame has been extinguished for the time being. We do seek to preserve the honor and rich history of the Jaguars, however. Those who go on this journey will have a fair voice in their future and their fate."

"No offense," the older scientist said, "but you are just a Nova Cat. This is not even your concern to begin with. I want to hear it from him—from Moon." He turned his icy glare back to the Elemental.

Baldur's eyes, along with every other eye in the room, fell on Paul Moon. *This is the hardest change for him—is he willing to fight for it?*

Moon looked uncomfortable, but rose to his full height and drew a deep breath. "We are creating this colony so that the best parts of the Smoke Jaguars will be preserved. I concede your point—" he locked eyes with Baldur for a millisecond, "—that we are not remaking our former Clan. There may come a day when we can reveal to the universe where we came from. For the immediate future, our origins need to be hidden."

"So you are comfortable with my scientists having a representative voice, *quiaff?*"

"Affirmative," Moon said solemnly, his voice sounding weary. "Those who go on this trek will be charged with forming their own government. There are far too few of the warrior caste to rule as we once did in the Smoke Jaguars. Some will not go," he acknowledged. "Their spirit has been too badly mauled between the Star League and the Goliath Scorpions. Others are scattered on Jaguar holdings throughout Clan space and the Inner Sphere. Some will stay and fight with the Jaguar, others will stay out of a sense of duty to a long-lost cause."

His answer seemed to satisfy Nicasio, who nodded.

"What of the caste system?" asked Merchant Factor Lagemann, the skinny, short leader of the merchant caste. He had pasty white skin that made Baldur wonder if he had ever been exposed to sunlight.

Baldur jumped back into the conversation. "That will be for those who go to decide. The people going on this exodus must have some say over their ultimate destiny. If order is imposed externally, we will be no better than the Star League coming here and disbanding the castes. Is that agreeable to you?"

Lagemann nodded. "You are asking much of my caste. We are critical to this effort. You need my pilots and ships."

"True," Inanna replied. "As a people, are you conducting much commerce now?" *She only asked a question she already knew the answer to...shrewd,* Baldur mused.

"*Neg.* The Star League ordered us here to Huntress until they make a policy regarding trade. The other Clans will not trade with us because we have no status with them. The Star League may have won the Grand Refusal, but they left my merchant trade in limbo. Treaties and agreements will have to be made between the League and the Clans. I have been assured by Paul Masters that he will address the matter, but it is a low priority for him, that much is clear."

"If you will transport us, you would be providing sanctuary to our people for the duration of the journey," Paul Moon said. "We cannot do this without your support."

"What happens once we reach Wayside V?" Lagemann queried.

"You would be free to remain," Baldur said. "Our colony will need to establish trade, albeit covert, with the Inner Sphere, especially in our first few years. Or you could return to Huntress. All we ask is that you keep our location a secret. The Clan Watches and the Star League will be very curious to learn where we went. While we would not pose a threat, as we have seen with the Goliath Scorpions, we would be a tempting prize—a target for them to conquer."

Lagemann's gaunt face winced at his words. "Come back and serve the Star League, *quineg*? I think not. The House governments will send their own merchant fleets to Clan space, now that it has been revealed. While I love the thrill of barter, facing external bidders with agendas we do not know makes for a dangerous marketplace. I fear the arrival of the Inner Spherers here will spell the end of commerce in Clan space. The Clans will be bought and sold a million times over, and are ill-prepared for such a violent change in the markets. *Neg*, those of us who go will remain on Wayside V. For better or worse, it is the best opportunity for us to thrive and still keep our most cherished traditions alive."

Baldur had expected a more vicious debate. *They feel the same way Paul and I do about this. Remaining on Huntress is untenable for the long term.* "We have two Smoke Jaguar WarShips that will accompany us on the voyage. Paul Moon contacted their captains, and they conferred with their crews. They would rather face the risks of setting up a new colony than have their ships confiscated by the Star League and be grounded for the rest of their lives."

"None of us are colonists," Udvar said. "You have a fairly exhaustive list of supplies and equipment to take, but there are inherent risks in setting up a new colony."

"There are," Baldur replied. "Wayside V has had a garrison for years, and from the records Paul Moon has obtained, the colonists have not suffered from any new diseases. There may yet be garrison troops there, it is difficult to know for sure. Yes, there are risks. Mistakes will be made—we are only human. However, remaining here is full of risks as well. You have all seen that the Goliath Scorpions have come. They are only the first of those who will come to Huntress to test the mettle of the SLDF and lay claim to what was the Smoke Jaguars. It is not a matter of if, but when."

A silence fell over the Hall of Commerce as everyone contemplated what he had said. *We are asking a lot of them, even more of their people. This choice may take time for them to digest.*

Udvar broke the quiet. "Where do we begin?"

Inanna activated the holodisplay. "Most of the merchant caste DropShips are grounded at the Lootera spaceport. We need to be discreet about loading them. We have identified warehouses and other buildings surrounding the spaceport that are perfect for staging the material we need to load." She pulled up a holographic map of the spaceport, and the identified warehouses glimmered orange around the perimeter. "We suggest loading the ships gradually, over the next few weeks, to avoid any attention from the Star League garrison."

Lagemann leaned in. "So far security at the spaceport has been light. We have no place to take those ships, so only a few guards patrol the area. Loading the ships over time, with a degree of stealth, should be easy. Moving the people onboard will attract unwanted attention, however. We are talking thousands of people. The garrison will know something is afoot."

"*Aff*, normally they would," Paul Moon said. "I will arrange a diversion for the SLDF. On top of that, our target date for departure is Founding Day, 24 August. The Star League has granted permission for us to hold some small celebrations, and all of those events require some degree of security. If we stretch their security thin enough, they will never know we have our people on the move."

"What about the trip to the jump point?" Lagemann queried. "Those DropShips will be vulnerable to the Star League's WarShips. If we cannot reach the JumpShips, this is all moot."

"We will arrange for a distraction that will draw the League's WarShips away from the nadir jump point, where the merchant fleet is located," Inanna said. "By the time they realize the ruse, it will be too late for them to intercept."

"They will pursue," Nicasio said flatly. "It is only logical."

"*Aff*, they may," Paul Moon said. "They also may not. Sending off their WarShips would strip Huntress of its first line of defense. Now that they hold this planet and have faced the Scorpions, Paul Masters and his subordinates are wary of other Clans coming to attack. They may come after us, but based on the meetings I have been in, I believe they will hold their forces in check."

"Why you?" Lagemann asked, looking at Baldur and Inanna. "This is an internal Smoke Jaguar affair. The Nova Cats stood down when we were attacked and even fought alongside the Star League. Are you now betraying them as well?"

Baldur opened his mouth, but Inanna cut him off before he could utter a sound. "Betrayal is a matter of perspective. We believe this is the right course of action. In fact, tomorrow our Khan arrives, and we intend to ask him if the Nova Cats can provide us safe conduct to Wayside."

"My colleague raises a good point. Why should we trust you?" Udvar asked.

Baldur tackled the challenge head-on. "If I were you, I would be suspicious of our motivations as well. Our Clan did what it believed to be correct: the demise of the Smoke Jaguars was predestined, as was the reformation of the Star League. There are times I do not fully comprehend it all myself; I do not have the foresight that some like

Inanna have." He cast her an assessing glance. *Since the time I met her, she has been guiding me down this path—I see that now.*

"The Nova Cats respect balance in the universe, though, of that much I am certain. Our cooperation and assistance is needed to set the scales back in balance. Our actions in the Great Refusal and turning a blind eye to the Smoke Jaguars' fate now demand an act of compassion. This is that action. I intend to go with you, even if you treat me as an outcast. I do this because I too have things I must set right in my life, and this is the best way to do that." *My burden is betraying these people. I have seen what my decisions have done to innocents as well as the guilty. I understand their reluctance, but I need them to understand my need to create my own balance for my actions.*

Inanna spoke up. "Baldur speaks the truth. I have seen what your people will become, and the role you yet have to play in matters. I will be joining you on this journey, putting my own life at risk with yours—if you will have me."

Her words surprised Baldur. *I did not know she intended to join the exodus.* He flashed her a grin. *She constantly finds ways to surprise me.*

Nicasio waved his hand at her words. "Foresight? Visions? *Neg.* I must look at facts."

Lagemann leaned toward Inanna. "What have you seen?"

She shook her head. "Echoes of the future—images of your people standing on Terra long before the Clans who turned their backs on you. I have seen reflections of a war to come where your people save others. Nothing tangible—" she shot a glance at Nicasio, "—but more of a feeling. I see greatness in what you will become."

Even Baldur looked at her in silent amazement. *She has never shared this much with me.*

The merchant smiled. "That is all I need. I have no qualms about help from the Nova Cats. We will need as much assistance as possible."

# CHAPTER 28

Khan Santin West's face was stern, his broad brow wrinkled, as he watched the end of the proposal Inanna and Baldur made. Paul Moon sat at the far side of the small tactical operations room, his arms crossed. West had said nothing during their presentation, though his face spoke volumes—but the message was, as yet, unclear.

When he did speak, his voice was crisp and deep, almost as though amplified. "You two do realize we sided with the Star League against the other Clans. That is why we are leaving now."

"Understood, my Khan," Inanna said.

"They will not be pleased that several thousand Smoke Jaguars have packed up and left—and that we would be offering them *safcon* under your plan, *quiaff?*"

"Agreed," Inanna replied.

"You are also talking about forming a colony of former Smoke Jaguars on a world and giving them the capability to be some sort of threat in the future."

"*Aff*, Khan West," was all Inanna offered.

*Why are you not trying to convince him, Inanna?* Baldur shot her a glance through narrowed eyes, but she ignored his unspoken message.

The large Nova Cat leaned back in his chair for a moment, the metal protesting slightly at his weight. "Their future is fraught with uncertainty—more than our own. Our former brothers and sisters all believe we betrayed them. No matter what arguments have been offered by the late Khan Leroux or myself, they have painted us as agents of evil. So much so that we are abandoning the worlds we tamed and conquered to go to the Inner Sphere. They refuse to accept fate and destiny into their vocabularies."

Khan West fell silent for a moment, then continued. "The Star League has accepted us, but only out of necessity and convenience. This I understand. We have thrown our lot in with them. Will they see this plan as a betrayal?"

"They may, my Khan," Baldur said firmly. "Consider this. The Star League is composed of member states. We are one of those. They have sovereignty to conduct their own affairs, and do so. This is little more than that. We are not relocating the entire population of Huntress to rebuild the Smoke Jaguars. We are simply taking the best of that Clan's remains and preserving it, nourishing it."

West nodded his head slightly. "If I were to undertake this plan you propose, I would anger both the Clans and the League. At the same time, that is its appeal. The Clans see us as puppets of the SLDF. This would demonstrate that we do exert our own authority and autonomy. It proves the same to the Star League. They would see us as independent, and perhaps with more respect than mere 'convenient allies.'"

"Yes, my Khan," Inanna replied. "And we will not fight our way free of Huntress. We will use subterfuge and guile to depart. The Star League has viewed what is left of the warrior caste as a thorn in their side for months now. That thorn would be removed. In some respects, the Star League might be grateful for the gesture."

"They will not," West countered. "We would be doing this without consulting them or aligning them to the cause. I do not delude myself that they will be happy if and when this happens."

He turned to Paul Moon. "You are a former Smoke Jaguar, Paul Moon. How will your people feel about accepting help from my Clan?"

"Most will dislike it," Moon replied with a remarkable lack of emotion. "Right or wrong, some have affixed the Nova Cats with part of the blame for what happened to our people. At the same time, they know if they remain here, their fate is cast to the wind. The Star League does not know how to treat them, and in time the other Clans will come to consume them."

Khan West said nothing for a moment. "It is ironic that you have chosen Wayside V. I fought the Smoke Jaguars there years ago. It is not the most hospitable of worlds. When the Smoke Jaguars came to take it back, we defended it with only two warriors. For us, more than anything else, that planet was a burden to defend. Do we know the fate of the garrison there?"

"Unknown," Paul Moon replied. "There was a Trinary stationed there as of the last updating of the *touman*—Zeta Galaxy, older warriors exiled to garrison duty."

The word "older" pricked at Baldur. It was one of the reasons Paul Moon had sent Trent back to Huntress in the first place. Because he was in his late thirties, it was assumed younger generations of warriors had surpassed him. That strict adherence to age and obsolescence had helped turn him against his people.

"Does the planet have an HPG?"

"*Neg*," Moon replied.

"So they may not even know the fate of the Jaguars, *quiaff*?"

"*Aff.*"

"That is a lonely world to be abandoned on. The atmosphere only clung to what had been oceans at one point. The old continents are devoid of life and air. What seas remain are shallow. I remember the storms when I was there. We left atmospheric processors running on the world, but I doubt things have changed much since I last saw it. It will take years for your colony to thrive, and even then it may be difficult."

"We are stronger than most believe," Moon replied. "Those who make this exodus know the hardships they may face. They are coming of their own free will. The loss of Huntress hurt us deeply, but in the end it will make us stronger." Baldur could hear the pride in his voice.

"What of the Goliath Scorpions?" West probed.

"What of them?" Moon replied.

"Do you think they will sit idly back and allow the surviving warriors to depart, *quineg*? I have dealt with the Goliath Scorpions before, and it would be wise to factor them into your plans. They are a dedicated people, as much as we are. They understand the importance of history, and they will react to the loss of the best of the Smoke Jaguars."

*We did not take them into account...an error on our part.* "React how?" Baldur asked.

"Huntress and its people are a prize. Losing the warriors means depriving the Scorpions of precious genetic material. They will pursue you."

Moon chuckled. "All along the Exodus Road? *Neg*. That is a long way to travel for such a small prize. After all, this generation of Jaguar warriors lost Huntress."

"You do not know the Goliath Scorpions as I do," Khan West said firmly. "They have sent their Seekers to the Inner Sphere. Our Watch has detected this. They see themselves as the archivists of our people and believe the future is tied to the past. They will try to follow your people, Paul Moon."

"Then we will need to be prepared for them if they do come," Moon said. Baldur nodded in agreement. *We cannot stop them from pursuit. All we can do is be prepared if they do find us.*

"I take it your plan for provisioning the DropShips is already underway?"

"*Aff*," Baldur replied. "It is happening all around us as we sit here—just out of sight of prying eyes."

West leaned forward. "Then this plan is going to happen, regardless of the Nova Cats' involvement. It stands a better chance of succeeding if we assist you."

Inanna responded first. "It will happen, my Khan. It is ordained in the stars."

"I have come to trust Inanna over the last three years—as did Khan Leroux," West said to Baldur and Moon. "She has an ability to foretell events. Even before I became Khan, I learned that it was foolish to ignore her unique insight."

He paused as if in thought, then continued, "I grant you whatever aid you need. We owe something to the former Smoke Jaguars. Offering your small fleet protection along the Exodus Road seems to be the least we can do. The Star League will be aggrieved by my actions. This is a good thing, in my eyes. Clan Nova Cat is not a pawn to be sacrificed or manipulated. We have our own destiny far beyond this Star League." He spoke with confidence and assurance.

"Well bargained and done," Paul Moon said, rising and extending his hand to the Nova Cat Khan. "We will wait for you in the Niles system. If you are not there by a prearranged time, I will order the fleet to continue on to the Inner Sphere. We can ill afford a reprisal strike by the Clans who seek retribution for the Great Refusal."

West shook it. "Let this bury the strife between our peoples once and for all."

As the group started to leave, Santin West locked gazes with Baldur. "Remain for a moment, Baldur, I wish a word with you."

Inanna and Paul Moon left, and the two were alone. Khan West gestured to the chair next to his as he sat back down. "Please."

Baldur looked up at the Elemental and for a moment wondered if he was about to be chastised. This was his Khan; private audiences were rare.

"Your plan seems solid—though it relies heavily on diverting the attention of the Star League Defense Force," West began.

"We have a meeting this evening to secure the assistance needed for that."

The Khan paused for a moment, as if searching for the right words. "I know who you were, Baldur. I know the role you played in these affairs."

"Yes, my Khan," was all Baldur could reply, unsure of where West was going.

"Given what you have done, providing the Inner Sphere with the Exodus Road—and what it resulted in—I am surprised that you are here planning to save the very thing you were instrumental in bringing down in the first place."

Warmth rose to Baldur's face. "I owe it to these people. I did not want to see the Smoke Jaguars destroyed, despite what Victor Steiner-Davion believes. I wanted them returned to a place of greatness. They had wandered off that path. I never expected them to face utter defeat, only a humiliating one."

"That does not fully answer why you are doing this."

"*Neg*," Baldur replied. "It does. My actions and mine alone caused this. In helping preserve the soul of a once-great Clan, I can redeem myself. I *have* to do this. My own soul is at stake. Sitting back and doing nothing would be more criminal than my original betrayal of these people."

"Does Paul Moon know who you are?"

"*Aff*, he does. We faced each other in a Circle of Equals, unaugmented, where I forced his support."

West cocked an eyebrow, silent acknowledgement of the accomplishment of besting an Elemental in hand-to-hand combat. "So you do this to restore balance, to right a wrong?"

Baldur nodded. "I do."

West smiled. "Then you truly are a Nova Cat. I grant your fleet *safcon* to Wayside V and our people's assistance."

# CHAPTER 29

Paul Moon led Baldur through the twilit jungle. He knew his forced Nova Cat ally felt some hesitation. The jungle was like that, especially at night. Despite weeks of training in the thick foliage, even the most skilled warrior respected the Shikari. There were dozens of poisonous reptiles and insects that demanded a wide berth. Even with the cooler autumn nights, when most insects disappeared for the season, it was a dangerous place.

When he glanced back, he saw Baldur force aside a large branch. Baldur...Trent...it was hard to process. He could hear Trent in Baldur's voice, but every other physical aspect of the warrior was different. This particular Nova Cat was a ghost, come back from the dead to haunt him. His very presence reminded Paul Moon of his role in the downfall of the Smoke Jaguars.

A part of him still hated his foe. Trent had sold out not just the Smoke Jaguars but the whole of the Clans. Moon's anger at him was tempered by knowing Trent had done so because of his, Paul's, own actions. *I created Trent the Traitor with my own arrogance. His actions are blood on my hands too.*

They reached the massive boulder of the Paseena Stone, now dotted with dead leaves from the deciduous trees that had already turned colors with the autumn nights.

Baldur moved around the boulder, touching it as he went. "The Paseena Stone," he said as if the rock had awakened old memories. "I never thought to see it again."

"Passing those survival tests was a major stepping-stone for warriors," Paul said, taking out his flat-pack canteen and sipping water. "Did you do well in your trials?"

"I passed, but barely," Baldur replied. "It was hard to sleep in the jungle. I got bitten twice by tree vipers...the medics thought I might die. I surprised them by finishing the tests with the rest of my sibko."

Paul chuckled. "I was bitten twice too. The second snake dropped on my shoulder and nailed me in the neck. I thought I was going to die that night. To this day, I kill any snake that crosses my path."

Moon caught himself in that moment. He was having an actual casual conversation with Baldur. They were not talking about the plan that had consumed their waking hours, but about shared experiences. They had things in common that Paul had always overlooked. *If we had done this years ago, would things have turned out differently?*

Looking at the man before him, he saw very little resemblance to the mangled warrior who had somehow survived Tukayyid, scarred and disfigured. *I do not think either of us is now the same person we were.* Glancing down at his bionic arm, he allowed himself a faint smile. *We have both changed–become different people.*

"We are early," he said, glancing at his watch. "He will be here as arranged."

Baldur took a sip from his canteen pack. "This place seems smaller now. I presume this is because of my age."

Moon turned to his now-comrade. "I feel compelled to ask you this. You do not have to answer, but I have to ask. You—your former self—you gave the Exodus Road to ComStar. What did you ask for in return?" The question had gnawed at him from the moment he discovered Trent was alive after the fall of Huntress. *They must have offered him a lordship or something else of great value for him to turn.*

Baldur chuckled, if only to himself. "I asked only for a field command—to lead troops in battle."

"Against the Smoke Jaguars, *quiaff?*"

"*Neg,*" the Nova Cat replied. "It never occurred to me what ComStar would do with the data I gave them. I did not think about that at the time. All I wanted was to fight—in battle. I am a warrior, that was where I belonged, leading other warriors."

"So it was never about revenge."

"*Affirmative,*" Baldur said. "Everyone just assumes that was what drove me. I was furious at how you and others treated me. That motivated me to gather the data on the Exodus Road. I merely traded it for a chance to fight once more."

It bothered Paul that Baldur was not the grand traitor he had built up in his mind. *In many respects he and I are similar.* That thought bothered him more. He turned his gaze away from Baldur and into the jungle...it was easier than looking him in the eyes. "Did ComStar honor its word?"

"*Neg*," Baldur said, standing next to him, leaning back on the boulder and looking out into the jungle as well. "Prince Victor Steiner-Davion did not want a traitor in his midst. He threw out the promise that Focht made to me. He was so convinced I was out for revenge that he could never look past it. The Nova Cats took me, bonded me, and made me a warrior. Khan Leroux understood me, though he never said it. He knew I wanted to fight again."

"You are still angered by the Davion prince, *quiaff?*"

"*Aff,*" Baldur said, taking another sip from his canteen straw. "He would not listen to me because he simply did not care. I was a tool, one he used and discarded when finished with the task. I do not know why he even bothered to bring me to Huntress with the Operation Bulldog task force. I assume so he could rub my nose in the carnage and death I caused. Oddly enough, Paul, he is the only person I still have a grudge against. The Little Prince whose own interests trumped those with any shred of honor."

Moon turned his head toward Baldur. "What of me?"

His former comrade and foe grinned. "We resolved our differences in a Circle of Equals. We both bear some responsibility for what happened to our Clan. That is why the two of us are the only ones who can set it right."

"We will do that."

"Who is it you brought me out here to meet?"

"An old acquaintance."

Before Baldur could respond, the foliage near the Paseena Stone stirred, and through it came two warriors led by Russou Howell. He was oddly cleaner than the last time they had met, though he had lost a few more pounds...it showed in his hollowing cheeks. His eyes, even in the twilight, were dull and red. As he closed on Paul and Baldur, Moon caught a whiff of alcohol from the Jaguar.

"Russou Howell," Baldur said with awe in his voice.

Howell turned to him. "Do I know you, Nova Cat? You seem familiar."

*How could he know this was Trent?* "*Neg*," Baldur replied—a lie. "We have never met. I am Baldur."

*They were once close friends...* Moon remembered that. Russou had turned to drink when he thought he had killed Trent. *We cannot tell him now.* He carefully turned his head and made eye contact with Baldur, who seemed to fully understand simply from the look Moon gave him.

"Our Watch had an image of you on file," Baldur said. "Your reputation precedes you."

Howell seemed suspicious, but disregarded the Nova Cat. "So, Paul Moon. The last time we met here, you left and formed a unit with this so-called Star League. I must admit, you hurt my recruitment efforts. Tell me, how did your Ghosts fare against the Goliath Scorpions?"

Howell was smug and quite possibly intoxicated. Moon deflected his verbal stab as insignificant. "We fought with honor. More importantly, we did what you cannot—we gave our people hope."

"And now you summon me here again," the Jaguar said with a smirk. "I take it we did not come to debate philosophies again."

"Truth," Moon replied. "I came to ask you a favor."

"Paul Moon is asking *me* for a favor, *quiaff*? Well, this is indeed an intriguing turn of events. What could I ever possibly do for you?"

"I need a diversion, something that will draw off the Star League Defense Force from Lootera. You and your people are best suited for this."

Howell cocked his head slightly and eyed him with suspicion. "Why would you need a diversion?"

Moon looked at Baldur, who gave him a nod of support. "We are planning to leave Huntress. In order to board and launch our DropShips safely, I need the majority of the SLDF out of Lootera, at least until we reach orbit. I would offer you and your people the chance to join us, but we both know what your answer would be."

Russou laughed, but one of his compatriots, Oliver Howell, spoke up. "True enough. Where are you going?"

"I will tell you—" he made eye contact with each of the three warriors opposite him, "—but it goes without saying that it must remain a secret. I only share it with you in case you choose to join us."

"I am intrigued," Russou said. "Where are you off to, Paul?"

"Wayside V. One of our outpost worlds in the Deep Periphery."

Russou kept his composure. "And what are you going to do there? Take up gardening?"

"Perhaps," Moon replied. "We are taking several thousand of our former Clan and going there to preserve the essence of who we were."

"You are reestablishing the Smoke Jaguars?" the warrior named Jester asked.

"*Neg*," Baldur replied. "We are saving the best of your people. If they are revealed as Smoke Jaguars it will spell the end of them. The other Clans will sweep down on them to take their warriors and materiel."

"Other Clans, like your Nova Cats, *quiaff*?" Oliver Howell asked.

"*Neg*," Paul Moon replied. "The Nova Cats have offered us *safcon* to Wayside V. They are...repentant, and are treating us with honor in providing assistance."

Russou paced in front of Moon and Baldur, watching them carefully. "This is unlike you, Paul Moon. You serve the Star League now. You are turning traitor against them. That is remarkable, given your penchant for hating traitors, as I am sure you remember. Why?"

The Elemental was not shaken by Russou's reference to Trent, especially since the man he spoke of was standing before them. "I was a bondsman to a non-Clan entity, the Eridani Light Horse. I have been made a full warrior, which honorably restores my free will. I am not turning against the Star League. I am taking no actions that would deliberately put their lives at risk. I am simply reprioritizing my objectives—making the saving of the Smoke Jaguars a higher priority."

"This is most audacious, even for you, Paul. An exodus. You must cast yourself as one of the Kerensky Bloodline to undertake such a move. Is this your ego, Paul Moon, or something else?"

Moon stepped toward Russou, which made his two comrades unsling their rifles. Paul was not deterred, but leaned forward and down to Russou, making sure they spoke face-to-face. "Ego is not at the root of this. I do not see myself as a Kerensky any more than I see you as Robin Hood of old. You are fulfilling a need for some of our people—as am I. Neither of us holds the only solution for our people's plight."

Russou paused his pacing and rose to his full height, crossing his arms. "Why would I do this for you, Paul?"

The question was valid. Paul Moon had anticipated such a query, but had no answer prepared. A part of him had hoped Russou would simply agree to what he was asking for. "Because we were and are both Smoke Jaguars. You may not like me. You may not approve of my plan. I could have sold you out on our last meeting, turned you over to the Star League. I could have done that tonight as well. You are honorable, Russou. You should do this because it is the right thing to do. If that is not enough, then think of it this way—you will be getting rid of me once and for all. I doubt that I will ever set foot on Huntress again after this."

Howell smiled. "That has some appeal. Assuming that I do this for you, what is in it for me and my people?"

"What do you have in mind?" Baldur asked.

"There are two WarShips in orbit," Russou said.

"We need them to reach our destination," Paul replied.

"Agreed. While I have little love for you, Paul Moon, I would hate to see any of our people die unnecessarily. And the other Clans, they will come after you—that much can be counted on. After you reach Wayside V, what use are WarShips to you?"

"What will you do with them?" Paul asked.

"I do not know. I do know that if I remain here on Huntress, it is only a matter of time before the Star League tracks me down and kills me. Having a ship offers a chance, an opportunity to carry my fight elsewhere."

Moon stared at him as he thought. Giving him two WarShips was out of the question. *If we had one, we could possibly defend ourselves should invaders come.* "One, Russou Howell. I can send *one* ship back here to Huntress with a volunteer crew, if they will make the voyage. It will jump to a pirate point and signal you upon its arrival. How you get to that ship and what you do with it, that is up to you."

Howell smiled. "Well bargained and done."

"You and your people could join us," Baldur said. "There is no need for you to remain here after luring away the SLDF."

Russou and his two warriors laughed out loud. "Behold the Nova Cat mentality. Let me explain things to you, Baldur. We exist to bleed our enemies to death one pinprick at a time. It is not the best way to wage war, but it is all we have left. I exist to whittle away at this Star League garrison one warrior at a time. They must be made to pay. If I am successful, they will grow weary over time, pack up, and leave Huntress."

Paul Moon listened and watched Russou make sweeping gestures with his hands, but all he could feel was a swelling sense of pity for the man. *He believes the story he weaves. His people think a victory may be possible. Now is not the time or place to debate his choice of strategy. If this is what Howell believes, it is best to leave him with his delusions.*

"I meant no insult," Baldur said. "I simply did not want to exclude you. You seem the kind of warrior who is worth saving."

"If I was insulted, we would be facing each other in a Circle of Equals," Russou replied confidently. He then turned back to Moon. "If you want a diversion, I believe I can provide one. We can stage an attack against the city of Chhaiya. A missile production factory there has armaments we need. I will hit it."

Moon knew the city. It was small, some thirty thousand in population—but sufficient distance from Lootera. "I can use my position in SLDF's intelligence to leak information of a guerrilla raid planned there the day before we depart. The Star League will be well on its way to intercept you by the time you strike. The cries from the local garrison there will only be for the League to accelerate their pursuit. We can use that as the window for us to lift off Huntress."

Baldur, off to his side, nodded.

Russou Howell smiled. "There is only one highway to Chhaiya, making it the perfect target. By the time the Star League forces arrive, we will have fallen back into the jungle—leaving them holding the bag. Any time I can humiliate these Inner Spherers, I consider it my obligation to try."

"Good," Paul said. "It is a plan. I will coordinate the exact details over the channel we have been using to keep in contact."

Russou pointed his finger at the Elemental. "Understand this, Paul Moon. I am going along with this plan to embarrass my enemy. I am not doing this because I endorse your little exodus. I do not want you to recruit my troops. I struggle enough keeping my force cohesive without outside interference." His tone was vicious and threatening, but Paul was unmoved by the words or the timbre of Russou's voice.

"I agree to your terms," Moon replied. *I will treat your words as a request, not a threat–but only because it fits my needs.* "It goes without saying that our discussion is to remain secret. Our target date is the twenty-fourth of this month."

"Founding Day," Russou replied. "How fitting that you are leaving on the day those of us who still hold faith with the Clans celebrate our formation."

"Goad me all you want, Russou Howell. We both seek the same thing in the end—preserving what we love." With those words, Paul Moon did an about-face with military precision and marched back into the jungle—with Baldur stomping behind him. Over his shoulder he called out, "I am relying on you, Russou. Do not make a fool of me."

All he heard in reply was the warrior at the boulder laughing, his voice consumed by the jungle's darkness.

# CHAPTER 30

"How reliable is your source?" Lieutenant Farnholtz asked as Paul Moon pulled up and zoomed in on Chhaiya on the holodisplay of Huntress's main continent.

"As if I got it from the Jaguar himself," Moon replied confidently. His words had been carefully chosen.

"How large is the force he plans on hitting it with?" Lieutenant Fisher asked.

"The best estimate I have been able to ascertain is a full Cluster of warriors, though not all of them have 'Mechs. This is going to be different than his previous strikes. He is not going to hit them with a Star or Binary—he's coming in force." Paul had exaggerated his own estimate of Russou Howell's force size. *I have to provide them a target large enough to necessitate moving most of Lootera's garrison in pursuit.*

Farnholtz whistled in awe. "Our estimates put his force as somewhat smaller."

Paul turned to the Light Horse officer. "I understand, sir. Our intelligence has only seen a few 'Mechs and vehicles at a time. This will be the first time he is striking with the bulk of his troops. He aims to take Chhaiya—and hold it."

His words hung in the air like the echoing of an ominous bell.

Lieutenant Fisher finally broke the silence. "Chhaiya is a problem for us. We have a company of Com Guard infantry there and a platoon of medium-to-heavy armor. If the Jaguar shows up with that kind of force, our garrison will be overrun."

Farnholtz nodded. "The Jaguar is making a point. If he can bleed us badly, it demonstrates that we are not in control of Huntress. It makes it easier for him to recruit and erode our political position here."

"And he is hitting us tomorrow?" Lieutenant Fisher asked.

Paul shook his head. "Founding Day. I would guess he chose tomorrow because it is symbolic...a holiday throughout Clan space."

"We are permitting some celebrations—though it seems redundant, given the change in government here," Farnholtz said. "Perhaps we should send out word to cease and desist all Founding Day celebrations."

*Permitting,* quiaff? Paul thought. *That is how you see it. This is not a change of government, no matter how much you like to view it as such. This is a military occupation. Still, we need those celebrations for our plan to work.*

"*Neg*, Lieutenant," Paul replied. "It is wiser to let them go on. Even here in Lootera, the parade is relatively small—as is the fireworks celebration. Taking that away will only galvanize the population against the Star League, which may very well play into the Jaguar's plans. The real issue we need to contend with is the planned attack on Chhaiya."

"He's right," Fisher replied. "We need to get word to the garrison there immediately, have them take up defensive positions. We'll need a relief force to head down there—otherwise the defenders don't stand a chance against a full Cluster, regardless of their condition and status."

Lieutenant Fisher's eyes widened more than usual, given the new threat. "Our forces are fairly spread out over the continent and our holdings on Abysmal. One thing the Jaguar has done is forced us to garrison a lot of potential targets. We would have to send in at least a regiment of troops to counter an attack of this scale."

"A regiment might not be enough," Farnholtz said. "This is an opportunity to put an end to these petty raids and sniping attacks. If the Jaguar is going to be there in force, we have a chance to take him out in one stand-up fight. If we do that, we will need more than one regiment."

"Only the garrison here in Lootera would be large enough," Paul offered coyly. *As Baldur coached...let them arrive at their own conclusion.*

"With the celebrations, that would leave the city only marginally defended," Lieutenant Fisher said. "Two Com Guard companies here."

"What choice do we have?" his fellow officer asked.

"We could leave my Ghosts here for security and defense," Paul said. "I do not think it wise to put them in a situation where they may face former Smoke Jaguars in the field of battle. I think they will fight just fine, but I do not want them to suffer any emotional repercussions after the battle is won."

"Good idea. That'll leave us with a strong-enough defense here in the city in case this is some sort of ruse on the part of these renegades," Farnholtz replied, unconsciously rubbing the long scar that ran down his right cheek and neck.

"The colonel has been wanting a chance to face these insurgents in a straight-up battle," Fisher said with a hint of excitement in his voice. "The downside is the distance to get to Chhaiya. It's a long haul on a large contingent, and with only one highway, it's going to take a while to get up there. We're cutting it close as it is." Inanna had been correct: their sense of urgency and opportunity blinded them.

"We need to get this to the old man ASAP," Farnholtz said, combing his hand through his brilliant red hair.

"He's going to want confirmation to mobilize this many troops on such short notice," Fisher nodded.

Paul Moon shook his head. "I received this from a reliable source, one who knows this Jaguar personally. If we wait for perfect intelligence, it will be too late. If we do not start moving now, we run the risk of the local garrison in Chhaiya being overrun or taken prisoner." *Time is a powerful ally in this kind of ruse. It forces action because they fear the results of doing nothing.*

"Sergeant Moon is right," snapped Lieutenant Farnholtz. "If we spend too much time trying to confirm this, it will be too late to act."

Lieutenant Fisher finally acquiesced and nodded. "You're both right. We can't afford to ignore this. We need to get word to the garrison at Chhaiya so they can hunker down in case we don't reach them in time."

Farnholtz slapped Paul on his massive forearm. While meant as a gesture of solidarity and thanks, it was merely an annoyance to the Elemental. He glanced at the spot on his arm where the lieutenant had touched him, then stared into Farnholtz's eyes.


**LOOTERA SPACEPORT**
**24 AUGUST 3060**
**0908 HOURS**


Aviation Flight Control Technician Jessup brought coffee into the control tower, as he did every morning. Warrant Officer Lucas Lubowitzki of the Eridani Light Horse thanked him and took the cup as he surveyed the packed spaceport. The control tower did not require a large staff, since most of the former Smoke Jaguar ships were grounded. The Star League had provided operational management, but the former technician caste retained responsibility of 98 percent of the actual day-to-day work.

Jessup took his seat and gave a cursory nod to Angelica, another former Smoke Jaguar technician who helped manage flight operations.

"Is it me, or is there a lot of tarmac traffic this morning?" Warrant Officer Lucas said, taking a cautious sip of hot coffee.

Jessup got up and looked out with his enhanced binoculars. "Maybe. I remember seeing maintenance orders for the *Tripoli* and the *Monocracy* come through yesterday."

Angelica set her coffee aside. "Correct. And I saw some cargo transfer orders from the night shift, saying they're moving some non-perishables aboard the *Steadfast,* the *Admiral Arrastia,* and *The Duke.* That's probably what you're seeing."

Lubowitzki took another careful sip. "The place has been a tomb, but in the last week it's been crawling with techs and laborers. Made me wonder if something's going on."

Jessup turned and smiled. "The Star League ordered our merchant ships to ground. Even sitting here, these ships require a great deal of work to keep them flight-ready. On top of that, we moved a large number of ships here from the Abysmal spaceport. Having this many ships in one place creates the illusion that there's more people out on the flight deck than usual."

"You're probably right," Lucas said, returning to his chair and taking a longer drink of coffee. "Having your merchant fleet grounded means we get to sit back and have a chance to relax."

Jessup moved into the chair next to him, cradling his coffee rather than drinking it. "Before your Star League came, the spaceport was always busy. Now we nursemaid a mothballed fleet."

Lubowitzki took a larger drink of his strong, hot coffee and sighed. "It is your Star League too, you know."

Jessup grinned, casting a slow glance over to Angelica, then back to the warrant officer. "My apologies. Sometimes I forget." He set his untouched coffee in its holder next to the blank flight operations console.

"Sorry," Lubowitzki replied. "Didn't mean that the way it came out. It has to be hard for you...both of you—" he glanced at Angelica, "—having been raised in your culture and us coming down and change all that."

"We will prevail," Angelica replied.

Her words seemed to not be the response Lubowitzki had been expecting. He took another, deeper drink as he turned back to Jessup. "Is it me, or is it getting cold up here?"

"It's autumn," Jessup said. "We've always had issues with controlling the air temperature here in the spring and fall."

Lubowitzki set down his coffee, and his face went pale. "Something's wrong. I...I don't feel so good." His gray eyes widened in a moment of panic. The Light Horseman went rigid, motionless. Stark fear bathed his face with sweat.

"What you're feeling is the effects of the pill I put in your coffee," Jessup said, rising and moving Lubowitzki's chair so he could be closer to the window. "Don't worry, it's not fatal. It's a paralytic compound. Your muscles tense up, your vocal cords lock, but your breathing and heart rate are unimpaired." He pointed out to the tarmac. "While you cannot move or call for help, you do have a front row seat for the great show."

Lubowitzki's eyes darted to him and to Angelica in near-panic. "Even if you could call for help, your other Inner Spherers are being secured as we speak. Don't worry, the effects only last forty-eight hours or so."

Jessup dumped the rest of the warrant officer's coffee into the disposal unit. Angelica moved gracefully to the only access door to the tower's control room and locked it. Short of explosives, no one was getting in.

"Cat Prime," Jessup said proudly into his wrist communicator, "this is Bird's Eye. The nest is secure. You may begin loading operations. We are uploading the package to the SLDF task force."

Angelica moved next to Lubowitzki and leaned in. "As I said, we will prevail..."

**SLS *INVISIBLE TRUTH*
HIGH ORBIT OVER HUNTRESS
1025 HOURS**

"Commodore Beresick," bridge comms officer Adept Howard barked. "I have a properly encoded flash message on a secured channel, sir... priority alpha."

Precentor Alain Beresick drifted over to the station. Since Huntress's fall, the only excitement from a space perspective had been the arrival of the Goliath Scorpions. After all he had been through, Beresick was not complaining about some peace and quiet. Though he reminded himself every day that being at Huntress was akin to being surrounded by possibly hostile enemies, a year from any help arriving. *The crew can afford to relax–I cannot. I still have nightmares about the Battle of Trafalgar.*

"Are you sure about that clearance level?" he asked. *Priority alpha? This can't be good.*

"Yes sir—verified by two officers."

"All right, pull it up."

"Text only, sir," Adept Howard said. "Sent from the Lootera Tower."

The precentor's eyes devoured the text:

*SLS* INVISIBLE TRUTH
*ALPHA 1551 FD*


*MULTIPLE SATELLITES DETECTED NEUTRINO SURGE CONSISTENT WITH MULTIPLE JUMPSHIPS ENTERING SYSTEM. POSSIBLE USE OF UNDOCUMENTED PIRATE POINT. RECOMMEND* INVISIBLE TRUTH *AND FIRE FANG PROCEED TO COORDINATES 0893-009-0133 TO INVESTIGATE.*

*EOM*

"Sensors, are we picking up anything at 0893-009-0133?"

"Sir," Adept Murphy replied, "those coordinates are on the other side of Huntress, near the Ktanga Asteroid Field. We are blind to it at this time."

*We were told to watch for other Clans coming here to prove themselves,* the precentor thought. *Why they are arriving at a pirate point? If that is where they came in, they will be on the move by now. Best to check it out.*

"Comms, relay this message to the *Fire Fang*. Helm, prepare for course adjustments. We are going to get there fast—tell the engine room to prepare for maximum thrust."

"Aye sir," came the responses from the bridge crew. There was a low hum and throb throughout the *Invisible Truth* as her fusion engines flared to life.

"All hands, this is Commodore Beresick. Set Condition One throughout the ship—general quarters. All hands prepare for immediate rapid acceleration." *We should be prepared for the worst.*


**HPG STATION**
**SPARKS AND GEARS (TECHNICIAN QUARTER)**
**LOOTERA**
**1140 HOURS**

Demi-Precentor Chong Hin looked across the primary HPG control console and only saw darkness where there should be a visual cacophony of lights and displays. He frowned and stared at the display for the hundredth time. At 0900 hours the core had gone offline, and now, almost four hours later, it was still down. Hyperpulse generators did go down from time to time, but the fixes were usually quick. His skeleton crew was out of the control room, working on the core itself to determine the source of the outage.

Ever since Huntress fell to the Star League and ComStar took over control of the HPG in Lootera, Hin had relied heavily on former technician-caste members to maintain the station. Despite being built on the same base technological concepts as Inner Sphere HPGs, the Smoke Jaguar HPG had only begun to yield some secrets of its operation. Centuries of parallel development had led to some Clan enhancements that outperformed Inner Sphere HPG technology.

Because the Inner Sphere's HPG network did not extend to Clan space, the Huntress HPG had received little interstellar traffic, the majority being encrypted messages to and from the Goliath Scorpions, the new occupiers on-planet. Scorpion techs personally delivered their comms packets and picked them up, giving him a rare glimpse at a Clan the other Inner Spherers had not seen. *Queer bunch, the Scorpions. They have very little interaction with us, as if they don't trust us.*

Hin knew reaping this technology would enhance his career. *When I rotate back to Terra, the data I've gathered on Clan HPG engineering is going to secure me one of the golden positions–maybe even First Circuit.*

He had also downloaded images of the Goliath Scorpions, meticulously noting their uniforms and insignia. A few years away from Terra would certainly propel his career to new heights. As he looked at the blank displays, he could not suppress a self-inflated smile.

The fire alarm shattered the silence. Hin jumped to his feet as red warning lights flashed, indicating the fire was in the primary core and alignment system. *That shouldn't be possible–we are powered down. We have to put out that fire!*

He rose from his seat only to see Technician Mikel leaning casually in the doorway.

"We have to put the fire out!" Hin said as he rushed toward the doorway, only to watch Mikel shift position to further block his exit from the room.

"That is unnecessary," the technician said between the blares of the fire alarm.

"There's a fire in the core! If we don't contain it, we'll lose the station!"

"It's being handled."

The cycling alarm and red lights told Hin differently. He tried to push his way past the technician and for the first time realized just how large and muscular Mikel was. The former Smoke Jaguar didn't budge.

"We'll lose the primary core," he insisted.

"The core is safe. The station is not."

"Get out of my way," Him said, once more failing to get past. "Mikel, if you don't move, we could lose the entire station."

"It already is lost," Mikel replied calmly.

The demi-precentor backed up. *This is not an accident!* "You—you did this!"

Mikel shrugged, slowly. "I assisted."

"Why?"

"First and foremost, we need this station to be offline...indefinitely. Second, your efforts to steal our technology did not go unnoticed. Did you really believe that you, someone much less technically and intellectually competent than us, could actually extract the data and samples you took without us knowing, *quineg*?"

"I...we—the *core*—we need to save the *core*!"

"The core was removed last night. A simple subroutine made you believe it was still in place. Think of it as a parting gift from the people you chose to invade."

*They removed the core? Why?* "What about the fire?"

"Oh, the fire is quite real. The building will burn, as will all copies of the data you stole."

*No! I have lost the HPG. My career—everything I planned—gone!*

"Please reconsider! You don't understand the technological advancements you are depriving ComStar of."

Mikel laughed. "ComStar, the Houses...you all see yourselves as above us just because you defeated our warrior caste. In the end, though, you have just come to pillage. You stole our technology, deprived us of our way of life. You are little more than Dark Caste thieves in the night."

"That core—it is of no use to you. There's no place on Huntress where you can use it."

Mikel's grin broadened. "You think small. We are not staying on Huntress." He raised a hand in front of Hin and sprayed something in his face.

The demi-precentor's vision tunneled, and the floor rushed up at him and collided with his jaw. Hin's last memory was of Mikel's boots walking away through the din of the fire alarms.


**ALPHA GALAXY COMMAND POST**
**RAKT-JABADA**
**1245 HOURS**


"Sir," Bozwell said as he stood before Galaxy Commander Myers. "A priority message just came in from the *Copperhead*."

Rik Myers set down his cup of morning coffee. "Proceed."

Things had been far too boring for Myers since he had carved out a piece of Huntress for his Clan. *Our WarShip is at the jump point. Perhaps someone arrived to do the same thing I did here. That could be entertaining, to say the least.*

"The *Copperhead* reports that the Smoke Jaguar merchant JumpShips have deployed their sails, sir. All of them."

"Did they say why?"

"The former Jaguar ships say they have been ordered to go to the Inner Sphere," Bozwell responded.

"What about the two WarShips?"

"They are at the perimeter of the jump point, sir. With all of the sails deployed, it is impossible for the *Copperhead* to get a visual on them."

*It took the Star League long enough to divide up this* isorla. Such a move was not entirely unexpected. "The merchant caste is of no interest to me. If the Inner Sphere wants these ships, let them have them. If they do not take them, Clan Snow Raven will. Only their warriors concern me. I am willing to bet this is what Paul Masters is coming here to discuss later this afternoon."

The Star League's official ambassador had moved his Knights of the Inner Sphere to Abysmal after the Goliath Scorpions' successful Trial of Possession. He had been lobbying for a face-to-face meeting, one that Myers finally assented to. He found the Star League so arrogant to demand such a meeting. *They still believe they are our equals simply because they won their Grand Refusal.*

"As you wish, Galaxy Commander," Bozwell replied.


## DROPSHIP *WANDERER*
## LOOTERA SPACEPORT
## 1300 HOURS

"Reports in that we just finished loading fifty percent of the ships," Inanna said. "No sign of Star League activity yet. We can start launching at any time."

"*Neg,*" Baldur replied. "When people start seeing the ships go up, they will know something is afoot. We launch together—per the plan."

*She is persistent, I must give her that.* The topic of launching the DropShips had been heavily debated, and settled. He did not like crossing Inanna, but in this instance he felt she was wrong, despite her worries about coordinating all the DropShips in-flight.

The logistics and planning that he, Inanna, and Paul Moon had put into their exodus were staggering. *I have never been tested as much intellectually as I have these last few weeks.*

The members of the merchant-caste team Lagemann had assigned to work with him were geniuses. Their longshoremen understood the loading sequencing needed to maximize space and weight. Constantly updating the lists of supplies and materials the castes requested had been daunting...yet oddly rewarding. *This is what I have missed my entire career: true leadership at a high level...planning an opera-*

*tion involving thousands.* Few were ever afforded such an opportunity. *Even fewer for such a noble cause.*

Inanna had tried to soothe him after the late nights of work. She had offered to couple with him, but he'd declined. It was a matter of priorities for Baldur. Physical satisfaction had to take second place to fulfilling the mission. *There will be plenty of time for us to join once we are free of Huntress.*

"The HPG station is fully ablaze," Inanna said, "but all of our people and equipment are loaded. The crew of the *Mist Stalker* is reporting problems with their engines."

"Repairable, *quiaff?*"

"Unknown."

*I do not want to leave a ship behind.* "Send the engineering teams from the other two ships to the *Mist Stalker.* Perhaps some more hands and eyes may be of assistance."

"*Aff,*" she replied. "Satellite telemetry shows the Star League WarShips have taken the bait. No activity yet from the Goliath Scorpions at the jump point. The Star League Defense Force in Lootera are almost all on the highway heading south—as per our plan."

"Good," Baldur said as he studied his own data. Paul Moon and his people were handling perimeter security with the efficiency he expected from his former commander. *He will not allow this operation to fail any more than I will. That and his last shred of honor are probably all that is keeping me alive in his presence.*

Baldur checked his wristcomp and saw the time. *There is one more thing I need before we depart, something I can only entrust to myself.* "Inanna, I need you to take command of the departure. There is something I need to retrieve from the Warrior Quarter."

Her face stiffened. "This is not the time for frivolities. We are in the middle of a large-scale operation. What are you going back for?"

"I will only be a few minutes," Baldur said. "It is something I must do. You are more than able to handle the dataflow at this time."

"What are you going after?"

Baldur flashed her a grin. "Do not worry. But if I am not back at the departure time, you are to leave without me. Understood, *quiaff?*"

There was an awkward silence.

"*Quiaff?*" he asked more loudly.

"*Aff,*" she said reluctantly.

Baldur headed to the lower decks. *I only hope my intelligence was correct on this.*

## LOOTERA SPACEPORT
## 1314 HOURS

Demi-Precentor Josh "Slasher" Ellis saw the truck disgorging people at the spaceport perimeter, many of them carrying luggage. It was odd—and this was the seventh or eighth truck he had seen in the last hour. With most of the SLDF garrison on its way to Chhaiya, his armored assault company of infantry and light tanks was the last element of the Com Guards left in the city.

The troops guarding the spaceport let these people through. The troops wore Eridani Light Horse uniforms, but he knew an Elemental when he saw one, and there were several in the team. Fighting for weeks to take and hold Huntress, Ellis had been wounded three times and had his Hetzer Wheeled Assault Gun blown up twice. Even the one he commanded now only had a handful of original parts—the rest had been cobbled together from a variety of other tanks that had been trashed during the battles.

Word had come down a month ago that the Light Horse had absorbed some of the former Jaguars. *That has to be them...the Ghosts, but this is damn peculiar.* He'd had reports from his division's intelligence officer of some unusual activity at the spaceport. Now, a block away, he saw it. *What are they up to? Better yet, where do they think they're going?*

He slammed his fist on the top armor. "Roll us down there, Finnegan," he said into the throat mic. "Go slow, though. I don't want to spook them just yet. The rest of you remain deployed here."

The Hetzer lurched slightly as it started down the road. Finnegan had survived three Hetzers being toasted, and bore the scars to prove it. He wasn't a smooth driver, but he was deliberate and effective.

As the Hetzer closed, the Elementals and other Light Horsemen noticed the approaching tank. They directed the last of the trucks through the fence, and one of the larger Elementals stepped forward, saluting Ellis.

"Sergeant..." Ellis looked at his fatigue shirt. "Moon."

"Sir," Moon replied.

"What is going on here? I've been watching a parade of vehicles heading into the spaceport for the last half hour or so. We were on patrol and noticed that the city is almost dead calm except here and at the south gate of the landing pads."

"This?" Sergeant Moon said, gesturing to the now-empty gate behind him. "Simply some cargo transfers."

"Cargo transfers?" Ellis asked. "Seriously? I've seen at least a hundred fifty people go through that gate. Those DropShips are grounded."

"I am merely following orders, sir," Moon replied flatly.

"Let me see those orders," the demi-precentor demanded.

The enormous Elemental climbed up the side of the Hetzer, standing somewhat above Ellis, who was halfway out of the command hatch. "I want you to know sir, I take no pride or honor from this," Moon said.

"From what?"

Moon grabbed him by the throat with one hand and lifted him clear of the hatch in a single, herculean jerk. Ellis struggled to breathe and tried to chop at the thick arm of the genetically engineered warrior, to no avail. As he struggled to gasp even a single breath, he tried to reach Moon's neck, but his arms were too short.

The Elemental turned. Ellis heard the driver's hatch open, and out of the corner of his eye saw Adept Finnegan flying from the Hetzer, tossed like a doll onto the ferrocrete. Finnegan tried to fight, crouching like the professional soldier he was. Two of the non-Elemental infantry went at him with the butts of their rifles. Ellis heard another cry of pain, this one from his gunner, Adept Blaney. He couldn't see the gunner, but knew the sounds of a hand-to-hand fight all too well.

Ellis began to fade, his strength diminishing with each breath. His ears rang as he glanced down the street. The rest of his Level II came into view, and he saw the Light Horse troops pulling the crew out of the Demon tank, and some out of the Goblin. While he had been drawn in by the commotion at the spaceport, the infantry had overtaken his unit without even a shot fired. Gas grenades were going off, forcing troops to abandon their vehicles.

*What have I done?*

"I recognize this is a court-martial offense, and I do not take it lightly," Moon said as his face filled Ellis's field of vision. "I simply refuse to acknowledge the authority of the Star League any longer."

*What is happening here?*

Just before he lost consciousness, Ellis felt himself being lowered the ground, Sergeant Moon's grip on his neck still firm and cutting off most of his air.


**STAR LEAGUE DEFENSE FORCE HQ**
**WARRIOR QUARTER**
**LOOTERA**
**1448 HOURS**


Baldur entered Paul Masters's office and was struck by how little it had changed from when it had belonged to ilKhan Lincoln Osis. He had only been here once before, to give a briefing early in his career, but the office looked exactly the same. Something was different, though...*aff*, the paintings were gone—commissioned oil paintings of the Khans of Clan Smoke Jaguar. On one wall he could see the almost-invisible outline of where one painting had hung.

The desk was as he remembered it—a single black-marble slab carved in the shape of the continent of Jaguar Prime. It was thick, dark, ominous—just as he remembered it. Osis's large Elemental chair had been replaced with something more befitting Paul Masters's size. It was leather and thickly padded, soft. *A chair unbefitting a true warrior.*

In all the hours of planning, Baldur had done some research on his own. There was one thing he wanted to make sure did not remain on Huntress. *Our people may have to forge their own future, but they should not be allowed to forget their past.* As he entered the office, he saw the back wall, a magnificent carved bookcase. There were not many books there, but some of the former Khans' small trinkets had not yet been moved to storage. Bits of armor on small pedestals still dotted the shelves.

Except for one shelf, directly behind Masters's chair. The big book was still there, just as his source in the laborer caste had assured him. Baldur stood before it. The cover of the ten-centimeter-thick leather-bound book bore only two words.

*The Remembrance.*

He reached down slowly, carefully, and felt the cool leather in his fingers, caressing the cover. Each Clan had a book like this, their history in poetic prose. There were parts of the Smoke Jaguar *Remembrance* that all of the Clans had in common, but the majority was the Jaguars' own story of achievements and valor. He lifted the large book in his hands with the reverence and respect it deserved.

"Excuse me?" came a voice from the doorway. Baldur turned slowly and saw a Knights of the Inner Sphere lieutenant stepping into the office. His name tag read *Colin Duffy.* "Who are you, and what are you doing here?"

Baldur took a step toward him, holding the book in front of him. "I am sorry. I came to take this, to preserve it."

Lieutenant Duffy, no doubt Paul Masters's assistant, looked more agitated than angry. "You are not supposed to be here..." he said, struggling to remember Baldur's name.

"Baldur of the Nova Cats."

"Baldur. This is the office of the Star League ambassador. Who gave you permission to be here?"

"No one," Baldur said, closing the distance between them carefully, making no sudden moves. "This book has special meaning. I do not want it to become some trinket a soldier took home as *isorla*—the spoils of war, as you would say. I am sure you understand." He deliberately kept his tone low to lull the lieutenant into a false sense of comfort.

"Look," Duffy replied in a diplomatic tone. "I'm afraid I can't let you take that. It is one of the ambassador's personal possessions."

Baldur looked down at the book. "I understand."

The lieutenant reached out for *The Remembrance*, and Baldur extended his arm as if to hand it over, then brought it up with every bit of force his bionic arm could muster. He caught Duffy under his jaw, snapping the man's mouth shut and sending a fragment of tooth into the air. He hit him so hard that the officer was lifted off the ground and flew backward, landing hard on his butt and back.

Baldur didn't hesitate; adding gravity to his force, he swung the book like a club, slamming the hard edge of the binding into the side of the man's head. Duffy's face and neck twisted under the staggering blow, and he rolled facedown onto the marble floor, blood dripping from his mouth and shattered jaw.

The Knight of the Inner Sphere was a fighter, that could not be denied. He was reeling from two savage blows to the head, but still clung to consciousness. Baldur kicked him hard, again, this time aiming his boot just behind the lieutenant's ear, lifting him slightly off the floor. Duffy dropped face first. A thin steam of blood oozed across the gray marble floor as he succumbed.

## DROPSHIP *WANDERER*
## LOOTERA SPACEPORT
## 1528 HOURS

"Where have you been?" Paul Moon asked from the tactical display as Baldur entered the room.

"There was something I needed to pick up before we departed," he replied. "I take it we are ready to launch? I saw your Ghosts are no longer on the perimeter."

"Right on schedule," Inanna said as Baldur moved to the holodisplay table to check the sea of green lights flickering before him.

"I also saw what looked like a Com Guard armored patrol stationed at the west gate," he said to Paul Moon. "Is there anything I need to be concerned about, *quineg*?"

Moon actually smiled at him, still a somewhat disturbing sight for Baldur. "*Neg.* Let's just say the Com Guard patrol is all tied up at the moment. Their vehicles are parked as if they are in a guard position."

"Sitrep?" Baldur asked.

"Fully loaded," Inanna said. "We had some last-minute replacements—mostly in the scientist caste. Some families got cold feet. Nicasio authorized other families from the approved list to take their place. Also, one shipment of industrial parts never arrived. We supplemented it with items from our auxiliary list."

"No reaction yet from the Star League forces?"

"None," Paul Moon said. "I did receive a troubling report, however, that the column heading to Chhaiya was ambushed some forty-two kilometers from their objective. It seems Russou Howell was not quite a man of his word."

*He used our plan to his own advantage. It lacked honor. The old Russou Howell would not have behaved this way. None of us are the men we used to be.* "That is regrettable, but nothing we can influence—nor does it impact our plans."

"*Aff*," Inanna agreed. "We are good to go. All we need is for you to give the word."

Baldur felt their eyes on him. He turned to face Paul Moon squarely, looking up at the man he had spent a lifetime hating. *We have gone a long way toward healing our wounds. That healing needs to be complete now if we are to survive.*

"*Neg.* Paul Moon, you led the counterattack on Huntress against the SLDF. They thought that fight was over. You are a true Smoke Jaguar at heart. Me giving that order, as a Nova Cat, and with my background, would be wrong. You lead them—as you always have."

Paul Moon nodded to Baldur, then picked up the microphone. "This is Ghost Actual to all ships. Today's codephrase is Charred Rabbit. We are only leaving Huntress behind—not the core of who we are as a people. We will prevail and show the universe what real honor and pride is. Our journey will be long, and we will face hardships, but in the end we will control our destinies, and one day we will resume our place in the stars." He paused for a long moment, and glanced at Baldur. "All vessels launch—I say again, launch!"

A roar under and around them made Baldur vibrate as the fleet began its journey. Paul Moon reached up and tore the Star League patch off his fatigues, followed by the patch for the Eridani Light Horse. "It appears, Baldur, that you and I have one more thing in common: we have both betrayed our word."

# CHAPTER 31

ALPHA GALAXY COMMAND POST
RAKT-JABADA
ABYSMAL CONTINENT, HUNTRESS
THE KERENSKY CLUSTER, CLAN SPACE
24 AUGUST 3060

Galaxy Commander Myers looked at Paul Masters and suppressed the disdain he felt for the man. Masters was a military man; that much he respected—Myers could see it in everything from his haircut to the way he wore his uniform. His "Knights of the Inner Sphere" were an affront, though. *How dare a House presume it possesses the honor a knight might cherish? These warriors of the Inner Sphere know nothing of true honor.* And as to the Star League that Paul Masters represented, that was a farce—a government in name only. Respect had to be earned.

"I appreciate you making the time for us to meet," Masters said as he took his seat. "I hope our peoples can become good neighbors now that you are on Huntress."

Myers grinned. *He begins from a position of weakness.* "I have no intention of being neighbors, good or otherwise."

Masters's face went pink at Rik's words. "Are you planning on leaving—or is that some sort of threat, Galaxy Commander? The Star League does not take such statements lightly."

*Good, he is easily upset.* "No threat. Your Star League Defense Force is formidable, but it can be defeated—I have shown that. Where the other Clans faltered in the Great Refusal, the Goliath Scorpions demonstrated that you can be bled...that you can be bested in combat. Even now my Khan is making sure the other Clans know this. How long do you think you can survive once the other Clans smell your blood?"

Masters girded himself against Myers's taunts, even forcing a grin. "Your people were defeated in the Grand Refusal. The Clans would be reminded what we did to the Jaguars. If you believe we are so easily crushed, we will devour any and all comers—just as the Smoke Jaguars learned."

"We are not the Smoke Jaguars."

"You are not. They were a proud, downright arrogant people. Their arrogance proved to be their ultimate downfall."

"On this, Paul Masters, I agree. I did not agree to this meeting to bandy words with you, though. It has been said by Nicholas Kerensky that every discussion between two rivals is a test of wills and words."

"I am not a diplomat," Masters admitted. "This role has been thrust upon me. I accept it because that is what men like you and I do. We adapt to survive. That is one of the things I admire about your people. You came here and tamed these worlds far from your home and grew into a great culture."

"Great *cultures*," Myers corrected his guest.

"Of course, cultures," Masters replied. "Your Nicholas Kerensky quote is not far off. I may have to use that myself sometime. We need not exchange harsh words, Galaxy Commander. You bested us in a Trial of Possession. We honor your traditions in this case. I am not here to be at loggerheads. I want to ensure our two governments can work together—that's all."

Myers nodded. "Very well then, Paul Masters. In the spirit of this kinship, perhaps you can explain to me what the Star League is doing with the Smoke Jaguar merchant fleet."

Clearly his question caught the Star League commander off guard. "We are not doing anything yet with the merchant fleet. It was my hope to open up trade with the Clans at some point, but we need to stabilize Huntress first."

*They are still struggling with this Jaguar and his band of raiders...that may yet be useful.* "We detected the entire Smoke Jaguar merchant fleet deploying their jump sails earlier today."

"That's not possible. We ordered those ships to hold in position."

"They are not."

Masters activated his wristcomp. "This is Knight Actual—patch me through to the spaceport immediately."

Myers could hear some of the terse words from Masters's tiny earpiece. "*What?* Why wasn't I contacted? I don't care if the comms-net was down. Someone should've gotten word to me or Colonel Antonescu."

There was another pause. "What do you mean, 'ambushed'? We were supposed to be the ones springing the trap. Who's in command of Lootera?" Another face-reddening pause. "Damn it—what is going on? Put Lieutenant Duffy on. What? How did *that* happen? Where is spaceport security? Have you contacted the Com Guards? They had a patrol in the city. *Damn it!* How did this happen? Contact the task force—get the commodore on the horn and let him know what's happening. They're deploying *where*?" The muffled voice was clearly attempting to explain what was happening, and with very little success, from the expressions on Masters's face.

"Would you like some privacy?" Myers said, doing very little to suppress his glee at the Star League ambassador's discomfort.

Paul lowered his wristcomp slowly and shook his head. "There's been a series of incidents on Jaguar Prime. The whole Smoke Jaguar DropShip fleet has taken off."

What had been funny a moment earlier suddenly hit Rik Myers differently. "All of them, *quiaff*?"

"Yes—that's right. They are burning to the nadir jump point."

"What of the warrior caste? Who is aboard the ships?" *And where are they going?*

"From initial reports, a percentage of the surviving warriors and the other castes were on board. The HPG is offline, along with our command network. Our satellite network is down—apparently the technicians working space control sabotaged the equipment. That's got to be why we didn't detect the JumpShips deploying their sails."

Myers was caught. He had WarShips at the jump point. *Do I offer assistance to the Star League, or let them falter?* What concerned him most was the warrior caste. *One of the reasons I came here was to harvest those genes for our own pool. Have I lost my chance?*

"I wish I could extend assistance," he said, "but that decision must be made by my Khan." That was not true. *I have the authority to act as I see fit. Until we know what is happening, this provides us with a good test of what the Star League is capable of.*

Paul Masters rose to his feet. "If you don't mind—I need to get back to Lootera and get this situation under control."

"Of course," Myers said, extending his hand. "Should you need any assistance, I would be happy to pose the matter to my Khan."

As Paul Masters left his office, Rik Myers moved over to the window and looked out at the clouding sky. *Those Jaguar warriors are going to settle somewhere—that is the only way they would have the cooperation of the lesser castes. This is not just their warriors—it is a possible colony.* A part of him was angry. He had sent Watch agents to Jaguar Prime. They had provided some wonderful reports on the Jaguar—Russou Howell—but nothing pointed to an audacious move like this.

"Where are you going?" he asked the empty room. "And what are your intentions once you get there?"

**DROPSHIP *WANDERER***
**OUTBOUND TO NADIR JUMP POINT**
**HUNTRESS, CLAN SPACE**

"We just received word from Commodore Beresick and the Star League task force," the communications officer aboard the Nova Cat DropShip said as he moved into the tactical operations room. "We are ordered to halt acceleration and heave to."

"Does Star Captain Ramsey believe they can intercept us?" Inanna asked from her seat.

"Negative," the comms officer replied. "He calculated the flight path and speed of the task force. It would be against the laws of physics for them to alter course in time to intercept us."

"Beresick is a skilled ship commander," Baldur said with all of the respect he could muster. "But he is chasing ghosts. We fooled him, plain and simple. Now that he is deployed, he cannot simply stop and turn around fast enough."

Inanna had chosen the bait carefully, something the commodore could not resist. There was an old Clan saying: "You cannot fight the math," and physics was all math.

"Any word from Huntress?" Paul Moon asked.

"*Neg*, Star Colonel," the comms officer said, honoring Moon's previous rank. "The virus we uploaded into their communications network is adaptive and resilient. Every few minutes a new variant of it pops up. They can purge their systems, but that will take time."

"Until we are clear of Clan space, we cannot assume we are safe," Moon said.

Baldur wholeheartedly agreed. *We have stolen from the Star League a valuable prize—a fleet of ships and the people of Huntress. They will not take that action lying down.*

"We have three aerospace fighters," he said. "Do we deploy them on CAP?"

"*Neg*," Moon replied as the comms officer left the room. "Three fighters would not be much protection. The DropShips' guns are ample firepower." He shifted in his seat as *Wanderer* continued to accelerate. "I must admit, our departure seems almost anticlimactic."

"It was the product of good planning and teamwork—including those who did not join us," Inanna replied, adjusting her black hair.

"*Aff*," Baldur said. The people that remained behind had been supportive. There had been competition within some castes to determine who among them would go, as there was more demand for seats on the journey than were available. *The spirit of the Smoke Jaguars still exists despite the Star League's victory. Now they are coming to grips with that reality.* "All we can do at this point is wait and monitor our would-be foes. Keep close eyes on the Goliath Scorpions. The Star League may press them for assistance. Our JumpShip fleet is largely unprotected. Many things can happen—things we did not prepare for."

"You worry too much," Paul Moon said. "Our plans are sound, and our cause is just."

Baldur looked at him solemnly. *Will that be enough?*

**CSJ *STREAKING MIST***
**NADIR JUMP POINT**
**HUNTRESS, CLAN SPACE**
**SIX DAYS LATER...**

The massive *Black Lion*-class battle cruiser felt almost roomy compared to the packed common space aboard the *Wanderer*. Baldur, Inanna, and Paul Moon drifted to the bridge, where a short, muscular Star Captain named Farland greeted them.

Baldur shook his hand. "I take it you had no problem in handling your Star League observers, *quiaff*?"

Captain Farland's grip was tight. "I asked them if they had ever seen the lifeboats on a *Black Lion*-class ship. They said 'no.' So my crew introduced them to the inner workings of several of ours. Alas, their comms system was disabled before they launched. We will squirt a signal to Huntress before we jump...they should be fine, if a bit rank, by the time they are rescued." He seemed quite proud of his accomplishment, as his sarcasm demonstrated.

"Are they healthy?" Baldur asked. The plan had been to avoid killing any SLDF personnel if possible. He was unsure whether Paul Moon had been able to live up to that in the confrontation with the Com Guards at the spaceport. He also did not press the matter with the Elemental.

"They were when I last saw them." Farland shrugged, his twisted smile making Baldur a little nervous.

"Any sign of activity from the Goliath Scorpions?" Moon asked, defusing the tension.

"Only a little," Captain Farland replied. "We used the jump sails to obscure the WarShips charging. The Scorpions were probing, trying to get an angle to see what we were doing. It wasn't until two days ago that we confirmed they finally got line of sight on us."

"Did they respond?" Baldur pressed.

"*Neg*," Farland said. "They are curious little bugs, but no one wants to pull the tail of a *Black Lion*. We deployed our fighters in CAP, and they backed off. Apparently they only wanted to see what we were up to."

"Any risk that the *Invisible Truth* will intervene?"

Farland grinned even more broadly as he shook his head. "The commodore, well, he is persistent. He and the task force did a sling-shot around Huntress and are on a high-G burn here. There are two problems he is facing. The first—he has accelerated to the point that he will pass right by us so fast he will be lucky to get off a shot or two."

"And the second?" Inanna asked.

"We will be long gone by the time he arrives. He is eighteen hours late, I am afraid. He is fighting both the laws of physics and the fact that we planned this well."

Baldur looked at the Star Captain and smiled as well. *The logistics had been taxing, but it seemed to be working.* "Are we ready to jump, *quiaff?*"

"*Aff*, once all ships are moored and secured. We have one jump sail still being retracted. There was an issue with her sail-winch, but it has been resolved. We can go in one hour or so."

"Excellent. Is there anything else we need to know, Captain?" Baldur pressed.

"The SLDF has gotten their ground comms to work. They have been broadcasting a message to the commander of this task force." Farland's eyes drifted to Paul Moon. "He wants to talk."

"I imagine he does," Moon said. He glanced over at Baldur. "Should I respond?"

Baldur nodded. "Affirmative. We want no ill-will if it can be avert-ed."

"It is a little late for that," Captain Farland said. "You have stolen his merchant fleet and two WarShips—not to mention a lot of person-nel the Star League felt were theirs. I would imagine that he is a step past slightly miffed."

"Best get this over with, then," Moon said.

Captain Farland led them to the comms station, and Paul straight-ened his uniform as the comms officer established the link.

"This is Paul Moon."

There was a delay, then the Star League ambassador came into focus on the display. Anger was written on his face, Baldur could see it. The bags under his eyes told Moon that matters on Huntress were not being taken lightly. "Sergeant Moon, this is Paul Masters. I order you to return to Huntress. If you do, we will waive all charges of trea-son and mutiny."

Paul was unaffected by the orders. "You will find I resigned my commission in the Light Horse just prior to committing these actions, sir—that is, unless your computer net is still down."

There was another delay. "Sergeant, I cannot simply allow you to steal these ships. They are Star League property."

"We are not stealing them," Paul countered. "We are merely bor-rowing them—for an extended period of time."

"Don't play semantics with me. You are taking those vessels without permission. If you jump, you will be considered a renegade fleet. I will send word to the Inner Sphere and the Clans. There will be no safe haven for you or your people anywhere." Masters was becoming more agitated with each word.

"We did not force these crews and people into this act," Moon said. "They came of their own accord. And as for your alerting the Star League, I suggest you have the commodore prepare for jump operations. Your HPG core is in the hold of the *Sharpsburg*. The Inner Sphere is a long way from here."

"This is high treason!"

"This is freedom," Moon countered. "I am doing you a favor, sir. I am taking away warriors who might fall under the sway of the Jaguar. I am giving hope to people who did not want to live under your rule. You conquered Huntress, but you never truly defeated what made the Smoke Jaguars the Smoke Jaguars. These people were unhappy on a Star League world. They want to set their own course in life, control their own destiny."

Baldur found himself nodding with Moon's words.

"Where are you going?" Masters asked.

Moon shook his head. "That is classified. Know this though—we do not see you as the enemy, not yet. As long as you do not interfere with us, you have nothing to worry about."

"You can't just go off and re-form the Smoke Jaguars," Masters cautioned.

"We have no intention of that," Moon replied. "We are going to create something better—something more in line with the true path of Nicholas Kerensky."

Masters turned his gaze toward the camera. "Baldur and Inanna of the Nova Cats...I thought your Clan was our ally."

Baldur moved into full view of the screen. "We are not enemies, but the Star League would be wrong to think that it holds sway over us and our actions."

"I ord—I beseech you all, stop this now," Masters said. "If you continue, you will go beyond our protection. I cannot guarantee your safety."

"We do not ask for your guarantee," Paul Moon replied. "Nor is any protection expected. Good life to you, Paul Masters. And remember my words. Do not look for us—you may not like what you find."

Before the Star League ambassador could respond, Moon killed the channel.

Captain Farland grinned and shattered the momentary silence. "That went well," he snapped sarcastically. "I suggest you settle in. We are about to begin a long journey. Jump prep begins in twenty."

## STAR LEAGUE DEFENSE FORCE HQ
## TWO HOURS LATER...

"Sir." Commodore Beresick sounded strained over the secured comms system in Paul Masters' office. "We've begun deceleration, but at best we're going to be a week or more behind them."

"Without a destination," Masters said, "what would be the point of trying to pursue?"

"Sir," the commodore pressed. "You can't just let them jump away. What will the Clans think of the Star League?"

Paul Masters leaned back in his chair and for the first time noticed something was missing from his bookshelf: the Smoke Jaguar *Remembrance. That was why they were in my office. I should have known.* "I will send word to the Clans that we exiled malcontents of the former Jaguar ranks. I will tell them they were aiding the insurgency and rather than execute them, we sent them off into the unknown—like their Dark Caste." *We can ill afford to appear weak. Huntress is surrounded by bitter and angry Clan warriors looking for any sign of weakness.*

"What about the Goliath Scorpions? They saw all of this unfold, didn't they?"

Masters allowed himself a thin smile. "Let the Scorpions think what they want. Our intelligence tells us the Clans rarely share intel with each other. One Clan knows what happened...so what? They won't tell anyone that they were as powerless as we were to stop what unfolded. That secret is safe because of the nature of the Clans."

"Where does our intelligence staff believe they have gone?" Beresick asked.

"They purged all the stellar cartography data stored by the Smoke Jaguars. We had already sent a copy back to the Inner Sphere with the rest of the task force, so the data will be there—but that is a year away from us even beginning a search."

"Are we going to search for them?"

Masters shook his head. It was a question he had posed to himself many times in the past week. "To what end, Commodore? If we did find them, they would rather fight us instead of returning to Huntress. Looking for them now would serve no purpose."

"Is that wise—over the long run?"

"Who knows? I would rather not have their offspring wanting revenge on us. Yes, they stole our merchant fleet, but they did not battle their way off-planet. Our casualties were minor except what we lost to the Jaguar. Let's focus on him. If Moon, Baldur, and Inanna want to go off and play colonist, I say we are better off without them."

"I hope you are right, sir," the commodore replied.

*As do I,* Masters thought. *Only the future can judge my actions now.*

# CHAPTER 32

CSJ *STREAKING MIST*
SYSTEM TW2016, ZENITH JUMP POINT
EXODUS ROAD
10 MAY 3061

Baldur was mentally exhausted from the discussions. When he had conceived of saving his former Clan, he did not realize how much bickering would be involved. Even coming up with a name for what to call themselves had become a heated debate—one still unresolved. The trip itself was a test of mental integrity—adding the political debate only made it seem longer. *It is not enough to make the voyage–now we are forced to confront our future.*

He sat at the conference table and eyed Paul Moon across from him. The Elemental's arms were crossed, and from the expression on his face, he was just as annoyed by the debate as Baldur was. Paul had been elected chairman of the ruling council, the delegated body attempting to figure out their destiny. He had not lobbied for the position: it had been thrust on him.

The droning of debate gave Baldur time to scan the faces in the room. Smoke Jaguars all, except for him and Inanna. The last three months had changed his former Clan's view of their comrades. Many disliked that the Nova Cats had turned against the Clans in the Great Refusal. Now they were jumping through the stars under the protection of the Nova Cat fleet. On some ships Nova Cat crews mingled with the ex-Jaguars, who came to respect the Cats. Even the delegates in the room treated Baldur with almost the same respect that Moon himself had. It helped that Paul Moon had told the ruling council that Baldur and Inanna had planned their exodus. Many were thankful, but there was something else—a respect a warrior received from the other castes. *Even when given their freedom, our people have been bred to defer to the warrior caste.* Moon had demonstrated extreme levels of patience in the debate. *I would have cut this conversation off two hours ago, yet he does not. He wants their opinions heard.*

Baldur took time to jot down notes in his notebook. It was an archaic tool, physical paper and pen. He preferred it to his noteputer. The things he wrote in the notebook were for him, not for computer storage, where anyone might access them. *Who knows, maybe one day these notes will help sort all of this out? We have been through a great deal, but there is more fire we must face—I know it. Who can say what will come out of that coming inferno?*

"I suggest that we break for the day," said Arahoff, the technician caste representative. "All of this talk...it's giving me a headache."

All eyes shifted to Moon. "Very well. We will pick this up to-morrow. However, tomorrow will be the last discussion of rotating families between ships. A decision will need to be made. We need to address more pressing issues—like the plans for constructing our housing once we make landfall." There were grumbles, but slowly the representatives left, leaving only Inanna, Paul, and Baldur.

"Why do you let them get mired in such debate?" Baldur asked, more out of curiosity than anything else.

"If I cut them off, they will tell their people their voices were not heard," Paul said, putting his noteputer down. "It will cause unneces-sary tension and resentment. Best let them argue themselves hoarse than to simply expedite things and make the decision."

Baldur grinned. "I never knew you had this kind of patience."

Moon looked somberly at his former subordinate. "I was impul-sive in my youth. I did things that I regret—things that led us here. We all must evolve and grow. I know that now."

The words hit Baldur like a PPC blast. His face reddened, and for a moment he felt a twist of guilt. *I have to remind myself over and over that this is not the same man who exiled me to Huntress to wither and die.*

"What is past is past," he finally managed to say. "We have all been forced to change, Paul. Look at me." He gestured to his face. "I am not the same warrior you clashed with so often. I have been through the fire of the Grand Refusal and come out a Nova Cat."

"That is the thing," Moon said, turning his head slightly but main-taining eye contact. "You look different—even sound a little differ-ent—but you are still Trent. Every time we are together I am faced with my mistakes—forced to confront my poor choices."

"Should I leave?"

There was a pause. "*Neg*," Moon said in the deep tone unique to Elementals. "I find that sometimes I need the reminder. My choices led the Smoke Jaguars to ruin, and even to the end of the Crusade in the Inner Sphere. Having you here makes me remember that. It forces me to be patient and take the time to make the right choices. You are a ghost, a shadow, always there to remind me of the ramifications of what I do."

Moon rose and left the room. Baldur was at a loss for words until Inanna came to his side. "He is a proud man. You besting him in that Circle of Equals, telling him who you were, it changed him."

*She may be right.* "Truth. I do not think I alone changed him. Paul experienced the greatest loss of all—Huntress. It was his responsibility to save the homeworld, and he lost it. He had to live as a bondsman to the Light Horse. He had to watch his entire life dismantled and erased by the Star League. Any one of those would have changed a man. All of those things, they made the man that just left here."

"They remade you too. You embraced the man who nearly destroyed you—who led you to make your decisions. A lesser man would not have taken Paul Moon into their confidence, even after a Circle of Equals."

"We needed him."

"*We, quineg?* It was not *us* who needed Paul Moon as an ally, Baldur—it was *you.* As much as you have become his conscience, you needed to complete the circle that began years ago with Paul Moon."

Baldur looked up at her for a long, silent moment. *She may be right, but that does not mean I have to acknowledge it.* Confronting Paul Moon had been a moment of hubris on his part, mixed with a hope that he could end the ruse he had been living since the Great Refusal. At the same time, he did want to end the rift between them. *I could not let that hate define who I am and what I have done to the Jaguars. I am Baldur, and yet the greater part of me is still Trent.* That he never admitted it out loud was an entirely different matter. "Inanna, there are times you make me want to punch you."

She grinned. "My words strike home, *aff.*"

"*Aff.*" He nodded. "I say we go and work off the frustration you have stirred up. Some combat drills with Woodall Winters might pummel those words from my ears."

She took his hand. "I have another idea. One just as physical, but with less chance of bruises..." She squeezed. As he looked at her in surprise, she smiled even more broadly, her eyebrows cocking upward in a way he had never seen before.

"Well bargained and done," he said in a throaty whisper, and rose from his seat.

## ALPHA GALAXY COMMAND POST
## RAKT-JABADA

Galaxy Commander Myers looked down at the hospital bed Oliver Howell was strapped to. The man was badly bruised, especially his face. The right side of his face was swollen, and his puffed lip was cracked and bleeding. Bandages covered the cut on his left shoulder where a chair had been broken over him in the struggle to apprehend him. *The Watch did not act with a great deal of honor in apprehending him. Good.*

Howell stirred as Myers moved to his side. "You are wondering where you are, and who I am, *quiaff*?"

"*Neg,*" Howell replied. "I see your Clan and rank insignias. You are Rik Myers of the Goliath Scorpions."

"Good, your brain was not damaged in your capture," Myers said. "And you may have surmised why you are here as well."

"*Neg.*" A bit of drool from Howell's damaged mouth ran down his cheek. "I was in a bar, and the next thing I knew, three men were on top of me, beating me."

"You are a warrior fighting with the Jaguar, *quiaff*?"

Oliver Howell stiffened at the mention of the Jaguar. He said nothing.

Myers moved around the end of the bed, hovering over his prisoner's face. "Do not deny it, Oliver Howell. The Watch has been monitoring you for two weeks. You are not like the warriors who chose to flee Huntress. You fight on. We are both Clan—that is something I respect, warrior to warrior."

"What do you want from me?" Howell managed, testing the straps that held him in place.

"Russou Howell has become a nagging pain for the Star League. I am not going to ask you to betray him. In that capacity, he serves the needs of the Goliath Scorpions as well. No, what I want from you is something else."

"What?"

"I want to know where this Paul Moon has taken the warrior caste."

The query surprised Oliver Howell; Myers saw it in his face. "What makes you think I know?"

"The Jaguar struck at the Star League at the exact hour Moon and his people left Huntress. Coincidence...? *Neg!* You are one of his most trusted aides. Russou Howell would not have attacked if he did not know the plans of Moon and his Nova Cat henchmen. You have been seen at Russou Howell's side, according to my Watch. I think you were with him, or he confided to you where they were going. I want that information."

Oliver struggled against his straps again, to no avail. "Why do you, a Goliath Scorpion, want to know—or care?"

"My people respect the past, and the past is where the Smoke Jaguars belong. Not on some world building a new colony to seek revenge or to strike when we least expect it. There is more, though I doubt you will understand. We are stewards of history. Those warriors represent the last generation of Smoke Jaguars. Their genetic material deserves to be preserved, or even used if worthy. While you may not like the idea of your fellow Jaguars being a museum exhibit, my people revere the past and what your Clan represented."

Oliver Howell laughed. "I was taught that about you Scorpions, but thought it was mere myth."

"I assure you," Myers said, "we are quite real, as is our desire to possess the Smoke Jaguars."

"If I knew such information, I would not share it with you."

Myers nodded as he moved to Oliver Howell's side. "I could make you a bondsman. You were bested in a fight. As my bondsman, you would be compelled to share the information with me."

Oliver tried to smile, but his battered face would not comply. Only the corner of his mouth raised slightly, twisting his grin. "I was not defeated in a Circle of Equals or a trial. I was ambushed in a bar. You can wrap a bondcord on my wrist, but I will not be bound by it."

Myers nodded. "I understand. You have a misguided sense of honor to a Clan that no longer exists."

"As long as Russou Howell lives, the Smoke Jaguars live," Oliver said defiantly.

"A shallow view," Myers countered. "If you will not share the information with me honorably, I am forced to use other means."

"Torture me if you wish," Howell replied. "I will not give you what you want."

Myers held up a syringe filled with a bright-green serum. "Have you heard of necrosia?"

Oliver blinked nervously. "I have. Your warriors drug themselves so they can see things that are not there."

Myers shook his head. "A misunderstanding of lesser minds. In the right dose, it opens your mind to visions of the past and future. My people use it to help us achieve focus, our *Cestra*, a view of how we are to proceed in life."

"You blur your thinking with a drug—that much I understand."

Myers licked his lips and smiled. *So narrow a view.* "You do not know that we have studied necrosia extensively. We know how it works on the brain, especially when combined with other drugs. In the proper doses, it can make someone under its influence susceptible to suggestion—even revealing one's innermost secrets. In the right mix, it can activate the pleasure centers of the brain when you speak the truth, or trigger agony when you withhold information—firing every nerve in your body to experience pain. Sometimes that pain feels like burning, other times it feels like millions of pins piercing you to the bone.

"I have seen warriors weather this storm, but in the end, the necrosia always breaks them. All talk eventually. There is a downside, unfortunately. The longer they resist, the more permanent damage takes hold."

"Permanent damage?"

"Fight long enough, and the damage to your brain is extensive. Some are left as vegetables. Others are crippled. For some, the pain does not end when the drug wears off. They live only a week or two in absolute agony as their brain fires off endless messages of pain to their bodies. In the end, they lie on a bed much like this one, festering in their own feces, vomit, and sweat, screaming until their vocal cords rupture.

"So, Oliver Howell, where did Paul Moon go?"

Howell glared up at Myers and at the syringe he held. His jaw locked. "I am a Smoke Jaguar. I do not fear a needle or your hollow threats. Bring it on, Rik Myers."

The Goliath Scorpion failed to suppress his grin as he jabbed the needle into Oliver Howell's arm.

## THREE DAYS LATER...

"You are planning *what*?" Star Colonel Ahrissta Lunde of the Eighth Scorpion Dragoons asked in stunned disbelief. "The Khan would never sanction such an operation."

"Watch your tone with me, Ahrissta," Rik Myers responded. "I am unaccustomed to my subordinates questioning my plans."

"With all due respect, sir," Star Colonel Adam Yeh said, "usually your plans make more sense. This is folly."

"I came to Huntress to reap the remains of the Smoke Jaguars," Myers said firmly, his gaze shifting between the two Star Colonels. "My interpretation of those orders has to be changed. The best of that former Clan has set off to this Wayside V. I intend to fulfill my mission. I will go there and claim what is rightfully ours." *What is rightfully mine.*

"Sir," Star Colonel Lunde said in an almost pleading tone, "the world you speak of is a year away. Khan Suvorov will never sanction you to take Alpha Galaxy away for that long a quest, no matter how visionary it may be. The rewards do not match the risk."

"I do not intend to ask the Khan for permission. There is no time. They already have a three-month head start. Waiting for approval would only give them time to establish their colony and prepare its defenses. It is best to strike now, before they become a greater threat. I will leave the Eighth Dragoons here as a garrison. I will only take my Thirty-fifth Cuirassiers. They should be more than a match for whatever paltry force the Jaguars have."

"Sir, you must realize we are not equipped for such a journey. It is almost all the way to the Inner Sphere. The Grand Council may misinterpret such a move by our Clan. There are political ramifications."

"I understand those, perhaps better than you."

"Your source for this information, were they reliable?" Star Colonel Yeh asked.

"*Aff,*" Myers replied. *Right up to the moment of death.* "He endured the Drink of Truth for two days. In the end, he gave me everything he knew." They both knew what he was referring to, and the implications of how he obtained the information. *That is right, Lunde–I am willing to go that far for the victory I deserve.*

"I have had a vision," Myers continued. "It gnaws at me in my sleep. We were deprived the rewards of taking this toehold on Huntress. I underestimated the Smoke Jaguars once...now they have fled to the stars. I must fulfill this mission, if not for me, then for our Clan."

"It is a year there and a year back," Star Colonel Lunde replied. "Much can happen during such a period. The Khan would never approve this course of action."

"If you wish to report it to her, go ahead," Myers replied flatly. "The HPG here is destroyed. By the time you jump to Roche and back, I will be gone. This *will* happen, Star Colonel, with or without your cooperation. If you desire a Circle of Equals, I need only remind you the results of our last one." Myers grinned at her like an animal about to feast. She had challenged him two years earlier, and paid the price of a broken shoulder.

"I am obligated to inform the Khan," she replied through gritted teeth.

"Very well. In the meantime, I want our best logisticians to begin loading our ships for the journey. I have a long voyage ahead, and I mean to get underway as soon as possible."

# CHAPTER 33

Paul Moon stepped off of the gangway of the *Wanderer* and out onto the tarmac of Wayside V. The air was slightly thinner than what he had been breathing for a year aboard the DropShip and WarShip. This air was not sterile or purified, there was dust—and pollen. Inanna sneezed behind him, and he understood her reaction.

The planet itself was what he had prepared himself for. The clouds hung low over what were once seas, but now were the only pockets of life. The trees were like mesquite, though leafier. The grasses were deep green, and moss seemed to grow more like grass, with strange stalks that billowed in the wind. The clouds were dark and high, like thunderstorms waiting to burst. The sunlight on his skin felt strange, warming. *I have been living too long in the same environment at the same temperatures.*

Across the tarmac, ten BattleMechs lined up in two rows of five. They were familiar to him, gray with black spots and white dots—long the camouflage of the Smoke Jaguars. Moon had been in contact with the garrison commander, Star Captain Av Weaver. The garrison confirmed Moon's peaceful intentions, and Weaver had agreed to meet them on the tarmac, which was little more than a flat field of stone that crunched under Moon's feet as he stepped out.

Av Weaver stepped forward to greet him. What struck Paul Moon first was his age. His hair had streaks of gray in its short-cropped cut. His face was wrinkled, his eyes sullen. He moved like a warrior, but to Paul Moon he was a warrior past his prime. *I need to watch that thinking. It made me misjudge Trent.* Moon carefully hid his surprise as Weaver saluted him.

"I am Star Captain Av Weaver of the Forty-seventh Garrison Cluster of the Smoke Jaguars Zeta Galaxy. I bid you a long overdue welcome to Wayside V."

"Star Colonel Paul Moon. These are my advisors—Baldur and Inanna of the Nova Cats." Both offered a salute, which Weaver reluctantly returned.

"Nova Cats? Why would a Smoke Jaguar be with Nova Cat warriors?"

"What was the last news you had of our Clan?" Paul asked.

"Seven years ago," Weaver said. "They posted us here rather than send us to back to Huntress. We were too good to die in battle, but too old to waste sending home. So we were sent here to garrison this world. We thought our people had forgotten us."

"Much has changed," Paul Moon said. "We should talk with you and your warriors—someplace private, perhaps."

Weaver escorted Moon and his small entourage to a series of military structures off the tarmac. As he did, other DropShips began to land, and clearly the number of them coming in caught his attention as they walked.

Paul Moon calmly told Av Weaver and his Binary what had happened. The re-formation of the Star League, the loss of the worlds in the Inner Sphere, then the loss of Huntress. He told them of their exodus and their plans to settle Wayside V. It took almost an hour, during which no one from the garrison even asked a question. Some shook their heads in disbelief, others sat with mouths agape, stunned at the news.

"You have come to rebuild our Clan, *quiaff*?" the Star Captain finally managed to ask.

"*Neg*," Paul replied. With that word, he saw the last glimmer of hope fade from the older man's face. "If we were to be the Smoke Jaguars here, both the Star League and the Clans would come at us. We are alone. Our intent is to preserve the best of what we are. In our hearts beats the Smoke Jaguar Clan. They cannot take our spirit from us. But to the rest of the universe, we must become something else—something new."

"Everything we were, everyone we knew, they are lost to us," said one of the other warriors, Star Commander McLean Hoyt.

"Some did not come with us," Moon said. "The fighting in the Inner Sphere and on Huntress consumed our ranks. Very few remained on Huntress, to wage a war of insurgency."

Reed Bowen, a bald warrior who wore his despair on his face, spoke up next. "You have come here, but this is not a good world for a colony. The atmospheric processors are terraforming the planet, but it is a slow process."

"We brought with us everything we need to make a viable colony," Inanna said.

"This is a harsh world," Bowen said. "It is unforgiving. Our laborers and technicians have done remarkable work—but terraforming takes many years."

"You warriors," Baldur spoke up. "You represent some of the last Smoke Jaguars of your caste. You have an important role to play in our plans. We will need your strength and leadership to rekindle the flames of what made your people a great Clan."

There was a long, awkward silence in the room. Finally, Star Captain Weaver spoke up. "We are set in our ways. I am not sure we can simply adapt."

"I understand," Paul Moon said. "I too was set in my ways. A lifetime of doctrine will do that to any warrior. From birth we are wired to a certain way of thinking. When something clashes with that pattern, we resist it, we fight it. It is alien to us. It was not our intent to disrupt your garrison here—but the Clan you were waiting for to relieve you is gone. You have been forgotten by everyone but our people. Despite what others might think, I believe you still have something to offer us. We can be better because of your training and your strength."

Reed Bowen nodded. "I hear your words, Star Colonel. You are asking a great deal of us. Many times we thought we had been left here to die. Now we find that our only salvation may be to change who we are. That is not an easy choice."

"Our caste was meant to rule," Weaver added. "You speak of the lower castes having a voice in matters. I would chafe at taking orders from laborers or merchants."

Baldur jumped in. "The castes are gone—left dead and buried on Huntress with most of the warrior caste. For a colony to survive, everyone must take on different roles. The old designations and rules would limit our growth."

"When I was a bondsman to the Star League," Paul said, "I worked as a technician. I resisted it at first, but I found I enjoyed the work. It taught me a great deal about myself and what it would take for us to survive. There are times that we are all laborers, techs, or whatever is needed."

Eny, one of the warriors who had been silent up to this point, spoke up. "I will not work as a laborer. I am a warrior. I was created for one purpose—for battle."

Baldur pounced on him quickly, but with a hint of compassion in his voice. "I hear your words, Eny. But there are no battles left for you to fight. I know it is hard to hear, but the Smoke Jaguars are gone. They were annihilated. The Clans were defeated in the Great Refusal. You wish to fight, but there are no more wars for you—for any of you."

His gaze swept across the nine Zeta Galaxy warriors in the conference room. "However, there may be a time when we need to fight. When that happens, we will join you in battle—gladly. For now, we need builders, not fighters. You see yourself as above the other castes. Well, it is now time for you to lead them, and the best way to lead them is by example."

Eny rose to his feet abruptly, sending his chair wheeling into the wall behind him, his face red with anger. He stormed out of the room.

Star Captain Weaver spoke, "He has not been the same since his sibmate Ballard died last year of a cancer we were ill-prepared to treat. I would ask you to forgive his attitude and offer understanding. He just learned the entire universe he has been living for is gone."

"It is not gone," Paul Moon replied. "We who are left are the heart of the Jaguar. He has people again, and with people there is hope."

"He may yet come around," Av Weaver said. "Though I must admit, I too find this hard to accept. I have been trained to never accept defeat—that death was preferable to submission."

"You were left here because your Clan considered you too old," Inanna weighed in. "You were seen as no longer useful. They placed you on a backwater world because it was easier than sending you back to Huntress. Our arrival means you have purpose again. Your people need you, Star Captain—all of you."

Her calm gaze held each of the other warriors. "We cannot force you to do anything. You must do it of your own accord. But those people in the DropShips outside, they will look to you—it is ingrained in their thinking to do so. Show them what it *really* means to be a warrior of the Smoke Jaguars. Adapt. Aid the weak. Show them your leadership qualities."

Weaver nodded. "We can try. That is all we can do."

"I can ask nothing more of you," Paul Moon said. "Now then, we have a colony to build."

Baldur watched Khan Santin West stride from his shuttlecraft across the tarmac amid the stream of personnel and materials being unloaded from the DropShips. The Khan stood tall above the masses, and as soon as Inanna spotted him, she grabbed Baldur's hand and they moved to intercept him.

Both of them saluted. "Khan West," she said, "your arrival was unexpected."

"We are close to our new home. I fought, and my warriors and I bled on this soil. The chance that I would not see this world again was great—as such, I thought one more visit was in order." West's eyes swept far past the spaceport to the skies and the hills in the distance.

*Is that nostalgia I see in the Khan's eyes?* "Is it much as you remember it?"

West drew a long breath and exhaled. "The air is thicker than I remember, but those clouds...those were one of the things I remembered most about this place. This is a hard rock to build on. It will give these former Jaguars a good foundation, but will test them sorely."

"They are up to the task," Baldur proclaimed.

"I believe they are, Baldur," West replied. "I cannot stay but a day. I want to meet with Paul Moon and this ruling council before I depart. I want them to know our Clans were once competitive rivals and comrades in arms, and I hope that we can remain as such, despite all that has come to pass."

"I am sure Paul Moon will appreciate your words," Inanna said.

"I also came," West said, staring at Baldur's partner, "to say my goodbyes to the two of you."

"You are staying?" Baldur asked Inanna. In all of their time together, he had never asked her to. He assumed she would depart with the rest of the Nova Cats. *She never spoke of her desire to remain.* She had been sending West a steady stream of reports, but Baldur had no idea what her final intentions were. *I am relieved she is staying–not just for the coupling, but for the companionship.*

Inanna only gave him a side glance, and a thin smile. "*Aff,*" she replied. "My fate is with these people. Your farewell is not necessary, my Khan. We shall see each other again—I am sure of that."

"Your voice and vision will be missed," West said. He then turned his steely gaze to Baldur. "And you, Baldur, you have almost restored balance to your life. You have always been with these people in your heart. Now you are a Nova Cat as well. You will be remembered with honor in our ranks—but I know you need to be here. Inanna is not the only one who has foreseen the importance of what you offer these people." There was a ring of prophesy in his voice that Baldur found both reassuring and unnerving.

"Thank you, Khan West. I am indebted to the Nova Cats. Khan Leroux saved me from obscurity. The Nova Cats gave me a new life. I will not dishonor them."

West bowed his head to him in an almost ceremonial manner. Instinctively, Baldur did the same. *Why do I get the feeling he knows we will never see each other again?*

# CHAPTER 34

For more than six months Paul Moon had worked to help his people establish their colony. Mankind had been in the stars for centuries, but there was remarkably little information to go on when it came to establishing a new colony. The Clans were conquerors, not colonists.

The existing garrison structures became the core of the small city they had built. The garrison had gardens and livestock for food, though nowhere near enough for the thousands of arrivals. Their gardening experience about what would grow well was a good starting point. Already two cycles of harvest had been brought in—and the results had been surprisingly plentiful. *I never thought I would find joy in harvesting crops.*

Shelter had proven more challenging. The temporary shelters were badly battered by the storms common to the planet. Mining the iron needed for smelting into construction material had taken three times longer than expected to get started, and required converting a BattleMech to mining operations. Soon, they had steel.

Oil drilling had proven much easier, which had led to plastic fabrication and much-needed lubricants. Limestone mining, mostly done in the near-vacuum of the old continents, provided stone and concrete—but that too took much longer than expected. Wood was in short supply, as the forested areas produced a short, gnarled species of tree ill-suited for lumber. Permanent structures were slowly built—and the garrison began to look more and more like a thriving community.

Everyone chipped in, regardless of the tasks. The ones who chafed the most at this division of labor were the warriors, especially those from the Wayside garrison. The idea that the colony was not a true Smoke Jaguar base for rebuilding the Clan led to constant clashes. It had required Paul Moon beating Eny in a Circle of Equals to get him to assist with the iron mining, piloting the mining 'Mech every day.

The solution Paul had arrived at was to drill the warriors regularly. He did not want them to lose their combat edge. They ran together each morning, did calisthenics, and practiced tactics. The rest of the time, the warriors were expected to work, just like the rest of the colonists. *The drilling gives them purpose and fulfills the need of keeping them prepared, should we ever need it.* This reduced the friction between the garrison troops and the colonists, but the underlying tension remained. As Inanna had put it, "They want to be part of something that no longer exists except in their hearts and memories."

The DropShip and JumpShip crews were tasked with locating water sources and mining rare ores in the system. Water had proved easy to find in space—there was a great deal of ice trapped in asteroids, which could be burned up in Wayside V's atmosphere. The technicians assured Paul that the asteroids were improving the atmosphere, but he did not yet feel the difference. *The rains here pour almost every two days or so. There are weeks where I yearn for the sun.*

Moon spent a great deal of time working with Baldur and Inanna, who had been completely accepted into the colony as if they had always been Jaguars. Baldur had demonstrated a knack for logistics, organizing complicated—and boring—construction schedules. Streets were laid out and eventually paved.

Baldur and Inanna's hands were everywhere in the production of the colony. Inanna had established a school for the children—including those from the sibko they saved on Huntress. Dealing with children, especially civilian children, was not easy for Moon. *They stare at me because of my size and my role in the community.* He sometimes ordered them to stop looking at him, but whenever he did, it only sent them scurrying. *Of all the things I have been trained for, I have never learned how to cope with children.*

The merchants had created a banking system and a crude form of currency. They wanted to call the currency a "Kerensky," but Moon vetoed that. He did not want anything that might tip off a future visitor as to their origins. As a compromise, it was simply called a "credit." He had also ordered that the Smoke Jaguar insignias be removed from the ships...under the pretense that at some point in the future, when the time was right, the symbol would be restored. Baldur pointed out that he was doing exactly what the Star League had done on Huntress, but Moon only gave him an icy stare in response. *I hated that comparison. I do this for a different reason, to protect these people.*

Paul had not been prepared for the human side of colony life. Fifteen colonists gave birth during the trip to Wayside V, and another dozen since they had arrived. One colonist committed suicide three weeks after their arrival—which puzzled him. *Why travel all this way only to kill yourself?* The colonists also had a thief in their ranks, and it took four months to finally track down the culprit. Moon himself sat as the judge for the man, who was sentenced to hard labor for his crimes. *In my youth I aspired to be a Khan, yet these are the kinds of things a Khan has to deal with—times ten thousand. I find these duties the hardest, because each decision has a potentially far-reaching impact. Like the other warriors, a part of me yearns for the smells and dangers of the battlefield.*

At his desk in the new administration building, he studied the day's tasks and sighed. A meeting with the merchants over pricing...a ribbon cutting at the new school...Baldur's committee on road naming. *This is not what I was born to do, but it is necessary for the colony.*

Moon's communications technician knocked on his door, shattering his moment of self-reflection. "Star Colonel, we have an incoming message from our JumpShips at the zenith jump point."

*The jump point—this cannot be good.* "What is it?"

"A JumpShip arrived and signaled them, asking to speak with our leader."

"What do they make of her?"

"It is the Goliath Scorpion destroyer *Bloodied Stinger*."

Moon's mind raced. *We have two WarShips in-system. Do I send them to attack?* "Contact Baldur and Inanna. Have them join me immediately."

It took twenty minutes for the three officers to gather and huddle around the communications terminal. "They must have pursued us from Huntress," Baldur offered.

"It does not matter where they came from," Inanna said. "What matters is that they are here now."

Moon nodded, and the comms technician began to broadcast. "I am Paul Moon, the leader of this colony. What is your intention in this system?"

The image flickered, and a man appeared in the black-and-gold dress uniform of the Goliath Scorpions. His face was drawn and pale. *They have come a long way in pursuit of us.* "I am Galaxy Commander Rik Myers of Alpha Galaxy, personal commander of the Thirty-fifth Scorpion Cuirassiers. I have come to harvest this colony, the last vestige of the once-proud Clan Smoke Jaguar, in a Trial of Possession. I intend to take you as a whole. Your remains will be preserved and stored in our hallowed halls, your genes will be ours to use as we see fit. I mean to take this world as our own—and your people will be my *isorla*. With what forces will you defend this planet, Paul Moon of the Jaguars?" Arrogance and bravado rang in Myers's voice.

"Stand by," Moon said and then killed the broadcast. "Everything we have built...he means to take it all from us."

"We cannot fight near the colony," Inanna said. We need a venue that will work to our advantage, but not put our civilians at risk."

"We have a single Cluster of troops," Baldur said. "The garrison Binary that was here, plus the Trinary of troops that came with us. That includes your Ghosts, Paul."

"This battle is all or none—we cannot afford to hold back. Our bid should include our WarShips, which I will immediately bid away. This allows me to tap them if we need them. We go with our entire Cluster. In the meantime, we need a place for this battle."

"They have been in space for nearly a year," Inanna said. "Remember how our training degraded on the journey here? They will not be at peak performance."

"You and Baldur will need to find us a battlefield we can leverage," Moon said. The two nodded as he reopened the channel.

"Galaxy Commander, the Clans and the Star League turned their backs on us, and as such, we are not Smoke Jaguars, but our own people. We have no score to settle with you, but if pressed to fight, we will do so with all of our forces, including one Cluster of warriors and two WarShips. However, I bid away my WarShips so we can settle this on the mud of the world you seek to claim. All that you bring to this world and all that orbit it are to be the spoils of war, should you lose. I further stipulate that, should we win, your vessel must erase its map to our location, and upon their return to Clan space, none of your people may reveal where we have settled. We will defend with all of our ground forces, one Cluster—a Binary and Trinary—on a field of our choosing."

"You expect me to surrender my entire force, our ships, and our BattleMechs should we lose?"

"Affirmative, I do. You have come to take all of us as your prize, likewise you must put all you have on the table. It is fair—and more importantly—honorable."

"Very well," the image of Rik Myers replied. "It is good to see you have not forgotten our traditions in your flight from Huntress. I will consult my commanders and determine the forces with which we will attack. You will soon feel the sting and snap of the Goliath Scorpion."

"And you will feel nothing, since you and your troops will be dead, far from home," Paul countered, then shut off the channel.

"Brilliant, Paul," Baldur said. "You told them we are not Clan—this means we are not restricted to Clan rules of honor."

"*Aff*," Moon said. "And I told him I bid away our WarShips—giving me the option of pulling them in if I have to."

"Do not delude yourselves," Inanna weighed in. "Rik Myers has come a long way for this fight. He has no choice but to win. Returning to the homeworlds with nothing to show for it will weaken his position in his Clan, and may cost him his command. Such desperation makes a warrior much more dangerous."

"It may be more than that," Baldur said. "We had to carefully plan for our provisions, not just to reach here, but to sustain us after we arrived. I wonder if he brought enough food to account for a voyage home, should he lose. This may make him even more desperate to win—simply to keep his people fed."

"Good," Paul replied. "Desperation can compel someone to make mistakes. At least he will have the same pressures on him that I do." He turned again to his two comrades. "Find us the right place to fight—the right place to win."

## THREE DAYS LATER...

"The Straits." Baldur pointed at the holotable display of Wayside V. "This narrow pass between the old continents is perfect for our needs. From what we have seen visiting there, it is a defile with steep canyon walls. Everything is channeled into a single canyon. It reduces any advantage the Scorpions have—forces them to bunch up, overlap their own fields of fire. Their use of Clan rules of engagement bottlenecks them. That opening is so narrow in some places that destroying a 'Mech will actually clog things up. We need to compel them to come into that pass."

Paul Moon surveyed the proposed battlefield. "The only thing that will draw them is our warriors. They want us as chattel, something to put on display in their museums, something to possess as a sign of prestige. We put enough of a force there, make it visible—the Scorpions will not be able to ignore it."

"It may not be enough," Inanna said from the same side of the holotable as Baldur. "Most of our BattleMechs are not top-of-the-line OmniMechs. They are older. That will still give the Scorpions an edge."

"I trust you have a suggestion, *quiaff*?" Paul asked.

Inanna smiled. "*Aff*, as always. The continents flanking the Straits, they are almost a vacuum. With the steep drop-off, taking BattleMechs or armor up there is not an alternative. It is not a battlefield anyone would willingly fight or maneuver across."

"Which," Baldur added, "is exactly what we propose doing."

"I thought we would hold them in the pass," Paul said, gesturing to the display.

"*Aff*," Inanna continued, "but your Ghosts can use that high ground to maneuver to their rear. We have one Star of Elementals which can operate in a vacuum and a point of infantry. They can be equipped with space suits from the DropShips—allowing them to maneuver on the high ground. While a force lures them into the mouth of the canyon—" she activated the force placements on the map "—the Ghosts creep along the edge and come down behind them."

"The infantry will not last long against the bulk of their force," Moon replied.

Inanna nodded. "Correct. They hit at the exact moment the rest of our BattleMech forces emerge from their hiding place at the far end of the Horned Sea to the north. The seabed there is a large plate of natural lodestone, highly magnetic. It obscures most passive sensors. The sea is not very deep, but enough to conceal line-of-sight on the bulk of our forces. While the team holding the Straits keeps them focused, we hit them from behind with the Ghosts first, then the rest of our force. They are encircled. We are not governed by Clan rules of engagement, so they will not escape."

Moon studied their plan intently. Baldur saw him taking in every detail of the terrain. "We will need to position our forces in the sea before the Scorpions make landfall. We are talking two days of sitting there underwater."

"Agreed," Baldur said. "Does this meet your needs?"

"*Aff*," he said. "Though the force holding the Straits will suffer the worst. They hold the cork to this bottle you have created. Everything will pour against them, and they must put up enough of a fight to keep the Scorpions engaged and focused on them. We must make the Goliath Scorpions think the bulk of our forces is beyond that pass—that the defenders are there to draw them in, grind them up."

Inanna looked over at Baldur, then back to Moon. "We have had some thoughts on that—things that must not leave this room."

Moon cocked his eyebrow. "I am listening."

"The original garrison force. They are the most resistant to our settlement plans. They still cling to the old Smoke Jaguar mindset and find the work of building a colony beneath them. If we use them to hold the Straits, they will suffer the most losses in the fighting, but it will give some the release they desperately seek."

"You talk of sacrificing them, *quiaff*?"

"*Neg*," Baldur said. "They will not be slaughtered, but those who survive will be few in number, meaning they will not be a vocal faction after the fighting. Many of the warriors in their ranks are older than I am by a decade. They seek one last chance to fight for a cause. I say we give that to them. One last glorious battle—what every warrior seeks."

"They are short a warrior," Inanna said. "Dresden was injured on a construction site two days ago. His arm is broken in three places and the mending will take time."

"He piloted a *Timber Wolf*," Baldur said. "Though his is not in prime condition. I have experience in that model. I can take his place." He and Inanna had discussed it at length. While she was against him taking part, she never said it out loud. Baldur respected that. *I long to pilot a 'Mech again in combat. This may be my last opportunity...my last chance to purge some of my guilt. Once more I will fight alongside Smoke Jaguars in combat.*

"You? Baldur, you could be killed. That force will be hard-hit in the battle to come," Moon said. *He is actually trying to save me. Odd how things have come full circle.*

"It is important that I take part in this fighting. I know you, Paul Moon. You will be with your Ghosts. I need to be in this fight as well. The future of our people depends on it."

Moon wanted to protest—Baldur could see it in his face—but he could not find the right words. After a moment of his mouth hanging half open, he finally spoke. "Very well, you shall be attached to that unit—at the rank of Star Captain. If anyone is to lead these older warriors, who better than you?"

"Some will challenge that."

"And if we were Clan, I would respect those challenges. We stopped being true Clan when we undertook the journey here. I appoint you at this rank, and our people must support it."

"Affirmative," Baldur replied. "If that is the price of victory, so be it."

# CHAPTER 35

The DropShips of the Thirty-fifth Scorpion Cuirassiers made a slow arc through the rolling purple clouds, visible most of the time only from the plumes of their engines as they descended.

Baldur watched them from the *Timber Wolf* he piloted. His hands caressed the stick and throttle controls of the OmniMech. They were familiar to him, like an old, comfortable uniform. This *Timber Wolf* had a defective hip actuator on the right side that gave it a bit of a limp. The technicians claimed it was impossible to fix completely without replacing an entire segment of the leg's endo-steel internal structure. On Wayside V such parts were rare, and while it could be manufactured, there was not enough time. It degraded performance by a few kph, but Baldur did not mind. *I am where I belong–one last battle with the Smoke Jaguars at my side.*

The steep, jagged gray walls of the Straits were dotted with molds and moss, which draped down in several places, swaying in the breeze. It was every bit as forbidding as when he and Inanna surveyed it. The *Warhawk* and *Peregrine* at his sides were painted in the gray with black spots of the Clan that they once served. Turning to look to his other side, he saw a *Rifleman IIC*, a battered *Mist Lynx*, a *Galahad*, and an *Ebon Jaguar*. His sensors told him a *Warhammer IIC* was in reserve behind him, all but masked by the mass of his *Timber Wolf*.

Inanna had overseen the paint scheme on his OmniMech: a base color of flat gray covered with light-blue streaks with hints of white in them in a crisscrossed pattern. He had the insignia of the Nova Cats, complete with the Star League's Cameron Star, and next to that, the pouncing Smoke Jaguar. He approved—a mix of both Clans. *Paul would hate to see the Jaguar there, but it will mean the world to my Binary.* Privately, he had authorized his warriors to paint the insignia on their 'Mechs as well.

There had been some questioning of why Paul Moon had put Baldur in charge. Av Weaver had all but demanded a Trial of Grievance to settle the matter. Baldur had taken the man aside and spoke to him in private. "I am here because I too have reached my later years. I too want one more time in glorious battle. I am here because I need to be here—with you and your warriors."

Weaver had been moved by his words, warrior to warrior, enough to retract his protests. "If this Nova Cat wishes to fight at my side, I will have him lead us."

A voice came on over the broadband channel in the clear as soon as the DropShips landed. "Smoke Jaguars, the Goliath Scorpions have come for you. Come out on these plains of this dead sea, and let us finish this quickly."

Paul Moon's voice responded. "It is not for you to determine how fast this fight goes. You should know better than to awaken the fighting cat in us." Then on the secured tactical channel, he said, "Baldur—draw him in."

Baldur switched to his Binary's channel. "This is Anvil Actual. All right then—it is time we show these trespassers what it means to fight true warriors. Alvarez—you are our fox. Go out among the hunters and bring them to us."

"It shall be done, Star Captain," the pilot of the *Mist Lynx* said. The light OmniMech sprang out and headed off into the distance to where the Scorpions' DropShips had landed.

### THIRTY MINUTES LATER...

"Galaxy Commander," Star Commander Azure Kirov said, "we are picking up a faint reactor signature on the outer perimeter—moving fast along our front. Recon class 'Mech—*Mist Lynx*. Configuration undetermined at this time."

Rik Myers nodded in satisfaction. *I was beginning to think they were going to remain in hiding.* "Excellent. Let us advance on that signal." He saw the plot for the signal on his tactical display and advanced his *Fire Scorpion* forward. The four-legged 'Mech could be a jarring ride for those unskilled at piloting it; not so for Rik Myers. This 'Mech had been his for five years, he knew every nuance of its movement—every sound it could make.

Wayside V was not the kind of world he would have chosen for settlement. Half of the world poked up beyond the atmosphere—the petrified forests testimony to a disaster that happened tens of thousands of years ago. *This is a forsaken world. When I am done taking it and the legacy of the Smoke Jaguars, I will leave it abandoned, as it should be. This entire grand experiment on the part of Paul Moon and his minions was doomed to fail from the start.*

"Sir," Star Commander Kirov said. "They may be baiting us with that reconnaissance 'Mech. I recommend deployment of forces to our far flanks."

Myers looked at the tactical display overlaid with the surveys from their descent. "Negative. Even if they had 'Mechs on the high ground, there is no way down for them unless their entire force is jump-jet enabled—and even then it would be difficult. We do not detect them there because they are not there. We have this *Mist Lynx.* Let us pursue it and see where it takes us."

*The Star League thought they destroyed the Smoke Jaguars two years ago. The truth is I will destroy them now, today. That is how history will remember me.*

"This is Alvarez, the fox has bugs in pursuit," came the breathy voice of the *Mist Lynx* warrior in Baldur's earpiece as he came into visual range. A string of distant explosions followed a few moments later.

*It has begun.*

Baldur checked his long-range scans as he made sure he was still on the Binary's tac channel. "All right. We are the anvil, the other forces are the hammer. We need these Scorpions to engage us. All 'Mechs, engage multiple targets. Draw them in."

"That lacks honor," replied Corbett from his *Rifleman IIC.* From the "*affs*" Baldur heard, others supported the stance.

"I know what you all think, but Clan rules of engagement permit this. In this case, it is the best strategy open to us. The majority of them will be forced to fight us, forced to try to defeat us. The better part of honor is victory," he said, quoting a Smoke Jaguar dictum.

That was all it took. "*Aff,* Star Captain," came back a chorus of voices.

Baldur flushed with pride.

On long-range sensors he saw the first Goliath Scorpions emerge at the limits of his sensor range. A *Fire Moth* and a *Kit Fox* were closing in on Alvarez's *Mist Lynx*, taking potshots at maximum speed. The rest of the Scorpions were closing in from a greater distance, hindered only by speed. *We will be showing up on their sensors by now.*

"Those of you with range, let them get a little closer," he ordered. "Pick multiple targets—stick to the plan. We do not move from here. They will come, and we will weather their attacks. Our goal is to snare their attention. Several infantry in harvesters will stir up dirt to our rear, to create the illusion that the bulk of our forces are there."

He paused for a moment as the Scorpions continued to close on them. "Remember, the fate of all of the colonists, former Smoke Jaguars all, depends on us holding this position. This is the battle every warrior dreams of, a desperate last-stand action where the fate of the world hangs on their actions."

Baldur waited and knew in the cockpits next to him, the other Jaguars were locking weapons. He brought his long-range missiles onto a single target-interlock circuit and drifted his targeting reticle with precise movements on top of a Scorpion *Stalking Spider*. A millisecond after hearing target-lock tone, he unleashed forty long-range missiles.

At extreme range, the missiles' smoke trails spun and churned in the wind as they arced to follow the *Spider*'s movements, then came the flashes of explosions followed by the distant rumble three seconds later. A quarter of the missiles missed their mark, one hitting a *Warhawk* behind the *Stalking Spider*. *That is even better. Now you must both engage me.* Baldur brought his extended-range large lasers onto separate triggers and looked to the right for another target.

Off to his side, a brilliant bluish-white flash of incoming PPC fire slammed into the *Ebon Jaguar* piloted by Aaron Ott. Armor plates seared and melted under the glancing hit, spraying liquified metal into the air. Aaron returned fire with his Gauss rifle and autocannon.

Baldur did not follow the shots downrange to see the results of his comrade's barrage; he had found another target—a four-legged black-and-orange-streaked *Fire Scorpion*. He zoomed in the targeting reticle and aimed at the center of the squat body, then fired. The lasers whined as they fired, the crimson beams stabbing out under the rolling purple storm clouds in the distance. Both shots hit the quad 'Mech hard, staggering it back a step under the impact as the warrior fought to maintain their footing. The heat in Baldur's cockpit spiked appreciably, but not dangerously—not yet.

Emerald pulses of laser energy slammed into his *Timber Wolf*'s right leg, boring a string of holes in three armor-plated sections. The damage flashed on his display. He ignored it. *We are still early in this battle.* Tukayyid had taught him that.

The silvery flash of a Gauss-rifle round passed right next to him in a blur and into Corbett's *Rifleman IIC*. The devastating impact cratered deep into the 'Mech's right torso. The slug itself, simmering hot, stuck there. Corbett dropped the 'Mech to one knee for a moment, then slowly rose, as if his *Rifleman* were angry at the audacity of the hit.

Baldur swung his pulse laser into the fray, blasting at the nimble *Fire Moth*, but missing as the speedy recon 'Mech darted across his field of fire. Stravag! *I should have hit him.*

Another laser beam, this one solid and crimson, seared a nasty scar just under his cockpit. The armor absorbed it, but the hit left a sizzling furrow there, the smoke drifting up around his canopy. He stepped quickly to the right, and a fusillade of autocannon fire hit his left arm and the canyon wall behind him, spraying bits of rock down around them. His damage display flickered for a moment, but Baldur refused to pay attention to it.

With deadly precision, he aimed at another 'Mech entirely, an *Ebon Jaguar*, sending another wave of long-range missiles spiraling away. The Scorpion MechWarrior was slow to dodge to his left, with most of the missiles tearing into the upper portions of his 'Mech in a cloud of black smoke.

"Pour it on, hit as many of them as you can," Baldur ordered through clenched teeth. "We must keep them focused here."

Galaxy Commander Myers glanced at his sensors and was puzzled. Only a Binary of 'Mechs was showing in the narrow canyon ahead, effectively blocking the pass. *Where is the rest of the enemy?* From the fire jutting out at him, it seemed the defenders here were inviting their own demise. *They are engaging the bulk of my force, some shooting at upward of four different targets. This is not the Clan way. It lacks honor. They know this, so why are they seeking their destruction?*

He raced through the scenarios. There was no sign of the rest of the enemy force. *Do they mean to grind us up against that pass, replacing fallen 'Mechs when they go down?* The dust cloud rising in the distance beyond the defenders betrayed where the rest of the Jaguars were hiding—waiting for him to strike. *It might work.* Luring them into the canyon negated him bringing the full firepower of his Cuirassiers to bear. It would make the trial a contest of attrition, not the way Goliath Scorpions preferred to fight. That seemed the likely tactic.

Myers pondered a variety of scenarios to counter the strategy. *I cannot go around them—getting out of this basin is nearly impossible. Stravag!*

There was another option. Did they have a force at his rear? Sensor sweeps showed nothing, but BattleMechs were fast. *If they catch me here, in the open, we would be caught in the crossfire. I have come too far to risk losing my entire Cluster here!*

"Lancer Star, this is Cuirassiers Actual. Break off and head to the south, spread out in a reconnaissance sweep. Make sure no one is coming at us from behind."

"As you command, sir," Star Commander Manning replied.

Another laser lashed out at his *Fire Scorpion*, hitting the body of his 'Mech near his cockpit. Melted armor splashed his cockpit canopy, leaving a blackened mark. "Reaper Stars One and Two, send in two 'Mechs to point-blank range. I want a reading to see if the rest of their force is waiting behind that Binary in the pass."

Star Captain Chiasson Brinker's voice came back quickly. "Sir, at that range—"

"I know what I am asking. Have them charge through the defenders. I have to know what else is there." He understood the hesitation—he was sending two warriors to rush into the enemy, and most likely, to their destruction.

*I have to know what they are up to.* He angled his targeting reticle on the *Timber Wolf* in the pass and unleashed his Ultra autocannon, filling the air between them with a burst of deadly armor-piercing rounds.

Paul Moon turned to look behind him. The progress across the desolate upper continents was ponderous. His Elementals did well, but the platoon of infantry in vac suits moved far too slow for his liking. "We need to pick up the pace," he commanded.

There were three ways down that he had plotted—all far too small for a BattleMech to traverse, but passible for his infantry. His infantry only needed enough room to shed their vac suits. All three avenues put him down in the flank, near the rear of where Baldur and Inanna had hoped to bait the Goliath Scorpions. Battles did not work that way, though, and that thought tugged at his mind as he moved forward. *Rik Myers is a Galaxy Commander. He did not achieve that rank without demonstrating skill on the battlefield. He will smell our trap. Baldur has to lure him in regardless.*

He checked the feed he was getting of the battle. So far it was working, but then he saw it: a Star of 'Mechs peeling off and heading into the Scorpions' rear—right toward where the rest of the force was hidden in the sea. Myers was proving himself as smart as Paul feared.

"Ghost Actual to Claw Three. Scorpions fanned out in a standard Wing formation heading toward your general area. Recommend you keep cover. Go passive, low-power mode."

Inanna's voice came back. "Roger that, Ghost Actual. We will stay swimming with the fishes until you give the signal."

The *Fire Moth* did not dodge side to side as Baldur would have expected. Instead it rushed straight at them, along with a jet-black *Mist Lynx.* They bore straight at the pass where he and the Binary of Smoke Jaguar veterans held. It was a charge—plain, simple, and direct. *They are light 'Mechs, it is such a waste. Unless...*

"Everyone concentrate your firepower on the two approaching 'Mechs," he commanded. "They are trying to scan past us, to see if we are alone here."

"As you command," Aaron said from his *Ebon Jaguar.* He unleashed a barrage that missed the *Mist Lynx.* Baldur opened up on the *Fire Moth* with his extended-range and pulse lasers. The brilliant red beams missed the Scorpion OmniMech, but the medium pulse laser found its mark on its legs—as did a devastating salvo of Streak short-range missiles from Brandley Bowen's *Warhawk*. The *Fire Moth* sprang right at his line but fell flat on its front torso, skidding across the rocky floor of the pass, throwing chunks of moss into the air as it skidded to a stop. A trail of fractured and ripped armor plates marked its path.

The *Mist Lynx* twisted midstride to try dodging the waves of energy and munitions pouring at it, but the LB-X autocannon and Gauss rifle from Aaron Ott's *Ebon Jaguar* ripped its left leg off, sending it spinning away behind it. The Goliath Scorpion warrior managed to hop three times, trying to continue forward, but lost their footing on the uneven ground and toppled next to the *Fire Moth*.

Baldur was about to congratulate Ott's shot, but a Gauss-rifle slug slammed into the *Ebon Jaguar*'s cockpit. The squat OmniMech shuddered under the hit. Baldur turned and saw a maroon smear on the fractured cockpit canopy under where the slug had impacted: blood. As if to add insult to injury, another blast, this time a brilliant blast of PPC fire, lashed into the 'Mech. The *Ebon Jaguar* rocked back, but caught itself.

*He's still alive? Impossible.* "Aaron..."

A breathy, agonized voice responded. "I still live—I still fight, Baldur." As if to make his point, he fired his own Gauss rifle at the slowly approaching wall of Goliath Scorpions. He struggled to pull his feet back under him, rising like a drunkard staggering about a bar.

Baldur's targeting reticle fell on a *Kit Fox* and he fired all of his lasers at it, mostly out of anger over the hit to Aaron's 'Mech. A fourth of his shots missed the faster, lighter 'Mech. The rest, including both of his large lasers, blasted off the *Kit Fox*'s right arm, sending it flailing into the nearby *Fire Scorpion*'s leg. The heat momentarily spiked in the cockpit, but Baldur ignored it. *Heat is the least of my problems.*

A burst of autocannon fire stitched up his left arm and into his long-range missile rack, mangling it into a box of worthless scrap. A handful of the missiles in the rack went off in a sympathetic blast. Bits of metal clashed against his cockpit canopy. Glancing at his damage display, he saw what he already knew: his left arm was badly mauled.

He stepped forward, putting the birdlike foot of his *Timber Wolf* on the downed *Fire Moth*, crunching its remains under the weight of his 'Mech. He brought his remaining long-range missile rack to bear on the *Fire Scorpion* looming at medium range, and fired another wave of missiles. They peppered the 'Mech's two front legs and its torso and cockpit. It was not enough to take it down, but it forced the enemy 'Mech to stop advancing for a few seconds.

One of the Scorpion BattleMechs, a hulking *Kodiak*, emerged from the smoke of the battle. "The *Kodiak*," Baldur said as he brought his targeting reticle down onto the claw-equipped 'Mech. "One salvo from all of us. Let us make it bleed. Now!"

He assigned his large lasers to the same trigger and blazed away, as did the other 'Mechs of the Binary that were still firing. A flash of silver from Ott's Gauss rifle—a precise shot—an identical salvo from Shell Rippon's *Galahad,* and a wave of fifteen long-range missiles from another Smoke Jaguar 'Mech all found their mark on the lumbering Scorpion 'Mech. Most of the shots hit high, and two Gauss rounds tore into the dead center of the 'Mech. The impacts lifted it off the ground, if only a few centimeters, then dropped it on its back—hard. The ground throbbed under Baldur's *Timber Wolf* from the impact of the *Kodiak* going down.

To his chagrin, through the smoke he saw it sit up—still in the fight. Blackened holes marked where it had been horrifically damaged, and it struggled to get to its feet.

An explosion went off to his left, and Aaron Ott's *Ebon Jaguar* toppled. A ripple of heat rose from it—one or more hits to its fusion-reactor housing. A heartbeat later, a series of autocannon blasts sprayed shrapnel along the line of 'Mechs, knocking Shell Rippon's *Galahad* off its feet.

A burst of brilliant green pulse-laser fire seared pockmarks all over Baldur's left torso, causing his *Timber Wolf* to reel slightly. The damage display flashed red to get his attention, but he ignored it. *It does not matter how badly I am damaged—as long as I can fight, I will.*

"Ghost Actual," he said, licking the sweat from his upper lip. "We are being crushed here. Sitrep."

No answer came back in his neurohelmet's earpiece.

"Ghost Actual!"

Paul Moon heard the calls, but was more intent on getting the last of his platoon down into the crevasse where they had assembled. The Elementals had shuttled the infantry down one at a time into the tight black crack in the old continent. The ground there was a gravel of crushed shells and fossilized crustaceans, and made far too much noise for Moon's preference.

At Baldur's last transmission, Moon turned to the narrow opening. From his concealed position he saw the battle raging off to his right. The Binary in the pass was obscured in a cloud of explosions, lit up with the flashes of energy and laser weapons. Baldur's *Timber Wolf* looked like a toy that had been chewed by a pet dog, its armor crumpled and blasted almost everywhere.

He was about to issue the order to spring the trap—but he checked his emotional response. *You only get one chance to spring a trap correctly.*

His sensors showed that, with the exception of a lone Star fanned out near the sea where Inanna's force was concealed, the Goliath Scorpions were entirely focused on the 'Mechs holding the pass.

Their advance was slow, but they were closing to deadly shorter ranges. *Even if they detect us, there will be no time for them to pivot and face the threat.*

A *Kit Fox* passed Moon's crevasse only twenty meters away, unaware of the infantry right next to it. It was unleashing its Streak SRMs at Baldur's battered defenders. Moon chose his targets from the number available. The nearly pristine *Kit Fox*, then find the prize— Galaxy Commander Myers's *Fire Scorpion*.

"This is Ghost Actual to Claw Three. You are a go. Repeat—you are a go. Take out that recon Star and hit the enemy's rear. Anvil, the storm is coming."

Moon turned to face his reinforced point. "We take this *Kit Fox* first, then the *Fire Scorpion*. Concentrate on their legs, shatter their knees and bring them down. We break them here...now!"

The Ghosts poured out of the giant crack and immediately swarmed the stunned *Kit Fox*. The Goliath Scorpion warrior panicked for a moment, staggering back as a salvo of short-range missiles devoured its leg armor around the thighs and knees. The black 'Mech reeled about, firing its small pulse laser wildly, missing the assaulting infantry.

Man-pack PPC fire concentrated on the Kit Fox's left knee, leaving it red hot and oozing lubricants and slick coolant like blood. The warrior tried to shift, like they wanted to gain some distance from the attackers, but could not. The damaged leg froze. It dragged thirty meters in an awkward limp, only to have the other leg attacked. Manmade lightning from the portable PPCs blew off armored plates and severed myomer bundles, leaving the loose ends flapping about.

The *Kit Fox*'s small pulse laser fired again, hitting one of the troopers. The energy bursts seared right through his armored chest plate and out through his spine. Smoke rolled from the hole as the man froze in place, then fell over dead. One of the Elementals rose on a plume of jets over the Scorpion 'Mech and unleashed two short-range missiles at the cockpit canopy. They exploded at point-blank range, even hitting the Elemental with bits of shrapnel.

The swift assault was too much for the light 'Mech. It toppled over on its side, its legs all but worthless. The 'Mech's impact made a sickening grinding sound on the stone. Moon swept the battlefield then saw the outline of the *Fire Scorpion*, moving toward Baldur's position. "This is Ghost Actual, follow me!"

Inanna switched to her own tac channel. "Everyone target one of the reconnaissance 'Mechs. The moment we emerge, unleash an alpha strike. We need to take them by surprise before they can warn the rest of their Cluster. We need to take them down and out of the fight, then run right at Anvil's position. Understood, *quiaff?*"

"*Aff*," came the Trinary's response.

"Engage!" she howled.

They broke the surface of the dull-green alkaline sea and Inanna saw an *Ice Ferret* only 100 meters from the edge of the sea. Her *Mad Dog* locked onto it immediately, and she let loose with her pair of large lasers and forty long-range missiles. The temperature in her cockpit went from chilled to hot in a matter of seconds. Both of her lasers hit the smaller 'Mech in its upper torso, cutting the *Ice Ferret* with nasty scars. The missile salvo landed a few seconds later, enveloping the Scorpion 'Mech in a series of explosions and almost making it disappear in smoke.

She was not alone. Star Commander Reid Chrisholm's *Shadow Hawk IIC* tore into it with short-range missiles and a blur of emerald pulse-laser fire. The *Ice Ferret* spun, much to its warrior's credit, letting its side and back take some of the damage in an effort to spread out the carnage. It staggered a few wobbly steps. Reid's *Shadow Hawk* did not wait for it to recover. Instead it rose on jump jets, rising up and over the *Ice Ferret*. Then, without a hint of warning, the jets shut off. Forty-five tons of BattleMech dropped straight down on the *Ice Ferret*, hitting the cockpit and shoulder with its footpads. There was a metallic grinding noise that she could hear over the shots being fired at the other recon 'Mechs around her.

The *Ice Ferret* never stood a chance; it crumpled downward, compacting as its internal structure fractured under the death-from-above assault. Sparks popped as Reid spilled off the fallen Goliath Scorpion, coming up on one knee.

Inanna scanned the other recon 'Mechs. All but one was down, and that one, a *Hellbringer*, had weathered the initial surprise assault. Its black camouflage with blue and orange streaks did an admirable job of hiding the damage her sensors showed it had suffered. Its gyro and engine had been hit, and it had lost a full third of its armor in the initial attack. It was firing back with everything at its disposal, PPC and laser fire, at a Jaguar *Jenner IIC*. The *Jenner* went down, but the *Hellbringer* did not get to enjoy its victory for long. A laser hit to the cockpit toppled the 'Mech backward. As the warrior rolled it to one side to stand up, a barrage of autocannon fire rained down on the *Hellbringer*. Explosions tossed aside armor plates and engulfed the Scorpion 'Mech in a cloud of grayish-black smoke. Its engine showed as offline—proof of its destruction.

As the heat trickled down, Inanna licked her lips. "Standard wide-u formation. Sweep forward!"

Galaxy Commander Rick Myers weathered another salvo of long-range missiles from the narrow rocky pass—courtesy of the *Timber Wolf*. He trained his LB 10-X autocannon on the *Galahad*, and the targeted burst ripped its left arm off, sending it spinning into the debris field already clogging the pass. The *Galahad*'s warrior staggered back a step, leveled their remaining weapon, and sent a Gauss-rifle slug just past Myers, slamming into a *Mad Dog*, crushing its missile rack.

Something was wrong; he could feel it. These Smoke Jaguars were not falling back, allowing replacements. They were fighting until they went down. Even when they went down, they crawled back up to fight.

Checking his long-range sensors, he focused on the reconnaissance Star he had sent to protect his rear. Suddenly the dots of light marking his warriors' positions winked out, all but one going out almost simultaneously. One, Ahrissta's *Hellbringer*, was falling back toward the Goliath Scorpions' main body. Two heartbeats later, it went down too, joining its comrades.

The realization hit him as hard as any weapon trained on him. The crimson dots on his long-range sensors confirmed it. The enemy was in his rear—a fresh enemy.

"Pinch Binary, about-face—we have enemy forces to our rear," he commanded. Then came the warnings on the tactical display: infantry right in the middle of his formation. "Alert. Elementals and infantry at our feet. All units, pull back, compress our line."

As he barked out the orders, he did the math…the mathematics of battle. This fight had turned. *All I can hope for now is to take them down and break their will before I lose mine.* Stravag!

Smoke and dust hung thick in the air as Baldur ignored the heat in his cockpit and strained to keep his battered *Timber Wolf* upright. There was a rumble in the distance and a flash of lightning. One of Wayside's thunderstorms was slowly creeping toward the battlefield.

Nearby, Aaron's *Conjurer* was still operational, but was missing its left arm at the elbow, and its leg barely resembled a functional limb at all. It was more like a pole with a charred wrapping of myomer. Slick green coolant formed a growing puddle around its foot. A fragment of the PPC assembly dangled from the severed joint by three myomer strands, still smoking from the shot that had torn off the limb. Brandley Bowen's *Warhawk* had taken up position behind the fallen form of Sorrentino's blackened *Mad Dog*, which still stood near a *Stalking Spider* that had tried to rush their lines. The quad-legged 'Mech had collided with Sorrentino, who had ripped off one of its front legs in retribution. A Scorpion *Piranha* lay at the far end of the line, its cockpit blown out from the warrior ejecting as it fell.

Through a billowing cloud of smoke Av Weaver emerged, his *Conjurer* blackened from the waist up, with twisted and gnarled bits of armor everywhere but on his legs, which were oddly pristine.

The 'Mech turned toward him for a moment. "You are no Nova Cat, Star Captain Baldur!" Weaver said on the tactical channel. "You are a Smoke Jaguar today!"

Baldur grinned broadly in his neurohelmet. He had longed for this moment.

For Baldur's own 'Mech, "badly battered" was in his rearview mirror. His gyro had taken a bad hit that made just standing a challenge. He still stood with one foot on the fallen *Fire Moth*, shifting his 'Mech's weight as little as possible. He had only one salvo of long-range missiles left. His right arm only had the ER medium laser still operational. Four of his heat sinks had either failed or been destroyed, so he was coping with heat problems as well.

The *Fire Scorpion* and the *Kodiak* loomed through the smoke, with the *Fire Scorpion* unleashing a dual barrage of autocannon fire on him—again. He contorted as he had just before the last hit, but a millisecond too late. Two rounds exploded on his cockpit, one penetrating the armored glass, bringing a deafening blast and a rush of air that popped his ears.

The *Timber Wolf* vibrated under the assault, but Baldur ignored that. A hot pain rose in his left leg, screaming for his attention. Looking down, he saw the torn flesh of his thigh, blood splattered everywhere. He smelled the acrid smoke of the battlefield through the holes in his canopy but could hear nothing.

*Got to tie that off before I bleed out.* The only useful thing he had was the feed for his coolant vest. He tore it free with his bionic arm and used it as a tourniquet. Every move of the leg, even to wrap the tube under it, felt like a hot branding iron, but he pushed past the pain. Coolant splattered on the floor of his cockpit, mixing with the blood to make a sickening ooze.

As soon as he tied off his leg, Baldur brought his targeting reticle to life, dancing it over the *Fire Scorpion*'s right front leg. He fired, sending his last twenty missiles streaking into the low-riding BattleMech. All but two missiles found their mark. The armor was nearly gone on the *Scorpion*'s leg, and the missiles took out what remained in a series of explosions that bent the leg inward and back, crippling the 'Mech. The warrior fought gravity as the *Fire Scorpion* dipped down hard, grinding what was left of its knee into the stone. It stood, barely, tendrils of smoke snaking from several of the missile craters.

The *Kodiak* fired four of its medium lasers at Baldur, who could do little but weather them. The *Timber Wolf*'s right arm sheared off in the attack, shifting his balance heavily to the left, forcing him to compensate. As he did, the searing pain from his leg wound made him see stars—brilliant, tiny flashes of light.

The damage display was all red—there was nothing left but his rear armor. The *Fire Scorpion* maneuvered to the side, preparing for another volley. The entire Goliath Scorpion line seemed to be shrinking; Baldur could just make that out between his visuals and the tactical display. *I may as well use the last bit of armor I have.*

Just before the autocannon volley unleashed, Baldur adjusted his stance on the *Fire Moth* and twisted his torso, presenting his rear to the enemy. The concussion of the explosions hit hard, tossing him violently against his safety restraints. His leg erupted with another wave of fiery agony. Breath left his lungs, and when he inhaled, he struggled to get enough air. His right ear popped again, and he was surprised to hear his own agonized moan.

The *Timber Wolf* slowly tipped forward, out of his control. The legs wobbled and gave way, and he heard the awful grinding of metal on stone and metal. The safety harness dug into his flesh despite the padding, and he felt dizzy. There was pain in his lower back, not the bone, but off to the left side. He ignored it and surveyed the battle before him. Shots stopped raining down on his battered survivors. Something else had stolen the Goliath Scorpions' attention.

*Inanna.* Despite the pain, he smiled.

Shifting in his seat released a new rush of pain, this time in his arm. Looking down, he saw a jagged piece of shrapnel had severed most of his bionic arm's myomer muscle near the shoulder. His organic shoulder ached, and he felt something stabbing him there. Baldur coughed, and a spray of blood hit his neurohelmet visor. *Shrapnel— right through my ejection seat.* He tried to lean forward, but his back throbbed, and his breath became increasingly ragged. The warmth and dizziness increased with each beat of his racing heart.

*I am dying.* The realization was oddly calming. *I have died before and remember nothing of it. I wonder what it will be like this time?* With his free hand, he juked his stick to adjust his 'Mech's torso for a better view.

In the distance, Paul Moon's Elementals were rising into the air over the *Fire Scorpion*, like wasps attacking a tarantula. Their short-range missiles were precise and devastating. Two of the Elementals landed on the *Fire Scorpion*'s back and attacked its weapons. The now-three-legged 'Mech spun in place, but could not shake off the battle armor. The Ghost infantry used the crippled leg to press their assault.

Baldur smiled.

The last thing he heard before passing out was Galaxy Commander Myers transmitting in the clear: "I yield. Our position is untenable. Smoke Jaguars, it pains me to my core as a warrior, but I submit..."

Paul Moon and Inanna watched the medtechs remove Baldur from the *Timber Wolf*. The 'Mech was almost a total loss. Inanna held tight to Moon's forearm as they carried Baldur out on a stretcher. He was heavily wrapped and had two IVs on the stretcher with him, but was ghostly pale.

*All the years I wanted to see him dead–now it tears at me.* "He is a priority," Moon commanded the medtechs who got him to the ambulance. Looking down at Inanna, he tried to comfort her. "It probably looks worse than it is."

"*Neg*," she said in a soft voice. "His fate was etched in the stars before we even came here." She glanced up at the thunderstorm, which unleashed a torrent of rain the moment she looked skyward. Thunder cracked and rumbled above them, and the cold rain pelted them.

"You knew this was going to happen?"

Inanna shrugged. Her face sagged, and the words were hard for her to muster. "We need to be there—at the end."

Paul didn't understand Nova Cat thinking when it came to visions. *It does not matter.* Belief was not something he had, not in a higher power or even in destiny. *I always convinced myself you make your own destiny. I do not like the thought that even my fate might be known to others, but not to me.*

At that moment, he came to the conclusion that his beliefs did not matter. What mattered was the moment. *In this moment, a Smoke Jaguar warrior needs me at his side.*

"You are right," he said. "We need to be there."

# CHAPTER 36

What was left of Baldur was barely recognizable to Paul Moon as he and Inanna entered the intensive care unit. Both of his arms were gone, his left a bandaged stub jutting out from his shoulder. His skin was wrapped in skin-graft packs and gauze—in some places showing a crimson stain from bleeding. In another spot on his lower torso, the stain was a sickly mustard yellow. His bionic eye had been removed and that side of his face wrapped, his skin burned off, from the little that Paul could see. It was as if he were mummified except for his eye and mouth. IVs hung all around him, their tubes dangling like jungle vines. The air stung Moon's nostrils with the stench of hospitals, mingled with an aroma of feces. Inanna drew an unsteady gasp of air at the sight.

The nurse moved between Moon and Inanna and her patient. "We have done all we can. He is awake—but not for much longer." Her voice was a near whisper.

"Will he survive?" Paul asked.

She shook her head. "He has refused to be further sedated. He said he wanted to talk to you."

Moon nodded as the realization hit him. Baldur—*neg*, Trent, was dying, and it upset him. *We were at odds for so long, there were times I wanted him dead. I ordered him killed. Now that he is dying, it seems wrong.* Baldur was not the man Moon thought he was. *He was only my enemy because I made him that. His love of honor is equal to or greater than mine. He was willing to sacrifice everything to ensure that we are preserved as a people.*

Paul leaned over Baldur and saw his eye flicker open.

"Did we win?" he croaked.

"Affirmative," Moon said, putting his massive hand gently on Baldur's shoulder. "Thanks to you."

"Was never about me," Baldur's voice creaked. He winced under the bandages, fighting a wave of pain Paul could almost feel. "Now I am dying. This time...not coming back." Moon was not sure, but he thought he heard a single chuckle.

Inanna leaned in. "Do not speak that way."

"Not much time," Baldur said. "Paul...you were meant to lead our people. Give them a vision, tell them their future." He coughed hard, licking cracked lips, leaving a bloodstain on the bandages around his mouth. "They must have hope as they move forward. They...and you... were always faithful. You know true honor. Show them that."

"I will," Paul said. "I swear it."

"I do not want to be remembered this way—as a traitor. You will tell them, *quiaff?* Tell them the truth. I do not wish to be the Defiler. I am more than that...I hope you see that now."

"I was wrong about you," Moon said. "You bear no guilt for your actions. It is mine alone to bear."

"The guilt was ours," Baldur said with a deep, gurgling sigh. "My warriors...did they survive?"

"Only three," Paul admitted. "Av Weaver managed to cheat death with a tenacity comparable only to your own."

Baldur tried to nod. "It was necessary. They were old Smoke Jaguars. They would have had the hardest time with our fate. It was... calculated."

"They died with honor," Paul said. *As will you...* Honor, that was what his former adversary was about. *He has given up everything for what is right.*

"If you ever meet Prince Victor...tell him he was wrong about me... in every way. My only regret...I cannot beat that into him." Another soft chuckle rose from the bed.

Moon smiled. "I will make him understand the error of his thinking."

"Our people, they need you to tell them who they are. Tell them that one day the whole universe will know where they came from. Keep their faith, Paul."

"I will honor you and your sacrifice, Baldur," Moon replied, his own voice wavering slightly.

"*Neg.* I was Baldur. I die as Trent. The last Jaguar—for now." Those last two words sounded like a promise, a commitment.

Inanna leaned in. "You have fulfilled your destiny, and more," she said.

Trent's lone eye watered. "In my room...my notebook. You and Paul read it. It has instructions, thoughts, things that might help. I am a true Nova Cat...it holds my vision. Also my last gift...under my bed. It is for Paul."

"I will find it."

"Take my *vineers*. They are all I have now."

Inanna fought the weeping, but her tears dripped down onto his wrapped chest. "I will."

"Take care of Paul. He will need you," his voice rasped. "Make him as strong as you made me." Trent's eye closed for a long moment. His breathing became labored. There was a low, muffled rattle from his chest.

"Forever faithful," he said in a dreamlike voice. "I can see that now. Forever faithful..."

Trent's breathing stopped, and instantly an alarm went off. The nurse, who had been hovering near the door, rushed in, feeling his neck for a pulse. She hit her communicator. "We need a crash cart in ICU Two now!"

Inanna touched her on the arm. "*Neg.* You do not. The last Smoke Jaguar has passed."

The nurse stopped in her tracks, then nodded. "I am sorry."

"As are we all," Moon said, wiping away the lone tear he had shed. "He died saving us all."

In Trent's small quarters Moon and Inanna sat on his perfectly made bed. She clutched a small leather pouch which Paul assumed were his *vineers*. She took out one of them, a battered Smoke Jaguar patch, and gently ran her fingers over it.

Paul opened the small notebook that Trent had scribbled in during their planning sessions. Some of the items were doodles, odd geometric shapes. Other notes dealt with issues from their meetings during the trip to Wayside V. Near the back was a page titled "The Future," which caught his attention.

Words jumped out at him: *fidelis*—Latin for "faithful." There were other notes on "The Hidden Destiny" and "The Road of Pain." Trent had even sketched out the military organization, consisting of a "Century" of one hundred warriors. Unit compositions were drafted, as well as notes on doctrine. Page after page laid out everything from new cities to street names. No detail was omitted. Moon was dumbstruck by the sheer volume of what Trent had documented. *Our entire future is here.*

"*Vision: In our hearts beats the soul of the Smoke Jaguars. But we cannot reveal this to the universe—not yet. Someday, yes, we will take our rightful place in the stars and our former brethren. That time is generations away, our Hidden Destiny. We must be something else, something that is neither Clan nor Inner Sphere. We must slowly work our way back into civilized space, but never reveal who we are until the time is right, until the time of the ilClan. This is our burden, our cause.*"

Paul Moon stared at the words and was stunned. "He had it all thought out. He said so little in the meetings."

"Affirmative," Inanna said. "In the end, I think he knew his destiny. He must have known we needed something beyond the voyage here to bring the people together. The battle with the Goliath Scorpions provided just what was needed. That was the Nova Cat in him—our contribution to your culture."

"Now that we have defeated the Goliath Scorpions, the time is ripe to tell our people who he was—and who they now are." It was suddenly so easy. Trent had given him a blueprint in the book for almost every aspect of the new society. *Why did he not share this with me when he was alive?* It hit Moon then. He could not. Trent's own words on the page spoke to him from beyond the grave: *"There can only be one Custodian–Custos–of our people."*

From under his bed, Inanna produced a large package wrapped in brown paper. Paul carefully pulled it open and saw the Smoke Jaguar *Remembrance.* "How?"

"He reclaimed it from the ambassador's office the day we departed."

Paul saw a note stuck on the cover. *"The Unopened Work,"* clearly a reference to something in Trent's notes. "He saved this for our future."

Inanna nodded. "That was his intention."

"Then we begin our journey on the Road of Pain today. The road to our future."

Rik Myers stood facing Paul Moon in the room where he had been locked up, still wearing his fighting shorts and T-shirt. When Moon stepped into the doorway, Myers noticed the Elemental barely fit without turning sideways.

The Galaxy Commander tried to put on as jovial a face as possible. "Paul Moon, I presume," he said with a hint of arrogance still in his voice.

*False bravado.* "I am Paul Moon." He let silence follow his pronouncement. This man had come to take everything away from him, to turn them into museum pieces for the Goliath Scorpions. More damningly, this man had killed Trent.

"I compliment you on your strategy," Myers said. "You sacrificed those infantry in the pass and hit us from behind. Those warriors were slaughtered but held. That was a daring move."

"If you seek a compliment from me, some pointless comment about your honor, you are wasting my time," Paul said wearily.

"My warriors—what is their fate?"

"You are prisoners of war. Even if I let you go, you do not have enough food for the trip back to the homeworlds. Your people will stay here and farm, tend livestock, do what is necessary to raise enough food for the journey home. Then those who want to leave, will."

"I anticipated a victory," Myers confessed. "I would have replenished my supplies from your own."

"I have ordered your JumpShip crews here as well. They will toil in the fields alongside us."

"This is not the Clan way," Myers protested. "We do not impress captives. We do not take prisoners of war."

"We," Moon said proudly, "are not Clan. Not now. Perhaps one day, but today we are something else—the faithful—the Fidelis."

"Am I to be your bondsman, Paul Moon?"

"*Neg*," Paul replied. "I will not give you that honor. You will work like the others. You may yet find such manual labor rewarding. I do not care. Your life was forfeit the moment you entered this system. If you work hard, you will be released and sent home under the escort of one of our WarShips. All references to our location will be purged, and you will be returned to Huntress to explain to your Khan your failure, and the price of such failure."

"I am a Clan warrior!" Myers bellowed. "I am a Galaxy Commander! I will not work as a slave! It is beneath me as a warrior and leader of warriors."

Paul Moon took a step toward him, leaning right into his face. "Then you will die," he said flatly. "Today, you killed one of the few people I respected. I would actually find ripping your throat out somewhat satisfying. The choice is yours. Do as I command, or we end this now."

Myers recoiled a step. *He understands how serious I am.* Paul felt a twinge of sorrow that he would not get to kill him then and there.

"You taint your heritage, Paul Moon," Myers said.

Paul forced a smile. "You are wrong. I am saving it. That is something a Goliath Scorpion should appreciate." He spun and left the room.


**THE NEXT DAY…**

Paul spent the night pouring over Trent's notebook, then met with the ruling council. There was, for the first time, remarkably little debate. *Some will say I bullied them, but in reality, I simply gave them focus and purpose.*

That morning, he asked Inanna to assemble the entire colony on the parade field that now served as a public park of sorts for the colonists. The usually purple-clouded skies over Wayside V were different that day. The deep yellow sun blazed overhead. Inanna had set up a small stage and podium, along with a sound system for amplifying his voice.

Moon had put on a dress uniform, one stripped of any rank or insignia. He took the stage in slow, careful steps. Public speaking was part of being an officer. *I am no longer an officer–I am a leader in a different capacity. Today we begin the healing. My healing begins too. They say confession is good for the soul...I will use mine to completely unify our people. Today we have our purpose defined–a vision set.*

"Yesterday, our gallant defenders met the forces of the Goliath Scorpions in a battle for the survival of our people. A handful of warriors, led by our greatest hero, sacrificed their lives to defeat this enemy. Their honor is without question, as is their bravery. And I am here today to tell you that they were victorious."

The crowd cheered. Several hats were tossed into the air. Applause filled the grassy field.

"Now, we must move forward. In doing so, we must become something else. We have always been faithful to the tenets of Nicholas Kerensky and his Great Father. Our former Clan lost its way—I know that. Our own arrogance and brutality forced the Star League to come and purge us. Yet we, the faithful, remained.

"The Latin word for faithful is *fidelis*—and that is who we are now. It is who we are, our name. Our past must remain hidden until the time is right. We will one day take our place in the stars as the rightful heirs of the Kerenskys. It is our Hidden Destiny—our future. For now, we must hide our origins, conceal who we are, until that time comes. This is the burden each of us must bear. But with such burdens, there is great honor. Not the honor of a warrior, but the honor of a proud people—which you all are."

There was another roar from the crowd.

Paul waited until it died down. "Any proud people must have those they look up to. The ruling council has asked that I serve as your leader. I do this not as a warrior, but one of you. I am your custodian—your Custos. My commitment to each of you is that I will see to your protection, and we will build a society that will be a beacon to the rest of the worlds. Any proud people must have someone to look up to, a hero. I am not that man. I have made mistakes in my past, horrible errors in judgment. I am not worthy of the title 'hero.'

"But there is one...one who died yesterday...died so you all could live. This man set out on a course years ago that led to the battlefield and his death. He sacrificed everything in his life...not for personal gain. He sought honor and righteousness where there was political backstabbing and cruelty." Paul paused. *It is time they know the whole truth, even my role in it.*

"His name was Trent—though you knew him as Baldur of the Nova Cats. He was called many things... warrior, traitor, defiler. Few know the truth about him, but his saga, and my own, are like a Greek tragedy. He was the soul of our people, though you did not truly know him.

"This is his story..."

# CHAPTER 37

Captain Farland of the Fidelis WarShip *Streaking Mist* had never antici-pated being back on Huntress, but it had been the will of the Custos that he escort the Goliath Scorpions there. Some of his escorted POWs had remained on Wayside V, joining the Fidelis. Their desertion stung the worst for their commander, Rik Myers. The rest had done their duty as POWs, as humiliating as that was. They came back, hav-ing lost three years of their lives to Myers's Folly, as they had begun calling the planet.

Paul Moon had given Farland specific orders for his return to Huntress. Jump to a pirate point known only to the Jaguars. Contact Russou Howell if he is still alive. Offer him escort to wherever he wanted to go. "Provide Howell with whatever assistance he needs."

Most of his original crew did not want to leave Wayside. A hand-ful of colonists had changed their minds and wanted to return, so Farland's people had trained them for the voyage back. They were not as skilled as his former flight crew, which had led to some main-tenance problems, but Farland had prevailed. *The Custos is a wise man, allowing any dissenters the chance to leave.*

To his surprise, Russou Howell had replied to his signal, and now Farland's DropShips had grounded—right under the nose of the dwin-dling Star League garrison.

The foliage shifted at the edge of the makeshift LZ, and a row of BattleMechs emerged. Most were clearly patched together, with arms and legs from other 'Mechs attached but not even painted to conceal their origins. Others showed unrepaired damage.

One, a *Warhawk*, stepped forward, and its pilot climbed out. He was nearly bald, with only a widow's peak of defiant hair in place. His uniform was more tatters than actual clothing. Farland felt out of place facing the man while wearing such a pristine uniform. Russou's beard had not been shaved in several days, and was peppered with gray hair.

"Russou Howell, I presume?" Farland said, extending his hand. A filthy hand grasped his and shook it.

"I wondered if this was a trap," Howell replied, and Farland caught a hint of alcohol on his breath.

"Custos Paul Moon sends his regards. I have been told to be at your disposal."

"*Custos?*"

"Much has happened since we departed Huntress," the captain replied.

"So he made it—founded his new home."

"Affirmative. *We* did," Farland corrected.

"Good," Howell said. "I have heard of a cache of JumpShips hidden by the Widowmakers. We will need them."

"You aim to continue to fight?" Farland said in dismay.

"*Aff.* Of course I am. Paul Moon has his way of saving the Smoke Jaguars. I have my own."

## ALPHA GALAXY COMMAND POST
## RAKT-JABADA, ABYSMAL CONTINENT
## HUNTRESS
## SEVEN DAYS LATER...

Galaxy Commander Rik Myers stood before Khan Ariel Suvorov in what remained of his dress uniform. While clean, it was heavily worn and patched, the cuffs frayed to dangling threads. The uniform was loose-fitting—Myers had lost weight during his time on Wayside. He could tell by the way Khan Suvorov looked at him that he had changed in his time away. Even the long trip home had not eroded the calluses on his hands.

"You live," the Goliath Scorpion Khan said. "I am not sure that is a good thing."

"My Khan, I took the actions I did because timing was of the essence. The responsibility for this is—"

"Silence!" she commanded, rising from her desk, the same one that had once been his. "I read the report you transmitted when you arrived in-system. You took one of our Clan's best Clusters and set off along the Exodus Road in hopes of capturing the Smoke Jaguar warriors. This was not for our Clan, but for your ego. You traveled all of that way only to fail. Now you stand before me, a Galaxy Commander who left the majority of his command in the hands of subordinates, with nothing to show for your efforts. Your Cluster lost all of its equipment. It is only by the grace of this Paul Moon that you were allowed to return here. Rarely has a warrior in any Clan ever failed as completely as you did and still live, Rik Myers."

Myers had played out this dressing down in his mind countless times while on Wayside. Nothing compared to the real thing. His fingers twitched at his sides, a side effect of necrosia deprivation while in exile. He wanted to protest, to justify what he had done. Words would never do that.

*She is right, I did fail. I let my ego guide my actions. Rather than harvest the Smoke Jaguar warriors, I was nearly wiped out by them. There were no trophies, no artifacts of victory. Only defeat.*

"Yes, my Khan," was all he could muster.

She paused and seemed to look at him from head to toe, taking him in. "You were their prisoner. Made to work as a laborer, *quiaff?*"

"As it said in my report, *aff.*" The humiliation associated with the jobs he had done still rankled. He had despised the manual labor, but some of his people found it pleasing. Worse though, a handful of his warriors chose to remain. *For Clan warriors to remain rather than return speaks volumes of their loss of honor, a loss I brought upon them. Mutiny—unheard of in the warrior caste.*

He saw the look on her face. Anger had been replaced with something else: pity. That hurt him even more than her fury. "Rik, you were one of my best warriors. Now you stand before me a broken man. What am I to do with such a warrior?"

"Redemption," he managed.

"What?"

"Allow me to redeem myself. I have learned a great deal about myself during my time away. I was broken by the Custos and remade as a new man. I have paid a price for my arrogance. I know I do not deserve another chance—but I ask for it regardless. Whatever you believe is punishment, I have endured already. I saw my unit dismantled and some of my own warriors turn their backs on our Clan and opt to stay with the Fidelis. I have learned a great many lessons. Allow me to present myself as a warrior, and restore my honor in your eyes."

She said nothing for a long minute, and the silence was as devastating as her words. "You have changed—I see that. Very well, you shall have your chance. You will need to retest for your position as commander of Alpha Galaxy. Then, should you succeed, I will tell you of my plans for the Eridani Light Horse."

Rik Myers forced a feeble smile to his lips.

# CHAPTER 38

Precentor Albany Clarke stepped off the shuttlecraft and was greeted by atmosphere thinner than what she had been breathing. Looking around, she saw this was not some ragtag pirate base or long-forgotten, struggling colony world. This was a thriving contemporary city. *Blake be blessed, it is more than I could have hoped for.*

A hulking man, clearly an Elemental, stepped forward from the delegation. *They are Clan, just as I had anticipated.* He stood in front of her party at the gangway of her shuttlecraft.

"I am Precentor Albany Clarke of the Word of Blake," she said. "I bring you greetings from Terra."

The man stood before her, arms crossed defiantly. "You ignored our signals to depart this system."

She smiled. *The fools. They think they can command us. We are driven by the Master's vision. I came to convince them, one way or another, to join us.* "I have been searching for you for some time. We discovered someone was selling HPG components on one of the Periphery worlds. They were not of our manufacture—and the Word of Blake controls interstellar communications—so I realized we had found a clue to your existence. It took some time, but I had to find you, come here, and meet you."

"You were told to stay away," the Elemental replied in a deep voice.

"I come to enlist your aid. I was sent here to liaise with your people, now that you have been located."

"We do not require liaison with the Inner Sphere or anyone else," the Elemental said coolly.

"I disagree. We have a common enemy—the Clans. Your people were betrayed by them and my Order recognizes their threat. I have come to enlist your assistance. We detected some of your BattleMechs on our approach. You too come from the Clans. We know who you are, and I came to extend our goodwill and ask that you join us in the war raging in the Inner Sphere."

"Until today," the hulking man said, "I had no concern of what happened in the Inner Sphere. I still do not. We have no ill will toward the Clans. We only take issue with those who seek to disturb our privacy."

"Perhaps if we went inside, sat down, discussed this in detail," Clarke offered.

A wry grin crossed the man's face. "We have nothing to discuss."

"And you are?"

"Custos Paul Moon," he said firmly. "I am the appointed leader here. I speak for the Fidelis."

*He is stubborn, but I have an ace up my sleeve.* "Custos Moon, the Word of Blake has much to offer you here. All we ask in return is your assistance in fighting our war. When that war is done, our intent is to take the fighting to the Clans. Surely that is worth us sitting down and talking?"

He shook his head. "We have nothing to discuss with you or your people. We have no desire to be a part of your war."

*Very well then. Time to make him understand what he faces.* "Custos Moon, as we speak, I have three DropShips with a battalion of troops on descent. They will land outside this city in a matter of minutes. We skirted your sensor sweeps. On my word, they will attack and take from you your 'Mechs and technology. This colony will become a staging world for the Word of Blake."

She paused, then flashed her famous smile. "But this does not have to end in bloodshed and battle. If you will listen to my proposal, we can become allies—good friends, in fact. Your force merging with ours could tip the scales of the war we fight for the freedom of the Inner Sphere."

"I was aware of your ships. I compliment you for attempting to hide their approach in-system. I am afraid you underestimate our technical prowess. Our satellite network is a little more sophisticated than your sensors," he replied flatly. "Your ships are of no consequence. My stand does not change with your idle threat."

"It is no idle threat, I assure you!" Precentor Clarke snapped. "We are more than a match for your forces. I implore you, sir. If we can sit and talk, you will find we have much in common."

"Perhaps," he replied, still unimpressed. "I suggest you contact your JumpShip first. I will lift our jamming to allow it." He nodded to one of his people standing at his side, who punched something into her noteputer.

*Jamming? We detected no jamming.* Clarke raised her wrist communicator. "This is Starbright Leader to the *Divine Wind.*"

A hiss and sizzle of static came back over the small speaker. "Precentor, their fighters came out of nowhere. Our jump sail is in shreds. We are stranded here."

Anger and fear hit her at once. "That does not stop me, Moon." She spoke into her communicator. "This is Clarke—execute Plan Indigo."

In the sky far off to the western horizon, the fusion engine plumes of DropShips burning in appeared, three ships aiming to land several kilometers away from the spaceport. "As you can see, I was not bluffing. If you will not join our Order, you will be crushed by it."

Moon lifted his own wrist communicator. "Captain Franks, you are authorized to engage two of the DropShips as soon as they land. Leave one intact." He turned to a woman at his side. "If you would, my dear, instruct Shane to take her Striker Umbra into battle against the lone survivor. This is our first chance in some time to test ourselves in actual combat. Let us not squander it."

"As you wish, Custos," the black-haired woman said, bowing slightly.

Rage and confusion swept the precentor. She watched the plumes near the ground in the distance. Suddenly, from the skies, came a brilliant barrage of naval-weapons fire. Two of the DropShips were hit, one after the other. Flames and a billowing black mushroom cloud rolled into the low skies of Wayside V.

Then, in the distance, a force of BattleMechs, vehicles, and infantry fanned out toward the third DropShip. *That is nearly a battalion—and that ship only holds two companies!* Weapons fire filled the air between her troops trying to get clear of the DropShip and the rush of oncoming forces.

It hit Clarke then. She had come into a trap.

"How?"

"Our WarShip, the *Hidden Destiny*, plotted your DropShips from the moment you arrived in-system. We took measures to make sure you did not detect it." Moon turned to watch the battle in the distance with a look of satisfaction on his face. "You were told to leave the system, but came here as invaders. You are fortunate that we take prisoners, Precentor."

"You will pay for this," she spat back in rage.

Moon disregarded her for a moment. "Inanna, when the fighting is over, I want teams to pull every bit of data from their data banks. I want details on this war that is being fought, and everything you can learn about the Word of Blake. Find out who they are fighting and why. Intelligence is our best defense."

The lithe black-haired woman nodded and headed off toward the battle in the distance, which was already winding down.

"When the Clans learn you are here, they will come and destroy you."

"Or," Moon said wryly, "they will meet the same fate as you. Besides, I am willing to bet you do not have good relations with the Clans, since you suggested we join you fighting against them. I have little to worry about—I assure you."

"They want your blood. The Clans hate the Wolverines. They will come and consume you and this little colony you've built."

Paul Moon laughed. "You think we are Clan Wolverine? The Not-Named Clan? That is the saddest and funniest thing you have said since landing."

*No! Our intelligence could not have been this flawed! They have to be the Wolverines!* "Then who—who are you?"

"We are the shadows in the night. The ghosts of the past. The retribution and the destined."

"You will pay for what you have done!" Clarke said as guards closed in around her and her party.

"I am sure we will. In the meantime, thank you for the salvage, the BattleMechs, and your ships. And for our new purpose."

"I don't understand..."

"The Word of Blake brought war here, to us, in our homes. We will seek out your enemies in this war and aid them. Your attempt to consume us will be repaid in full. It is long past time for the Fidelis to prove themselves in battle."

The guards ripped off her communicator and seized her party quickly and efficiently. As she was led away, Clarke fumed at the debacle she had led. *If they are not the Wolverines...then who in the hell are they?*


**SEVEN MONTHS LATER...**


Precentor Martial Victor Steiner-Davion and Devlin Stone, leader of the alliance against the Word of Blake's Jihad, both looked up as Paul Moon and Inanna entered the conference room.

Moon watched the prince, waiting for recognition to hit him. He saw it. *Yes, that is right, I am the bondsman you met on Huntress. Much has come to pass since then, Prince Victor.*

"Paul Moon," Victor said, rising to his feet and slowly extending his hand.

"You know this man?" Stone asked, also rising and extending his hand, which Moon shook—ignoring Victor's.

"A Smoke Jaguar warrior," Victor said. "He led the counterattack on Huntress. So that's what this is about. You are the Smoke Jaguar survivors—the ones who left. Now it makes sense."

"I *was* a Smoke Jaguar. We are now the Fidelis."

Stone looked at both men as if he could sense the tension between them. "We received your invitation to come here to negotiate for your assistance in the Jihad. I had no idea you were the last of the Smoke Jaguars."

"Does it make a difference?" Moon had reviewed the intelligence data from Precentor Clarke's ships. The Word of Blake's Jihad had already slaughtered billions. It was a struggle between a techno-religious ideal and the last bastions of freedom. It had been tempting to do nothing at all...just let the war go on.

But his people were chafing. His warriors wanted battle, not just simulated fighting. And the colony, despite his leadership, was taxing its limits. *We need a new home. This war offers us a chance for a bigger future, perhaps a new home.* In another ten years, Wayside V would no longer be able to support the colony's continued growth.

Paul took his seat across from the delegation. "We need each other. I have two Centuries of warriors, each with one hundred warriors trained in covert operations and specialized tactics. We have one WarShip as well. You need troops and ships. I offer my pledge of assistance, if we can reach agreeable terms."

Victor and Stone glanced at each other, then back at Moon. Stone spoke first. "This is incredible. Of course we want your troops for our cause."

"We are not invested in your 'cause.' We fight for our own goals."

"And what is it you want?" the precentor martial asked.

"Not a great deal. Should we prove ourselves worthy, we want a new home. Wayside cannot handle our population growth. We want a new home, close to Terra, a place we can call our own."

"I think that can be arranged," Stone replied.

"Another condition—our origins must remain a secret shared by those in this room. We are not yet prepared for the universe to know who we are. The Word of Blake came to crush us, drag us into your war. We are simply paying them back for their arrogance."

Devlin Stone nodded. "Your secret is safe with us."

Moon surveyed him carefully then nodded. "Very well. When you land on Terra, we will be there."

"Having a Clan land on Terra would be problematic," Victor replied, shooting a glance at Stone.

"We are not a Clan, Victor Steiner-Davion," Moon replied. "We will earn our right to be there—but we will stand on Terra before the other Clans. It is symbolic—and not up for negotiation."

Devlin Stone spoke up. "Assuming you are not going to claim you are the ilClan, I think we can work with that." He cast the precentor martial a look that calmed Steiner-Davion's discomfort.

"Good. That leaves only one other thing. I need to talk to Prince Victor—alone."

"I don't understand...," the precentor martial said.

"I have something to tell you, in private. Something you need to hear."

Stone looked at Victor, who nodded. "We agree," Stone said.

"Excellent. My wife, Inanna, will take you on an inspection of our troops while the prince and I speak." Moon rose to his feet, as did the two other men.

"That was it?" Stone asked. "You don't want payment of any sort for your services?"

"We are not mercenaries to be bought and sold, Devlin Stone," Moon said. "The Word of Blake came here to coerce us, then devour us. They brought this Jihad of yours to our home. They established themselves as a threat, and we will respond in kind. We will not do it for money, but for our future. And if you betray us, you will pay a similar price in blood and vengeance." It was not a threat, but a statement of fact.

Inanna gestured for Devlin Stone to follow her, leaving Victor alone with Paul Moon. Paul said nothing for a few long moments, looking at the man, measuring how he had aged since the last time they met. *We are both getting older, and starting to show it.*

Victor chose to break the silence first. "So here we are, old enemies. Is this about what happened on Huntress, Paul?"

"*Neg.*" He frowned. "This is about Trent."

"Trent?" Victor asked...then Moon saw the realization hit him. "The traitor?"

*Neg—you fool. I am here to change your thinking, make you see the truth.* "What I am telling you stays in this room, understood?"

"Of course. But what can you tell me about Trent? He died with the Nova Cats fighting the Ice Hellions."

"No, he did not," Moon said. "In fact, if not for him, we would not be here to fight alongside you now."

"He lived? Damn. The Nova Cats. Of course..."

"You were wrong about him. You were wrong to treat him the way you did. You agreed to let him fight, and then denied him that honor. In doing so, you created us. Your misjudgment sent things awry, Victor Steiner-Davion. There is much blood on your hands, many hardships you caused, many lives changed."

"I—I didn't mean to...I mean, you have to understand—"

"*Neg,*" Paul Moon said, clearing the distance between them in a single stride, looming over the diminutive prince. "I do not have to understand. You do. You have been wrong all of this time. We are going to talk, Victor, you and I. You will see the error of your ways. You will walk out of here understanding true honor. You will come to know what you set in motion all those years ago.

"Then, and only then, can you come to face your own demons..."

# EPILOGUE

As the drop hatch of the *Stalwart* opened, Paul Moon saw the Blue Ridge Mountains in the distance. His Fidelis had drawn a special assignment, taking out a series of bridges along the Potomac to limit the Word of Blake's response to the main landings. This was the kind of "special operations" assignment Devlin Stone had been giving them. He called his Fidelis "Stone's Shadows," and they fulfilled their promise with grim determination. Considered special forces, Stone's Shadows were both feared and cursed in the Blakists' mouths.

Paul stepped down the gangway. "All units, remain aboard until I am done."

He reached the bottom of the gangway, but stopped short of standing on Terra. He opened his Elemental armor's hatch and let the hot late-summer breeze of mankind's homeworld hit him. *Our people have waited long for this Great Redemption, as Inanna named it. Our chance to prove that we and we alone hold the true honor that the Clans claim to cherish so dearly.*

Moon pulled out a small metallic canister and opened it. "You were here first, my old comrade," he said, spilling the contents onto the red clay of Terra. Trent's ashes blew in the breeze across the dry grass. "You are the first of our people to touch Terra. This makes you the greatest of the Clan warriors and us the ilClan, regardless of what Devlin Stone and Prince Victor have been misled to think." When the canister was empty, he tossed it into the distance.

"We have remained faithful—and always will." He closed his suit and activated the tactical channel again. "Fidelis—deploy!"

**SANTA FE, NEW MEXICO**
**TERRA**
**REPUBLIC OF THE SPHERE**
**11 DECEMBER 3130**

Victor Steiner-Davion looked at the words he had just typed, narrowing his eyes and squinting through his reading glasses. "'Little did I know that my ignorant mistreatment of Trent would form the Fidelis...a unit integral to our success in winning the Jihad. The most formidable monsters we face in life are those we create. My own arrogance and obliviousness inadvertently forged a weapon I would need to wield later in life against the Word.'" It was the final paragraph of three pages discussing Trent and his role in excruciating detail, including all of the parts Paul Moon had told him.

*Paul told me I needed to honor him. This does that.*

Then, with a deliberate stab of his finger, Victor deleted the last pages, back up to the point where Trent was thought to have died fighting the Ice Hellions. They were gone—erased. He left in the battle results and Trent's role in the Grand Refusal, how he had been critical to the Nova Cats' victory. Gone was the material about the Fidelis. Deleted was the untold story of Stone's Shadows, Wayside V, and the truth of how Trent had really died fighting the Goliath Scorpions. There was a sense of loss as he deleted the material he had spent so long documenting.

*The universe is not ready for the full truth...not yet.* The Fidelis lived on New Earth in blissful isolation. *They are a ticking time bomb. At some point they will reveal their origins. I have no idea how the Inner Sphere or the Clans will react to that. But I cannot be the instrument of that revelation.*

He saved the file, the deletions lost forever. *Why do I feel like I just deleted a part of my soul?*

In the early morning hours, Victor settled back in his seat. *I was wrong about you Trent...we all were. But me most of all.*

# AUTHOR'S NOTES

This book was a trip down memory lane for me, filling a gap I had created years ago with *Surrender Your Dreams*. When I created the Fidelis for the Dark Age era, I was asked by Catalyst Game Labs to explain just how that happened. I wrote a single page that had to be approved first. After all, I was resurrecting the Smoke Jaguars. Randall Bills approved the proposal and I wrote the book. Easy, right?

The fans did what fans do—they argued with themselves as to whether these were the Fidelis or the Smoke Jaguars. Some even swore they were the Wolverines. My head shakes sadly side to side as I type that...How did the Fidelis come to be? Were they really Clan or something else?

That is all good—because it meant people wanted to know how the transformation of the Clan had taken place. That one-page outline literally became the outline for this novel. That's why I never delete anything off my drive.

There were some challenges with this story. The majority of it takes place in the post-Twilight of the Clans era. It also spills over to the Jihad and to the Dark Age.

This is not a story about the Clans, though, at least not below the surface. This is a story of two men, bitter enemies, who mirror each other in many respects. It is how they bury their hatred with a common cause. It is a story about what defines honor and the importance of vision and sacrifice. These two men were destined to clash and come together. Both were cloaked in guilt, bitterness, and the desire to redeem themselves. By the end of the book, the two men become one character, or that was the intention.

I liked writing about the Goliath Scorpions in this book. We have seen little of them in the fiction. I also enjoyed taking the Eridani Light Horse out for a test drive as well. What happened on Huntress after the invasion is murky at best, a period that has been overshadowed by the Jihad and the Wars of Reaving. Yes, the Star League had conquered, but conquest differs greatly from ruling a world surrounded by other hostile worlds.

In writing this book, I had to set some things right about Victor Steiner-Davion's treatment of Trent. No offense to Mike Stackpole, but I never liked how he handled Trent and Victor's last exchange. I felt he had missed the point of Trent, what he really wanted. This book gave me a chance to set that right (grin).

Writing a book should always be fun and fulfilling. This one was. It is good to be back in the saddle again.

# ABOUT THE AUTHOR

Blaine Pardoe has been writing *BattleTech* fiction for decades, starting with the first *Technical Readout*. Blaine has been involved in the gaming industry for decades, writing for a number of companies and universes. His true-crime books earned him a spot on the *New York Times* Bestseller List, and his military-history books have been lectured on at the U.S. Naval Academy and the U.S. National Archives.

When he is not writing or solving crimes, he is a fan of *BattleTech*. He can be reached at bpardoe870@aol.com or via Facebook.

# LOOKING FOR MORE HARD HITTING BATTLETECH FICTION?

## WE'LL GET YOU RIGHT BACK INTO THE BATTLE!

Catalyst Game Labs brings you the very best in *BattleTech* fiction, available at most ebook retailers, including Amazon, Apple Books, Kobo, Barnes & Noble, and more!

### NOVELS

1. *Decision at Thunder Rift* by William H. Keith Jr.
2. *Mercenary's Star* by William H. Keith Jr.
3. *The Price of Glory* by William H. Keith, Jr.
4. *Warrior: En Garde* by Michael A. Stackpole
5. *Warrior: Riposte* by Michael A. Stackpole
6. *Warrior: Coupé* by Michael A. Stackpole
7. Wolves on the Border by Robert N. Charrette
8. *Heir to the Dragon* by Robert N. Charrette
9. *Lethal Heritage* (The Blood of Kerensky, Volume 1) by Michael A. Stackpole
10. *Blood Legacy* (The Blood of Kerensky, Volume 2) by Michael A. Stackpole
11. *Lost Destiny* (The Blood of Kerensky, Volume 3) by Michael A. Stackpole
12. *Way of the Clans* (Legend of the Jade Phoenix, Volume 1) by Robert Thurston
13. *Bloodname* (Legend of the Jade Phoenix, Volume 2) by Robert Thurston
14. *Falcon Guard* (Legend of the Jade Phoenix, Volume 3) by Robert Thurston
15. *Wolf Pack* by Robert N. Charrette
16. *Main Event* by James D. Long
17. *Natural Selection* by Michael A. Stackpole
18. *Assumption of Risk* by Michael A. Stackpole
19. *Blood of Heroes* by Andrew Keith
20. *Close Quarters* by Victor Milán
21. *Far Country* by Peter L. Rice
22. *D.R.T.* by James D. Long
23. *Tactics of Duty* by William H. Keith
24. *Bred for War* by Michael A. Stackpole
25. *I Am Jade Falcon* by Robert Thurston
26. *Highlander Gambit* by Blaine Lee Pardoe
27. *Hearts of Chaos* by Victor Milán

## NOVELLAS

1. *A Splinter of Hope* by Philip A. Lee
2. *The Anvil* by Blaine Lee Pardoe

## ANTHOLOGIES

1. *Shrapnel: Fragments from the Inner Sphere*
2. *Onslaught: Tales from the Clan Invasion!*
3. *The Corps* (BattleCorps Anthology vol. 1)
4. *First Strike* (BattleCorps Anthology vol. 2)
5. *Weapons Free* (BattleCorps Anthology vol. 3)
6. *Fire for Effect* (BattleCorps Anthology vol. 4)
7. *Counterattack* (BattleCorps Anthology vol. 5)
8. *Front Lines* (BattleCorps Anthology vol. 6)
9. *BattleTech: Legacy*